CLAIMED BY FANGS AND DARKNESS

MAGGIE SUNSERI

Maggie Sunseri
PO Box 1264
Versailles, Kentucky 40383
https://maggiesunseri.com

Publisher's Note: This is a work of fiction. Names, characters, places, and incidents are a product of the author's imagination. Locales and public names are sometimes used for atmospheric purposes. Any resemblance to actual people, living or dead, or to businesses, companies, events, institutions, or locales is completely coincidental.

Cover Design by Story Wrappers — storywrappers.com

CLAIMED BY FANGS AND DARKNESS/Maggie Sunseri 1st ed.

CONTENT WARNINGS

For a list of content warnings please visit Maggie Sunseri's website: maggiesunseri.com.

For my readers. Thank you for trusting me with your hearts, however ephemerally. You deserve all the love & beauty this world has to offer.

Oh, and I've enchanted this book with healing magick. I hope you find what you need. <3

1

EVIE

eath is not the end. It's just another beginning.

In the pit of darkness, a voice found me, the sound echoing in lyrical resoluteness. When at first I thought I was lost to eternal nothingness, I now saw a sliver of light above—a shimmering, iridescent crescent moon. Or perhaps it was a solar eclipse seconds away from totality, and I was bearing witness to Selena swallowing her solar sister before the inevitable miracle of rebirth.

I was not a child of Helia, but I was going to chase those rays anyway.

Life and I weren't finished yet.

I was curled in the fetal position, bathed in the safety of some primordial womb. I craned my head toward the light. I stretched my legs, one and then the other. I spread my arms wide. I remembered who I was.

And I screamed. The sound that escaped me shook my bones. It tasted like freedom, like forbidden bites of chocolate stolen at the markets when I was a child and Mama wasn't looking—decadence I'd been denied, lest it ruin my prepubescent body marked for marriage.

I got to my feet, and in the darkness, I reached my hands out. My fingers brushed against something solid, slick and damp, like moss on stone. I traced the solidness in a circle around me, still unable to see anything but the tiny sliver of light above. I was trapped inside a pit, or perhaps an empty well.

And I knew I had a choice. I could sink back into the blissful liminal space and rest for a while. I could take a new form. I could say goodbye. There was love in death, more love than I'd ever found in life.

Not yet, I thought.

And it was that *yet* that surprised me. It was that *yet* that drove me forward and had my fingers digging into the slimy walls, searching for purchase.

Maybe it was foolish—to choose uncertainty, pain, grief, and suffering. It was foolish to choose life, but I did it anyway.

The Fool tarot card came to mind as more of myself and my memories seeped through the cracks. The Fool took that first, courageous leap of faith. Number zero in the major arcana, the beginning, square one.

How exciting.

I laughed. The sound was easier without the block inside my throat. My voice was a river undammed.

With a grunt of exertion, I hoisted myself up, finally finding some protruding slab of stone to grab. My legs shook, my arm muscles spasming.

This wasn't my body.

I was spirit walking.

As soon as I had the thought, things became slightly easier. My mind melded with the environment. I dragged myself up, one foot at a time, resisting the call of eternal rest. I imagined my hands and feet meeting sturdy points of leverage, and they did. Still, I ached, I trembled, I unleashed raspy cries.

The sliver of light was bigger now, nearly within reach.

Where was my body?

In sharp, excruciating flashes, my last moments crashed into me. Kylo's betrayal. The sound of Idris's skull cracking against a jagged rock. The scorch of unfathomable heat that melted the block in my throat. The truth that had dragged me into the nothingness: my parents allowing a vampire to harm Idris when he was a child and the shadows that had poured from my soul to feast on my coven until only ash remained.

The image of blood pooling under Idris's head, his face frozen in shock, overtook my vision. My foot slipped, and the shaking in my arms became unbearable. I screamed as my hands began to slide.

If I fell, I wasn't sure I'd climb up again. I wasn't sure if I'd even have a choice.

I found my footing again in the darkness, but it was too late. A loud booming sound filled the cavernous space, and then all I could hear was the sound of my own scream. I remembered the shadows that had poured from me, that had likely killed my brother just as they had killed my parents all those years ago.

I lost my grip.

But instead of falling, a hand shot out from the light and into the darkness that threatened to consume me again. And then another.

Fingers circled around my wrists and held tightly. My legs dangled. There was no more air left in my lungs. My suspended body was lifted by a dark form above me, obscured by the bright light behind them, grunting and panting heavily.

As soon as I met solid ground, I scrambled away from the pit of darkness, and my eyes adjusted slowly to the world around me.

Thirteen-year-old me stared into my eyes, swiping a hand across her dewy forehead. I stared back, my lower lip trembling.

We both stood, and I didn't hesitate, not this time—not anymore.

I closed the distance between us, and I pulled her into a hug.

"Thank you," I whispered, inhaling the scent of my childhood home—the hints of candle smoke, sage, and soil. "Thank you for protecting me."

"I'll always protect you," she replied.

I pulled back, peering into her wide, frightened gray eyes. She worked hard to erase the fear from her determined features.

I took her hands in mine, even if it made me squeamish, even if I didn't know how to be warm, maternal, and comforting. It had never been taught to me; it was a foreign language that felt wrong and clunky on my tongue.

"It's not your job to protect me," I said, my eyes pooling with tears. "It's my job to protect *you*."

I noticed the instant softening of her tense, raised shoulders, and the exhale from her lips.

Her blonde hair was messy, her black dress slightly too small, her sneakers streaked with dirt and grass stains.

"Your only job is to play, explore, and be loved."

She shook her head. "She doesn't love us," she said, heartbroken. "Mama doesn't love us at all."

We were back in our childhood home, sitting together in the corner of the room as doors and cabinets slammed beneath us. My thirteen-year-old self sobbed, half afraid of being heard, half yearning to be heard—to be seen, to be held.

I felt Princeton's presence somewhere close, and I remembered all of his guidance from our emotional healing sessions. Grief clenched my heart, and the yelling from the kitchen downstairs grew louder.

"That was her loss," I said, lifting my wobbling chin. I pulled her hand into mine again. "We aren't here in this house anymore. You know that, right?"

She stopped rocking. She stared at me in confusion, shaking her head slowly.

"We can leave. We don't have to stay here," I said. "We *already* left. I have my own place, somewhere far away. We live with someone who loves us—Mena, our adoptive grandmother. Idris lives close by."

She looked around, still perplexed by my words.

"I have a closet full of pretty dresses, none of them black."

At this, she smiled.

"We never have to come back here again," I said, mirroring her smile, watching her eyes light up with relief. "*I love you. You're safe now.*"

The room lit with a faint purple glow, Hekate's fierce, protective maternal energy drowning out the noise from downstairs.

"I let you down before," I told my inner child, the part of me that had been burdened with too much pain, too much responsibility—all that had been denied and suppressed for over a decade. "But I'm taking over. You were never meant to hold any of this for me. You're free."

Her tears stopped, her face relaxing.

"Do you trust me?"

She nodded. "I can try."

I could see through her words to the truth beneath. Of course, she trusted me. All she'd ever wanted was to let go.

She didn't want to be a savior. A protector. An angel or a monster.

She just wanted to be a kid.

We hugged one more time, and my next exhale was as long and cleansing as hers. When I opened my eyes, she was gone.

I watched from the window as that thirteen-year-old girl ran through the tall grass, a rosy-cheeked Idris trailing her as he waved around a butterfly net.

As I whispered my goodbye to my childhood home, to the secrets beneath the floorboards and the whispers in the walls, a sharp pain sprouted at the side of my head.

I winced as agony set in, and a voice cut through the haze.

"Please, baby," a voice called, panicked, gruff, and in pain.

A voice that made my heart flutter. A voice that didn't belong here.

"If you don't stop, you're going to kill yourself! *You're going to hurt Idris!*"

Slowly, I remembered the events that led me here. Idris's crumpled body on the forest floor.

The sun grew brighter above the rolling hills of Isolde. I reached for the rays, clawed for them, begged for them.

I want to live. I promise not to waste it.

Please let me live.

I want to live!

2

KYLO

Idris's eyes closed. My shield trembled, a fissure rippling through the wall of shadow.

A rare tear slid down my cheek. I looked to the angel of death.

"Come back to me, baby. Hold on, Idris. Hold—"

The fissure ruptured. My shield exploded. My life flashed before my eyes: my childhood in Morha; plotting and scheming with Aisling; her lifeless body, desecrated by the soulless born; finding a chosen family in Blade, Harmony, and Princeton; the euphoria of my higher purpose serving the clan; and my precious Evie and her beautiful, vulnerable heart.

The world, once deafening and dark, became so instantly still and bright in a split second that all I could do was gasp for breath. I clutched my chest with one hand and still held my blood-soaked shirt to Idris's head with the other.

The angel of death dropped back down to the earth. The shadows evaporated, leaving a scorched, deadened wasteland in their wake. The late afternoon sun peeked out from behind heavy clouds.

Evie loudly sucked in air, and the proof of her miraculous

aliveness drew an incomprehensible, strangled sound from my lips. She was on her side; her arm was bent awkwardly beneath her. Her heartbeat was labored and slow before growing far too faint.

My first instinct was to run to her—to scoop her into my arms and assess for injuries—but Idris's eyes were closed, his body slack as I tried desperately to stop his hemorrhaging.

A heavy mass was lodged in my throat. My vampiric hearing strained to find his heartbeat, desperate to witness another miraculous promise of life.

Evie tried to stand, and I watched helplessly as she fell back down. She held her likely broken arm against her chest as she let out an exhausted, muffled cry.

My mouth opened, and I realized I didn't know what to say. It was remarkably unusual for me, this state of uncertainty and paralyzing horror. I was used to knowing exactly what to do at all times, especially when it came to my angel.

That rare tear fell from my eye and down to the earth, joining the river of Idris's blood.

"Slowly, baby," I managed to say, the words a gruff rasp.

Evie was dragging herself to us, her white dress now coated in black ash and gods-knew-what from the born vampires' remains.

Idris and I were on the only circular patch of untouched grass in this decimated plot of forest. The only source of green —of life—in sight.

Except the grass was consumed by crimson, and Idris's heart had stopped.

Still, I held the useless, drenched fabric to his head as my jaw trembled. Evie's wail shook my bones and crushed my soul.

My brows were drawn close, my face crestfallen as I stared from Idris's body to Evie. She was within arm's reach. I wasn't sure the last time my hand had trembled, but it did now, violently, as I slowly let go of the bloody shirt.

"He's alive," she croaked. The inflection was like a question as she nodded her head and reached to feel for Idris's pulse. She homed in on my stained hand, the rag I'd dropped now swimming in a pool of blood.

The nodding turned into a vigorous shaking of her head. "No, no—"

She touched Idris's cheek, her eyes scanning his body.

She wailed again, her chest rising and falling rapidly, her heart working too hard.

I pulled her into my arms. At first she fought me, hurling a slew of curses and begging me to help her save him.

Then she relented and slumped in my arms.

"He's gone," I said, confirming what she already knew. "I'm so sorry, Evie." My voice cracked.

"I—" Her next words were unintelligible, but I intuited their meaning.

"It wasn't you—it wasn't your fault."

I assumed the born had been responsible for Idris's injuries. Evie had to understand that her outburst hadn't killed her brother. I'd shielded us from her shadows.

From my arms, her head was still turned toward Idris, her hand twisted in his shirt as she sobbed.

"I made the wrong choice," she said, letting go of Idris's shirt as she buried her head in my chest. A tremor rolled through her.

She needed a healer. Her heart wasn't beating right.

"I should've died," she said.

"You should've, but you didn't," I choked out. She'd been terrifyingly close to death—far, far too close—and this brave, resilient girl survived the impossible anyway.

"I should've chosen to die."

I realized I'd misunderstood her the first time, and her true meaning was a devastating blow to my already shattered heart.

I clutched her tighter before remembering my vampiric strength and her broken, fragile body.

9

Her speech became slurred, and I pulled back to study her. Her eyes fluttered. Her breathing turned slow and ragged.

"What was the point? Was there ever a point?" she asked. "Maybe they were right… the nihilists…"

Evie lost consciousness.

THE BEST HEALERS in the city tended to Evie, while others cleaned up Idris, preparing him for a death rite.

Evie's loss was what finally broke through my own protective barriers, the walls I'd erected in the wake of Princeton's death in order to lead effectively. I hadn't allowed myself to grieve. I didn't have the time for it.

If you don't grieve properly, that pain will leak out in far less desirable ways. Feel it, Kylo.

Princeton's voice echoed in my mind—what I'd imagine he might say if we were in a healing session.

That choked sensation was back. It was so human, so raw.

All I could do was stare at Evie, her chest rising and falling more evenly now as a blood witch delivered fluids and healing tinctures straight into her veins. She was still unconscious, lying on a cot in the healing wing of our hidden, underground facilities.

"The city is panicked. The Servants of Lillian are calling it an act of Lillian's wrath, a sign from the gods in favor of their religious delusions. The born—"

"Phineas," Harmony snapped, her gaze fiercely sweeping from me to my most trusted, lethal eye.

Phineas straightened, but he stopped speaking. He was doing his job. Reporting on the city and all that he'd gleaned from behind his glamour of shadows.

When it became apparent I wasn't going to speak, Harmony took over completely.

"Is there an emergency that needs our immediate action?"

"Well, I suppose that depends on one's definitions of the words *emergency* and *immediate*," Phineas said.

"Sounds like a *no*, mate," Blade grumbled.

My gaze flitted from a frustrated Phineas to my protective comrades to the blood witch, who was staring at Evie's stained-black clothes with rising concern.

It was always a risk bringing mortals into the underground, but we had a wealth of protective measures in place to ensure both loyalty and safety. Only the turned could make it past our magickal wards, for starters. Mortals needed an escort at all times.

Estella was fiercely loyal to the clan. Her entire coven of healers was. Regardless, I hated what they now intuited about Evie. Especially in the wake of Princeton's assassination, with the culprit yet to be identified.

Evie was one of us now. Even if she'd run from me. Even if this wasn't what I wanted for her. Even if she no longer wanted to be alive at all.

There was no going back.

I hadn't noticed Phineas leave, likely ordered away by Harmony. Nor did I register Harmony's hand on my shoulder, her worried eyes on me.

"Evie's stable," Harmony said. "She's strong. She's powerful. She'll heal quickly."

Estella and the other healers filed out of the room, and Blade shut the door behind them.

I sank to the ground. Blade and Harmony sat with me as I unraveled, for the first time since Princeton died. For the first time in many years—too many to count.

Blade patted my back, this massive brick wall of a man. His eyes pooled with understanding. "Cried like a baby after Princeton died," he said softly, his lips curving. "Isn't that what he always said? That if you don't look like pure shit after, then you didn't grieve properly."

Harmony nodded, rubbing her thumb in circles on my hand in hers. "Doesn't apply to Kylo," she said softly. "He's too pretty of a crier."

My choked sob turned into a bark of laughter. "Fuck off."

Harmony grinned, her tan cheeks damp. "She's going to survive this. We will *all* survive this. Because we have to."

"In life, death is the only certainty," I murmured, channeling the words of my mentor.

"Another Princeton classic," Blade said.

The shared laughter lightened the weight pressing against my chest. I felt strangely lucky to share this grief with my best friends, as much as I wished I could shield all of my loved ones from suffering.

But then I studied Evie again, and the weight was heavier than before.

"It's different for her," I said, devastation racking through me in waves.

Evie had spent her entire life protecting her brother. Twenty-four years devoted to ensuring his safety and happiness.

"No, it's not," Harmony said gently. "Find one house in this city unmarked by grief, untouched by death. It *feels* different because you love her."

"She's one of us now," Blade said. "She will survive because so did we."

I shook my head. "This is my fault," I said, staring at the ornate purple carpet, avoiding either pair of eyes. "I fucked up. I let her down, and she ran from me, and the born killed her only living family—her reason for living."

Harmony shook her head. "Look at me, Kylo."

I slowly met her empathetic dark irises.

"Someone else cannot be your reason for living," Harmony

said sharply. "You know that." She took a steadying breath. "I don't know what happened, but I believe you when you say you fucked up." She tilted her head up, holding my gaze fiercely. "You fucked up, so you will take accountability and fix it. Because that's who *you* are. But the *born* did this. You didn't kill Aisling. Nor Princeton. Nor Idris. You are not responsible for every life in Ravenia. You are only responsible for yours."

"Not quite true," I said bitterly. Evie was absolutely my responsibility. My most cherished, in fact.

We were all channeling Princeton now, Harmony's words serving as proof. I felt him in the room with us. I could almost see him out of the corner of my eye.

Or perhaps the lingering poison in my veins was making me hallucinate.

An inappropriate smile curved my lips. "She stabbed me with a poisoned bone needle." I rubbed my chest, moving the grief around as it continued to engulf my spirit.

Blade grinned. "Sexy."

I glared at him lightheartedly. "Far from it."

I rubbed my eyes. Visions of Idris's corpse assailed me, and I could hear Evie's inhuman wail as if she were still screaming.

"How long?" a raspy voice jolted me from these torturous visions.

All heads swiveled to face the bed. Evie was staring at the rubber tubes delivering fluids and healing tinctures into her veins with an expression on her face I clocked immediately.

"Nope," I said, rushing to her and grabbing her hands before she could rip out the needles.

Her gaze followed the tubes up to the glass bottles of faintly pink liquid next to her, no doubt assessing their magickal properties.

Her eyes locked on mine with indignant fire. "How long were you dead before Princeton turned you into vampires?"

3

EVIE

My arm fucking hurt. But unlike before I lost consciousness, I could move it. Someone must've mended my bones.

Which was perfect, because I needed all of my limbs in working order for magick of this magnitude.

Kylo, Harmony, and Blade merely stared at me, no one answering my incredibly simple question. Kylo let go of my hands.

This time when my eyes returned to Kylo's, I actually saw him. The unending pools of pain in his blue irises, the grief I'd been searching for since Princeton's death. The sorrow he'd been carefully concealing poured through every crack in his mental shields. His face was slightly flushed, his lips turned down. He'd been crying—crying for my brother. Crying for *me*.

I swallowed and looked away. "How. Long," I repeated.

"It wasn't like that," Blade said, earning a glare from both Harmony and Kylo. "Wait, how do you know we had to die first?"

I was back to staring angrily at the tubes in my arms, the bondage currently keeping me from my brother.

"From Princeton, in the spirit realm," I said, my words coming out quickly and impatiently.

Blade glanced from Kylo to Harmony. He scratched his head. "Right..."

"Congrats, you're all getting exactly what you've always wanted from me," I spat. "You should be very pleased with yourselves."

Blade and Harmony feigned confusion, tilting their heads. All eyes moved to Kylo, who was uncharacteristically silent.

I didn't want to look at him. I didn't want to see his pain, the pain that contradicted all of my most paranoid thoughts. I had neither the time nor the energy to overthink or overanalyze.

Idris was all that mattered.

"Princeton will help me," I said. "As will Hekate."

I bluffed more confidence than I truly held, as my time with Princeton before regaining consciousness was brief, mostly wordless.

Death is not the end. It's just another beginning.

His white shirt had billowed in the wind, his bone amulets emitting a faint purple glow.

I connected the dots on my own, and Blade just confirmed my intuition.

"There has to be a point to all of this," I said, quieter this time, slowly meeting Kylo's heartbroken, bloodshot eyes. "I chose life for a reason. I—I did what Hekate asked of me, and what Princeton told me I needed to do in order to reconnect with my power. I'm not blocked anymore."

Kylo's frown deepened. "Evie, you have to understand that you were never a pawn. This wasn't some master plan to recruit you. I broke your trust. And I'm so—"

"Where is my brother?" I hissed. None of that mattered. It was a distraction from the only thing that meant anything to me right now. I had to *move*.

I reached for one of the tubes in my arms.

Kylo grabbed my wrist, thwarting me yet again. "Evie, please," he said, in a voice I nearly didn't recognize. "You need to heal. Do you have any idea how close to death you were a few hours ago? *They were scared your heart was going to give out.*"

"We're wasting time," I said, hating the way my lips trembled and voice shook. "I can rest after."

"After *what?*" Kylo snapped, his eyes alight with anger before he took a deep breath. He loosened his grip on my wrist.

"After I turn Idris!" I said, nearly hysterical. Was I speaking a different language? Why weren't they rushing to help me? This was good for them either way. If they were evil masterminds, then this was their way to ensure I was bound to the clan forever. And if they cared about me at all, they would want to help me save my brother.

"You have to choose to be turned," Kylo said calmly. "It's not a way to save a life that's already been lost."

"Then Idris will be an exception. Magick is malleable. *My* magick is malleable," I said, putting on an air of authority that was beautifully foreign. Authority that was necessary.

Authority that was *mine to take.*

"He's just a kid," Harmony said, stepping closer to us. Her eyes were wide and glassy. "We don't turn anyone under twenty-five."

"He's almost nineteen," I said. "And this was what he wanted. Kylo knows that—he knows my brother and how much he wanted this."

Kylo shook his head, and anger boiled my blood. I didn't understand why they weren't helping me—why they cared so much about these arbitrary rules. Where was Kylo's sense of goodness, grace, and nobility when he'd slaughtered Jacob and then lied to me about it for months?

"Evie, you have no idea how sorry I am," Kylo said fiercely, pleading with his eyes as if *I* were the one who wasn't listening. "Death is only a part of the ritual—a ritual with a specific protocol that must be followed. Things have to be done in a certain order. It's not the kind of spell to ad-lib or fuck with—I've seen firsthand what can happen when things go wrong. Did Princeton tell you to turn Idris?"

He searched my eyes, knowing I couldn't lie to save my life.

Rage was sticky and volatile under my skin. My teeth ground together.

Kylo's exhale was shaky. "Death must be accepted."

"That's easy for you to say!" I yelled.

The lights flickered, and black spots erupted in my vision. My stomach lurched, a tendril of shadow leaving my palm and curling upward like a snake poised to strike.

Harmony and Blade stared at the shadow with mouths agape.

Kylo laughed dryly. "Like hell it is, Evie," he growled. "Like fucking hell it is."

The fury in his voice made me flinch. It wasn't something I'd ever heard from him before, especially not directed at me. I hadn't realized how much it would affect me. It became harder to swallow as I stared at Kylo's feathering jaw. Tears pricked my eyes, beyond my conscious control. My ribbon of shadow stared at him too, waiting.

His face softened. "I'm sorry. I shouldn't have raised my voice. I'm sorry, angel."

I hated the power he still had over me, the way a simple pet name was able to draw such rich, unwanted emotions from my depths.

"If you don't let me do this…" I began, my desperation overtaking everything else. So many threats ran through my mind all at once, and I weighed each of them for what would hurt Kylo the most.

In the end, I didn't need to vocalize any of them. Kylo saw it in my eyes—the resoluteness, the immovability. His face crumpled, as if it were *me* he was grieving.

I let my shadows bleed. The glass bottles of healing fluids rattled against their trays. The floor trembled.

I blinked away the exhaustion, the alarmed protests from my body.

I hadn't realized Kylo's hand had slipped down from my wrist to intertwine his fingers with mine.

"I'm going to remove these needles now," I said.

Kylo nodded, his brows drawn tight. "I'll help you." Something in him had crumbled.

"Kylo," Harmony said, with that same tinge of horror in her voice from when she'd called Idris a kid. "You *can't*. You can't do this."

I removed one needle from my arm, and Kylo removed the second one, his touch gentle.

He didn't look like himself. His eyes were endless wells, seeing too much of me as they always did.

The way he stared at me wasn't possessive, angry, or cold. He shone with a quiet, all-consuming intensity that burrowed into my chest against my will.

He was terrified.

Blade and Harmony stared at their leader, waiting for him to speak. The room was silent for three long beats.

"I need Evie to live," was all Kylo said.

The sound of his voice cracking melted my desperate anger, my readiness to destroy anyone who stood between me and Idris.

I reabsorbed my shadows.

Kylo sank to his knees. "*I need you to live, angel.*"

~

HARMONY AND BLADE protested Kylo's decision, regardless of his leadership position. Harmony pleaded with me not to do this to Idris, not to do this to myself. Blade ran through a list of possibilities that could go wrong.

What if I killed myself trying?

At this, a tremor had rolled through Kylo—his hold on my hand tightening.

What if it didn't work? What if I traumatized myself all over again?

To that I said, *so what.* I was already traumatized.

I held onto Kylo's arm as we walked to the morgue. Not because I'd forgiven him or had simply moved on from his betrayal—but because his authority and power were helping me save my brother. Without him, this all would be far more difficult and messy for me.

That, and also I was still woozy and needed him to keep me balanced and upright.

"What if he's not himself when he comes back?" Blade asked from behind us, refusing to let us go so easily. "His skull was fractured, and his soul is already with Helia. This isn't how—"

"He didn't choose this!" Harmony exclaimed.

I stopped walking and turned.

The chandelier above us exploded. Kylo shielded all of us from the spray of glass with his shadows.

After the dust had settled, I straightened.

I faced down Blade and Harmony. *"He wasn't supposed to die."* My voice was venomous, a charge of power that rattled the walls.

When my shadows leaked again, Kylo stroked my hair, soothing me beyond my conscious control.

"This is what is supposed to happen. This is what's going to give everything meaning. Can't you see that?" I sounded deranged to them—I could see it in their faces—but I couldn't stop. "Hekate, The Tower card, Princeton, my shadows and my past and all of my trauma, bringing fractured parts of myself back to wholeness, climbing my way back up from death, the

orchid in the flower shop telling me to *bloom...*" I made an exasperated sound and looked at Kylo. "Do *you* understand?"

I wish I could say I didn't know why I asked Kylo this question, why I needed him to see and understand me. But of course I knew why. My wounded inner child certainly did too.

Kylo stopped his soothing strokes through my hair. He kissed my forehead. "Of course, angel. You're following the cosmic signs from the otherworld."

"Who the hell is Hekate?" Blade whispered to Harmony, who shrugged and shook her head in frustration.

I ignored them, my lip trembling as I searched Kylo's eyes for the truth. In the end, it didn't matter if he fully understood. His words of support comforted me anyway and eased the tightness in my chest enough to turn my back on Harmony and Blade completely.

"Kylo—"

"Enough," Kylo said, staying by my side. "I understand your concerns. I told you my decision. I'll find you as soon as we're done."

He believed in me.

After everything that happened, Kylo choosing *me* still affected me deeply.

But the temporary warmth in my heart snuffed out the moment I entered the morgue. The moment my gaze collided with Idris's pale, lifeless body, his soft brown eyes that saw nothing at all.

4

EVIE

I couldn't help the sob that crashed from my lips seeing Idris like this, confronted with the brutal reality that he wasn't here anymore.

No aura. No heartbeat. No jokes at my expense. No warm laughter.

I froze up completely as I stared at his motionless form on a cold porcelain table. They'd cleaned him. They'd been preparing him for death rites.

Kylo took over. He lifted my brother into his arms with mournful tenderness.

The room's chaotic, deadly energy swarmed me. I could sense there were some extremely unhappy spirits haunting this space—no doubt captured and tortured born vampires.

I shuddered at the oversized drawers in my periphery, housing more bodies.

Kylo cradled Idris to his chest and followed me out of the room.

"Do you know where you're going?" Kylo asked curiously.

"Yes," I half-lied. I'd figure it out as I went.

Since the block on my power had melted, everything was heightened. Even despite my poor, depleted body.

I'd always been tapped into energy, the layer of spiritual reality that existed atop our physical one.

But now, it was a far more powerful connection than what I'd become accustomed to. Colors were brighter, the world more alive and open to be bent to my will.

Princeton. Hekate.

I invoked them both, tethering myself to hues of purple, black, and green. Healing, death, destruction.

Rebirth.

An invisible thread of connection tugged me forward, showing me where to go. I sensed Princeton's power that still weaved through the halls, growing stronger the closer we got to his spell room.

Each vampire who passed us in the winding underground halls stared at us in utter confusion. I wondered what they assumed from the sight—Kylo holding a dead human boy, a witch covered in ash at his side.

The healers had cleaned me up the best they could, but I was still in the same stained white and floral dress.

I found Princeton's spell room without even a hint from Kylo.

The relief was evident in Kylo's face, even if it was coupled with that same terror that had never left him.

He wanted to believe in me. But he was scared of losing me more.

"Can you... are you talking with Princeton now?" Kylo asked quietly.

"Sort of," I said. "It's more of an energy thing."

The words came out on autopilot, as my attention lay elsewhere, toward forward momentum. I ran my hands along the bookcase in Princeton's innocuous study, searching for the hidden trigger.

A book on sex magick stared me down.

I reached for it.

"Wait," Kylo said. "There are wards in place. If the space doesn't recognize you as Princeton, it could—"

I tried not to look at Idris's pale, lifeless form. But I could see it in my periphery. His spirit, his energy, was nowhere to be found. All of him was gone.

I reached for the book before Kylo finished his warning. I pulled it off the shelf, nearly smirking when I realized the cover was an artsy drawing of a man in a latex hood with a ball gag in his mouth.

Of course a book on kinky sex magick rituals was the door to Princeton's evil lair.

If I had the ability to laugh right now, I would've.

I'd save it for when Idris was alive again.

As the bookcase trembled and began to move backward on its own, all I could see was Idris's expression of pure determination when he rushed the born, weaponless, powerless. He was trying to stop them from taking me even knowing it would only ever end in his demise.

He knew it was a futile effort, and he did it anyway.

I wiped a stray tear from my cheek. I stepped into the dark unknown.

My foot touched hardwood floor, and warm-toned witch lights flickered to life above.

I turned back to Kylo, shuddering again at the sight of Idris.

Kylo stared at me in awe, in reverence, even as fear for my life oozed from his splintered heart—the heart he made vulnerable only for me.

"I can help you talk to Princeton," I said. "When this is over, I can help you connect with him."

Kylo's eyes rounded slightly, his jaw tensing. "Thank you, Evie."

Embarrassment reared its ugly head. Kylo's betrayal, my

grief and terror over Jacob's death, past trauma, and sleep deprivation had all formed a dangerous mix the past week. I hadn't been thinking clearly.

What Kylo had done to Jacob was real. It was wrong.

But I was deeply ashamed about some of the more delusional, paranoid possibilities I'd entertained. Like the possibility that Kylo and his clan had intentionally killed Princeton to replace him with me, someone they could more easily control.

I knew that wasn't true. I didn't know what, exactly, the truth was yet—but Kylo loved Princeton, adored him, and I feared he felt the same for me.

"I'm going to set Idris in the center of the spell circle," Kylo said.

"Thank you," I mumbled, still sticky with shame as I took in our surroundings.

The room was spacious, the lights emulating a layer of warmth that might've otherwise been lost to the eerie darkness of the underground. Bookshelves loomed against a wall, and multiple altars stood in various focal points. There were statues of all three major goddesses present, and I struggled to make eye contact with Lillian's. Other figures were depicted in the art displayed on walls or decorating altars, and there were many magickal objects, workings, and supplies spread out across shelves, furniture, and the floor.

In the center of the room, Kylo had already laid Idris down in the center of a large circle drawn in white chalk. Various sigils were drawn around and within the spell circle. Clearly the spirits and protections in place didn't mind Kylo's presence here. From the way he spoke, it seemed as though Kylo had witnessed Princeton's mysterious, reality-bending rituals on plenty of occasions.

The bookcase swung back into place. Power was ripe and

chaotic. I could feel Princeton's lingering guides and helpers around me, in mourning.

"Thank you for allowing me to be here," I said to them.

Something poked at me, and I gasped at the strange sensation of pressure and coolness at my palms, my feet, my neck.

Kylo was quick to train his gaze on me. "Everything okay?"

I wasn't used to seeing Kylo this jumpy and unsure. And in a way I wasn't expecting, it humanized him, making me even more ashamed of who I thought he was in the wake of his betrayal.

I nodded. The spirits released me. As I walked to the center of the room, whispers grew louder. My first instinct was to shut them out, before remembering that wasn't who I was anymore.

No more running. No more repressing. No more weakness.

Kylo once again looked at me in some holy reverence, and I realized a thin mist of shimmering shadow had gathered around me—like a dark, starry night.

It reminded me of the room of stars in the art exhibit where Kylo told me he loved me.

I'd never done magick in front of anyone before, not like this. The occasional tarot reading or tiny working, sure. But not an elaborate ritual. I'd certainly never allowed anyone to see me in communion with the otherworld, with the spirits and energies whom only I could hear. It was too vulnerable, and I'd been too ashamed.

I hadn't forgiven him, but I also couldn't deny that Kylo might've been the only person in the realm I was comfortable revealing this side of myself to.

He'd never feared or shunned my darkness. My power. My secrets. He'd only ever encouraged them, pried them from my depths with a sweet, coaxing tongue.

It wasn't until I reached Kylo and Idris, the circle and sigils activating with a faint glow, that I remembered I had absolutely zero ingredients or instructions for a turning spell.

"I always suspected you hailed from the stars," Kylo said softly. He stared down at me, Idris between us.

My cloud of onyx and starlight swept through the space, and several pillar candles sprouted flames across the room. I recognized my own guides, ancestors, and helpers as they flooded the area, including Hekate.

"I'll get a statue for you soon," I promised, a whisper.

Kylo raised a brow. "I'm not sure that would be good for my ego."

"Not you," I muttered.

It was the most inappropriate time for jokes, but my lip twitched anyway. Kylo homed in on the movement, his own lips curving ever-so-slightly. I could just nearly make out that silly dimple.

"Princeton didn't write down any of his workings, Evie. Especially not this one—for obvious reasons," Kylo said softly.

"I figured." I avoided looking at my brother, keeping my eyes on Kylo's. "I was being groomed to take Princeton's place, but I'm not *him*. And I don't need to be. The ritual will probably need to shift now that I'm the one doing it."

"I wasn't grooming you for that," Kylo said, studying me.

I closed my eyes. I slowed my breathing. A wave of my righteous anger dissipated into fine mist. "I know you weren't."

My higher self had already taken over, because that's what this magick needed from me. I needed truth. Focus. Centered calm.

Idris's life was at stake. There was no room for error.

When I felt a shift, I slowly sank to the floor, my eyes still closed as my head dropped forward.

I heard faint static and then a few popping sounds as my spirit began to float.

Show me what I need to turn my brother, I said, calm but fierce.

It wasn't a request, my usual method of crafting new spells as a chaos witch.

It was a command.

I opened my eyes, staring down at my cross-legged form below. Kylo was sitting now too, watching my physical body in rapt attention.

I floated up, past the ceiling, past the layers of stone and sediment. All the way up to the forest floor. Trees were lush; wildflowers were in full bloom. Under a dark sky, the smell of incense smoke was rich in the summer air.

This time when Hekate appeared to me, she was unhooded. Her striking dark hair and deep brown eyes were sharp contrasts to her fair skin.

She held a large, golden snake draped across her shoulders. Her smile was soft. *Proud.*

Something about the show of maternal approval sent a stab of pain into my heart. I'd finally received something I'd been starved of since birth, my once-parched tongue now supple and satisfied.

"Your friends were right," Hekate said. "This is not the way to turn a human into an immortal. You are not a goddess, my child."

My throat tightened, tears pricking my eyes. "That's not fair," I said, anger sliding into my tone. "The ritual is already unnatural—already an act of the gods, a cheat of death."

Hekate didn't answer. She didn't need to. She knew I could tell the difference, that my arguments weren't rooted in truth. They were rooted in desperation.

"I know this isn't how it's supposed to go," I whispered. "I will *never* do this again. I'll do it the right way next time, and all times after."

Earlier today, I thought I was escaping the clan forever. And now I was offering my soul on a silver platter. My wooziness returned, and I ran a hand across my warm forehead.

"You have given me *nothing*," Hekate said.

The firmness in her tone triggered my mother wound, and I had to take a steadying inhale. This wasn't the same—she wasn't my mother. No one was disappointed in me. I was safe.

"I will," I vowed, holding her sharp gaze even as I trembled. "I will give as much as I take. You have my devotion. I'm not afraid anymore."

"Bear witness," Hekate said, her voice a resonant thunder. Heavy clouds collected overhead. Fat rain drops poured from the sky like tears.

"You cannot do this for him. You must do this for the realm or not at all."

Her snake hissed, and my knees buckled. My hands dug into the soil, and roots closed around my wrists.

My eyes rolled back.

5

EVIE

At first, I thought I really had died and ended up in one of Lillian's hells to suffer for an eternity.

Because I wasn't back in my childhood bedroom. I was in another little girl's bedroom, watching a woman in all black punish her in the name of the Dark Mother.

"Recite your prayers. May Lillian have mercy on your soul."

The girl's dark brown skin was wet with tears as she said, "I wish I was a witch like you. I wish I was full of witch blood so I don't have to get married."

My heart dropped. The girl transformed into another child, and then another, and on it went.

Of course, I knew I wasn't the only child born to a cult. I'd wondered where the other children from our coven had gone after I'd killed their parents with my plague of shadows. It was yet another thought I'd become proficient in banishing.

Was I being punished for my selfishness? For focusing on my and Idris's survival and no one else's?

You are not being punished, Hekate whispered, her voice a soothing balm. *You must choose this for you. You must choose this for the realm. Or this magick is not yours to wield.*

It could've been me standing before an altar of Lillian, dressed in white for the first time, my small palms resting in the hands of a monster. I watched the human boy's eyes brim with tears—no older than fifteen—as he stared into some wealthy born woman's soulless voids.

The scenery shifted again, this time to a feeding club, where mortal women appeared drugged as they were passed from born to born. The demons laughed, their tongues circling wounds or bathing in elixir. Mortal lives meant nothing to them.

What did they even live for? What was the point of an immortality devoid of meaning? Devoid of love? What was the *point*?

Why were they the ones ruling the realm? Why must we mortals bow before creatures that chased pleasure for the sake of pleasure, power that was unearned, undeserved?

Shouldn't the realm be ruled by those who were in love with life instead of removed from it entirely?

These questions seemed stupid as soon as I thought them. They were downright asinine in their obviousness. They probably *were* those things to the turned. But I'd spent the past decade in hiding, terrified of anyone knowing who I was and what I was capable of. Petrified of seeing my brother and adoptive grandmother in danger because of *me*.

I hadn't had the bandwidth to think such obvious thoughts before.

For a moment, I saw the forest again—Hekate's wise, knowing eyes—the snake that slithered and coiled around her.

Then I saw a group of tattooed turned, dressed in all black, exiting a mansion with a group of terrified, wounded mortals—some of them teenagers.

I focused on the turned man in front, the man with thorny branch tattoos and dark eyes, power that thrummed through the air. The vampire commanding his comrades to be careful, to make sure the humans were delivered to a care center safely.

I was looking at Rune, the turned lord of Aristelle, rescuing trafficking victims from the born.

Rune, who had overthrown the born on the island of Valentin centuries ago, forcing King Earle to recognize him as the semi-autonomous island's new ruler. He was Kylo's idol.

The next images I saw were not as heartwarming.

Born sex parties, which mostly involved torturing mortals for their own amusement. Born hunting humans in the streets, murdering someone's daughter, someone's father or sister or high priest.

I saw corpses like Idris. Bodies tossed away with little concern. Eyes that stared into nothingness.

I wondered who those drugged mortals, child brides, and victims could've been if the born didn't exist. Would they have been healers? Artists? Would they have spent their days laughing? Or in the arms of a lover?

The last image I saw was of myself, suspended in midair, shadows leaving my mouth and my limbs in fits of screams and darkness.

I watched as my shadows feasted on the born and the witch who served them, as Kylo protected Idris with a shield of shadow.

Flesh ripped from bone. Bones crumbled to ash. Souls returned to their Dark Mother.

I felt no shame. I felt no fear. I felt no regret.

My eyes opened back up to the lush forest.

The roots released me, and I rose to my feet. New intuition flooded my mind—intuition about what could be sacrificed in exchange for my brother's immortality.

"I'm still going to be selfish to save my brother, because I'm mortal. And that's just who I am," I whispered unabashedly. "But you were right."

Princeton stood next to Hekate now, his smile as mischievous as ever.

"I won't be devoted to the clan because of Idris. I'll be devoted to the clan because I begged you for my life and I promised not to waste it."

A tear slid down my cheek. Princeton's smile grew.

"I have enough magick to change the world. I have enough power to rescue children the way I always hoped someone would rescue *me*. I don't want to play defense anymore."

I remembered the dark pit, the realization that I hadn't experienced nearly enough love in this life. Not *yet*.

"I no longer fear death. I fear not living."

Princeton's eyes sharpened. "Stop trying to be good, Evie. Be you."

My chest opened, and my shoulders released some unconscious burden.

"Be the motherfucking Tower."

I smirked. The once terrifying tarot card suddenly became a source of power, an image of ultimate freedom.

Princeton twirled a hand, his messy curls lifting in the wind. "When it's called for, of course…"

"Of course," I whispered. My smile was shaky, still tainted by the violence of the realm I'd born witness to.

"You must pay for this spell, performed improperly. And you cannot make the same payment twice." Princeton said. "Do you understand that?"

"Yes."

I needed my brother. He had more love to experience too. I loathed that he would do so as a vampire, a life I'd never wanted for him. But it was better than no life at all.

"You must be quick. His soul will already be difficult to retrieve," Princeton warned.

I nodded.

"What are my shadows for, Evie?" Hekate asked.

I walked to her. In her outstretched hand, a heavy brass key rested.

The old me would've said violence. Destruction. Oblivion. Chaos.

"Revolution," I answered.

My fingers closed around the key. The protector of the downtrodden, the mother of witches, the keeper of the keys, and the guardian of the crossroads—Hekate in all her forms formally invited me to become her daughter.

For the first time in my life, I belonged somewhere.

"I NEED BORN BLOOD," I said, slowly raising my head.

Kylo's eyes were wide for just one second before he smirked. "Your wish is my command."

He rose and carefully exited the spell circle, avoiding stepping on any of the glowing markings.

I squinted when Kylo waited in the corner of the room, staring at absolutely nothing. One of his sigil tattoos faintly glowed on his arm.

My body moved on autopilot when a being manifested before Kylo, suspended midair in some strange white mist. I scrambled to my feet, my heart pumping hard.

"Shhh, baby," Kylo said. "Let's keep that heart settled for me, please."

I rubbed my chest. "Who is that?"

The man held in magickal imprisonment glared at Kylo with raging hatred, though he couldn't move his face. All of him was frozen, including his sickly, dark born magick. Lillian's magick.

"He's your born blood," Kylo said, his eyes dancing with humor as he glanced back over his shoulder at me. "Warwick

Ganzor. He was once the lord of Morha, before his mysterious disappearance."

Warwick's eyes were ice, a sharp contrast to Kylo's sadistic grin. Morha was Kylo's hometown in the northern region of Ravenia and close to King Earle's capitol city, Prospyrus. It was where his best friend Aisling was brutalized and murdered by the born as Kylo was forced to watch.

"Powerful wielder of fire magick, often used against his dissenters, or anyone who dared question the borns' violence," Kylo explained. "We figured out that powerful born blood worked best for these activities. And I had a personal vendetta to see to its satisfying conclusion."

Kylo's words no longer made me squeamish. I had no urge to run. No desire to hide from this violence that began and ended with the born. Kylo's satisfaction mirrored my own.

"Can you please bring me a vial of his blood?"

"Gladly." Kylo reached for a ceremonial knife resting on a nearby altar, along with a bowl marked with sigils. He'd clearly done this before. "Perfect manners as always, angel."

My stomach fluttered against my will, and Kylo laughed at my small noise of irritation.

I suddenly realized why the spell circle was so large—I imagined that Princeton performed this ritual in waves, turning multiple human recruits at once. It was likely an incredibly draining ritual, and it couldn't be performed too often. It wouldn't be safe for Princeton to be chronically exhausted and vulnerable, especially when the entire clan ran on his magick. When the clan *needed* him.

Like they now needed me.

I left the circle to hunt for more ingredients and tools. I didn't need as much this time, as Hekate knew what my sacrifice was going to be. She would be lending me far greater power in exchange. It was a one-time-only sacrifice, as I only possessed one soul. The next ritual would need to be far more involved.

Unless my heart gave out. Then there would be no more rituals.

I closed my eyes for a moment, shoving the thought away.

Princeton had told me to be quick. I grabbed objects hastily, my intuition leading the way. This wasn't ordinarily how I practiced magick. I was used to being careful, meticulous, and well-researched.

You are *well-researched,* one of my guides gently reminded me.

I remembered the book on Hekate and her magick that I'd been reading, the book I'd once been frightened of. I'd asked the chaos witch section in Etherdale University's library to show me what I needed, and the book had flown at my head.

Hekate had always been preparing me. Supporting me, guiding me. Even when I'd been too in denial to listen properly.

"Kylo?"

He'd been wordlessly taking objects from me to place on our makeshift altar in the center of the circle. Helping me without question, without any doubt in my abilities, despite me having only reconnected with my unpredictable, chaotic magick hours ago.

"Yes?" he asked, quickly scanning my eyes and body.

"Have you ever tattooed someone before?"

"Many times." He glanced at Idris. "I already gathered those materials for Idris. He will need clan tattoos."

My next breath was deep. "After we bring Idris back, I will also need you to tattoo... me."

He took a step forward. Something shifted in him. He released a shaky exhale, his eyes burning with a different, darker intensity than the grief or fear. They dropped again to my body, landing on my fluttering jugular.

I reacted to him subconsciously, despite where we were and

everything that had happened. It was beyond my control. The way I tilted toward him, my skin warming with anticipation.

Kylo was close now, and I didn't back away. He didn't touch me; he didn't need to. His words were a cool caress down my spine.

"I would love nothing more."

6

KYLO

Despite what Evie believed after my breach of trust, I'd never intended for her to join the clan. My drive had always been to protect her innocence, her dreams, her autonomy. I'd sooner die than make her feel used the way her parents had used her.

Even when she'd told me she wanted to join us, before she found out I had murdered John-Jarod-Whatever-His-Name-Was, I still had never fully agreed. I'd been resistant, consumed by my own protectiveness.

I didn't want this for her.

Not after I'd been powerless to save Aisling. And certainly not after the last witch in this position—my friend, brother, and mentor—had been slaughtered and was still without justice. All we knew was that Princeton's killer had been a masked mortal who'd gained access to our erotic dungeon, likely a witch. It was a maddening, unanswered question that served as yet another threat to Evie's life.

Yet I couldn't deny the way it felt to be working with her now, to be in the presence of power she'd finally freed from its cage. To have my purpose bound to hers after I thought I might have lost her.

Blood bond or not, I would've searched every inch of this realm until I found my angel and brought her home.

Luckily, my blood still coursed through her veins, through her fragile, beautiful heart. I wasn't sure what I would do if, gods forbid, another choice needed to be made during this ritual. To save Evie's life or let her die trying to save her brother's.

I didn't want to think about that.

I wanted to focus on the pleasure of serving Evie, making sure she had everything she needed. The ecstasy of her dark, starlit power flooded the room.

She was a dark goddess, a being that didn't belong in this realm. I was lucky to be near her, blessed merely to witness her brave, ethereal magick.

"I'm going to close the circle now," she said.

Such strength in that heart-melting, sweet voice. I didn't even feel guilty about the way it made my cock twitch in her direction.

"We won't be able to leave until the ritual is completed," she said. "No matter what, I need you not to interfere, not even if you think I need help. You could destroy us all in the process."

I wasn't sure if Evie's warning was a plea for me not to choose her over her brother, or if it was the cold hard truth. I resigned to believing it was a mixture of both.

These were powerful forces she was dealing with.

"I understand. Thank you for letting me be here."

Her mouth opened and then closed. I easily read her mind. She didn't want me to think she'd forgotten or forgiven me. Even if her body knew who it still belonged to. Even if her bright soul still reached in search of mine.

"Thank you for helping," she managed.

Evie began her workings, and my smile evaporated. I needed

her to live. That was why I'd allowed this, why I'd shut out Blade and Harmony. I needed Evie to see that I believed in her. So she would choose life. So she would allow me to stay close.

I knew I shouldn't make someone else my reason for living, but I'd never claimed to be a perfect, holy man or an ascetic monk.

I was Etherdale's rightful lord, a vampire born from magick and blood.

And Evie was mine.

Evie invoked the four elements and cardinal directions. She called upon the celestial realm, the heavens. She hesitated only a moment before calling on the chthonic realm and the hells. She invoked Hekate and the rest of her allies.

I noticed the small tremble in her hand when she spilled her own blood. And I saw the way her eyes lit up with surprise—maybe even delight—when the room surged with power the moment those drops of crimson touched the ground.

She set down the ritual knife, the knife I'd watched Princeton use countless times before. I was envious of Evie's connection to the other side. My once-human heart yearned to hear my mentor's voice again, rather than rely on my hopeful imagination.

Evie had been ignoring her brother's lifeless body since I'd retrieved him from the morgue. I could tell how much it disturbed her seeing him like this.

The circle's perimeter lit with leaping purple flames. They reflected in her eyes as she chanted, words flooding from her lips that were no longer recognizable, as if spoken in the tongue of the gods.

I couldn't help the unconscious, reverent smile that slipped when one of Evie's shadows slithered across the floor, acting as extra limbs to bring her a bowl of water and herbal oils.

Evie could no longer ignore Idris now. She frowned deeply as she consecrated the black bowl with lunar markings, blessing it in the name of Hekate. I homed in on the faint dew of sweat that had gathered on her forehead, the way her breathing was already labored.

As I sat in respectful stillness, she brushed the holy water across the crown of Idris's head. Between his eyebrows. His throat. His heart.

She blessed each of his major energy centers.

I had to swallow a gasp when she began to recite Princeton's usual turning ritual speech, only altering the language slightly in reverence to Hekate.

"Hekate, anoint this body and soul with the spirit of the revolution," she said. She touched a drop of her blood to Idris's third eye. "Though shadows may belong to Idris, so too shall he belong to the shadows. In exchange for eternal life, he pledges his service, his devotion, and his loyalty to a power greater than himself. He will become one part of a whole. He will be a..." Evie faltered, only for a beat. "A brother, in a family that will always stand with him, whom he will protect and uplift just as they will guide him through this transition. He will be a protector of the realm, of Helia and Selena's mortal children. He may be masked today, but tomorrow, he will wear his clan tattoos proudly in a liberated world."

Shadow whispers grew louder, gusts of wind sweeping through the circle. Evie braced herself as the wind slammed against her. She closed her eyes as her body shivered.

She was being tested by the powers she'd called. I held my breath every second until the winds calmed and Evie opened her eyes again.

Princeton's version of this ritual was far more theatrical, but he enjoyed putting on a show.

Evie set the bowl of blood next to Idris's head. She paused for a moment before looking at me.

"We're usually, um, still *awake* for this part," I whispered.

She nodded. "Can you please lift his head?"

I followed Evie's sweet, polite command wrapped in a question without hesitation. I gently parted Idris's lips.

The blood trickled from the bowl down Idris's throat, some of it spilling out and down the side of his face and neck. Evie was gentle, her face contorted with effort and exhaustion.

She pulled back, placing the remaining blood back on the altar at the northern edge of the circle.

"I offer you the blood of a born vampire," she said to her spirit allies. "Please nourish yourselves as you aid me in this rite."

Shadows circled Evie's feet, and I felt her heart flutter through the bond. I wanted to tell her to be careful, to keep the channeling of power nice and steady. I wanted desperately to guide her through this, but I'd promised not to interfere. I bit my tongue so hard it bled.

"From born blood we rise."

Evie changed before my eyes. She bloomed from her chrysalis, shadows swarming her from each focal point of the circle. Instead of releasing shadows, Evie now devoured them. They entered her mouth, her heart, her solar plexus, claiming her the same as she had finally claimed them.

A voice boomed from the cloud of holy darkness, a feminine power that rattled my bones.

"And from this day forward, the Masked Order will be renamed in honor of its patron goddess. The Hekate Clan, the rightful rulers of Etherdale and the spark of Ravenia's revolution."

I bowed my head. I closed my eyes. My body knew I was hearing the voice of a deity, a dark goddess of the chthonic realm.

Not Lillian.

Hekate.

It might've been wrong to do when Evie was already asking so much, but I said the prayer in my mind, anyway.

Please protect her. Thank you.

Evie's own voice left her lips over the boom of wind and screaming shadows. "I will initiate myself as Hekate's daughter under the light of the new moon, a vow I make with blood and shadow."

My heart squeezed, knowing what such a vow meant. If unfulfilled, Evie would perish.

"Turn my brother."

Some unholy bargain had been struck, and I didn't have enough time to process these monumental recent developments. The moment Evie turned back to Idris, the shadows swarmed him next.

I was thrown back, away from them and to the southern point of the circle.

Evie closed the distance between her and Idris. Her palms were outstretched, her face twisted with exertion as she channeled raw, unearthly power in and through. The purple flames shifted to black, leaping toward the ceiling.

The sigil markings began oozing crimson as if painted in blood.

Evie fell to her knees, closed her eyes, and held Idris's hand in both of hers.

When a tear fell down her cheek, her heart skipped a beat, and a strangled cry left her lips, I scrambled to my feet.

I took a step toward her and was blown back, barred from approach.

My teeth ground together. I struggled not to see Aisling, torn to pieces by the born while I watched, powerless to do a damn thing.

Evie was strong.

More than that—she'd been right. There had to be meaning to all of this. To the series of beautiful, cruel, horrifying, grueling, celestial moments that had led us here and would lead us into the revolution. I wanted to believe.

I *did* believe. How could I not when Evie herself was the greatest evidence for miracles and divinity there was?

"Come on, baby," I whispered. "Prove them wrong."

Had Idris's other hand twitched, or was it my hopeful imagination again?

It was hard to see through the chaotic web of power weaving around them. In a move that was all Evie's, she placed a pink flower over Idris's heart.

I tried to read her lips, her voice no more than a whisper. "It's your turn to bloom, my knight in shining armor."

Her lip wobbled. Then her head dropped, and it seemed like the power was settling. Draining, even.

I'd never been so tense, so terrified of my intuition proving fallible.

The sigils leaked, streams of blood creating a morbidly beautiful floral design around Idris and Evie. It reminded me of the stained-glass window in my library.

All I wanted was to be back in that room, reading to Evie while she sat in my lap where she belonged.

I was mesmerized as a stream of blood broke free from the formation, moving along the floor until it met Idris's head.

As if the blood he'd lost was flowing back inside his wound.

I had no more room for obsessive worrying. All I could do was stare in unshakable awe.

My angel was raising someone from the dead.

The power was definitely fading, redirected toward Idris. She was doing it. Evie was going to accomplish exactly what she said she would, and then I was going to force her to rest and heal.

"I can't find his soul," Evie whispered.

I heard the exhaustion weighing down every word. I wanted to help. Gods, I wished there was something I could do to help her.

I couldn't lose faith. Not when Idris remained motionless,

and the shadows quelled, and the winds no longer held me back from her.

"Come back, Idris," she said, nearly a sigh as her shoulders slumped. "Come back for me. For Mena. We have more love to experience."

Sweet girl. I wanted to be close to her again so badly it stabbed my heart.

My feet moved tentatively. One step and then the other.

Did we act too hastily? Did we miss a step that was crucial? Was she too drained? Was her deal denied?

Idris's hand twitched again. This time I was certain of it.

I was a godsdamned heretic to question her.

When Evie gasped, my heart stopped.

"Yeah, yeah," she whispered. "A *thank you* would've sufficed."

Her words were slurred. Who was she talking to?

One single gust of wind moved from the ceiling in a veil of white mist, colliding into Idris's body with a *pop*.

His eyes flew open. Evie's wilted body slumped. She was mumbling nonsense now.

Idris gasped for air, gulping it down, his body spasming.

I approached carefully, a few feet away now.

And it was a good thing too, because it only took three short seconds for Idris's pupils to blow wide, his mouth to open.

He bared his fangs. His nostrils flared.

Evie tried to lift her head. Her glassy eyes attempted to find her brother's. In her failed attempt to do either, she seemed unaware of Idris's movement.

Unaware that Idris was entering his first bloodlust.

When he reached for Evie, I tackled him.

7

KYLO

Idris growled, his face strained and eyes wild as he breathed raggedly. He stared at me without a glimmer of recognition. There was no room for humanity in a mind overtaken by bloodlust.

Luckily, the condition didn't last forever. All cravings could be ridden out.

Blood helped.

I'd placed a jar of human blood beneath the altar for exactly this purpose. Princeton's spell room was nothing if not well-stocked.

Idris fought and writhed against me. He snapped his jaws like a beast gone feral.

I glanced at Evie, but she'd never gotten back up after falling backward. Her breathing was slow, and she was fighting and failing to open her eyes.

It was time for me to take over. In a swift maneuver, I released Idris only to pull him into a headlock. I dragged his flailing body toward the altar. He flexed his newfound strength, but it was no match for mine. His movements were clumsy and hampered by urgency.

I'd had the foresight to dose this jar with a small amount of blood onyx, a paralytic poison to vampires. It wouldn't do any long-term damage, just enough to immobilize him and calm him down.

As soon as the lid was removed, Idris yanked the jar from my hands.

"Careful, now," I said, knowing my words went unheard.

The liquid sloshed against the sides, some of it spilling out as he lifted the glass to his lips.

As he chugged, he stopped fighting against me. I released a breath.

Luckily, as a newly turned, he had no comparison for this blood. Older, preserved blood was certainly a stale, unappetizing alternative to fresh.

And nothing compared to blood straight from the veins.

I gritted my teeth. I was starving. I hadn't fed since before Evie ran from me. And Evie had been so mysteriously broken that I hadn't felt comfortable feeding from her this morning or last night. I hadn't understood what was going on with her, so I'd taken to caring for her rather than taking. And like an idiot, I'd chosen to forgo blood altogether.

Because Evie had ruined my taste for anyone but her. It felt like disloyalty to sustain myself with another's blood, not to mention the lackluster, downright sickening taste. I was addicted to Evie and only Evie.

It was still irresponsible of me. Starving myself put her in danger, not to mention what it did to my power reserves. It was in her best interest for me to keep myself fed no matter what.

Watching Idris drink and settle down was both soothing and triggering to my hungry, overworked mind.

I needed to feed. And Evie needed to heal. More than that, she and her alluring, humanlike blood needed to get the fuck away from a newborn vampire.

She'd accomplished the impossible. She'd called a soul back

from Helia, and now I was certain she would never leave me again.

"What..." Idris slurred.

He'd gone limp, so I took back the empty jar and released him. He sat upright as he stared at me in utter confusion. His pupils were no longer saucers.

"I don't—" He swallowed, his gaze dropping down to his own body in utter terror. "Where am I?"

He stared at his palms as if not recognizing his own skin. I'd always felt paternal toward Idris, and those feelings had never been stronger.

"You're safe. I'm going to explain everything to you and answer all of your questions. If you want more blood, you're going to let me give you basic clan markings. Additional tattoos are earned. I will explain each step as we go."

Idris's eyes flashed on the word *blood*, even if he didn't yet understand why. I wasn't sure how much more of my words he truly comprehended after that one. His poor fangs were likely on fire right now.

"You were turned, Idris," I said. "You're one of us now."

I MOVED QUICKLY AND EFFICIENTLY. Either Idris was in shock, or the blood onyx had worked a little too well, because he hadn't spoken another word to me since awakening. He fought me only initially when I began to tattoo his skin with magickal ink, but after soothing words and reassurance, he settled.

These initial markings were for underground clearance, a signifier of his essence so he would be recognized by the clan and our magick, as well as glamour activation for appearing human or masked.

So far, the remnants of Princeton's workings had held up in the face of his death. But I wasn't sure how long our supplies would last. Eventually, Evie would need to craft her own ink and sigils.

Our tattoos and vampire essences were a union between our maker's magick and our own, which was why no vampire's gifts, skills, powers, and appearances were the same. The only constant was our shadows, which I now believed belonged to Hekate—even before she'd formally presented herself through Evie.

The mortals and turned had a goddess on our side, for reasons I was only beginning to understand. I'd always known greater forces were at play, made obvious by the numerous clans of turned rising up across Ravenia, but being a part of something so cosmically grand humbled me.

I'd been keeping careful watch of Evie as she napped on the floor behind us in a puddle of shadows. They roamed over her protectively.

It was fucking adorable.

I wanted her away from Idris, but her spell circle remained steady. We needed the concentration of magick and intention until Idris's markings were in place.

My own exhaustion was starting to reach me as I carefully needled into Idris's chest. I'd asked him where he wanted each sigil, and he'd just shaken his head as his brows drew together. I carefully chose for him.

I smiled when one of the sigils' onyx hues turned midnight purple, like a few of mine.

"Kylo?"

Evie's groggy voice reached me right on time.

"Angel, I need you to release the circle now," I said, striking a balance between commanding and soft. I kept my eyes on Idris, watching for a change.

I carefully set down the bone needle and enchanted ink in a box of magickal supplies.

Evie decided to be a good girl, and I immediately felt the

energetic shift in the room. There was a sudden stillness when the circle's misty border evaporated.

At the flash of Idris's fangs, I executed the correct next steps.

"I'm going to take you somewhere to feed. I'm also going to find some of your turned friends and classmates to be with you."

Idris needed familiarity. He was a bright kid. He likely suspected which of his older classmates were part of the clan. When I'd blacklisted him from recruitment per Evie's desperate request, I'd learned he was already on our list of potentials.

He was going to have more support than he knew what to do with. He was going to be okay.

I helped Idris to his feet and supported him as he leaned against me, still half-paralyzed.

Evie was making an admirable effort to stand.

"Stay put, angel," I said, and this time the command was sharper. "Idris is okay, but if you approach him, he will try to eat you. He has no control over it, and it will be rather traumatic for you both."

Her eyes scanned Idris rapidly as she swayed on her feet. Tears spilled down her cheeks, her lips wobbling.

She nodded. "Okay."

"Good girl," I whispered. "He's not going anywhere. You'll be able to see him soon. I'll be right back."

I headed to the door. "You can go back to sleep. I'll carry you somewhere more comfortable when I return."

Those big gray eyes were wide, her soft pink lips parted slightly.

"Evie, you just rose someone from the dead. *Rest.*"

8

EVIE

I rose someone from the dead.

I'd heard of such a thing in myths and legends, but never in magickal case studies—never in the realm of verifiable reality. Witches were not meant to cheat death. Not like that. Not after a soul had already been returned to Helia.

It had all been a haze. I'd been almost entirely in a trance state, and it often felt as though other beings had taken up residence in my body throughout the rite. Words and actions had poured from me beyond my conscious awareness.

Never in my life had I channeled such power. Certainly not intentionally.

I wish I could say I was terrified—of the consequences of breaking the laws of reality, of my own capacity for world-bending—but there was a high to this power I couldn't deny.

All my life, all I'd ever wanted was safety. Running and hiding hadn't worked. But this?

This could work.

I *was* the motherfucking Tower.

Ironically, I was thinking these thoughts in a half-conscious state. My body remained vulnerably mortal, my strength not without limits.

When I detected Kylo's scent, I snuggled closer to him. I inhaled deeply and easily, letting the notes of mint, leather, and woodsy musk cocoon me in comforting familiarity.

Lips brushed across my forehead as arms held me tight.

Another mortal limitation made itself painfully apparent. I hadn't forgotten what Kylo had done, but I pretended as if I had in this groggy state.

Because I wanted to be close to him. I wanted to feel safe in his arms.

I didn't want to admit that I was glad I'd failed in my efforts to dig out our bond and leave him forever.

That was my most mortal limitation of all.

"I HESITATE TO WAKE YOU, but it has been an impressive twenty-two hours," Kylo murmured.

I stretched like a cat, basking in a pleasurable and strange groundedness in my body that only came from oversleeping.

Slow to process and remember, my gaze swept from Kylo to his familiar bedroom before I frowned deeply.

"Don't you have a spare room?"

My voice was soft and kissed by sleep, effectively erasing the anger I'd been trying to conjure.

Kylo smirked, perched on the edge of the bed as he watched me. "Seeing as you never actually broke up with me, I thought it might be strange to make my sleepy, incapacitated girlfriend recover in the guest bed."

"A poisoned needle in your abdomen wasn't obvious enough of an ending for you?"

Kylo's eyes narrowed for a split second before softening back to their gentle blue.

I braced myself for something cocky to leave his lips, something classically brazen and Kylo that would both make my body squirm and also wedge wider our divide of broken trust.

"Evie, I need to apologize," he said instead. "Would you prefer coffee first?"

I blinked. I fucking loathed this man.

I glared at the ceiling and away from his deceptively earnest eyes.

"Coffee first," I grumbled.

Kylo's low chuckle felt like a defeat.

And of course, because Kylo was Kylo, he did effectively create a coffee hostage situation until I drank a glass of water and took my first bite of food.

"I don't scare you at all, do I?" I muttered as I sipped my blessedly warm, caffeinated beverage at the kitchen island.

Kylo threw me a devastating grin from his place at the sink. "Aw, do you wish your big scary shadow powers frightened me, angel?"

I glowered.

"You know what's better than being feared?" He paused, turning to lean over the island between us as he pinned me with his gaze. "Being respected. I want to worship you, Evie. I don't fear you. I only fear losing you."

Kylo and his stupid, perfect words. I suppressed the urge to growl in frustration. I knew what he had done to Jacob. I poisoned him and ran from him—the one thing he'd commanded me never to do. I'd challenged his control, his authority.

Yet there was no grand, sinister mask slip. He didn't move to punish me. To gaslight me. To make me feel guilty or wrong or stupid.

Kylo was still Kylo, the man I'd fallen in love with.

The man who betrayed me and covered it up.

"Idris is safe?" I asked again, even though he'd already

answered this question a few times in different ways as he'd cooked me breakfast.

Kylo didn't show a hint of irritation. "Yes, baby. He's just a little shocked and doesn't remember what happened. He's being expertly cared for."

Kylo had told me that he'd checked on Idris multiple times while I'd been asleep. I knew it wasn't safe to visit him yet, but the urge was as strong as ever.

"Did I hurt anyone? Besides the born and Servant of Lillian?"

Kylo's eyes darkened. "No, not to my knowledge. The shadows scorched quite a bit of land, and the surrounding area experienced high winds, property damage, fear for their lives..." His lip curled. "Did the witch know who you were? Is that why they attacked you?"

I shook my head. "No."

Anger rattled my bones. I felt my shadows yearning to break free, and for the first time in my life, I was easily able to soothe my dark magick back to rest.

Because I no longer feared it. *And* because I promised to deliver my darkness its next desired meal.

"This was the fucking Whitfields."

Kylo was perplexed for only a moment before he put two and two together. His face dropped from wrath to guilt in the next breath.

The sound of Idris's skull splitting had me seeing red. "They killed my brother. I'm going to see to it that they get everything they deserve."

Kylo sighed. "Reasonable. And also sexy," he drawled. "But we can't afford another magickal explosion. Not now. Not with all of Ravenia's eyes on us."

All of Ravenia? Oh gods. The old Evie reared her fearful head for only a brief moment.

"Then I won't explode," I said simply. I took another gulp of coffee and bite of eggs as visions of righteous violence flashed across my mind's eye.

I hadn't realized I'd been smirking until Kylo's eyes were glued to my lips. His arm muscles flexed, something potent sparking the air between us.

He seemed to shake himself out of it with monumental effort. "We are still glamoured. We're on the precipice of war. And when the born strike, I need the clan to be prepared. Not taken off guard and forced to adapt, especially with our new chaos witch only just learning to wield her power. I have been building these forces and forging our path carefully for eighty years."

My eyes widened. He really was grandpa-aged. Maybe even great-grandpa. I comforted myself with his beautiful, masculine features and bulky tattooed muscles until my stomach settled. Vampires were *old*.

Kylo's brow lifted. "Angel?"

"You aren't allowed to be the only one to deliver *justice*, and I use that term lightly when it comes to you," I spat. "If I'm truly not a prisoner or a means to an end, then you will stay out of my way." I straightened, making my once people-pleasing demeanor unyielding instead. "I am going to pay the Whitfields a visit. Today."

Kylo's jaw ticked. "No longer scared of war, are we?" he asked, his voice low and slightly condescending.

I bristled.

"Your brother isn't ready for battle either, Evie. He's going to want to protect you and Mena. And to do so, he needs training and *time*."

I opened my mouth to state the obvious—that even without another magickal explosion, the born could move in at any moment. Kylo already knew this.

"I can't have you revealing your identity," he said. "You are already the most coveted kill in the city."

We stood in a silent, calculated stare-off. So much was said, and so much more remained unsaid and painfully obvious.

"I don't suppose you know how to keep a death neat and tidy then, do you?" I said, faux sweetness layered atop my poisoned, bitter tongue.

Kylo didn't back down. "It's in my wheelhouse."

I made a soft noise of derision before finishing my food and coffee.

This kitchen was where I discovered what Kylo had done—what he'd hidden from me after promising to never let me down.

"How could you do that to me?" I asked finally. "Do you have any idea how ruinously you broke my heart?"

Kylo's face fell, his hands dropping to his sides as he stared at the marble island.

My voice quivered with anger, with grief I hadn't been able to fully feel yet. Not when I had tunnel vision, determined to get me, Idris, and Mena far away from Kylo and the clan. And certainly not after Idris had died.

It was here now, rage slowly melting into that crushing heartbreak.

His gaze returned to mine with a gentle steadiness. "I'm so sorry, Evie. I should've told you. I told myself I was protecting your heart, but I know I was protecting myself most of all. I didn't want to see you in pain, especially over someone who didn't deserve it. It breaks *my* heart to know I broke yours." He shook his head. "It took unfathomable bravery for you to trust me in the first place, and I broke my promise. I let you down. I hate what I did and how it could've led to me losing you for good."

Now it was my turn to stare at the countertop. I'd crumbled in his arms, telling him how scared I was to love him, how brutally shattered my parents had left me with their abuse and cruel apathy.

"And?"

I waited.

Kylo blinked.

My lips turned down, my nostrils flaring. I clenched both fists. My heart panged, begging me to stay focused on Kylo's genuineness, his apology and accountability for his actions. I wanted to fill the void he'd dug into my soul and never feel so empty again.

But there was one action he had *not* taken accountability for. And it was glaring.

"I'm not sorry for killing Jacob."

My mouth dropped open, and my eyes snapped to his.

"He saw you get attacked on the street outside the restaurant, and he ran the other way. He didn't yell for help. He didn't fight to protect you. The born vampire noticed him, and he chose to save himself."

The words were more daggers to my bruised heart. I remembered what I'd seen when I touched Kylo's dagger. Yes, Kylo had brutally killed Jacob after humiliating him and making him piss himself. But Jacob had also offered me to Kylo in exchange for his life. He'd said he wanted nothing to do with me anymore. It was painful to know that Jacob wasn't just a selfish, dismissive cheater, but he also didn't care whether I lived or died.

And I'd allowed someone like that to be in my life. To see me naked. To crush my feelings with no remorse.

I shifted in my seat.

"I know it was extreme," Kylo said. "But *I am extreme*. Especially when it comes to protecting those who deserve to be protected."

I felt his intensity charge the air, circling us.

"You said you wanted to kill him just for touching me."

"And I resisted the urge," Kylo said with a shrug. "You weren't officially mine yet, even if it felt like you were. I killed him because he put you in danger, and he was always going to put you in danger. I'm not sorry for that. I'm sorry for keeping it from you and creating a web of lies by omission."

My mind replayed all that I'd assumed when I'd learned the truth. I thought Kylo had been love bombing me, manipulating me, isolating me. Even if that didn't quite make sense. The paranoia in the wake of his deceit had taken completely over.

"It's still fucked-up," I snapped. "So you're just going to kill people close to me whenever you feel it's justified?"

Kylo's eyes told me the truth before he could. Before I could snap at him again, he spoke first.

"I will never kill someone close to you without your prior knowledge ever again."

"Without my *approval*," I hissed.

Kylo smiled, that silly little dimple working overtime to melt me into useless, pliable goo.

"You're so sexy when you're negotiating, baby," Kylo purred. "I remember our first negotiation like it was yesterday..."

An image of Kylo holding me underwater while his shadows roamed my body flashed against my will.

I stiffened, my body coming alive, yearning to be closer to him.

Kylo inhaled deeply, and my glare became scorching. At the first hint of his smile, one of my shadows burst free. Kylo grabbed it with his own shadow, and soon the smoky tendrils intertwined in the space between us.

I huffed. "*Traitor.*"

The shadow ignored me, only tracing Kylo's jaw when she finally reached him.

Kylo's grin was dangerous now.

I yanked my darkness back inside me and away from his. "We aren't negotiating, Kylo. It was wrong of you to kill my boyfriend."

"Ex-boyfriend."

"Urgh! It was wrong of you to kill him, and I never want to feel like you don't respect me enough to give me a say in my own life *ever again*."

The words came out fierce despite my natural, trauma-induced doormat tendencies. And it felt good to be strong, to stand up for myself the way I hadn't always been able to. I didn't want to keep letting myself down.

"Or you can't be a part of my life," I finished. "Not in any meaningful, intimate way."

Kylo's smile vanished.

Our fates were bound together now. But I still had a choice. We didn't have to be romantically involved to work with one another. We could merely be allies, for the good of the revolution.

I remained strong even as my heart panged, my parental wound begging me to give up all of my boundaries just so Kylo would continue to love me.

I was terrified, conditioned to believe that my feelings didn't matter. That if I wanted someone to love me, I had to give up my intuition, thoughts, and desires. Because mine were wrong, too much, and not to be trusted.

But I saw the truth now. My soulmate would show up for me in the way I needed him to, and if that wasn't Kylo, then I would learn to live with that. No matter how badly it would hurt, no matter how long I would be devastated trying to come to terms with the inconceivable.

I hadn't realized I'd started to cry until a tear dropped to the counter, and Kylo was by my side in an instant.

"I don't think powerful witches should cry as much as I do," I muttered.

Kylo rubbed soothing circles on my back. "Yes, they should. Because it means they're tapped in. It means they're beautifully mortal." He stroked my hair next, and I melted into his touch. "I never want to make you feel like I don't respect you. I want your approval on any decision that might affect you, so long as it's not a matter of immediate life or death. I wouldn't be truthful if I were to apologize for taking Jacob's life. But I am sorry for the way I did it and everything that came after. Most of all, I'm sorry for failing to protect your heart. If you will allow me to, I will work tirelessly to earn back your trust. As long as it takes."

My head found itself resting against Kylo's chest as he continued his comforting touch. Tears still fell from my eyes, emotions hitting me from every conceivable direction.

It had been a long fucking week.

"I'm still so angry," I whispered. "I want to believe I know who you are, but I'm afraid of getting the rug pulled out from under me. I want *us* to have meaning—and it was shattering to think that nothing about us had any at all. That it was a lie from the start."

Kylo lifted me into his arms, and I allowed him to. He brought me into his lap in a chair in the living room. He cradled my face in his hands, those beautiful lips downturned.

"What an agonizing thing to hear," Kylo murmured, pain ripe in his solemn voice. "That you might not believe we were made for each other anymore."

I stared down at his chest, brows drawn. He tucked a strand of hair behind my ear.

"That's okay, angel. I'll believe enough for both of us."

He'd never felt real. Perhaps that was why it had been so easy to believe the worst.

"Be as angry and distrustful as you need to be, for however long. Didn't much bother me before," he said, humor easing back into his voice.

His smile still held notes of pain that I traced with my expanded witch sight. My own lips twitched in spite of myself.

"I think I know what might cheer you up."

I nodded. "Me too."

"Let's go kill the Whitfields. Neatly and tidily."

He finally got me to smile.

9

EVIE

The Whitfields had hired guards. Loyalist shifter vampire hunters, to be exact. While the majority of mortals detested the born and stood on the correct side of this impending revolution, there would always be those who ignorantly fought against their own interests. Whether because they thought they were preserving their place in the wealth and power hierarchy, or they'd succumbed to the borns' asinine propaganda machine, it was hard to say. Usually a mix of both.

That had never been me. Though, after the widespread, unspeakable cruelty Hekate had me witness, I still felt a thick layer of shame from my own complacency.

Shame is wasted, a shadow whispered. *It will only weaken you. You did the best you could with what you had at the time. Move from devotion now.*

"I don't feel good about killing the guards," I admitted to Kylo from our spot on the outskirts of the Whitfield estate. Kylo's shadows protected us from prying eyes, though we were also concealed by meticulously manicured shrubs. The moon was the thinnest crescent above.

It was the middle of the night. Tomorrow was the new moon and the night I would dedicate myself to Hekate and the clan, lest I be consumed by shadows. It was the night Kylo would tattoo me, which he was *far* too excited about.

"They'd feel just fine about killing you," Kylo said. "I am certain the guards are fully aware that the Whitfields offered Idris as bait to lure you away. And I guarantee they were fine with that too."

That second point was enough for me. I gritted my teeth. My shadows were starving, my rage a delirious, intoxicating buzz.

Because now, I could actually *do something about it.*

"But won't people suspect this was me? If their hired help knows, wouldn't they have told their friends?"

"It's possible, but I doubt it," Kylo said. "That's not how powerful people operate. They don't show their weaknesses and open themselves up to more attack. Especially not a businessman like Roger. They're both well-aware that their high-class circles are filled to the brim with snakes, and they certainly don't want the clan or our allies after them. Even if a few people suspect you..."

"Like Jacob's friends and Kailey, the woman he cheated on me with," I interjected.

"Remind me again why I'm supposed to feel sorry for eliminating that rodent?"

I elbowed Kylo, and he grabbed my arm, turning to tower over me. "Careful, angel. I bite." He inhaled deeply. "Even if they suspect you, they're humans. They're not going to do shit. They will have seen what happened to the Whitfields after they targeted you, and they'll have even more reason to keep their mouths shut and avoid getting on our bad side." He lowered his head, his lips close to my ear. "On *your* bad side."

To say the Whitfields were on my bad side was putting it mildly.

"Okay, we've scouted and discussed, I'm ready to move," I said impatiently.

Kylo groaned. "You have no idea how sexy it is to see you as starving for violent retribution as I am. How many couples can share this intense, intimate bonding activity?"

He stroked my cheek, and I yanked back. Kylo smiled.

"Is *murder* the bonding activity?"

I shook my head, even as my lips threatened to form a begrudging smile.

"No, baby." He looked like he wanted to reach for me again but refrained. "It's revenge."

He tilted his head, wordlessly indicating for me to follow him. It took him a couple seconds to remember that my shadowed powers didn't include super speed or strength. My short legs were no match for his.

He shot me a sheepish, apologetic look as I glared at him for almost leaving me behind.

We must've set off a magickal trigger, as the guards began hissing orders the moment we crossed a certain threshold.

"We need to take them out quickly, so no one else is alerted to our presence," Kylo said, in a tone that was rarely used with me. It was all-business, authority that spanned decades. "Remember everything we discussed."

I nodded. The two guards on the front porch were scanning for us. One was armed with a crossbow, and another wielded a dagger in each hand, weapons no doubt imbued with blood onyx.

A growl ripped through the night.

"Fuck, I'll take out the beast," Kylo whispered. He eyed me with hesitation for only a blink before kissing the side of my head.

A large black panther sniffed us out immediately—a shifter in animal form. It barreled for us.

All of my senses heightened at once. I called on my power, channeling every drop of rage I'd suppressed all my life.

I wielded my shadows with control, careful not to allow too much through.

No strange weather, I commanded the darkness.

The glamour dropped. I visualized a shadow as sharp as a blade, like I'd seen Kylo wield before. My mind melded with my magick, and a third and fourth limb sprouted from me.

The shadows shot forward, and with a degree of clumsiness, I impaled the two burly men the moment they leaped for us. One of them clutched at his chest, crimson blooming in the center of his green shirt. The other had been impaled at the throat, and he dropped immediately as he gurgled and choked. I quickly tilted my head, maneuvering the second shadow to finish off the man bleeding from his chest before he could yell.

The shadow sped through the air. My stomach lurched when it sliced clean through his neck, unintentionally removing the man's head from his body.

Kylo had made his own move at the same time as I had, his shadows lassoing around the panther and snapping its neck. Now he was beside me, barely exerted, chuckling softly.

"They were really sharp! And I didn't want him to scream," I hurried out, horrified as I turned toward Kylo.

Kylo laughed harder. "Angel," he mock scolded. "Absolutely ruthless." He stepped forward, staring down at the severed head on the bottom of the steps. "And *very* messy. Bad girl."

His voice was a sinful purr. My body was reacting to his words incredibly inappropriately, given the context.

Or maybe Kylo and I had the kind of sick minds that couldn't quite tell the difference between sex and violence.

"Cleanup crew will handle it," he assured me as my lips twisted. "Come on," he said, still laughing and shaking his head.

I followed him up the steps. A grand marble pillar was now splattered with blood.

Kylo lifted another brow, and I glowered at him.

A voice from beyond the ornate, polished front door startled me. My ears pricked with recognition.

"I'm sure it's fine, Cindy. Just another false alarm like last week," Roger called from behind the door. His voice nearly carried the façade of a doting husband, but irritation bled through the cracks in abundance.

Like father like son.

"I heard a *growl!*" Cindy's shrill voice called. "And commotion!"

"Oh no, not *commotion*," Kylo whispered.

I bit my tongue on a laugh.

The door flew open, and Kylo moved quickly to shove a cloth gag in Roger's mouth before he could utter a sound.

"Roger?" Cindy called, whiny and pathetic.

Like mother like son, too.

We slipped inside, and I closed the door behind us as Kylo kept a dagger to Roger's throat. The sight of his favorite blade and its spilled secrets pissed me off, but I decided to use that as fuel too.

Kylo had fucked up. But Jacob and his family had fucked up *far worse*.

"Make a sound, and Roger loses blood," I said flatly as soon as my gaze collided with Cindy's.

She stood cowering in the spacious foyer, halfway down one of the lavish staircases. The house was even gaudier than I remembered, sparkling with fine crystal and shitty art and gold *everything*.

"Get the fuck down here, Cindy," I hissed.

As I did, my shadows crawled from me like snakes, making their own hissing sounds.

She trembled, and I could tell it wasn't even authentic—her movements exaggerated as her mouth wobbled, and she fought the urge to wail.

Likely inebriated on one or more substances, Cindy shook her head and clutched the railing for dear life. She mouthed the word *Roger* dramatically, her puny mind working on overdrive for a few beats before she leveled a cold glare on me.

"You killed my son!"

Kylo slashed Roger's face. Roger hissed in pain, reaching for his wounds in shock—as if he'd never had to consider his own mortality before. He stared at the blood that came away on his palms in horror.

"I warned you," I said sweetly to Cindy. "Do you want to walk down here yourself or do you want me to force you to come down?"

My shadows slithered closer, curling around the banister.

Roger stared at me as if in unrecognition. It was the first time his gaze hadn't oozed with lust. Probably because I was no longer so naive and vulnerable.

I had power now, and that wasn't a quality Whitfield men wanted in their women.

Cindy's shoulders slumped, sobbing with a quiet histrionic flair. As soon as she made it to the base of the stairs, I wrapped one of my shadows over her mouth and pulled her forward as if she were leashed. Her cry was muffled.

Kylo merely followed my lead. *His* gaze, on the other hand, absolutely oozed with lust.

I led my prisoners down to the basement, the basement in which I'd given Jacob blowjobs without any degree of reciprocity.

Witch lights responded to our presence, flickering on overhead. *Dim,* I commanded.

I shoved Cindy to the floor.

"Good thing this basement is soundproof!" I said cheerfully. "That's what you always used to joke, right Roger? How no one would be able to hear me scream? Violence against women is hilarious!"

Kylo pushed Roger to the floor next to his wife, and he was far less gentle than I'd been. Roger removed his gag with shaking hands. Kylo's lip curled as he regarded Roger with wrathful disgust.

We were in the center of the basement, a space for entertaining high-class leeches or mistresses. Roger and Cindy were positioned on the opulent marble floor, up against a wall separating the kitchen from a drawing room.

"Congrats to you both," I said, my power growing slightly less stable as I allowed more anger through. The walls shook, and Kylo ran a hand through my hair. "You killed Idris. You killed my eighteen-year-old brother. You murdered an innocent, human university student."

Roger averted his eyes to the floor. Cindy vibrated with emotion. I let her gag fall.

"We didn't tell anyone to kill that boy," she said. She appeared to be fighting hard to keep from saying what she truly wanted to say. She wasn't known for her restraint. "We wanted justice for Jacob. He was our son! We only wanted the authorities to investigate what had happened to him."

I laughed dryly. "The *authorities*. You mean born vampires tasked with murdering witches? Born vampires who throw away human life like it means nothing at all?"

"These were respectable individuals," Cindy said, shaking her head. "They wouldn't kill anyone who was truly innocent and law-abiding."

"You're either a fucking idiot or a fucking liar. Which one is it, Cindy?"

A gust of wind shot her back, her head striking hard against the wall. It wasn't nearly as sickening as the noise Idris's head had made. She cried, rubbing her skull.

No apology. No remorse. All Cindy did was defend the monsters in power.

"Why are you always so quiet?" I screamed at Roger, who

reached for Cindy's hand and mumbled something useless about how it was all going to be okay. His eyes were slow to meet mine. "Saying less makes it easier for you to get away with your own atrocities, doesn't it? Open your mouth too wide, and I bet all manner of harrowing admissions might fall out."

I'd always detected Roger's putrid soul with my witchy senses, but its stench was even stronger now in the face of my power.

Roger's face reddened, one of the first signs of his true emotions I'd ever seen from him. "This whole neighborhood knows what you are, girl," he hissed. "They will know who harmed us. You and your criminal boyfriend will be hung up in the streets."

There was that carefully concealed venom.

I grinned. "But if given the chance, I'd bet you'd still try to fuck me, huh Roger?"

Kylo was glued to my side in an instant, his hand on the back of my neck in a clear show of dominant possession. Heat radiated from his every pore.

"Remember how you tried to take advantage of me? When I was in tears after Jacob mistreated me yet again?"

"I offered you *comfort*," Roger stammered, pretending to be appalled by the notion. "And I would never involve myself with a vampire clan's whore."

Kylo threw his dagger. It collided with Roger's shoulder with such force that he slid backward, hitting the wall as he yelled in pain.

I glanced up at Kylo, the menacing cold of his blue eyes and dilated pupils. The flash of his shiny fangs.

"My hand slipped," he said with a shrug.

His hand gripped my neck harder, but not enough to reduce my airflow. My core turned molten.

Yep, those sex and violence wires were definitely crossed.

Oh well. One of my shadows yanked the dagger out of

Roger's shoulder and delivered it back to Kylo's waiting hand. Cindy was wailing in that irritating way she did, pressing on Roger's wound. Blood still dribbled from Roger's cheek where he'd been slashed.

I kept them both pinned against the wall, shadows curling around every limb. I moved closer now, soaking up their hatred as the whispers grew louder in my ears.

My shadows were hungry. Not for violence for violence's sake. But for retribution, for the eliminating of soulless creatures devoid of humanity. People who would sentence an innocent human boy to death without a second thought.

Loyalists who defended cruelty so long as it kept them comfortable in their tacky, haunted mansions.

They both writhed against their bindings. In them, I saw my parents, offering up their children as tithing.

I didn't feel remorse when my shadows grew uncomfortably tight, inching closer to their necks and faces.

"You had my brother kidnapped, tortured, and then killed in cold blood. Everything you accused *me* of." I crouched in front of them, spitting out each syllable.

"Well then I guess we're just as good as you are, aren't we?" Roger asked, his mask finally all the way off. His brown eyes were nearly black now, like two empty voids.

I thought I wanted to see them beg. Or admit what they'd done, what they were truly capable of. Like a trial before an execution.

But now that I was here, absorbing the cool emptiness of their gray, useless souls, I realized that I didn't really want to talk it out.

There was nothing left to say. I understood everything about them.

"You were probably just a victim, at one point," I said to Cindy as a shadow reached for her eyeballs. "I do feel sorry for you, on some level. But you're not the only one who has been abused by narcissistic men. And instead of wanting better for your son, you chose to stay comfortable. You let him become another monster."

"I don't think she was ever merely a victim," Kylo said from behind me, his body heat at my back. "I know her family. But I do love your empathy and optimism as always, baby."

I shrugged. "Anyway…"

Roger's evil hissing and insults transformed quickly into terrified sobs as the shadows entered his ears and mouth.

"You killed my brother, and you don't give a fuck. If I had it my way, this would've been an execution worthy of artistic immortalization. Your entire estate would've been returned to Lillian. But we have to keep things *neat and tidy*." I jutted my bottom lip with a cock of my head.

I let the shadows plunge into Cindy's eyes, showing her the truth of what she'd done to my brother—a loop of his suffering that played over and over—before she stopped fighting, and life was drained from her.

Roger only saw himself, eaten alive, as shadows stole his last breaths. A man like him had never considered his own death. I bet he'd deluded himself into thinking he'd live forever.

"Death, the great equalizer," I murmured.

No more wailing. No more vitriol. The people who'd tried to have me killed no longer existed.

Best of all? They'd failed at killing Idris too.

I was truly the only winner here.

My shadows crawled back to me, and I turned away from their lifeless, ruined bodies. The mansion was quiet save for the low hum of our combined power.

Mine and Kylo's—the tall weapon of a man whose focus was devotedly trained on *me*.

My nerves were achingly alive, my sight and hearing sensitive and in tune with the fabric of this world and the great beyond. Would touch feel similarly as intense?

Taste?

I stared at Kylo's lips.

When his hand slowly reached for my cheek, I didn't pull away this time.

"You've got some blood on you, angel," he said, voice low but strong.

I wanted to bathe in his strength, cede myself to it. I was blissfully free, the looming threat of the Whitfields no longer hanging over me.

"I don't forgive you," I whispered before tugging Kylo's head down toward mine.

Our lips collided. Kylo's tongue teased mine. He grabbed my waist, pulling me against him as his cock grew and hardened against me. I moaned into his mouth. The room filled with dark power.

10

EVIE

Kylo's kiss was painful. His fangs were out. He sucked and nibbled and devoured, and I tasted every ounce of his intensity on my tongue.

His kiss was a command for me to never leave him. His hands at my waist were a mark of possession.

My legs wrapped around him the moment he lifted me. Before I knew it, we were on a fur rug, soft and luxurious under my flushed skin.

Kylo wrapped his hand around my throat. "Damnit, Evie," he hissed. "*Don't you ever fucking do that to me again.*"

I bucked against him, but before I could speak, two of his long fingers were in my mouth. My teeth scraped against them.

Kylo grinned. "Try it. See what happens."

I bit down.

Kylo had me flipped onto my stomach and pinned to the floor before I could taste blood.

"You can be a bad girl to your heart's content," Kylo hissed. "With anyone but *me.*"

He shoved up the fabric of my lavender dress as my legs flailed.

"Oh, how I've missed those adorable kicking feet."

His shadows curled around my ankles. Kylo's hand came down against the curve of my exposed ass.

I gasped. I could fight back. I'd barely exerted myself killing the Whitfields.

But I didn't. My shadows contentedly curled up inside me for a nap, satisfied and well-fed.

I merely squirmed as Kylo spanked me and held me down. A quick succession of slaps until I screamed and my legs shook.

He paused to study me, my cheek pressed against the rug.

I nodded, silently affirming what he already knew.

"Limits?" he asked. He tongued his fangs, his eyes dark and hungry.

"The same as before," I breathed, before my overthinking brain could change my mind. I didn't want to live the way I used to—overintellectualizing and ruminating and denying myself.

I deserved to indulge, to let flesh be flesh, to satisfy yearnings dark and shadowed.

"When was the last time you fed?" I asked, curious.

Kylo grabbed my ass painfully until I winced, and he delighted in my pain, drank it in as ravenously as he did my blood.

"While you were sleeping."

My frown was immediate. I detected a note of avoidance in his energy, like he was hiding something. His touch was soft now as he trailed his fingers along my skin. They crept across my panties, teasing.

I arched my back, a soft moan leaving my lips. My ass cheeks were radiating heat and stinging, my pussy surging with need.

"Are you upset?" Kylo asked.

"Yes, but I know that's not fair of me. Considering there was no way in hell you were going to be feeding from *me*."

Kylo's eyes darkened, a wrathful chuckle sending a chill

down my spine. "My unforgiving angel wants me starving for her, hmm? Shall I waste away, unable to feed entirely?"

"Yep."

Two of Kylo's fingers plunged inside me without warning, and I yelped at the sudden fullness.

"Greedy little thing," he growled.

He bent and sank his teeth into my shoulder, marking me without feeding.

I cried out, attempting to lift up before Kylo shoved me back down and placed some of his weight on my back with his knee. He fucked me mercilessly with his fingers until I'd melted into the carpet, moaning and opening myself up to him.

"What a soaking wet mess you are," he taunted, removing his fingers the moment I reached a tall peak.

I whined in frustration.

"I should mark your pretty face with cum and then take you home unsatisfied," he said cruelly. "But even that doesn't sound like nearly enough of a punishment."

"For biting your fingers?" I asked, knowing full well that was not what Kylo was punishing me for.

He bit me again, this time on one of my stinging ass cheeks. Another scream escaped me.

"I don't like this new attitude, baby," he said. "You were never one to brat off."

"Things change," I growled. "Adversity will be good for you. It might strengthen your character."

Kylo's laugh rumbled through me. I had no time to react before he'd lifted and peeled me off the floor. I kicked and fought as he dragged me, my back to his chest and his breath skating over my ear.

"You don't want to be my good girl anymore?"

He pulled me into his lap as he leaned against the wall, forcing my legs apart as he held me tight.

"Shhh," he whispered, tickling my ear.

I shivered, and his lips brushed against the shell before his tongue teased. I melted into tingling, undeniable pleasure.

I settled.

"Mmhmm," he wordlessly praised.

One of his shadows roamed my body, encircling a nipple before squeezing. Before I could yelp, Kylo's hand was over my mouth, muffling the sound.

And when a second shadow slipped under my panties, cutting them clean off, I was utterly still. It was soft and solid when it met my clit, vibrating softly.

I began to grind, arching my hips to meet the intoxicating sensation.

"There's my good girl," Kylo purred.

And damn him, the praise was a stronger drug than resisting him. He was right, but I didn't want to admit it.

I wasn't a brat, at my core. I just couldn't let him off the hook so easily for breaking my trust, for crushing my heart.

For forcing me to believe our connection wasn't written in the stars.

His cock pressed harder against me, Kylo's hips grinding the same as mine.

I was snug against him. And it felt safe, to be this close and tightly held. His fangs skated across my neck, and I tilted my head to give him easier access.

Kylo didn't hesitate, a feral, possessive noise crashing through him from deep inside his throat. He sank his fangs into my flesh and sucked.

He gripped me tight enough to leave bruises, and I didn't make a sound. Only one long, relieved sigh. A shadow plunged inside me, and I exploded in a sweeping orgasm that brushed the cosmos.

After an eternity of ecstasy, Kylo's tongue closed up the wound as his venom coursed inside me.

"That's it, angel," Kylo said, his voice filling the entire room with its power.

I hung on his every word like he was my God. Waiting, listening, melting.

"Show me how much you don't forgive me."

He moved me gently now, ever so careful with his good little doll. I stared up at him with hooded eyes as he loomed over me, between my spread thighs. His cock sprung free, as large and frightening as always.

"You, covered in enemy blood and staring at my cock with rapt captivation and fear, is my new favorite sight." His grin slowly spread as he squeezed both my breasts beneath the fabric. "Deep breaths. You'll warm up to me soon. We'll just need to be more consistent."

My eyes rolled back the moment his cock impaled me. My brows drew close, but it was easy to relax when I was venom drunk and hooked on Kylo's praise.

"Eyes on me, angel," he commanded.

Kylo's jaw was tight, his gaze fiery. A shadow curled around my throat.

He gripped my cheeks between his thumb and forefinger. "I'm getting you a fucking collar."

My eyes widened, but I only reached for him, tugging his head closer to mine.

Kylo smiled. He happily acquiesced, lips melding with mine softly at first before becoming just as violent. His body jerked, and he buried himself deeper. My legs shook. His tongue conquered my mouth, tasting me as desperately as I tasted him.

He drove into me, hitting my cervix and drawing a scream from my lips despite the delirious haze of vampire venom.

He pulled back an inch. He didn't adjust his pace, only driving deeper as I lost myself to the painful, delicious intensity.

"I *was* starving for you, you vengeful little creature," Kylo admitted with a deep frown. "You were deeply upset before you ran, and you wouldn't tell me why. So I didn't feed from you. It didn't feel right. I knew you didn't want it. But I also couldn't stomach the blood of another, even if it was a faceless, connectionless chalice of blood."

I was lost in those pools of blue. His thrusts were slower. They landed so deep inside me that I had no hope of ever being free of him. My body only opened up, allowing Kylo as much access as he wanted.

"It was horribly irresponsible. I must keep myself fed to keep you safe—to keep all of Etherdale safe. But I only want *you*. I am only addicted to *you*. I force myself to stomach unappealing blood so I don't hurt you. But if it were up to me, I'd spend an exorbitant amount of money to keep you on blood replenishing potion and never drink any blood but yours until the day we die."

The day *we* die, as if it was obvious we'd only ever die by each other's side.

I smiled.

Kylo rolled his eyes. "Like I said, *greedy*."

He was rougher this time when he buried his fangs in the other side of my throat and drove into me. He pushed me into the rug as one of his hands buried in my hair and the other pinned my arm down.

I made a sound that was a cross between a sigh and a breathy moan. It faded into a gentle hum of contentment. My body curved and melded with Kylo's as if trying to become one with him.

I couldn't get close enough. My true desire was to crawl inside Kylo's ribcage.

A giggle fell from my parted lips.

Kylo went rigid. He clotted my wound and slowly rose to meet my eyes.

"My first giggle in days, maybe even a week," he murmured in wonder. "You have no idea how much I've missed that sound."

"Dramatic," I whispered.

His thumb brushed across my lips before plunging inside. My tongue swirled against it.

"I need to taste all of you," Kylo growled.

He slowly pulled out of me and made his way down my body, leaving a trail of kisses. All I could do was bend toward him like a flowering vine in search of the sun.

For one tiny moment of clarity, I realized we were having some version of makeup sex in my ex-boyfriend's basement while his parents' corpses rested in the next room.

Now I *really* giggled. I covered my mouth with my hand. This was fucked-up. I shouldn't have been laughing.

And because I shouldn't have been, I laughed harder.

Kylo grinned, his eyes sparkling. He lifted a brow at me, his head now between my thighs as he stared at my pussy in awe.

"What in the heavens is so funny?" He shook his head. "Hush, baby. You're distracting me from worship."

Telling me not to laugh didn't help at all.

But him biting above my womb sure did. My pussy fluttered, and I was back to giving Kylo my full attention.

"Good girl."

His tongue flitted over my clit, and my breathing turned ragged in anticipation.

The place Kylo had marked was intimate, primal. It reminded me of when he'd said he wanted to see me swollen with his child.

When Kylo's mouth closed over my clit, it was aching for him. The deepest, basest part of me found the notion more than sexy.

Kylo pulsed, and I went wild, legs squirming before shadows held them in place. Moans rolled through me. All I could think about when my eyes rolled back was how good of a father Kylo would be, how dangerously protective he'd inevitably become of me if I was filled with his seed.

It was a fantasy that couldn't ever be realistically fulfilled, but I was surprised by how much it worked for me.

Kylo forced another orgasm with ease.

It *undeniably* worked for me.

He was too beautiful. I stared down at his satisfied, unnaturally perfect face. I couldn't help but run my fingers through his soft, gentle curls of black hair.

"Tell me what you were thinking about just now."

My lips clamped shut, and Kylo tracked the movement with growing amusement.

"I'm glad to know you still can't hide those big feelings and sinful secrets from me to save your life," he taunted. He kissed my sensitive clit once before slapping my thigh. "Now, angel."

I gasped. "Um." My cheeks burned, and Kylo loved it. I looked up at the ceiling. "You impregnating me. Or something."

Kylo's dark gaze grew even darker, his smile melting. He flipped me over on my stomach. "Ass. In. The. Air."

Stars danced in my eyes as I followed his instructions, heady from all the orgasms and venom.

I arched, and Kylo wasted no time driving into me. "Good little angel," he whispered. "*My* good little angel."

All of me ceded to Kylo's dominance, just as I'd originally desired. I cried out at his increasingly rough claiming. But I also relaxed, taking him gratefully, slipping into a feeling of safety that couldn't be put into words. Like I no longer had to think or worry or make any decisions at all—because despite Kylo's breach of trust, I knew his devotion was the most real, unending, powerful force in Etherdale.

"You know I'd love nothing more than to mark this sweet body and even sweeter soul as mine for all of eternity. In all ways." His fingers dug into the flesh of my hips. "It's good I'm a vampire, or you'd already be pregnant. I wouldn't be able to help it."

I'm not sure I would've been able to either.

I arched deeper, ignoring the uncomfortable fullness and basking in the pleasure instead.

Yes, I definitely wouldn't have been able to help it.

"I will always love you, Evie. I broke your trust. But I never stopped loving you. Never stopped protecting and caring for you. Do you understand that?"

"Yes."

"Good. Because you deserve that kind of consistent, reliable love, as intense as mine may be. I know how much you deserve it."

I shut my eyes tight before they could well with tears. It was just like Kylo to make me cry from his sweetness as he assaulted me with his monster cock.

In my paranoid state, I'd thought Kylo had used my parental wounds, my primordial heartbreak, to manipulate me.

I'd never been more grateful to have been wrong.

"I don't forgive you," I forced out, as Kylo pulled my back to his chest, still inside me.

He chuckled in my ear. "That's okay, angel. So long as you still love me."

It was unfair of him to start playing with my clit, whispering sinful, condescending teasing in my ear.

I was impossibly full of him, filled to the brim as I shuddered.

"My perfect little doll. Can't help but come on her God's cock, hm?"

I tried to fight it, but Kylo bit my shoulder. I immediately spasmed and clenched around him. I cried out as the most intense orgasm of the night tore through me.

Kylo shoved me back down as I remained pliable, boneless, thoughtless. He drove deeper and deeper until his cock twitched inside me. When warmth flooded through, it landed right at my cervix as he made one last feral noise. His hand was closed around the back of my neck, forcing me to take every last drop of him.

"Oh my god."

I went rigid at the distant sound of a voice.

Kylo eased out of me, tugged my dress back down, and pulled his pants up in the next blink.

He pulled me to my feet and stood in front of me, a protective rage radiating from him as his shadows leaked.

At first, I heard footsteps down the basement stairs, but they stopped.

"Are you guys *fucking* down there?"

I heard muffled laughter from above. "Harmony, get your ass back up here before Kylo decapitates you next."

I cringed at the reminder of my headless victim.

Kylo glanced at me, still wrathful even as a slight smile tugged at his lips. "Are you going to tell them, or shall I?"

11

KYLO

I'd been practicing extraordinary restraint with Evie in all ways since she'd discovered my betrayal. I refused to harm her further. Hearing her tell me I ruinously broke her heart had killed something inside me.

It made me desperate to mend that beautiful soul—on my knees if that was where she wanted me.

Then Evie had all but begged me to feed from her and fuck her, and now I was struggling to maintain any amount of self-control. I couldn't keep my hands off her, especially not after she'd provoked my deepest fantasy to claim her. With my cum inside her, dripping down her thighs with every movement, I kept Evie close—always within my grasp.

She'd been turned on by revenge and violence, the same as me. I might've been shocked, given her previous aversion to such activities, but I'd always known there was more to her story than she'd let on. Princeton taught me that the stronger a person's fixations, the stronger their psychological shadow. Evie had hated everything dark and wrathful because that was exactly the true nature she denied. All these years, she'd been running from herself most of all.

Evie's fair cheeks were pinker than ever the moment we left the basement and faced Harmony and Blade. Blade's arms were crossed over his hulking body.

I knew on a conscious level they were my friends, whom I loved and trusted absolutely, but their smirks and eyes on Evie still made me edgy and possessive on a level I had no control over.

"Since when are you two on cleanup?" I lifted a brow. I tried and failed to subdue my primal urges as I looped my arms around Evie and kept her pressed against me, her back to my chest.

She was far more agreeable with my venom in her blood, squirming only for a moment before settling into my hold.

"We were curious," Harmony said, sweeping her long black hair behind her shoulders. "As you could imagine."

"You kept us out of the loop," Blade added. "On something as interesting and enjoyable as killing spineless, rich loyalists."

I rolled my eyes at the sadness in Blade's light brown eyes. "This was Evie's fun to be had, actually."

Blade and Harmony both focused back on Evie, whose cheeks were flushed bright red. My cock was already hard again and pressing against her, merely from her embarrassment and the bright fang marks dotting her throat.

"They killed Idris," Evie said simply. "So I killed *them.*"

My cock twitched. Who knew such ruthlessness lived beneath such a sweet, innocent exterior? I'd had my suspicions, but gods was it sexy to see Evie finally this *free.*

I heard my crew getting to work on disposing of the guards' bodies outside. Out of an abundance of caution, I decided to make everyone here disappear. It might have been obvious what had happened to those in the Whitfields' trusted circle, but we could do without the heat of a brutal massacre during a time like this. Propaganda was at its peak as war loomed. The clan faced enough obstacles as it was.

I wanted Evie to indulge in her sexy violence guilt-free.

"We also wanted to apologize," Harmony said.

"For being wrong?" Evie asked, a strong note to her voice I was still getting used to.

I loved strong Evie. I kissed the top of her head, inhaling her floral shampoo.

Blade uncrossed his arms. "For not even trying to listen. We were trying to protect you, Evie. We were scared for you."

"And there's a good reason we don't turn young humans," Harmony added.

Evie stared at the ground for a moment. I prepared to calm her down, but as always, Evie took me by surprise.

"I know," she said. "I never wanted any of this for Idris in the first place, let alone at his young age. I wasn't able to listen to you two either."

"What's done is done," Harmony said, her face becoming gentler in the face of Evie's humility. "We won't always agree, but we are always family. You're one of us now. And we want to welcome you into the clan. We didn't want you to think our warnings had anything to do with our level of respect for you as a person and witch."

Evie sighed. She'd clearly believed in the wake of my betrayal that the entire clan was against her, that this had all been some elaborate ruse to recruit her and manipulate her. She shifted a little, as if uncomfortable. Maybe even ashamed.

I'd destroyed not only her trust in me, but I'd also damaged her faith in her new family. And we all needed each other now more than ever. There was no room for weakness within our ranks.

"Thank you for saying that," Evie said. "I know I'm not Princeton. And I won't try to be."

I stroked her hair, reveling in her shudder as she leaned against me.

"I want to do what's best for the realm," she finished. "And I'm still learning."

"I think that's a lifelong process," Harmony said with a small smile. "Can I give you a hug?"

My glare was immediate and entirely unavoidable.

Blade raised his beefy hands in the air before scratching his beard. Harmony rolled her eyes.

Evie twisted to glance up at me in confusion.

I wiped the feral expression from my face. With begrudging effort, I released her from my hold.

"Sure," Evie said tentatively.

Harmony's face lit up, hugging Evie notably briefly. She was incredibly empathic, even to a magickal degree. She likely understood Evie wasn't used to such displays of warmth. But Harmony just couldn't help herself, and it pulled a grin from my lips to see Evie embraced by my comrades.

"Welcome," Blade said. "I would say I'm glad Kylo has someone to balance out his intensity, but I'm not sure you effectively accomplish that."

Evie stepped back. She lifted a shoulder. "Kylo should be able to balance himself at his old age."

Blade and Harmony laughed. I even heard a soft chuckle from outside.

"Well, at least I didn't decapitate a poor feline shifter," I retorted.

Evie glared at me. Harmony and Blade exchanged a shocked glance before shifting their incredulity to Evie.

"Brutal," Blade said with the widest grin. "The surprises keep coming."

Harmony shook her head. "I'm not surprised. You'd do anything for your family. That's how I know you belong with us."

Evie wanted to come with me to see Idris, but I'd explained once again how traumatizing it would be if Idris tried to eat her.

We'd gone straight to work on educating him about his new nature and building up his tolerance for bloodlust.

But it was a slow process. It took time, and he still wasn't quite himself.

"Still don't remember what happened?" I asked.

He shook his head. He sat at a table in one of our many casual gathering areas underground. A few of his older classmates were here too. They regarded me with enthusiastic respect, clearly grateful for the opportunity to do something meaningful for me. The way they looked at me felt strange on my skin, but I knew it was the same way I admired Valentin's turned leader Rune. Like he was more God than vampire. We all needed figures to look up to.

The lights in the room mimicked sunlight, and several potted plants brought another degree of life to the space.

"I remember walking to my professor's office. Then nothing. Just anger, darkness, a tunnel of light, and then this fucking *hunger*," he bit out.

Newborns were moodier than the most angsty teenager. Everything became bigger in vampirism. Our feelings, our senses, our urges. We were beings of shadow, and that didn't come without its drawbacks. It was the reason many vampires shut it all off completely, giving up on their humanity. I'd built intricate structures within the clan to guard against this—emphasizing philosophy, art, depth, and comradery to guard against the apathetic call of immortality.

We would never be like *them*.

"Why did you want to become turned, Idris?" I asked him.

His frown eased. His pupils halted in their widening. He processed. "To protect Etherdale like the city has protected me and Evie. And to protect Evie like she protected me." He glared at his feet. The words came out gritty and irritated, but I sensed a bit more of *Idris* peeking through the cracks.

"Do you feel that inside you? It's not the same as hunger, is it?"

He took a momentary pause before his eyes met mine. "I can feel it. It's different. Like a buzz in my chest and—" he gasped, clutching at his ribs.

One of his sigil tattoos glowed faintly. I could make out its outline through his burgundy shirt.

Idris exhaled as if it were his first deep breath in days.

I smiled. "That's your anchor. Through all of these exercises and training sessions, and for the rest of your life, that feeling is your anchor." I tilted my head toward the younger vampires playing cards at a table over and pretending not to eavesdrop. "Everyone here has been new before. We all remember what it's like. Every time you feel yourself sliding, come back to your *why*. That's what's going to ground you and remind you who you are."

Idris's shoulders were hunched as he stared at the table.

"We usually turn in groups. It helps us feel less alone when we know others are going through the same painful process. As soon as Evie is able, she'll be initiating her first round of vampires to join the clan."

We needed all the numbers we could get. Princeton's death had halted a new wave of recruits we'd been preparing to turn for the past year.

Idris's eyes flashed. His laugh was strained, bitter. "None of this feels real. My body. This place. But least of all: *Evie*. I need to see her. I want to believe you that she's safe and working for the clan, but that's the last thing I could expect from someone who *begged* me not to join only a couple of months ago."

"I assure you it's as hard for me to wrap my head around as it is for you," I said.

"Not possible," Idris snapped.

His classmates stopped talking, glancing over at us in utter shock. They couldn't believe a new recruit, or any clan member, would ever speak to the leader of the Masked Order that way.

Or rather, the leader of the Hekate Clan.

"You're right," I said over the astonished murmurs. "You're her brother. You know that Evie has been hiding from herself for a long time. But she's not running anymore. She's chosen to fight, just like you. If you want to see her, you'll take your sessions seriously. You'll keep grounding yourself, and you *will* get better. Just as we all did."

A woman from the other table cleared her throat. I gave her a nod.

"I'd never wanted anything as badly as I wanted to be turned," she said. "But after my first bloodlust, I freaked out. I was worried I wasn't meant for this life, that I regretted my decision. But I leaned on my new family, and they carried me through. All the anger and hunger—it doesn't pass, not completely. It transforms into something that works *for* you instead of against you. The sooner you get through basic training, the sooner you can see your mortal loved ones." She smiled. "And the sooner you can rip into some born scum and satisfy yourself in a way that surpasses all your wildest fantasies."

The three men around her all nodded in agreement.

Idris shifted in his seat. His forehead crease ran deep, and in his eyes, that hunger churned. A small shadow twisted around his thumb.

"She wants to see you just as badly," I said.

At this, Idris released a breath of tension. "*That* I believe."

12

EVIE

"You look tired," I said.

"Rude." Kylo's grin was nothing short of heart-stopping, his dimple making my stomach flutter.

He shielded from another of my shadow strikes. I'd spent the first half of my day reading in Princeton's library, communing with the otherworld, and patching up minor clan-related spells and wards.

Kylo encouraged me to rest, but there was no time for that. The born could strike at any moment. A reality that Kylo had accepted, as his protests against my exertion fell flat.

And now we were training with my shadows at the back of his estate, building up my combat skills. The breeze and descending sun were a gentle relief from the summer heat.

"I'm worried about you," Kylo said with a shrug. "I love seeing you strong. But I also know what that means for your future. I'm still getting used to the idea of you being anywhere near battle."

I nodded. "Me too."

"I'd much rather your only job description include being my spoiled good girl, but alas."

Another shadow solidified, slamming into Kylo's shield with such force that he skidded backward.

His smirk grew. Underneath it, I saw evidence of his emotional burden. He'd been caring for me and Idris for the past two days without reprieve, and he was still recovering from his own grief.

And damn him, I cared.

"I can tattoo myself," I offered. "You should rest."

Kylo went rigid. "Like hell you will," he growled.

"How hard could it possibly be? Place magickal needle on skin and draw symbols." I shrugged.

Kylo's intensity radiated from him in a thick mist of shadow. "Angel, no one else gets to mark your body but *me*. Not even you."

My core turned molten, my nerves lighting up even as my face contorted with anger.

Kylo charged me, his speed catching me off guard. He pinned my wrists behind my back, snaked an arm around my torso, and gripped my throat before I could blink.

"Learning shadow control is great. But you need new tools to combat vampire speed. We'll work on that next time."

In his tight hold, my traitorous body relaxed.

"Maybe training with me isn't the best option," Kylo murmured, his breath fanning across my ear. "I don't want anyone else fucking touching you. But I also can't have you turning into a wet, needy mess every time I threaten your life."

His grip on my throat tightened, and I struggled not to rub my thighs together.

I opened my mouth to deny what Kylo could obviously detect through my scent, my heart rate, my breathing—but he beat me to it.

"I'm curious, baby," he purred. "What is it about your life in my hands that turns you on?"

He let go of my wrists, his hand moving to pinch a nipple and tug. I whined, squirming in his arms.

"The threat of pain?" he whispered.

One of my shadows yanked his hand off my throat. I wriggled free as my extra limbs moved in varied degrees of precision to deflect Kylo as I put distance between us. But once his thrumming, violent power had been switched on, my bones rattled. It became harder to focus, my blood yearning for me to submit. I panted, raising my arms defensively as I leaked a fine mist of shimmering shadow.

Kylo's predator gaze was trained on me.

Our shadows moved at the same time, growing tangled in the space between us. I grunted in exertion, and strong winds circled.

One of his limbs broke free from the tangled mess and swiped my legs out from under me before pinning me to the earth.

Submit, a voice whispered, commanding and steady.

I lost my thread of control.

"Or," Kylo said softly, now standing above me as more and more shadows crawled across my body to weigh it down and suppress my magick. "Is it not really about the violence at all?"

My hands twitched. My arms were rooted in place. It was like being under a weighted blanket, all of me snug and bound.

Kylo's beautiful, ruthless face reminded me of a war deity— something I could become lost in, an anchor amid the storm.

The winds settled.

"I wonder if your pretty little pussy is merely reacting to the safety of my power. The idea that if your every breath belongs to the most powerful vampire in Ravenia, there is no greater danger that can reach you." Kylo smiled, a shadow plunging inside my mouth, cool and smooth.

I melded with the earth, feeling her energies embrace me the same as Kylo's. I gagged when the shadow expanded, and Kylo's eyes lit up.

"Your needy pussy is right, angel. I am indeed the only thing in this world you have to fear."

"Arrogant prick," I tried to say, but the shadow gag jumbled the sounds.

The way Kylo stood above me, arms crossed, only added to his air of authority. He was right, and he knew it. He knew *me*.

And deeply, truly knowing me provided me a far greater sense of safety than his hand around my throat.

"My shadows are going to play with you while I catch up on some correspondence. You need to rest your witchy powers for tonight."

My eyes rounded, incredulous. The shadow slithered out of my mouth. "What—"

I couldn't even finish the thought before my bondage became tools for both pleasure and pain. I gasped, a shadow already playing with my clit and robbing me of my ability to form words. The low vibrations became stronger as another shadow eased inside me. Others played with my breasts. Grass tickled my cheeks as I lay helpless, overwhelmed with pleasure and sensation.

Kylo watched for a moment longer, adding to my humiliation, my depraved undoing.

Then he simply pulled out a small leather journal from his back pocket, turning his attention to the magickal notes delivered from across the city, or perhaps across the realm.

He had many of these magickal linked journals, but I'd come to learn that this smaller one acted as a hub for all important messages. I wasn't sure whether Princeton had expanded upon this technology or if it came from elsewhere.

The shadow angled inside me, hitting a spot that turned off my ability to think. Thank the gods Kylo's backyard was incredibly private, obscured by tall trees and fencing, not to mention wards.

Even still, I felt exposed and degraded, intensity rolling through me in delirious waves. It was like being touched, used, tormented by too many hands to count. The darkness itself was having its way with me.

Kylo's shadows knew me and my hidden depths just as well as he did.

"Oh, gods," I moaned.

"Come," Kylo commanded without even looking up from the page. "*Now.*"

It was only when I began to shake uncontrollably, the shadows pulling my first orgasm, that I met Kylo's hooded, pleased gaze. He was able to praise me without words, filling my stomach with warmth before returning his careful attention back to the journal.

"I want to hear you sucking on that shadow as if you were gagging on my cock, angel," Kylo said.

The filthy words reached me in my puddle of satisfaction. I took his shadow deep inside my throat.

I wished it were Kylo instead.

"Same."

My eyes flew open. At my muffled speech, the shadow retracted.

"Did you just read my thoughts?" I asked, horrified.

Kylo peeled his eyes off the page, confusion passing over his features. He stared at my mouth—the mouth that had obviously been preoccupied.

"Well, that's new," he said. "I heard you whisper it."

The shadows had paused their meticulous assault. "It's them," I said. "Our shadows."

"Hot," Kylo said. His eyes moved back to the words on the page.

My mouth fell open.

"Come again, angel. I'm not releasing you until you've had at least three orgasms. No more thinking—your thoughts will still be there, waiting for you."

"But—"

A shadow tightened over my mouth. Another caressed my hair. Was he really not concerned at all that our shadows were speaking to each other? That they were spilling our secrets?

But he wasn't. Kylo wasn't fazed at all. As if he no longer had anything to hide.

If anything, he merely looked delighted, reveling in the idea that we were bound together in yet another way. By blood and now by shadow.

Sometime between the second and third explosive orgasms, Kylo's thoughtful gaze took a turn. A frown developed and then deepened.

I watched it all, spasming around his darkness, letting him consume me from within. I watched him move from worry to acceptance to cold, impassive determination. He snapped the notebook shut.

He watched me come a third time, how I imagined he might watch his forces move into battle at his command.

As I came down from my ultimate high, he scooped me into his arms. His lips met mine, his tongue conquering my mouth. He tasted, savored, claimed.

"Sometimes, the world has to get worse before it gets better, angel," he whispered. "The born are making their move. And we're going to let them."

13

KYLO

"If you're not going to stop this, then I need to get to Mena!"

Evie didn't understand. She didn't have the context of a century's worth of careful planning, learning, and thinking.

And I couldn't impart that kind of knowledge and perspective to her. I could only do my best.

"Baby, Mena is protected. You can visit her tomorrow. I know it feels like the end of the world, but it isn't. This is the necessary beginning. And if you don't complete the initiation ritual by midnight, you will be destroyed by shadows."

We walked quickly to the main deliberation room, where my inner circle and commanders, eyes, and other high-ranking officials awaited. Maybe it was my proximity to Evie, but I swore I could sense the spirits of the catacombs awaken around us—the stacks and stacks of remains from a failed moral uprising centuries ago.

They said Etherdale's catacombs were cursed. There were warnings about diving below ground level. But that had never been a problem for us, and it was obvious why.

These vengeful spirits were on our side.

Evie was angry with me—it was rolling off her in waves. She wanted to go to Mena anyway, but she knew she risked running out of time. She was bound by her own magickal oath.

In the wide hall before the deliberation room, over one hundred turned had gathered and spilled into the adjacent rooms and halls. A grand chandelier and candlelight from sconces illuminated the deep blue walls, the various statues of deities guarding the space. The crowd parted for us and went reverently silent.

My clan needed to see me. They needed to feel my strength, my calm resoluteness. They needed to understand how prepared I was for war.

Evie's mouth was agape at the size of the crowd, knowing it was only a fraction of our numbers. Her wide gray eyes found mine, and at the sight of her heightening anxiety, I stopped moving.

I took her second hand in mine and lowered my head. "Remember your *why*, angel," I whispered. "You're here for a reason. All moments have led to this one. Your story does have meaning, and that meaning will carry you through."

Evie's chronically worried mind halted, those bright, starry eyes bleeding curiosity and hope. She frowned, but she was no longer scanning for the worst possible outcome.

Now she was searching for the best one.

With her small hand on my arm, I led her into the deliberation room. So many pairs of vampire eyes on her made me grateful for the pink bite marks on her neck.

When the commanders closest to the doors reached to close them, I raised a hand.

"Don't. Let my voice carry. I want as many of us to hear these words as possible," I commanded. "We'll close the doors once it's time to dole out directives."

Blade and Harmony were already waiting for us on the small dais in the center of the room. Turned were seated at a long

CLAIMED BY FANGS AND DARKNESS

wooden table behind us. Others were gathered in huddles around the room and in the seating areas, now turning to face us.

I led Evie to stand by my side. Harmony stood on Evie's right. Blade on my left.

Evie's heart hammered. I glanced down at her adorably pensive features. She was gathering information with that powerful, frightened mind of hers.

"You belong here," I whispered to her. "Not just by my side. But in front of all of them."

"I haven't earned it," she whispered back.

I smiled. "Not *yet*."

Another hush fell over the gathered vampires as everyone settled into their spots. Through the open doors, I made eye contact with as many of my comrades as possible.

"Nearly two weeks ago, Princeton was brutally murdered by the born, his body desecrated," I began.

A few gasps broke through the silence. Some muffled sobs escaped. This was the first time I was publicly acknowledging the atrocity. My inner circle had already been made aware, but the broader clan had been kept oblivious out of an abundance of caution until we filled the power vacuum Princeton had left behind.

Evie reached for my hand and intertwined her fingers with mine. Sweet girl.

The show of tenderness despite her own mending distrust and heartbreak allowed a trickle of my own grief to leak through.

I glanced at Blade, his eyes glassy.

I let my eyes shine with loss. I wanted my clan to see my humanity, the way it did nothing to detract from my power that surged through the room in a steady hum.

"He was my mentor and my oldest friend. He was our maker.

His magick will live inside this clan forever. Death is not the end. It's just another beginning."

Evie jolted, staring up at me. I wasn't precisely certain of the reason for the sudden curve of her lips, but I let it fuel me, anyway.

"Do not fear grief," I said. "We are not the born. Parts of us are still human, and we must never forsake them."

My voice filled the space, booming with the weight of my power. I wondered if the entire underground could hear me.

I decided to give few details about the nature of Princeton's death, especially with his killer still at large. I could see the panic ripe in the eyes of the crowd. They were looking around, assessing each other's fear. An undercurrent of anger ripened at the same time, accompanied by smoky shadows circling at our feet.

"The born slaughtered Princeton," I said, inhaling the strong notes of anger that permeated. Vengeful curses and hisses coiled up with the shadowed whispers. "And he chose a successor to take his place."

Evie straightened. This brave, resilient woman showed not an ounce of the fear I could detect in her rapidly beating heart. Every pair of vampire eyes was on her petite, mortal form.

My hand moved from hers to the small of her back. We both stepped closer to each other at the same time, the subtlest of movements that were certain to have been tracked by everyone in the room.

I couldn't help the slow curve of my lips. The clan knowing that Evie belonged to me, formally and officially, was like a shot of the strongest elixir straight into my veins.

"Princeton will be avenged," I said, a sacred vow. The crowd erupted in uproar, and I allowed the din to rise and peak before lifting a hand. My clan hushed. "But we are stronger than ever. You will likely read and hear through the borns' propaganda machine that it was an act of Lillian that destroyed a plot of forest two days ago."

I grinned down at Evie. She took a steadying breath, choosing to stare into the crowd instead.

"But the truth is, it was Evie who birthed the strongest witch-conjured storm in over a century, and she did so to defend against the born and Servants of Lillian," I said with beaming pride. It felt like I'd been waiting for years to brag about my girlfriend. "The acts of the gods Etherdale has seen in the past few months—they have *all* belonged to the witch by my side."

The fear of what Princeton's death meant for the clan swiftly turned into a frenzy of excitement, a readiness that mirrored my own. It was a careful balancing act, the art of leadership in a time of turmoil. I had to move with the moods of the crowd, gently guiding, never letting my mask of ultimate authority slip.

"The rumors are true. The born will take Etherdale tonight."

No one on the dais flinched. Shadows slithered along the floor. Murmurs turned into battle cries.

All attention settled on me, desperately searching for answers.

"The born will expect us to drop our masks and come out from the shadows. And believe me when I tell you this was indeed my primary instinct," I said. "But it would be a mistake. King Earle may be losing his ancient, psychotic mind, but his council remains keen strategists. This is an intelligence-gathering mission. It's a ruse. They want to operate from the strongest position possible, luring us out of our stronghold and remaining a step ahead. It was intentional for us to know they were coming. The born suspect we are stronger than we've let on, and they're frustrated by their lack of understanding. They're also hoping our anger, grief, and panic in the wake of Princeton's death has weakened our magick and our judgment. On all accounts, we will not bend. We will not play their game.

The longer we remain formless, the more decisively we can push the born out of Etherdale for good."

I'd trained my clan in a wide array of disciplines in the realms of psychology, philosophy, war strategy, and mythology. It wasn't about *what* to think. It was about *how* to think. We weren't a disorganized mass of adolescents like the born hoped we were. We'd been strategically underestimated for decades.

The born had no fucking idea who they were up against.

"They're not going to make this easy," I said. "Our restraint must become its own weapon. We need as many mortals on our side as possible, and the born temporarily taking Etherdale under their control will be that catalyst. Loyalists must see the consequences of their own actions and inactions. Reality must grow darker before the shadows can deliver us from tyranny. This is the nature of the world."

Minds processed, including Evie's. I looked down at her, the furrow of her brows and the frown on her pink lips.

"We *will* fight from the shadows. Rest assured that pacifism is not my decree. But we are an example to the realm now. This is our story to write. We must craft a convincing narrative for all of Ravenia, a call for revolution that cannot be refused. Etherdale will be the first of many. More turned clans will join our coalition. We will destroy the current system together. King Earle himself will fall. The born do not deserve this world; and we were made to take it from them."

I felt Evie's power surge now. The crowd erupted in cheers and hollers. Every source of light in the space turned deep purple, illuminating the shadows with an iridescent sheen.

"We have a new goddess on our side, a protector of the downtrodden, a defender of mortals and their magick. She is the source of our shadows, and I suspect she is the reason for all turned clans here and in Valentin."

A wind from the chthonic realm swept through the purple-lit space as if to drive the point home. My clan was no stranger to magick and divinity. Princeton would often tell us that Spirit was on our side. What greater evidence for our cosmic support than our own defiant immortality?

Evie tugged on my shirt. "Let me."

I faltered, taken by surprise. Evie didn't even like talking to strangers, let alone having multiple people's focus on her.

Yet she opened her mouth and spoke with such command that it stirred something potent in my depths.

"Her name is Hekate," Evie said. Power rippled in an undeniable charge. "Our clan will now be renamed in her honor. She is guiding us to a realm free of the born." She steadied herself, her blonde strands of hair rustled by the wind. "I may be Princeton's successor, but that doesn't mean you know me, nor I you."

The crowd listened. My inner circle's gazes were sharper than ever, and the vampires spilling into the hall were rapt with curiosity, craning their necks for a better look at the small blonde by my side.

"I was born into a Servants of Lillian cult," Evie said.

Now she *really* had our attention. I almost let my own mask slip, surprised by Evie's bluntness about a truth she'd vehemently concealed since we'd first met.

"My mother was a high priestess," she said, a fact not even I knew. "My father was human. They willingly offered up their half-witch daughter and human son as tithings to the born. If we hadn't escaped, we would've been married off to born elites as children."

My comrades' faces twisted with disgust and rage.

"We had no one to fight for us. The family we were born to was not our family," Evie said, her eyes sparkling with tears and buried strength. "The shadows were my only friends, and they were my salvation. Through them I found a home in Etherdale. And now they've led me to you." She released an exhale. "My brother and I could've only dreamed of having a family like this to protect us. And now it's our job to protect this city and all mortals who are unable to defend themselves from the vile predators in power."

She was fucking perfect. Her speech was succinct, powerful, and humanizing. I didn't feel comfortable sharing Evie's story without her consent, but I knew how important it was for my clan to trust and respect her. They may have held my judgment in high regard, but being a part of a turned clan meant maintaining distance from outsiders. It was a survival mechanism. Loyalty was everything, and it was something Evie would need to earn and develop over time.

This was a beautiful start.

A loud clap sent the rest of the crowd into a show of support.

"I am so stupidly in love with you," I whispered, unable to help myself.

Evie looked away, a flash of reluctance in her proud, relieved eyes. "I'm still mad. But I stupidly love you too. Emphasis on *stupid*."

Harmony snorted, clearly eavesdropping over the roar of the crowd.

"You didn't seem very unforgiving during our training session today," I murmured.

Evie made an adorable, growly noise. "I was using you."

I laughed, quelling my urge to continue our banter.

Instead, I addressed the crowd once more, bringing the public portion of our gathering to an end. We needed to discuss more intricate details with my inner circle before I could tattoo Evie.

My cock was alert the moment the image crossed my mind.

With the love of my life at my side, surrounded by the clan I'd risen from blood and shadow, I'd never felt more brutally alive.

14

EVIE

The energy in the air was electric—intoxicating, even. It was hard not to become drunk on the revolutionary spirit.

I still hadn't told Kylo what I'd done to the coven who raised me, the reason I'd blocked all of my power and my buried darkness.

I was ashamed to admit that a part of me didn't want to ruin the image Kylo held of me in his mind. The girl in pretty dresses who grew and arranged flowers and read smutty fantasy novels in her spare time.

I knew Kylo loved my violence. But this was different. I'd obliterated my own parents with my wrath.

I wasn't the girl Kylo first fell in love with. At what point would I become so far removed from my original form that he no longer even recognized me?

In some moments, it was hard for me to even recognize *myself.*

Yet, here I sat, in a room full of vampires who no longer regarded me with blatant distrust. They absorbed me into the fold, the bulk of their energy and attention focused on the horizon now. The promise of a better tomorrow.

I wanted to be there too. I didn't want to imagine the born above us, moving into the city and instating unjust laws. Were they burning more ancient texts? Rounding up witches?

My fists clenched, my skin hot and itchy.

"We're going to infuriate them," Kylo said. "Commander Lachlan, your unit is going to continue protecting these kids. Born authorities will target professors and students and try to replace all curriculum with their own propaganda. It's the oldest trick in the book."

A tendril of Kylo's power curled around my ankle under the table, as if in a show of comfort.

"Take out as many as you can. When they're on their way to feeding clubs. When they're on the hunt. The moment they think they've gotten away with something, take them out like the rabid beasts they are," Kylo said. "Calculated, never passive."

Lachlan nodded. "Understood."

He was mid-height, blond, with angular features but soft brown eyes. He could almost pass as Idris's brother. I was focusing on remembering everyone's names and magickal signatures so I wouldn't dwell on the idea of mortals in danger. Lachlan oversaw the clan's presence on Etherdale University's campus.

"Can we make sure libraries have added protections?" I asked Kylo. "Or perhaps move certain texts underground?"

"We did that for witch texts," Lachlan offered. "They'll likely target social sciences next, particularly history."

Kylo nodded, sweeping his dark gaze to mine. "Of course, baby."

His pet names in front of this powerful room of vampires made my stomach flutter and cheeks heat.

"Don't be afraid to speak up," he said to me. "You're a part of this."

The conversation continued, and I learned more about the inner workings and far reach of the clan than ever before.

"How much time does the Serpent Clan need?" a lithe, lethal-looking woman with a shaved head asked. Her hands were in her pockets, her green eyes sharp.

"Two months minimum," Kylo responded. "Their forces combined with the clans of Terasette and we could absolutely withstand King Earle's army and keep Etherdale in our grasp. We'd become the central hub of the revolution."

In his eyes was a righteous fire, his words a command to the fates.

"The born don't want war. They know what war means for their precious mortal blood supply. Their hope is pushing us into battle quickly, crushing us absolutely with a large fleet, and being done with it all. That's what they did to Zander's clan. They believe we're mostly isolated, dispersed, and weak. But once we take this city, combine forces, and solidify alliances with shifters and witches, we will be poised to take the realm the same as Rune took Valentin."

Blade nodded. "We've already put in the groundwork. Anyone on the fence will be forced to choose, and their choice will become obvious. We have an entire web of allies across the realm. And perhaps Valentin would join us once the clans have all risen from the underground."

At this, Kylo's eyes sparked. It was cute how much he looked up to Rune.

When Kylo first told me the born were going to replace all mortal leadership and institutions with their own and employ force to do so, I was aghast that the clan would allow that to happen. But after listening to the intellect, power, and steadiness of the surrounding vampires, I'd been sufficiently humbled. They didn't want Earle to send a fleet before we were prepared to face the full might of his army. Right now, we were only dealing with the regional forces of Lord Conrad.

I was new to all of this. But these vampires had been at it for decades. My anxiety would remain, but at least Idris was safe underground.

We didn't just have safety; we had real *power* now.

No more running. It was the borns' turn to run.

"We're low on magickal supplies," a man in the back of the room said. "Looting Valentin's imports is becoming far more dangerous, especially with their own clan conflicts. Not to mention King Earle's obsessive hoarding. He wants us starving for weapons, poisons, and blood replenishing potions."

"Why does Rune still allow exports to the kingdom?" a woman muttered angrily.

Kylo shook his head. "He has no choice. He's doing what's best for the mortals under his protection. No one wants war. As inevitable as it may be."

Something was brewing in Kylo, at the mention of his most worshipped idol. I wondered what he was thinking. He glanced at the clock.

"Evie and I need to break for the night for a critical ritual." He threw me a dark look. "We have a potential solution for the blood onyx scarcity. Continue to discuss avenues for magickal supplies, and I'll weigh in as soon as possible."

At this, I smiled, remembering fondly poisoning and thwarting Kylo after he obliterated my trust.

"I've developed a new poison," I elaborated for the room as Kylo and I stood.

Blade and Harmony exchanged a brief, quiet laugh, and Kylo shot them an irritated frown.

It was new, this feeling of usefulness that didn't leave me feeling *used*. The eyes on me weren't hungry to take; they were hungry to give as much as receive. We were in this together.

The closest I'd gotten to this experience of power was when I was working for Celeste's and planning on opening my own witchy shop. But then the born stole *that* from me too.

Kylo finished his goodbye as we moved to the doors.

"Good luck," Harmony said with a wink.

Blade offered us a lazy salute.

Kylo and I departed as a unit, just as we had entered. The crowd outside had moved into huddles of vampires scattered around, deep in conversation. Their energy was rowdy, the low rumbles of thunder before a downpour.

It was a solace to see so many bodies ready to defend this city.

As was the unflinching confidence in the man at my side.

"One small step after the other," Kylo murmured. "That's how we'll take the realm."

"You're good at making it all sound easy."

Kylo chuckled. "Things tend to run smoother that way. Focus on the difficulties, and you'll be sure to encounter every single one. Assume ease, and you might find it. Much like magick, I'd imagine." Kylo's hand found the back of my neck, his thumb stroking softly as I shivered. "It won't all be easy, angel. Everyone here knows that. But we'll get it done because there's no other choice. This is the path. Only way out is through."

The spell room awakened to our presence, and my stomach turned over remembering Idris's corpse on the wood floor.

"I don't want to do this here," I said as I stopped in my tracks.

"Baby, we only have a couple hours..."

"I know. But I need to work under the new moon. I need to feel the world around me—the wind, the earth, the sky. I need to see the stars."

Kylo nodded. "Okay. Tell me what you need. Let's move."

I tugged his head down, kissing him softly, briefly.

"You love that I can't say *no* to you," he said darkly, gripping my hair in his fist.

I smiled.

WE EXITED the underground through a hidden passageway beneath Kylo's estate. I'd wanted to go somewhere more natural, like the woods on the outskirts of town, but Kylo's agreeableness had a limit.

Getting held up by the born would guarantee my demise. It was best we stay within the turned-controlled neighborhood where my magick could be concealed.

Where I truly wanted to be was my garden, my own magickal space I'd carefully nurtured for a decade. But I couldn't put Mena in danger either.

I picked out a spot underneath a canopy of trees. I immediately discarded my shoes so I could feel the grass and soil beneath my toes.

"This is where I like to read," Kylo murmured.

"It's so sexy you know how to read."

Kylo lifted a single brow.

"What? Most men can't."

His face shifted with displeasure. "Can't or won't?"

"Uncertain."

Kylo sighed heavily. "The bar is truly in Lillian's hells."

I wasn't sure Jacob had ever read a book front to back in his life. Yet he sure did love to shit all over the genre of novels I enjoyed.

"Maybe men just need eighty years to reach full maturity," I said as I set up our magickal area. I used a branch to dig protective sigils around us. Then I sprinkled salt in a circle.

Kylo laughed. "I've thought about this problem quite a bit, actually. It's the reason for my expansive education system before and after clan initiation." He watched me move with a curiosity and tenderness that warmed me from within. "Men need a higher power, or they will become their own. Whether that higher power is group consciousness, the spirit of the revolution, or devotion to one or more gods—there has to be a system of meaning that exists beyond their own egos. Greatness is derived from connection. A man's unchecked ego breeds alienation, profound spiritual loneliness, and insecurity. And instead of self-betterment, those lost souls will falsely believe that conquering, dominating, and stealing others' light is the only way to fill the bottomless voids they themselves created."

I paused, half of my pillar candles lit, and turned to face him. "Your soul is beautiful, Kylo."

His pensive face melted into something adorably human and vulnerable. I craved this side of him, the side he saved for me.

"Thank you, Evie. You already know how I feel about yours."

I grinned. This soon-to-be warlord almost appeared bashful as my compliment sank into his chest.

The rest of my candles sparked to life. I thought about Kylo's words as I cast my circle, as I wrestled with this inescapable dichotomy between light and dark, sex and violence, retribution and sublimity.

Kylo had turned my entire world inside out. He wasn't perfect, nor had he claimed to be. But the shadows inside me had always called to his. I'd known since the beginning of *us* that he was safe.

When the circle had been cast, I invoked Hekate. I called to the four cardinal directions. I channeled the heavens and the underworld, and I opened myself up to the power of the new moon.

Death, darkness, and rebirth. A new beginning.

An initiation.

I leaned into the certainty of Kylo's presence as I held his hands in mine. On our knees, our foreheads touching, my muscles unwound.

Never in my life had I imagined I could be so close to a man. To share my spirit world, my magick, and my devotion. I thought there were parts of myself that would remain hidden and private forever.

"Hekate, I offer myself to thee."

Kylo brushed his lips across my forehead. Behind my eyelids, I saw the cosmos.

"I initiate myself as your daughter, marking my body with your ink and chosen symbols forever. I initiate myself into the Hekate Clan, blessed by the shadows to protect all mortals. Here and now, ever and always, I devote myself to our shared will. I dedicate my body and spirit to a power greater than myself, and I vow to always strive to abide by your guidance, wisdom, and infinite blessings." I let power swell, and winds whistled through the trees above. "Thank you. Thank you. Thank you."

After consecrating the ink, blessing it in the name of the goddess of witches, I lay on the long, cushioned green bench Kylo had carried out from his house.

Kylo grinned the moment his hand gripped the needling tool. Shadows from the candles danced across his beautiful face.

I closed my eyes.

"I need to tell you what happened the night Idris and I ran."

15

EVIE

"Okay. I'm here to listen."

I opened my eyes again.

Kylo appraised my body for a moment. "But first, you're wearing too much clothes, angel. I need to see my canvas before I decide where each piece will go."

I slipped out of my casual, soft blue dress, leaving myself bare in a matching white bralette and panties. The energy in the circle was pleasurable, dark, and potent, immediately sending me into an altered headspace.

"Perfect," Kylo praised. His slow trail of fingers down my sternum made me shudder. "Now please be a good girl and relax, stay still, and tell me what you need to tell me."

I lay back, staring into the new moon and her accompanying constellations. Before, the lump in my throat would've been heavy with shame. Now, my voice was mine and only mine.

Through my hand on his torso as he kneeled beside me, I fed Kylo visions from the otherworld—the symbols or sigils Hekate had chosen for me. He gasped, his eyes widening in awe before he was able to bring himself back to center.

I let myself become a vessel, a conduit, placing my trust in this dark goddess and my Dark God.

"There's my sweet girl," Kylo praised, staring at my body as he wielded the needle dipped in magickal ink.

The ink was spelled to burrow into skin, to seek refuge in flesh and become a living, breathing source of magick. It was akin to a charmed piece of jewelry, but more permanent and melded with its host.

Kylo's gentle touch filled me with ecstasy, his fingers tracing my curves, my bones, the swell of my breasts and my full lips.

As he lorded over me, it felt as though I was on a sacrificial altar. And while that should've terrified me, my body was reacting in opposite, predictable ways.

"I know exactly where this one needs to go," Kylo said.

I kept my hand on him so the channel would remain open.

The words fell from my lips easily, no longer buried under my defensive fear. "A vampire hurt Idris, and I found out about it."

Kylo paused, the needle inches away from the delicate skin over my left hip. "When you were thirteen, and he was..."

"Seven," I hissed. "He was seven years old."

Kylo placed his free hand on my upper thigh. "Breathe. I'm listening. Keep breathing."

I inhaled deeply, the scent of pine and smoke ripe in the air. The needle touched my skin, just above my hipbone. I gasped. The pain was a mix of ice and fire, the ink rooting into my flesh as Kylo carefully drew.

The sensation melted into heady pleasure, making it even easier to continue speaking. "I heard my parents talking about how the vampire had ruined his purity. To them, it was an inconvenience and loss of material opportunity. Not the violation of a child."

Kylo's strong, powerful jaw ticked. His eyes lit up with rage.

"I'd been reading forbidden texts and talking to people

outside of the coven when no one was watching. My mind had been opening, and I started to understand that there was an entire world outside of my coven. My mother taught me that my reality couldn't be trusted. That everything inside me was wrong and stupid and selfish. I don't know how I broke free from her abuse. But I know how greatly my shadow magick helped. The shadows whispered things to me—which books to steal, where to go in order to eavesdrop important information. My once dark and miserable life lit up with meaning."

Kylo continued to draw, stopping only for a second to kiss above my heart. His touch on my thigh was a soothing source of comfort. I spoke through the pain, the mounting pleasure sweeping through to my core.

"When I overheard my parents admit what happened to Idris, everything clicked into place. Marrying me off to a born lord was one thing…"

Kylo's wrath was palpable, and the pain increased as he pressed the ink harder into my skin. I gasped, nearly wiggling away. "Stay still, angel," he rasped.

I closed my eyes.

"… but allowing a vampire to harm my brother was the last straw. I let the darkness overtake me. I told Idris to hide. I went downstairs, where the entire coven and their disgusting born vampire guests had gathered to celebrate a successful first harvest holiday. My magick exploded for the first time. I killed them all. The witches. The vampires. And my own parents." I swallowed. "I took Idris and ran. I thought he didn't remember that night, and I tried my best to forget it too. But the past refuses to stay buried without being processed—I see that now."

The words rushed out, and then I clamped my mouth shut.

"Open those pretty eyes for me, Evie," Kylo whispered.

I opened one eye and then the other. My hip was surging pain as if pierced with pure ice. A pool of wetness had gathered in my panties.

Kylo raked his eyes from mine down to the half-formed tattoo. "Don't look yet. I want them all to be a surprise."

I kept my eyes on his face instead. His features relaxed with an understanding that was steadily growing.

"Finally, it all makes sense," he said. Sadness and wrath battled in his blue depths. "Thank you once again for being so vulnerable and brave, Evie. I see now why you blocked your power, why you tried desperately to keep yourself and Idris away from all vampires and all violence." He shook his head. "You are a fucking miracle."

There was no evidence of repulsion for what I'd done, for who I truly was at my core. No hint of him falling out of love with me.

My lip quivered. My hand tangled in Kylo's dark blue shirt, the color he wore so I never had to see him in all black.

He'd been protecting me since the beginning, before he even knew why I was on the run.

More pieces of me fell into place for him; I could see it in his thoughtful gaze. All of my little quirks and fears and hopes and triggers. He saw why I was the way I was, and how excruciatingly difficult it was for me to finally stand my ground and *fight*.

"I feel cut open before you," I admitted.

Kylo grinned. "Good. I fucking love to see you so exposed." He returned to his careful needlework. "You're mine, baby. Mine to take care of, to admire, to cherish, and to worship. And the funny thing is?"

I tried once more not to move my thighs together as Kylo marked my body forever.

"I think being seen and understood in your entirety is what you've most wanted all along."

I exhaled. He was right.

All of me lay bare to him. I was clay to mold in his broad hands, a cut of marble to sculpt delicately into art.

Kylo inhaled deeply, a familiar look eclipsing his eyes as they darted to my soaked panties.

"Godsdammit, Evie," he cursed. "I love everything about you." He strained, and a glint of candlelight reflected in his aching fangs. "*Everything.*" His voice was gravelly, his touch becoming rougher where he gripped my thigh. "Now stop distracting me with your sweet, needy cunt. Allow me to stain this perfect body with darkness before I lose control and start marking you with far different substances."

My breath hitched, my core molten. "Distract?" I asked. "I've done nothing of the sort."

Kylo growled, manhandling me roughly to shift to my side before biting the flesh above my ribs. I squealed. It was a shallow bite, a brief burst of pain without the breaking of skin.

"The cute noises you make when I hurt you only encourage me to hurt you more," Kylo said with a sigh. "It's most unfortunate." He brought the needle back down as I panted and faced away from him. "For you. Not for me."

The next noise that left me was more of a moan. Kylo's inhale was rough.

"You smell so fucking good, baby," he said. "Is my angel of darkness in another dimension right now?"

"Maybe," I admitted.

This mix of magick, pleasure, and pain was a symphony of head highs.

Kylo chuckled. "Enjoy it. Let yourself be my pretty little canvas and nothing more."

"Are you still able to see the symbols?" I asked, realizing I was no longer holding onto him.

"Mmhmm," he said. "One of your shadows is curled around my ankle."

"Oh," I breathed. That breath became high-pitched the moment the needling became harsher, more throbbing.

"Huh," Kylo said. "Well, that's new."

I opened my mouth to ask, *what?* but refrained. I took my hands off the wheel and let Kylo steer the ship.

When gentle fingers trailed along the freshly tattooed skin, I flinched with a sharp hiss of pain.

"Shhh," Kylo soothed. He pressed his fingers into my raw skin. *"Wow."*

My curiosity wasn't as strong as the pleasure of submitting to him, so I abstained from peeking.

I slipped into the pain like it was a warm bath. I took everything he gave me as if my artistic suffering was an offering to the gods.

Kylo rotated me again, this time to my stomach.

"Next piece," he said softly. "You're being so good for me, baby."

When he kissed the base of my neck, I relished the tingling pleasure that radiated from where his lips touched.

The needle met where Kylo had kissed. I made a soft, pained noise before settling deeper.

"My strong, intelligent, fierce, loyal girl," he praised.

Ecstasy wrapped around me like shadows. I was held by the earth below, supported by the starlight above.

"Your words are made of drugs."

Kylo paused his tattooing to laugh. "No talking, my subby, spacey, pliable angel. Just listen."

I sighed contentedly, relaxing into Kylo's gentle, painful worship.

"You are a rarity in this world. The fact that you once argued against your own specialness astounds me. What you did for your brother and for yourself—not only when you were a child but also recently with your healing, growing, and breaking free from your internal bondage—it's more than most will accomplish in their lifetimes. You should be immensely proud of the woman you have become. And it's a privilege to know you. And your shitty mother, father, and coven?" He paused, his voice reverberating through the dark night. "Their fucking loss, angel. *Their fucking loss.*"

A sob broke free, and I recognized the wounded inner child that took up residence in this space. Tears rolled down my cheeks, dropping to the bench below.

Kylo ran a hand through my hair as he consoled me, as he told me how worthy I was, how much I deserved to be loved and protected.

And for the first time, I didn't tell him to stop. I didn't tell him the past didn't matter, or that I didn't want to be psychoanalyzed. I didn't shun this vulnerability and what it meant for my wounded heart and love-hungry soul.

It *did* matter. Every moment that had led me to this one, limbs intertwined with his—they all mattered.

"I'm not sorry," I said suddenly, with a small shake of my head.

The words became some holy mantra, a spell of their own.

"Say it again."

"I'm not sorry."

"Louder."

"I'm not sorry!" I screamed into the night.

The words rattled in my mind, over and over, healing some deep part of me. My tears dried up, and raw power moved down my spine.

"Heavens above," Kylo murmured, tracing my back.

I didn't wince this time.

"Last one," he said. "Sit up for me, please."

I sat to face him. The fire in my eyes complemented the pride in his. He kissed both sides of my lips.

"Arm," he said.

I lifted my arm, and Kylo took it into his strong hand. I didn't look down. Sharp, icy pain met the tender flesh of my forearm. I let myself be marked for a third time as magick charged the air.

All my life, I'd apologized to everyone for everything. I'd strived endlessly to atone for sins that had never belonged to me.

I lifted a hand to the smile that had formed on my lips. It felt like a radical, revolutionary act to take up this much space, to tell the world I was done carrying excess weight.

My next exhale was long and easy.

"All done," Kylo said, after a much shorter length of time. "This one needed to be more visible. It's a clan sigil."

I didn't want my body to be fully covered in tattoos, yet I couldn't help the disappointment that it was already over.

"You're a masochist, baby," Kylo whispered, the darkness in his voice matching his eyes as he leaned close. "Rest assured there are endless ways for me to torture you. All you have to do is ask very politely."

My arm and hip and neck were on fire, coursing with new magick and purpose. I tangled my hands in Kylo's soft, dark hair. I crushed my lips against his. He tasted like power.

Now it was my turn to devour, for my tongue to explore and conquer and claim.

The future vampire lord of Etherdale was *mine*.

16

EVIE

"Open."

I opened my eyes. In the long, ornate, gold-framed mirror, I saw my hip tattoo for the first time.

My shocked features and Kylo's grin existed in the periphery as I stared at the art.

"I assure you the ink did more work than I did," Kylo murmured. "It sort of did its own thing as I drew."

A serpent was coiled up a beautiful, decorative key adorned with sigils and surrounded by blooming flowers. It was the perfect size—a tasteful amount of complexity extended down my thigh, above my hip bone, and toward the curve of my ass.

"Watch this."

Kylo gently brushed the raw, aching skin with his fingers.

I inhaled roughly, leaning into him, as the onyx ink came alive. The snake moved, its skin shimmering in iridescent, deep hues of blue and purple like Kylo's tattoos. The black flowers turned a shade of rosy pink, gently unfurling.

Kylo retracted his hand, and the tattoo shifted back to its

inky black stagnancy. Though a touch of shimmering purple hues remained.

I had no words. As deeply devoted as I'd become to Hekate, I had to admit I was nervous to be marked in this way. I liked my body as it was, and I was nervous for it to take a form I didn't recognize.

But this art was *me* in a way that had my eyes brimming with reverent tears. The key and serpent were sacred to Hekate, but the flowers were all mine.

Hekate knew who I was the same as Kylo, protecting me the same as him. My heart swelled with gratitude. She'd been so patient with me as I learned.

I twisted gently , and Kylo handed me a handheld mirror so I could see my back. He lifted my long blonde hair.

"Oh," I gasped. A burst of surprise laughter escaped my lips, and Kylo couldn't help but mirror my smile.

It was a rendition of my favorite tarot card, The Star, in a gorgeous, minimalist form. Stars—one larger with seven smaller—twinkled above a nude woman pouring water into a gently flowing stream below. In the water, there were more tiny sigils. The imagery might not be obvious to a non-card-reader. I'd recognized it immediately.

"Do you know what it is?" I asked Kylo.

He brushed his fingers over the art, and the stars lit up with his touch. A shadow coiled up the woman like a snake. The sigils grew darker, and the water became a deep blue hue. When Kylo retracted his hand, the shadow disappeared back into the water's depths, and the ink returned to static onyx once more.

"A tarot card, right? The Star?"

I was trembling, overcome with watery emotions as the magick and awe enveloped me.

"The Star is number seventeen in the major arcana. It's the card that directly follows The Tower," I explained. "The Tower demolishes, but it also liberates. Everything must fall, including all limitations. The Star displays renewed hope, tranquility, and beauty. It's a shimmering beginning that can only be accessed after the destruction of all that we once knew."

"The rebirth that follows death," Kylo murmured. He kissed my forehead. "I love when you teach me about magick, baby."

It took enormous effort to peel my gaze off the tarot-inspired tattoo in order to finally admire the underside of my forearm, where an elaborate sigil marked my fair skin—several symbols that overlapped in bold black ink.

These etchings were heavy with magick that was certain, inarguable. This was the mark of the clan, a reminder of my duty and responsibility.

Kylo revealed the underside of his own arm, putting it next to mine. He had more tattoos than me, but the central, largest sigil on his arm mirrored my own.

"It's not a collar," he said. He pulled me against him, his large, frightening cock poking my stomach. "But for now, it will do."

NOTHING COULD'VE PREPARED me for Etherdale's new reality. More born than I'd ever seen in this once mortal-dominated city flooded the streets, even in the vampire-free zones on campus.

There was no such thing as vampire-free zones in Etherdale. Not anymore.

"Keep walking, baby," Kylo said. "You have to keep walking."

In broad daylight, a group of born were sitting at a university café, sipping martinis as they ogled young adults milling around campus.

The energy was heavy, mournful. As I studied the kids who passed, I noticed their bloodshot eyes, their puffy skin, and the shocked disbelief that marred their features. I was surprised they felt safe enough to be outside today, but Etherdale

University students had never shied away from acts of bravery and defiance. Instead of irritation or fear, I now brimmed with solidarity and duty, a drive to protect these young humans.

"She's not going to want to move," I said to Kylo. "And I don't blame her. *I* don't want to move."

The tiniest flash of hurt passed through Kylo's eyes before it melted into understanding. He knew what my cottage and garden meant to me.

We were on our way to see Mena. My heart pumped erratically, overcome with input from both my heightened senses and my expansive witchy sight.

I struggled to ground myself. Princeton's techniques and guidance were the only things keeping me from accidentally leaking shadow.

We kept moving through the grief-stricken streets. I counted three dead bodies. One was clearly turned, my sigil burning as we passed. The others were mortal, perhaps dissenters caught in the crossfire.

Kylo and I mirrored grief, his hand squeezing mine in response.

Ten minutes from Mena's house, we turned a street corner and ran into a fight between a group of masked turned and born. A giant wolf roared, snapping its jaws at the born. Humans scattered, running for cover. One of the born wielded explosive, fiery magick. In the blink of an eye, it had shattered through a shop window and obliterated everything and everyone inside.

A feral yell built up in my throat.

Kylo grabbed me and pulled me backward before I could make a sound.

"We have to—"

"I know," he said.

Relief washed over me. We were both hungry for a fight, even if that protective, hesitant fear lingered in Kylo's eyes. The agony of potentially losing me and his unhealthy need for control made him hesitate for a brief moment.

"Mask up," he whispered.

Kylo wanted to hold me back, to shield me from reality, but he set me free instead.

I activated my new sigil for only the second time. The first had been a trial run. I hadn't realized how soon I'd need the skill, but at the same time, I wasn't surprised.

I shivered at the strange sensation of shadows crawling across my face and bleeding into my hair, obscuring my identity. They turned my blonde strands black, and they created a hard, protective mask that covered the entirety of my face.

"Remember, do not give anyone time to realize you're not a vampire," Kylo hissed. "And if I give you an order, obey it."

I nodded. Just like Kylo killed his urge to hold me back, I killed mine to question him. It wasn't the time for ego battles. We were a team.

Another crash boomed, and we moved back around the corner.

"They killed my daughter!" a woman screamed. "They killed her and left her body in the street!"

I homed in on the human woman who'd burst out of a storefront, tear-stricken.

One of the born women rolled her eyes before mimicking the woman in a grating, high-pitched whine. "You stupid, insolent mortals will break the law and assault your rulers and then act surprised when you face consequences. If your daughter hadn't attacked one of Lord Conrad's men, she'd still be alive."

The born man who wielded explosives shot another at one of the turned, who managed to deflect with a shield of shadow in the nick of time. The other four turned were engaged in hand-to-hand, weapons reflecting the afternoon sun. Blood sprayed. Shadows flew. Bodies moved too fast to track.

The wolf shifter lay motionless in a pool of blood between us and the born. One of the born suffered a nasty gash in his chest, I assumed from the wolf.

A turned woman screamed as a rod of conjured ice impaled her through the shoulder.

"You're all a bunch of worthless, bratty children who don't live long enough to learn," the born woman rattled on. "Look beneath this city overrun with vermin. There's where your choices lead. Piles and piles of skeletons, meaningless and forgotten."

As soon as her eyes turned black and she lifted a palm, Kylo and I wielded shadows at the same time. I cut off the woman's hand. Kylo lifted her off the ground and crushed all of her bones and organs.

The man with explosive magick turned the entirety of his attention on us. He raised a palm.

Kylo erected a shield of shadow, but for some reason, I knew it wouldn't be strong enough. So, I conjured wind. Bright, fiery light shattered Kylo's shield and stopped when it met my air-based magick.

I yelled, shoving my hands out as if I were moving the weight of an entire planet. The ball of fire shot back toward the vampire with such speed that he had no means of counteracting it.

I grinned as a loud crack shook the earth, and all that was left of the born vampire was the scorched ground where he had stood.

Kylo took his chance to move toward his comrades. He threw his favorite dagger straight into a born man's neck. The man gurgled and choked on his own blood.

I wanted to help, but I knew my slow movements were too much of a liability. We didn't want anyone to know I was a witch, let alone a shadow-wielding chaos witch. I couldn't showcase too much magick out here in the open. Not yet. If a born vampire had witnessed this battle, they would have assumed I was merely a turned woman gifted in air magick. It wasn't entirely unheard of, as each turned was blessed with different powers.

Manipulating the weather or conjuring a natural disaster, on the other hand, was out of the question.

I moved to the human woman, who stood her ground as her fists shook with fury, staring at the born with seething hatred for killing her daughter.

"It's not safe," I said gently. "We're going to take care of them. You should go back inside."

Her haunted eyes were slow to meet mine. "I don't care if I live or die. They drained all the light from my world."

The words were simple, poetic, a sharp jab to the heart. Hearing a mother speak this way about her daughter hit somewhere deep, and for a moment, I wanted to escape.

I stayed put instead.

"I'm so sorry," I said. "She was lucky to be so loved."

The woman gritted her teeth, her eyes puffy and cheeks damp. "Get them out of here." Her voice was gritty and raw. "You hear me? You get these demons out of our city!"

"Angel!" Kylo yelled.

I turned just in time to see an inky, indiscernible creature leap toward me.

What the ever-loving fuck—

The *thing* tackled me to the earth. Time slowed down as I struggled to breathe, an impossible weight crushing my ribs. Just before a full mouth of jagged, razor-sharp teeth ripped into my face, the beast halted.

Its bright red eyes stared down at me. The long slits below audibly sniffed the air.

The repulsive black flesh smelled of hellfire and death, and visions of The Tower overcame me. My shadows heaved, wrapping around the four-legged, mysterious animal's neck. A snap rang through the air. Strong hands shoved the creature to the side.

I gasped for oxygen.

Kylo stood over me. He bled onyx, his face twisted in confusion.

"You okay?" he asked quickly, tearing his eyes from the motionless beast next to me.

I nodded. "What *was* that thing?" I rasped, still fighting to replenish my lungs.

Kylo only shook his head, eyes wide.

He helped me up, and we surveyed the area around us as everything stilled and quieted.

The turned had prevailed. The born instigators had been annihilated. Bodies littered the street.

"Disperse," Kylo commanded to his comrades.

A turned man bowed his head slightly in respect before leaving with the others in opposite directions. They each dropped their masks and reactivated their human glamours to camouflage back into the city.

Kylo and I returned our attention to the demented, disfigured canine in utter horror. I'd never seen anything like it, and by Kylo's reaction, neither had he. Perhaps I'd read about similar beings in myths, or horror novels.

An elderly human man stumbled out from behind a merchant's cart. "It's another act of Lillian," he cried. "Look what you people have done!"

17

EVIE

Mena fretted and spoke with increasing dramatic flair as she moved about the kitchen. "Sit, sit!"

Kylo and I exchanged a glance before we sat at the circular table in the adjacent room. Through the tall windows, I gazed at my garden with immense longing. Grief rooted in my chest.

"It's not forever," Kylo whispered, back in his human glamour. "We're going to live long, peaceful lives after this war has been won. I vow it."

He couldn't vow something like that, and yet I cherished his sweet promise anyway.

"Quit reading my mind."

"Never."

"Are you pregnant? Is that the big news?" Mena blurted, her mouth dropping open as she waited for the kettle to come to a boil. "Oh, my heavens! Well, you are an adult now, so it's not exactly a scandal, but gods, Evie, you're really quite young. You have options, you know. And what about your plans for a witchy shop? I'll help in any case. You know how much I'd—oh my, should I make you some food?"

I choked on a strangled half-laugh. "Mena! I am not pregnant!"

Kylo's blue eyes were molten, staring at me so intensely I had to swallow and avert my gaze.

"That's a relief. No offense to either of you." She frowned. "Did the born accost you? Is that why you look so disheveled?" Mena paused her rummaging of the pantry. "Well, *you* look disheveled. Kylo looks fine."

I made an incredulous, indignant noise as Kylo smirked. Mena winked, almost forgetting her dedicated fretting.

"Have you heard from Idris? I've been so worried about you both I can hardly eat."

"Yes, he's okay," I assured her.

I left out the *he died, but don't worry, I signed my soul to the clan and rose him from the dead, but I can't see him until he calms down and stops trying to eat me* portion of the truth.

"Good, good." She sighed deeply. "Chamomile?"

"Perfect, thank you," Kylo said.

Mena made an impatient gesture for me to speak.

"As you know, the born have decided to shun Etherdale's traditions and institutions and take the city by force," I began. "Additionally, the Whitfields believe I'm one of the witches the born are looking for. We no longer think you're safe here."

It didn't feel good to lie by omission, and it made me a hypocrite. But the less Mena knew, the better.

"The Whitfields went missing," Mena said. "Disappeared into thin air. That's what Missy told me during my afternoon stroll. She was tending to her rose bushes down by the road, which very obviously didn't need tending to. She just wanted to gossip with anyone and everyone who walked by."

Getting Mena to focus was like herding cats. Best to approach with gentle redirection.

"That is most unfortunate," I said.

"Not really." Mena slowly smirked.

"I was trying to be polite, but yeah."

I smiled, which only delighted Mena. She never failed to make spite look chic, as she stood in her leopard print tunic and dramatic gold earrings. Her lips were painted trademark Mena-red.

For a moment, something clicked, and Mena's head tilted as she glanced between the two of us.

"Like I said, I no longer think you're safe here, even with the Whitfields gone," I said, hoping Mena wouldn't ask the obvious question poised on her tongue. "I don't think either of us is safe here. Not for a while, at least. I have a place we could stay, and we can come back once the dust settles."

Mena's sharp, former-professor mind parsed through my words. She studied us, those perceptive eyes analyzing everything said and unsaid.

"Someone needs to take care of the garden," she said simply. The kettle whistled, and she reached for three mugs. "I've lived in this home for over thirty years. I picked out every single piece of furniture, art, linen, rug... this home is an extension of myself, and without it, I would be incomplete."

"Well, that's how I feel about you," I said.

Mena shook her head. "It's not the same, doll. This is my life, and you must let me live it. My parents wanted me to settle down and abide by their values and traditions, and I made my life full and rich and *fabulous* instead. This isn't my first brush with danger, and it needn't be my last."

The desperation in my eyes wasn't enough, and for a moment I felt helpless and triggered. I remembered Idris's motionless body.

Kylo traced circles on my back.

"You're becoming *you*," Mena said as she placed a plate of biscuits down with our tea. She finally sat, her spine straight and her chin lifted with a regal air. "I insist you leave this house. I will grieve your absence just as I did Idris's, but I will celebrate your growth with equal fervor." She bit into a biscuit and took a sip of tea. "Rebellion is not reserved for the young."

She reached for my hand, those amber eyes alight with mischief and knowing.

"It is a revolutionary act to stay in your home despite the threat from oppressors. To continue to laugh and take strolls and steal joy and orgasms and acts of indulgence, small and large. To refuse to live in fear is radical. I will dance and make art. I will fill vases with freshly cut flowers, and I will make my bed every morning. Do you understand what I'm saying?"

I wanted to shake my head and beg her to change her mind. But Mena had never been selfish with me. After boldly defying her parents' expectations and refusing to live a traditional life, she'd welcomed two children into her home without a second thought. She'd taken care of us better than she even took care of herself.

"I was made to understand your beautiful visions, Mena," I said.

She grinned and gave my hand a squeeze. "And that's why you're my favorite girl in the world."

"Do you write?" Kylo asked. "You have an enviable way with words."

Mena lit up, falling deeper in love with Kylo. "Poetry, mainly. But I'd love to turn my journals into a memoir. I have been documenting my life since I was ten years old."

"I would kill to read that memoir," Kylo said.

Mena angled her head, studying Kylo.

"You're right, by the way," Kylo continued. "About all of it."

"More of my favorite words! Go on." Mena sipped her tea with an impish grin.

Kylo's smile was nothing short of heart-melting. It was a hazard to society.

"The realm needs your wisdom. Preserving our ability to experience joy and levity is essential, no matter how heavy the oppression," he said. "They may not realize it, but I believe the born envy our mortality, the way it expands our capacity for humor, art, and love. The knowledge that one day we will die gives everything we do such vivid color and meaning. The born have never lived with the fear of death, so they will never truly experience life. They wish they were as brave and bold and creative and hopeful as we are. But they will never know anything more than their own hollow, unquenchable emptiness."

Even as my heart ached in my chest, still I sat here with Mena and Kylo and accepted the choice I always knew she would make.

Every laugh and joke did indeed feel radical, an act of defiance that rivaled my hungry, ruthless shadows. The tattoos hidden beneath my glamour told a story of rebirth and grief and radiant constellations.

"You should be with Idris for the, well, you know," Mena said.

"For the trauma anniversary," I said. It was in two weeks. This was when Idris and I experienced the peak of our nightmares and painful echoes from the past.

Mena nodded. She scanned my eyes curiously, unaccustomed to my bluntness. She hadn't yet learned that I was no longer afraid of my own shadow.

"Of course I will." I'd discovered that Idris remembered everything about that night—that he saw my greatest shame as an act of heroism, the reason he wanted to join the turned to protect me like I protected him.

"He's going to want to fight," Mena warned.

I held Mena's gaze, unflinching. "We'll fight together."

Surprise crested on Mena's features before it fell into a gentle, lulling wave of understanding. She glanced at Kylo again.

"Nothing will happen to either of them," he said with all the confidence of a vampire lord.

Mena sat back in her chair. "Good."

"Thank you, Mena," I said. My chest ached as I smiled. "For the tea."

Mena winked. "Always."

I'D ALREADY MOVED a great deal of my things to Kylo's estate, but this second round of packing and harvesting from my garden felt like a much more permanent goodbye.

A goodbye to who I once was. The version of myself that had hid from the world. The version of myself that had kept Idris and me safe the best she knew how.

Kylo kissed my temple as I dug my fingers into the soil and closed my eyes. The summer breeze kissed my skin, the sunlight a soothing balm. I was blessed to be a child of both Helia and Selena, the sun and the moon, an eternal dance of light and dark.

"Whatever you need to feel comfortable, baby, just let me know," Kylo said. "I don't care what it is, how expensive or how hard it is to make or find, I will get you anything you desire to make you feel at home with me."

I carefully pulled back my hands. "Thank you."

The reverent words were for both Kylo and the earth.

"And of course you know I'll do everything in my power to protect Mena and this land."

I'd be sure to add more of my own protection spells and wards too.

I nodded, leaning into his touch as I surveyed the gardens. I took in the birdbaths and marble figures, the tiny table where I loved to read, and the space between rose bushes where I often lay out a picnic blanket. Lastly, I studied the looming cottage with its cozy pastel interior and spell room with a pink altar.

I knew I wouldn't be far, and I'd always be welcome here.

But it would never be the same again. My roots had shifted to new land, new people, and a new purpose. I would become a visitor to the place that raised me, the place that used to be the center of my world.

My world was infinitely bigger now. Still, I grieved. My breath was shaky, my lips wobbly. I let Kylo hold me as I said goodbye to the childhood I never had, the adolescence Mena graciously made safe, and to the woman I became through blood and sacrifice and devotion.

Thank you.

18

KYLO

In my study, I reflected on the progress I'd made with Evie these past two weeks. I worked tirelessly to rebuild our trust. I answered all of her questions, even when I feared she might see too much of me.

It healed something deep inside her every time I read to her or washed her hair or cooked her food. I forced her to say her new mantra, *I'm not sorry,* at every opportunity. I watched the way it lit up those pretty gray eyes with the light so many had tried to steal.

Evie had also made progress in learning Princeton's magick and wielding her shadows, and Idris improved in controlling his bloodlust.

Generally, it wasn't this difficult for clan newborns to temper bloodlust, as we'd developed a system that began even before turning to mitigate the aftereffects. Idris's process was different, but he was also strong. Just like his sister.

"There have been additional sightings of those unidentified rabid beasts," Blade said as he entered my study in the underground. "Word on the street is that the turned and our chaos witch allies have disrupted the natural order of the universe and ripped open a portal to Lillian's hells. The Dark Mother is punishing us, and the only way to return to *normalcy* and save the world is to submit to the born and ask for atonement."

Blade's lips formed a thin, hard line, and his auburn brows lifted.

"And by *word* you mean the borns' carefully curated spin to paint us as the problem and them as our reasonable, benevolent protectors," I muttered. "They're so predictable, it's almost boring." I shook my head. "Whatever these beasts are, they're clearly of born origin. Yet another scare tactic to control the narrative."

Blade murmured his agreement.

After a careful pause, he asked, "Is she truly ready to turn a new class of vampires? We're up to one hundred who are ready for initiation."

My stomach flipped, but I didn't show my nervousness.

"She can do it. She has already started prepping, and I'll be assisting her. She'll just need to rest before and after, and we will need to create a window of time around the new moon where there's minimal clan activity."

"We can't predict what the born will do," Blade said, stating the obvious.

I sighed. "Whatever is happening, we can't drain her. Just as with Princeton, any big ritual will come at a cost. She won't be able to pour her magick and strength into anything else during that time."

Blade's lips tugged down, and he scratched his head as he looked at the floor. "Does she talk to him?"

An image of our maker and friend overtook my mind's eye. I saw those wise, mischievous features and long, wild curls of hair.

"Yeah," I said softly. "She says it isn't the same as talking to the living. Princeton won't answer questions about his death or speak in plain language, usually. It's mostly metaphor and symbols when it comes to spirits."

Blade nodded. "I bet he loves being cryptic and difficult as a ghost as much as he enjoyed it in the flesh."

I smiled. "Me too."

After a beat of shared grief and love, we began going over my current draft of the war plans. I spread out the pages of notes and charts in an intuitive order across my long, mahogany desk.

Blade was always my first pair of eyes on any plan or scheme. His appearance often led people to underestimate him. Underneath his meaty, hulky exterior lay a sharp mind built for keen strategy.

He was a crucial part of my creative process. I was a madman when it came to my obsessions and ideas—I followed my intuition recklessly, mapping out future possibilities and synthesizing data from the past and present as I worked it all out. My intuition was solid, but I needed someone who could put my wealth of meticulously cataloged information together in a digestible format.

Blade was made to understand *my* visions, and he made sense of my madness with ease.

I explained each step, bouncing ideas off him as we moved.

"Do you really think Rune would help us?" Blade asked as we neared the end. "I know you've read everything you can about him and Valentin. But these are all secondhand accounts. We don't actually know him, you know? I'm not sure if anyone truly does. He's made himself into more myth or god than a man."

"He wouldn't help us *yet*," I agreed. "But I think he would once we prove ourselves. Once we take Etherdale, push the born out, and create a hub for the revolution. We need a story for him to truly believe in, for the whole realm to believe in. We will go to him only when it would be impossible for us to be denied."

"*You* want to go to him," Blade said with a slowly growing grin. "Would you even be able to handle the excitement?"

I rolled my eyes. "Fuck off."

After one more round of teasing and retaliative banter, we found our groove again.

So far, our tactics were working about half as well as I'd hoped. Our mortal allies and supporters' patience wasn't infinite. While some rallied around our small-scale assassinations and guardianship, helping us to defy the born at every opportunity, others felt disappointed and betrayed that we'd allowed the born to take the city and university.

They were unable to see through their fear and anger to the other side, where a vast, powerful army awaited King Earle's direction.

The born were only showing a fraction of their capacities. While they attempted to provoke us, we succeeded in provoking them. As we infuriated them with our unpredictability and formlessness, we gathered information just as they had hoped to do with us.

We were mapping out exactly who was in charge, their precise numbers here in the city and where other born cells were stationed beyond Etherdale's mountains.

Lord Conrad was here. He'd rarely deigned to grace Etherdale with his presence, preferring to rule this region from his remote estate, surrounded by his court of elites and their human slaves.

He was despised by all non-loyalists. He was the reason for the uprising centuries ago, the stacks and stacks of mortal skeletons beneath our feet.

And nothing had changed. He'd squashed the rebellion, pretended to make concessions until that generation had mostly died off, then he'd gone right back to not giving a single fuck about what his people thought of him.

Now he was here, no longer scared of being assassinated. He

boldly took up residence in an estate in the center of the city that resembled a small castle, where he gave orders on who to round up, which oppressive laws to enforce and books to burn.

"We will all need to move as one," I murmured. "No clan can get cold feet. When King Earle declares war, all turned clans' fates will be intrinsically bound."

Blade opened his mouth to speak, but Harmony burst into the room without so much as a knock.

"Something's happened," she rushed out. She gulped in air, her brows drawn and her frown deep. "Where's Evie?"

I was on my feet in an instant. "Princeton's spell room. Why?"

"I don't know—it doesn't make sense." Harmony's tan skin was flushed, her eyes glassy. "An entire building on campus was scourged from the earth, reduced to nothing but ash. Students were in there, a great many of whom were potential initiates. The sky turned dark and rained blood."

My heart shattered immediately for the lives lost. "You saw this with your own eyes?"

She shook her head. "But other turned did. And the evidence is there for all to see."

Harmony's face crumpled, and Blade reached for her hand.

"Why did you ask where Evie was?" I demanded, my emotions raw in the face of this tragedy.

"The born aren't claiming this. No one saw who or what did it." Her tone was increasingly urgent. "And you just told the clan that all acts of the gods belonged to Evie."

Understanding dropped low in my gut, my blood pumping fast and hard.

"This was an act of the gods," Harmony said. "We know Evie didn't do this, but… we don't know what *did*. This wasn't born magick. It was something more."

It was becoming harder to think straight as my mind flashed

through several emotions, possibilities, and future events in quick succession.

"I'll go get her." I paused, unleashing a curse. "They slaughtered a building of university students as if it were a move on a fucking chessboard."

Disgust and rage and horror warred in the space. Shadows curled at our feet, hissing and hungry.

"Phineas is torturing our newest born prisoners in the dungeons," Harmony hissed. "It's rare. But we know they crack every once in a while. Even if they don't mean to."

"I'll head there next. I'll think about our official statement while I cut off someone's fucking appendages," I said as I stormed out of the room.

I quickly accessed Evie's location through the blood bond.

My stomach sank. *Fuck.*

Evie was above ground. On Etherdale University's campus.

19

EVIE

On a cliff's edge, I practiced writing important clan sigils—sigils Princeton had used for wards, glamours, and initiation rituals, and new symbols I was creating with Hekate.

Behind me wisps of light floated about a dark forest of tall evergreens, and creatures, earthen and otherworldly, roamed.

My body was back in Princeton's spell room, safe within a circle of salt. Here in the spirit world, I was open to far greater magickal influence.

I used a pen with a wide tip to draw on my sketchpad until the ink began to move on its own.

The ink split into hundreds of threads that flowed across the page in all directions. My finger brushed across the page, and the thin lines of ink swirled in a circular formation around my touch.

Fate weaver, something whispered, a presence at my back.

I lifted my finger. The threads of ink coalesced and formed The Magician tarot card, number one in the major arcana. The creator. The weaver.

This time when I touched the page, the threads pulled apart and moved vertically.

Weave, I commanded.

They braided together, intertwined, creating a tapestry of connection that covered the page.

Something powerful curled up my spine. I set down the sketchbook and turned, finding several non-corporeal entities. Some were balls of light, others hazy, nearly translucent outlines. One was a black hound.

She threw her head back and howled.

The ground shook, and my sense of power slipped like sand through an hourglass. I experienced the distinct sensation of running out of time, a frantic race against peril.

Princeton appeared from behind a tall tree.

He ran toward me, eyes wide. His mouth fell open, and he screamed, but sound didn't come out.

I scrambled back, stopping at the edge of the precipice behind me. The plunge into some great unknown.

Princeton continued soundlessly screaming. No words. Just a warning that echoed through every fiber of my spirit.

The forest shook. Trees expelled their leaves and needles. The sky turned blood red, and in the distance, I made out an Etherdale University academic building.

I turned toward the bottomless chasm.

The Fool card flashed in my mind, but I didn't leap.

I shut my eyes tight and opened them back up again in my physical body.

The dim light of the spell room was blinding as my eyes adjusted. I sucked in air as I jumped to my feet, broke the circle of salt with a frantic swipe of my foot, and ran for the door.

I didn't stop to think or explain myself to the perplexed turned that encountered me on my way to Kylo's private underground stairwell. My calves and hamstrings burned as I ran up the winding steps, witch lights illuminating my way through the darkness.

The sun beckoned me back up to the surface. I knew I was racing against inevitability. Princeton's warning was a shot of adrenaline to my heart.

For the first time in my life, I wasn't running away from the threat of danger. I was running straight toward it.

I sped through the secret passageway that connected to Kylo's aboveground study. Then I barreled out the front door of the estate.

"You all right?" Allie asked, my dedicated bodyguard who sat on Kylo's front porch with his other guards.

"Yes!" I said as I rushed down the steps. I couldn't have anyone slowing me down. "All good, just time-constrained witch business!"

It was a sketchy-as-fuck thing to say, but it wasn't a lie. And no one stopped me. I was one of them, after all.

Even still, I assumed someone would write to Kylo to be safe.

My lungs heaved as I barreled through the invisible barriers at the edge of the neighborhood. I passed the rows of shops and apartment buildings on the next block. My legs pumped. Someone shouted at me, and a shot of fear coursed through my blood.

"Hey!"

I kept running.

"Demon spawn on twelfth street!"

My next breath was less shaky as it burned through me. "Thank you!" I shouted without looking over my shoulder.

I avoided twelfth street, and it cost me time and oxygen.

Students stared at me as I raced through campus. I stopped only when I reached the quad. The building for physical sciences lay to the north, students outside holding books and speaking in huddles. A few ate their lunches on the steps before the entrance.

This was the building I saw in my vision.

I took a step forward.

An ear-splitting sound ripped through the calm afternoon. Fractions of a second later, a surge of wind and power crashed into me, sending me flying through the air.

I was too breathless to scream. My back hit the earth. The sky above darkened, and thick black clouds obscured the sun. Thunder boomed, and fat rain droplets fell and splattered against my skin.

I wiped at my eyes. Screams and shouts hit me from all directions. With great disorientation, I managed to push back up to a crouched position. My head spun; my ears rang. The cacophony of loud voices and commotion were muffled.

A rain drop touched my lips, and instead of salt, I tasted copper.

I studied my hands. Watery crimson smeared across my fair skin. Another drop landed, the same shade of red.

The clouds darkened further, dipping from the sky and wrapping around the academic building already collapsing. Several of the students who'd been chatting or eating now lay motionless on the ground several yards away. A few people attempted to haul unconscious bodies as they fled.

The shadow-like clouds impaled the building in rapid bursts. I stumbled forward. I scanned for the source of this magick—magick unlike anything I'd ever witnessed.

Apart from my own.

The air was charged with death, and all I could remember was Princeton's voiceless scream as the building exploded into ash and rubble.

I covered my head as debris flew in all directions.

Panting, confused, I still didn't run. I spun around, even as vertigo threatened to make me retch. I spotted a couple of born, but they were crouched and taking cover, which made little sense if they were the ones causing this destruction.

Whoever was doing this could've been on the other side of the building, obscured from my sight.

I took another wobbly step. The world was apocalyptic, stained with blood and darkness as mortals screamed and sobbed.

Tears burned my eyes. How many young mortals and professors had just died? A hundred? More?

More of my hearing returned. Something prickly moved up my spine, like a thousand tiny needles. My head swiveled, and I caught sight of a figure cloaked in white slip behind a statue of Helia. The statue was poised between two buildings opposite the destroyed physical sciences building.

It had been only a brief glimpse of flowing fabric that disappeared as soon as it had been perceived.

An older human man was yelling at the students to take cover, a difficult command after an entire structure had been demolished. Nowhere was guaranteed to be safe.

Once again, I ran toward danger, toward the phantom cloaked in white.

I dodged sprinting, panicked bodies.

A few pairs of eyes met mine, and my hidden clan tattoo burned. The turned women wearing human glamours scanned my body in confusion as I barreled toward them. One of them whispered frantically to the other.

I sprinted past them both.

Helia loomed, her golden crown of sunrays dull, her eyes weeping blood.

On the other side of her was a space where students typically rested or studied on benches surrounded by shade trees and flowering bushes.

The garden was empty as I passed through.

Yet, I felt a keen, predator's gaze on me, a sensation I knew all too well from Kylo's obsessive stalking.

My ears pricked at the sound of laughter, almost too distant to make out. Those sharp, prodding needles were back, skating across my spine.

I couldn't run anymore, or my heart might explode. I walked quickly through the wrought-iron gate at the back of the garden. Behind the buildings, I only saw mortals and turned running to or from this hellish scene. No flowing white robes.

A slip of paper carried in the wind, and I was quick to snatch it from the air.

What beautiful eyes you have. Play soon?

As soon as I read the deep red script, the note caught fire. I let go, and the paper was reduced to a few scorched crumbles before meeting the earth.

"Evie?" a woman asked.

I jolted before spinning around. The two turned women from before were behind me, keeping their distance as they scanned me up and down.

"Did you see someone dressed in all white?" I asked, rubbing my chest. "I think it was a man. You were standing close by when he entered the gardens."

The women exchanged a glance.

"Before or after the attack?" one of them asked, her dark brows knitted. She swallowed, her face racked with horror.

"After," I rasped.

Something about the way they were watching me put me in a state of unease.

I was well-accustomed to others' subtle body language, no doubt a survival mechanism from my abusive mother. All my life, I'd encountered people who'd assumed the worst about chaos witches like me. Or mortals who simply didn't like or trust me without fully knowing why, perhaps because I was untrusting and withholding myself. Too different to fit in anywhere, I'd spent most of my life in solitude, save Mena, Idris, and those I came to know through Celeste's.

But I was proficient in reading people and their perceptions of me, even if I'd so often kept my distance.

The women stepped closer to me, angling their heads as they studied me.

"Where's Kylo?" the red-haired woman asked.

The hairs on the back of my neck stood. I felt cornered.

I stood my ground, even if my instinct was to bolt. There was no way these vampires suspected that *I* was behind this. The entire clan knew who I was by now. I'd been initiated. I couldn't betray the clan even if I wanted to, as my oath and dedication were bound by magick.

"He's underground," I said, trying to keep my voice level. I was practically bathing in adrenaline.

The sting of their distrust was a brutal slap in the face after everything I'd gone through to be one of them.

More than wanting to prove myself to these strangers, I needed to find the writer of that strange, taunting note.

Could born demons wield magick like that? It was rare for anyone, but especially the born, who tended to fit into neater and tidier magickal specialties that ran through bloodlines.

The magick was dark, but it wasn't the same kind of shadow that belonged to me and the clan. I felt no connection to those clouds of darkness. They were foreign.

Whoever did this wanted it to look like a cosmic reckoning, a punishment straight from the chthonic underworld. And I had to admit, it was convincing.

I scanned our surroundings again. Nausea bloomed in my guts, the aftereffects of the adrenaline surge rearing its ugly head.

"There was a figure in white," I said uselessly. "He was fleeing the quad through the gardens. He left a note." I stared at the ground, not finding any evidence of the scrap of paper, as the pieces had already scattered to the wind. "But it's gone."

Shit. I sounded crazy. I could hear it, but it didn't change anything. I brushed a hand across my damp, hot forehead. The gravity of what had happened was slowly starting to reach through the haze. Idris could've been one of those piles of ash; he'd had a class in that building.

I closed my eyes, remembering every detail of my spirit walking journey leading up to Princeton's warning.

Out of desperation, I attempted to channel through more visions, perhaps to make contact with Princeton again.

"Maybe if I—"

A sharp boom of thunder had me jumping out of my skin, and a tendril of shadow escaped my palm.

The women charged me, fully masked and in vampire form. I yanked my shadow back inside.

I didn't have time to process or move on anything more than pure instinct. My own gust of wind shoved them back. One of them hit the gate with a *smack*, crying out in pain. The other landed awkwardly on the stone path.

"I'm so sorry," I said, backing away, hands raised defensively as I fought the urge to wield my shadows. Not in public, and certainly not *now*.

I finally gave in to my most innate, cherished survival mechanism. I turned, and I fucking bolted.

My legs were jelly at this point. I could barely feel them.

I didn't make it far before my world went dark.

Someone tackled me to the ground and pinned my hands. I thrashed until a blade pressed against my throat.

"Write to Kylo," one of the turned women hissed.

Angry, betrayed tears burned my eyes. This was supposed to be my new family, my new life's purpose.

I was supposed to finally belong somewhere.

There was no use fighting. Whoever instigated the initial attack was long gone.

"He won't answer," the other replied.

I lay motionless, helpless, for the first time since my shadows had broken free. I thought I'd never feel this weak again.

A man's feral roar shook the earth.

"Get the fuck off her!"

20

KYLO

Evie's heart fluttered through the blood bond. Rage was hot and thick in my blood at the sight of two of *my* clan members on top of her, holding her down with a blade pressed against her throat and a shadow blindfold over her eyes. Mortals ran in all directions in the distance.

The moment they heard my command, the two women ceased. Evie was slow to sit up, her skin flushed, her eyes frantic. When I detected the slightest tremble of her lower lip, I almost fucking lost it.

I'd managed to mask myself before I emerged from the underground, prepared for anything that awaited.

This was *not* what I'd expected.

"Explain," I barked. "Now."

Claudette cleared her throat, pushing strands of red hair behind her ears as she carefully lifted her gaze from the ground to my wrathful eyes.

"We saw her standing there right before the attack. Then, after, she took off running," Claudette said.

My gaze shifted to Evie. Her features warred between anger,

embarrassment, and something far more wounded and vulnerable. I moved to her immediately, helping her to her feet.

"Are you okay?"

She searched my eyes, and she released a breath when she'd found what she'd been looking for. "Yes. I saw a premonition. Princeton was warning me about something, but I didn't understand what it was—I only saw the location. So I ran here, but I was too late." Her voice cracked.

Her eyes filled with tears.

Both women shifted on their feet. I couldn't tell if they were doubting their initial judgments or merely pretending to in my presence.

Either way, my clan would never dare question *me*.

Evie attempted to squash her emotions down as she avoided my eyes. Her fists clenched at her sides. "I saw someone in white, a robe or cape or something, fleeing the area. A man, I think. I had an intuition, so I followed him and then—"

She stopped herself and glared at the two women.

"He got away."

The two women exchanged a glance as if fighting over who was going to explain their way out of this mess.

Evie huffed and lifted her arm.

One of the women tensed. "She *attacked* us."

"You charged me first," Evie snapped. She kept her outstretched arm steady as she flipped it over.

Evie's clan tattoo broke through her glamour for a few brief seconds before she lowered her arm. Claudette swallowed.

"We were doing what we were trained to do," the brunette said.

She was relatively new, and her name escaped me.

"It seemed like the right call after a natural disaster rotted hundreds of people alive," Claudette added. "But we didn't know the context, we didn't know—"

"That this was Princeton's successor and my partner?" I whispered harshly. The entire clan knew who Evie was.

Both gazes fell back to the ground. Rage rippled through me, and Evie looked relieved I was standing up for her.

Which irritated me even more. Of course, I trusted Evie's word. She didn't deserve to be treated this way by those who were supposed to be on her side.

"I'm sorry, K—"

A shrill, surprised laugh broke through the air.

"Born," Claudette hissed.

I moved in front of Evie instinctively, and my comrades flanked me. Though we were masked, Evie was not. I fought the urge to curse. To onlookers, she was a random mortal. To the born, they might've even mistaken her for a human, given her alluring, human-scented blood.

Still, it was safest for Evie to only be spotted with us when she was glamoured. Or when we appeared as humans.

Soon none of this would fucking matter.

The whole realm would know my name.

I made a mental note to ensure Claudette and the brunette faced consequences for how they'd treated Evie. A reprimand wasn't nearly enough of a punishment. But for now, I shoved that wrath aside.

A group of five born kept their distance, watching us from afar. The three in front were clearly guards, dressed in wine red, and the two behind...

Evie made a strange, strangled noise from behind me.

"No," she breathed.

Her heart hammered fast and hard like a rabbit on the run from a wolf.

My own chest clenched when I recognized one of the men obscured by his guards. Lord fucking Conrad.

But that wasn't who stepped forward. The man who stepped forward was grinning wide as his nostrils flared and pupils dilated. His flashy, archaic clothing oozed wealth the same as the lord next to him.

He stared forward, lips parting in shocked glee. "It really is you."

Who was he talking to? He was almost looking at me, but not quite.

"You're alive."

I fought the urge to glance back at Evie, who was clearly struggling for air. I didn't want to take my eyes off the enemy.

The born elite threw his head back in pure delight. His amber eyes were nearly red, a contrast to the cool blond of his hair. He looked like an arrogant politician, oozing charisma that was rare to born scum.

I shoved my confusion to the side as I plotted out what was about to happen. Could I take them out? How many more born had gathered nearby, waiting for us to make that attempt?

We weren't ready to kick off war. Everything had to happen according to plan. Or what I'd built for nearly a century would be for nothing.

No one moved. Lord Conrad smirked. The three guards were stoic. They kept their distance, tracking us with subtly exposed fangs.

The gaze of the man leading the pack took a strange turn. The look in his eyes boiled my blood and provoked my starving shadows.

Lust. Hunger. And even if it didn't make sense, I swore I saw possessiveness in those demonic eyes.

Evie's small hand gripped the back of my shirt. Her heart thumped in a distracting cacophony.

The next words out of the born man's mouth were a shocking punch to the gut.

"Hello again, my bride."

Now it was my turn to struggle to breathe.

My lip curled, my shadows singeing my skin.

Evie vibrated behind me with fear or anger or some combination of the two.

I worried I might crack my jaw with how hard I was clenching my teeth. I reminded myself, over and over, that we stood in a trap, another calculated born game to secure the upper hand. I couldn't lose control.

The blond man's eyes flitted from Evie to me and back again. I wanted to rip those eyes from his skull and shove them back down his undeserving throat.

He made an audacious, condescending clicking noise with his tongue against the roof of his mouth.

"It would be a pity," he drawled. "If such unique, perfect, *delicious* blood was ruined by impurity."

A low hum of power began to build. Evie tried to step to my side, but I gently stopped her with an outstretched hand.

I finally stole a glance to find that her fear had transformed into fiery rage. Her face was twisted with it, her palms twitching at her sides.

"By a blasphemy, a bastard of Lillian, no less," he said with a sigh. "I hate to see a child of Lillian so lost and confused."

I wanted to comfort Evie, but I didn't want to give away any clues about who she was to me, or who I was to the clan. They were fishing for information with every word.

Even if it was horrifyingly apparent that Evie's identity was already compromised.

Don't, I hissed at my shadows internally, begging them not to give in.

The words *my bride* rattled around in my skull in compulsive repetitions. Thank fuck for my mask so I could seethe and strain against my power without the born seeing a fraction of my fury.

Evie was mine. Fucking *mine.*

Lord Conrad stared at me, sizing me up. He barely paid any mind to the turned women next to me, as if already deeming them irrelevant. The born refused to let their beloved tradition of misogyny die, no matter how many centuries had passed.

In the distance, I could make out the sound of several heavy footsteps approaching. The sickly sweet smell of the born multiplied.

Every born vampire reached maturity in their mid-twenties and halted. But with a keen eye, you could detect the ancientness in their permanently youthful, enticing features.

Lord Conrad's dark hair framed a face made stoic and frigid through centuries of immortality. His blue eyes were so cool they were nearly ghostly. There was no sign of life in their cold depths.

"Fuck you," Evie said, piercing through the silent stand-off.

I tensed. The man smiled, delighted by the sound of her voice.

Evie was unaware of the born moving in to watch how we handle ourselves in the aftermath of their massacre.

"I was a child," Evie said, prodding at my protective, enraged heart. "That was why you wanted me, right? Because only someone who didn't have a choice would ever be with a vile, decrepit monster like *you*."

The man's smile dropped. I held my breath, silently pleading with Evie to resist making a move, pleading with myself to do the same.

Lord Conrad was a lethal force, possessing devastating pain magick. Could I take him? Maybe, if I moved quickly. But I didn't know the nature of the other borns' magick, and I could only assume the second predator was rich in power as well.

We were outnumbered. I hated that the most strategic choice was also the least satisfying.

"Still so feisty," groaned the man I wanted to rot from the inside out. He failed to hide the anger that had eclipsed his once easy charisma. "Rest assured we have ways to tame even the most murderous little creatures."

I'd never been more tense in my long fucking existence. Vision after violent vision played out before me. I wanted to claim Evie, to fuck and feed from her, while this man choked on his own blood, limbless and forced to watch.

He knew. Whoever this man was, he knew where Evie came from. He knew what she'd done.

"Disperse," I finally spoke, low and distorted through my mask. The word scraped from my throat like a knife. "*Now.*"

I didn't give anyone time to think, least of all myself. A thick wall of shadow rippled from me, defensive rather than lethal as I truly desired.

I scooped Evie into my arms.

And we fled. The ground shook, and my shadow glamour obscured us from sight as the cloud of shadow at our backs deflected the borns' offensive strikes.

They hadn't expected that. I *did* enjoy the thought of their confused frustration.

The atmosphere crackled with energy, a war of shadow and cruelty. Shouts came from all directions, orders to hunt us like rats.

Evie gripped me as we moved. A tremor rolled through her. She balled my shirt in her fist again and buried her head into my chest.

"When?" she growled.

She didn't need to finish the question. I knew what she was asking. *When could we finally fight back?* My jaw feathered with tension, my glamour dropping as we reached the nearest underground entrance.

I pushed her up against the stone wall inside as the darkness embraced us.

"Soon, angel." The bottom half of my mask fell. Our lips melded. My tongue dominated hers, tasting her violence that mirrored my own. My fingers dug into her waist as she moaned and ground against me. "Fucking soon."

21

EVIE

"Why didn't you tell me?" Kylo asked, pinning me against the wall with his tall, immovable form. The rest of his mask dropped and was reabsorbed by his shadows.

Too many raw emotions racked me to discern. This strange, hot shame that didn't make sense—like my body was under a microscope, being examined for impurities.

Dirty, contaminated. That was how it felt to see that man again. My mother's voice had become far quieter and more infrequent these past two weeks, but it had never been louder than when the born lord had essentially called me worthless.

No longer pure.

I looked away, but Kylo gripped my face and stared into my eyes until my gaze returned to his.

It was contradictory to feel this ravenous for him—aching, yearning—in the face of all my anger and disgust.

"Because it didn't matter," I whispered. "I'd only met him once. Before I'd been promised to him. Then at the coven ritual before I exploded, *Lillian* had declared—through my mother, of course—that I was to be wed to Lord Aster, the highest ranking born in the region. Because of course I was."

The words burned through me, my shadows finally escaping in this dark, secluded stairwell. They encircled Kylo, intertwining with his.

"Of course my power-hungry mother would want her daughter to serve Isolde's lord," I spat. "I wished he'd been there that night. But he wasn't. I guess he assumed that Idris and I perished with the rest of our coven."

"Then you exploded again, in the same fashion here in Etherdale... " Kylo finished. "So he put two and two together, followed a hunch, and discovered you were alive."

Kylo's strong grip on my waist was a comfort, but not nearly as comforting as when one of his hands slid up to close around my throat.

"And that it was me who killed my coven and the group of born celebrating with them," I finished.

He gritted his teeth. Anger and horror eclipsed his eyes which mirrored my own.

"Did that really just happen?" I gasped, tears forming as I remembered the stench of death. Too much death. "Did they kill a bunch of innocent *kids* to lure us out of hiding?"

Kylo's forehead touched mine.

Through the shadows, we shared our emotions and repressed urges. Disgust, rage, sadness and love burned through us. In the end, Kylo and I landed on the same thing: a thirst for retribution and justice that was maddening, all-encompassing. A drive that couldn't be properly released, at least not yet.

His fingers pressed into my airways, and my mind grew calmer the less I could breathe.

We stayed like this, my gasps for air transforming into tiny, high-pitched moans until our pent-up urges reached an undeniable peak. If we couldn't yet slaughter the born, then *something* had to give.

Kylo's gaze was a brand, a mark of his ownership over every inch of my skin and the depths of my soul beneath. His next inhale was shaky.

"I need your blood inside me and my tongue buried in your sweet little pussy," he said. "*Now.*"

"I need violence," I whispered. "I need pain."

Kylo grinned, but it was humorless and cruel. "As you wish, angel."

KYLO PRACTICALLY DRAGGED me into his bedroom—*our* bedroom—with a firm grip on my hair and another on my hip.

"Is this fucked-up of us?" I panted.

"We're self-aware, so it's fine."

"Hmm." I nodded. "Okay. That sounds right."

We all had different coping mechanisms, I guessed.

Kylo chuckled dryly, but in the same beat he manhandled me to the floor. His lips brushed across my forehead. "Kneel." He rose to his feet.

My cheeks flushed. And yet, I moved to kneel before him.

"Good girl," he purred. "Stay."

"I am not a *pet.*" My pussy throbbed as Kylo lorded over me.

Kylo made a mocking pout. "Aw, aren't you though?"

He turned his back to me and rummaged through a drawer in one of the dressers.

I glimpsed a delicate pink strap of leather and lace.

"That better not have a fucking bell on it," I grumbled.

Kylo laughed. "I thought about it. I truly did. But I settled on a pretty pink bow." His smile was sadistic, taunting. "For now."

I eyed the collar, my previous shame transforming into a form that was safe. I enjoyed when I was under *Kylo's* microscope, when he was my judge, my executioner, my higher power. It was some holy alchemy, this ability to relish the degradation and objectification from my lover that had traumatized me as a child.

Because Kylo wasn't examining me for purity or obedience. He was watching for my pleasure, my enjoyment, my sense of safety and trust and love.

Eye-level with his imposing, frighteningly large cock, my mouth watered.

He didn't move to collar me. As I knelt, he towered above, slowly inching closer until the bulge of his black pants met my face.

"Worship your God, angel."

He gripped my hair and pulled me forward, rubbing my face against his cock. The fabric between our skin was frustrating, a tease.

My mind melted as I obeyed, tentatively kissing his pants. I felt where his cock began with my mouth, the swell of his balls, and I kissed along his shaft until I reached the tip.

"Scenting the fear in your blood every time you see my cock will *never* get old," Kylo said. He rocked his hips and gripped me tighter. "Good girl," he cooed.

My kisses became sloppier, more desperate, hoping I could break him and end this merciless teasing.

"Such a greedy, mindless little slut for my cum, aren't you?"

The degrading words created a self-fulfilling prophecy, as I only became more floaty, unrestrained, and needy for him.

He continued rocking, grinding against my face as I swirled my tongue and sucked at the fabric along his shaft.

"You're *my* pet, little witch. My very good pet."

He released my head and undid the top button of his pants. I salivated, holding my breath in anticipation.

When his cock sprung free, I opened my mouth before Kylo could command it. He gripped himself, slowly stroking. I looked up at him, knowing how much he loved my eyes on his. I tilted forward, but Kylo pulled back.

"Ah-ah, not yet," he said. He stepped out of his pants.

The authority in his voice made me feel like one of his students in the sexiest, dirtiest way.

"I want you collared, baby," he said. "Do you know what it means to be collared?"

I shook my head. I sort of knew, as I'd read *plenty* of kinky romance novels. But I wanted Kylo to explain it to me, to teach me and guide me like I truly was a vampire's pet.

"Pretty girl," he praised, stroking my head. "It means you're mine. When you feel this collar around your throat, you'll be reminded that every breath, you breathe for me. I'm going to give you everything your needy pussy is begging for, because I take care of my perfect little mortal doll. You're going to swallow every dose of pain and venom and cum with gratitude. And you will thank me for every inch of my cock in your tight little holes."

I had to remember to breathe as I stared up at his strong, authoritative gaze.

After a quick reassurance that I knew I still had limits and a voice, Kylo settled back into his role.

"Beg."

I shook my head. "Take it," I said instead.

I wanted more intensity—more than we'd ever played with before. Instead of ceding my submission, I wanted him to take it from me instead. I wanted to know so deeply that Kylo dominated me that I could feel him inside every dark crevice of my mind.

Kylo's eyes darkened. "Bad. Girl."

He grabbed me and pushed me onto my back. The carpet was soft beneath me. A shadow slipped under my dress, and I shivered.

It sliced clean through, and Kylo finished the job as I flailed and fought him. He discarded the strips of lavender fabric as his gaze hungrily roamed my exposed body. He gripped a breast, fingers pinching my nipple as I cried out.

The flailing ended when Kylo pinned my arms beneath his knees. He stroked his thick cock above me and dangled the collar in his other hand.

My own shadow slithered free, slicing Kylo's shirt in retaliation as I fought for air.

He glanced down at his partially exposed chest and chuckled. "Okay, angel. As you wish."

His cock and the pretty pink collar both rested on my chest now as he pulled off the rest of his shirt, revealing a sculpted body that must've been chiseled by the gods. His sigils were nearly luminous in the candlelight, onyx with the occasional shades of midnight blue and purple.

"Too stunned by my body to remember you were pretending to be a brat again, baby?"

An indignant, defiant noise left my lips.

"See? How can I not treat you like the precious little creature you are when you make such adorable, growly noises?"

He shifted forward, finally placing the collar on my neck.

When I lifted my head—my first instinct to be helpful—Kylo laughed, and I scowled. Fuck. I really had forgotten my objective. My impulses would always lean toward obedience.

And it was hard to think with his cock this close to my mouth.

I wriggled, but the lacy pink collar was already in place, not too loose or too tight, providing just a touch of pressure to my airways.

Now I well and truly forgot how to think. A low buzz of relief rolled through me, every last one of my worries washed away by a flood of surrender. The present moment, with my body against Kylo's, was the only thing that existed.

"Is the collar enchanted?"

Kylo shook his head, his grin widening. "No, angel. The magick is *us*. It always has been. Let go. I've got you."

When the fire in my gaze didn't completely fade to blissfulness, Kylo pressed harder against me.

"That's okay," he said softly. "I think I know what might help."

His features shifted back to their dangerous, vampiric form. The dark, hungry eyes of a predator.

But instead of feeding from me, he yanked me back up to a kneeling position and fed me his cock instead.

My hands found his thighs, gripping hard as my eyes watered and his cock filled my throat. I gagged, but Kylo didn't relent.

"Feel the collar around that pretty little throat and remember that you're mine to use however the fuck I wish."

I remembered from previous instructions that relaxing made it easier to take. The collar was a pleasurable, steady sensation, a surge that traveled all the way down to my clit. I stopped fighting as Kylo slowly rocked his hips, going deeper with each thrust. My fingers dug into the flesh of his thighs as I gagged again, but I fought the urge to pull away.

"Good little pet," he praised, stroking my hair. "You were made to swallow my cock, angel. This is your highest purpose. Serving your vampire master, who takes exceedingly thorough care of his perfect good girl."

Kylo's hypnotic, soothing words were a spell of their own. They were a break from reality, a temporary reprieve from the duty that rested heavily on my shoulders.

I held him deep inside me, and when he slowly pulled away, I worshipped his cock without his command. I tongued his shaft, gazing up at him as tears and saliva dripped down my face.

"There's my good girl," he groaned. "I always know exactly what you need, don't I?"

I leaned into his palm as it cradled the side of my face. "Yes." And it was true, within and beyond this depraved roleplay.

"Kiss it, angel, and then use your manners," he said, calm yet stern.

I kissed the tip of his slick cock, tasting the bead of pre-cum that had gathered there. "Thank you, Kylo."

"For?"

I stared up at him, already drunk without a single dose of venom in my blood. "For letting me worship you."

Kylo's moan and his pleased, satisfied eyes made my stomach warm with satisfaction.

"I will always keep my captured angel well-fed," he said, his lips curved as he stared down at me.

Gods, he only became filthier, and I only craved more of it.

"That perfect response has earned you a reward, baby." He grabbed a throw pillow from a nearby loveseat as I knelt in wait. "It pays to drop the bratty façade and melt into your authentic self."

His tone was that of a professor, a guide who knew what was best for me. And the wounded parts of my psyche found delirious safety falling into these roles with him.

All I'd ever wanted was to be protected. For someone to see all of me with an unfaltering, steady love.

Kylo lay back on the rug, his head on the pillow. Those abs flexed, and I was once again mesmerized by the planes of his muscles and the perfect, masculine shape of his form.

He smiled. "Come here, my pretty little pet. I want to drown in you."

22

EVIE

I almost stood, but Kylo stopped me.

"No. Crawl to me, baby," he whispered.

My cheeks burned, and I hesitated for only a moment before I shifted to my hands and knees. I kept a little arch in my back as I closed the distance between us. Embarrassment and lust burned through me, but Kylo's intense, contented gaze was an anchor.

When I made it to him, I kneeled at his side, unsure what I'd been commanded to do.

His dimple appeared, and my stomach somersaulted. "Now ride my face and let me taste my perfect little pussy."

A surprised gasp left my lips. I remembered seeing someone do this at the sex dungeon. Was this really something men wanted?

"Did I give you permission to think?" Kylo said, his sharp tone pulling me back to him. He gripped my collar and yanked me down, crushing his lips to mine. He inhaled deeply, and I melted all over again, lost to the warmth of this kiss and his comforting scent.

He slowly released me.

"I know you can do as you're told, baby. Or do we need a leash?"

A pleasurable note of anticipation and dark curiosity swept through me at that thought. I tentatively shifted closer, placing a knee on one side of Kylo's beautiful face and then the other.

He wasted no time gripping me and pulling me lower.

The sound of pure ecstasy that left Kylo's lips the moment he kissed my clit had me unraveling.

"I'm obsessed with this pussy," he growled.

His fangs teased my flesh, and I went utterly still, my breath catching.

"*Mine.*"

His mouth closed over me, his tongue circling, tasting, teasing. A second moan vibrated against me, and all my previous doubts melted away. I slowly relaxed, my thighs no longer shaking as I allowed more of my weight to meet Kylo's ravenous, devoted worship.

Of course, Kylo enjoyed this. Even when I'd expected the opposite, conditioned by my lackluster first boyfriend, Kylo had always shown me just how much he adored my body and my pleasure.

It turned *him* on to drown in me.

I lost myself to the sensation as Kylo kissed, sucked, and devoured. His hands gripped me, occasionally roaming my body. My hips delicately rocked, chasing a delirious peak.

Something shifted in the room, though I was too lost to fully comprehend it. Power hummed. Darkness permeated the space, and when one of Kylo's shadows wrapped around my torso, I heard two words clear in my mind through our telepathic connection.

My bride.

I tensed, but Kylo didn't let up. He only devoured me with deeper intensity, as if these words were driving him. And I was too far gone not to melt back into place, to allow Kylo to claim me with his tongue.

The peak was in sight. I reached toward it, my head falling back, my pussy grinding against Kylo's perfect, sinful mouth.

My legs shook. A breathy moan escaped.

Then, Kylo bit me.

I screamed.

The shock of pain was cataclysmic. It shot through the nerves between my thighs and spread through the rest of my body in a violent, disorienting rush.

But the pleasure that followed was equally devastating. Kylo's venom locked me into an orgasm so ruinous that I worried it might kill me.

And I didn't think I'd much care if it did.

His fangs pierced above my clit, which meant he was both swallowing my blood and sucking my pleasurable center at the same time.

I came on a loop for what felt like a century.

Kylo was both holding me still and keeping me upright, his shadows wrapping around me possessively as he fed.

Just when I was on the verge of blacking out completely, he closed the wounds with his tongue, lifted me up, and then pushed me down to the plush carpet to straddle me.

His eyes were infernos; his lip curled with holy wrath. Blood dripped from his mouth, staining his brutal fangs. His hand found my throat. His fingers slipped beneath my collar and pressed on the sides of my neck until the whole room blurred.

Kylo drove inside me, and my moan was high-pitched and strangled. I could hardly feel the pain of this impossible stretch through the haze, only the fullness of him.

No part of me could be empty with Kylo buried deep inside.

I'd asked for his violence, and he delivered, thrust after thrust.

"Good pet," he said, gripping my face as he spit inside my mouth.

I sank into the floor, swallowing everything Kylo gave. "Thank you."

He shoved two long fingers into my mouth. "Now, tell me who the fuck you belong to."

I gagged, eyes watering. "You," I attempted to say around his digits. The sound was muffled.

Kylo grinned sadistically. "Try again."

He pumped his fingers, training my throat to take more and more as he drove deep inside my cunt.

"Can you say a full sentence for me, silly girl?"

"I belong to—" I started, the words incomprehensible as I choked. I struggled to breathe, my vision spotty as a tear escaped the corner of my eye.

"Aw," Kylo cooed. "Poor thing."

He kept his fingers in my throat as he bent down to lick the fallen tear. His tongue was warm and soothing against my skin.

His fingers slowly retracted. The deep blue of his eyes was hypnotic. I was sensitive to Kylo's every word and facial expression, only satisfied when he was. It was liberating to have such an easy purpose, to let someone else decide my every thought.

"Try one more time, angel."

He increased the pace of his assault, impaling me with his cock as he gripped my thighs and pushed them back to get as deep as possible.

"I belong to you," I managed to cry out shakily.

Kylo turned his head to the side and sank his fangs into one of my calves. I yelped in surprise at the quick burst of stinging pain. Pleasure radiated from the bite. He fed for only a moment, pulling back as if with extreme restraint.

"You only have so much blood," Kylo whispered. "And I plan on feeding from you all night."

He played with a nipple as a shadow found my clit. I came again, and against all odds, I managed to have my first coherent nonsexual thought on the comedown.

"But what about—clan stuff?" I breathed.

Well, it was almost coherent.

Kylo's eyes darkened. "You're taking the night off," he growled. "I cannot, but that doesn't mean you can't be a good girl and serve me while I work."

I should've been appalled by the visions that overtook my mind, but then Kylo spoke them out loud, and my core tightened.

"The possibilities are endless. Feeding from that pretty little throat while I torture born scum. Holding you in my lap while I give orders. Having you kneel under my desk and worship my cock while I write to our allies and prepare for war."

Yes, I should've been disgusted. But I wasn't. I knew that outside of our games I was Kylo's equal.

Which was why I let him treat me like I was his plaything instead.

His coaxing shadow drew another orgasm from me as I trembled beneath him. Kylo captured my lips with his, drinking my release and accompanying moan. He rocked gently as I settled.

The break was short-lived. Kylo manhandled me into various positions, his goal always to hit as deep as possible. My back was arched now as he took me from behind, every once in a while delivering spanks and getting high off my cries of pain.

The shadow that had played with my clit now rested on my thigh, and I heard those two words again, words that were clearly tormenting Kylo just as they'd once tormented me.

My bride.

And the more violently Kylo claimed me, the safer I felt in his strong hands. Because I knew he'd never let me go. My Dark

God would always protect me from the true monsters that plagued this realm.

He pushed me down onto my stomach, still inside me. My legs trembled as he slid in and out. His fangs pierced the fleshy part of my shoulder, feeding as his cock twitched inside me.

I sank deeper into the carpet as Kylo drank from me and held me down, using me to his satisfaction.

He pulled back and flipped me over. His eyes were appraising as he studied my body. I was lost to the waves of venomous pleasure coursing through my blood.

His hand rested above my womb. His gaze was dark and final. "It's extremely difficult for me to decide where to mark you with my cum," he hissed. "I want it dripping out of every single one of your pretty pink holes."

And it was hard for me to disagree with that sentiment in my current state, suddenly empty without him inside me.

I watched Kylo stroke himself as he continued to appraise me like I was a piece of fine art.

Suddenly his eyes snapped to my face and stayed there.

Bathing in pleasure, I reached a hand to my collar, perplexed by the immense relief it afforded me. My eternal quest for certainty was at long last quenched.

A feral noise escaped Kylo. Two shadows yanked my legs apart and bound them. Kylo slapped my pussy, his eyes lighting up when I yelped. The sound of pain quickly transformed into mewls of pleasure as a shadow filled me, angling against my internal center of pleasure.

"Good girl," Kylo soothed.

He kneeled by my face and stroked my hair. I relaxed, subdued by yet another mounting release. He lifted my head, cradling it as his cock slowly eased inside my mouth. I closed my eyes and sucked as Kylo continued to praise me.

"I'm going to mark this pretty face," Kylo said. "I need to see you painted with me, baby."

I moaned against his cock, and the shadow inside me expanded.

When Kylo forced another violent orgasm from deep inside me, I barely noticed him withdrawing his cock from my mouth. His hand closed over my collar.

"Keep that pretty mouth open."

I obeyed, and warm liquid fell against my lips, my tongue, my cheeks. The addictive, masculine taste of him was some kind of drug.

"What a perfect angel," he said softly. "You look so pretty with my cum on your face, sweetheart."

His throaty groan was equally addictive. I waited patiently, mouth open.

"Swallow."

I slowly opened my eyes as I licked my lips and swallowed his seed.

He thumbed the pink bow at the center of my collar, his gaze roaming over my face with immense satisfaction. The intensity hadn't lessened.

And the intensity didn't lessen as he praised me, only touching me gently now. He showed me careful tenderness as I came back down to earth. But his protective possessiveness was a steady thrum of power as he bathed me and made sure I felt safe.

It was unwavering, this shift in him. I knew without a doubt that he was imagining every single way he could murder Lord Aster, as mercilessly and as soon as possible.

Even from my cocoon of blissful subspace, I envisioned the same as I lay curled in his arms.

23

KYLO

E vie was perched on a chair in the dungeons. Groans of pain broke through the air, and *not* the fun kind.

Well, they were fun for *me.*

One of the born was strapped down to a blood onyx altar, much like the altars on which these demon spawn enjoyed torturing mortals.

I glanced back at Evie, only to find her eyes squeezed shut.

"You don't have to be here," I reminded her.

She'd been adamant about coming with me after we'd finished aftercare. As much as I would've preferred forcing her to stay home and recover, I would never actually abuse my authority as her dominant to strip her of agency.

"Torture makes me squeamish," she whispered. "But I'm okay."

Adorable, and also hilarious. Murder, shadow impalement, and decapitation? Fine. But Evie drew the line at peeling off skin and severing appendages.

Honestly… that was fair.

"We all have our limits, baby," I affirmed to her.

Not me, of course. My brain was sufficiently broken. In only sexy and desirable ways, obviously.

I chuckled to myself as I did something to this vermin's eyelids that would've made Evie retch.

"Are you laughing?" she squeaked. "During torture?"

"Don't pretend that comes as a shock," I drawled. "I've proudly worn my badge of insanity since day one."

She grumbled something under her breath. She was still floaty, riding the high of innumerable orgasms and shots of venom.

"All a part of the process," I said.

"What do you mean?"

"I've been brainstorming and plotting this whole time, of course. Drafting my address to my inner circle, my messages to the clan and our allies. There's truly nothing like born suffering to get my creative juices flowing."

"I don't want anyone else getting your creative juices flowing," Evie huffed. "If *that's* what we're calling it now…"

I laughed harder. The born under my knife yelled into his cloth gag.

Evie managed to giggle, a hand over her eyes. She peeked out from a gap in her fingers to meet my gaze.

"Uh-uh. I'll tell you when to look. I don't need you getting sick."

She stole one glance at my bloody tools and obeyed without question.

I continued my meticulous dance. Pain followed by relief and questioning followed by more pain. The trick with the born wasn't necessarily to get them to spill all their secrets. It was more about what we could get them to inadvertently reveal with their microexpressions and slips of the tongue. The more I could disorient, starve, confuse, and scramble their soulless little brains, the easier they were to manipulate.

The born weren't used to being deprived nor tortured. They

hated unpredictability. They were accustomed to order, indulgence, and their own supremacy. When their reality was flipped, they crumbled.

That was the thing about power that hadn't been earned. It paradoxically created an avalanche of weakness to exploit. Those who struggled for power, who fought with something to lose, built an inner strength that was harder to crack.

This born man was one of our most valuable captives, which unfortunately made him less prone to slips. Even so, I was getting the sense that he knew *something* about the attack earlier today. There was a smugness he refused to conceal, a slight twitch in his lips every time I mentioned the massacre.

After the next round of questioning, Evie gasped.

"The person that fled—their note said I had beautiful eyes," she said.

I whipped my head around. "What? I mean, you do, but—"

"Yeah, yeah. You want to murder them for noticing," she said impatiently.

I smirked. "Are my unhinged antics really that predictable to you? I need to try harder."

"Eyes," she repeated, as if that word was supposed to illuminate everything.

Her own eyes were shut, and her knees were pulled to her chest. I set down my tools and walked closer.

Her frown deepened, opening her mouth and then closing it. She took a shaky inhale. "Whoever killed Princeton had carved out his eyes," she said softly. "Were they ever found?"

My heart sank, all humor evaporating in the space between us.

"No. They were never found."

~

I DIDN'T MISS the several pairs of nervous gazes on Evie as we moved through the underground, nor did I miss her hurt defensiveness. The doors to the main deliberation room closed behind us as we entered.

In the aftermath of the unthinkable, tensions were high. Everyone wanted answers. There were potential recruits in that building. Comrades and friends. Innocent mortals and professors who'd been fighting the good fight.

I couldn't shake the intuition that something was unraveling, something I couldn't entirely control.

And I fucking hated that feeling. It wasn't one I was willing to accept.

I pulled Evie into my lap at the head of the long table. There wasn't a space for her yet, which had been an oversight on my part. But I wasn't going to complain about the solution.

Surprisingly, Evie didn't fight me. Beneath her façade of innocence, Evie had a cunning streak. Perhaps she saw the advantage of being so close to me in this critical moment.

She was also coming down from our temporary distractions, the horror of the day hitting her hard. My closeness was a comfort to her.

Blade spoke first, a deep grief in his voice—a grief that permeated through the entire city. "There are reports of water turning to blood, more creatures from Lillian's underworld roaming the streets, and magick that doesn't belong to this realm. The general sentiment is leaning toward a portal or a tear between worlds." Blade paused dramatically. "It's as if the gods themselves are at war."

A hush fell over the room. We'd all read myths about the gods and their wars before they left our world to occupy the heavens and hells. Mythological beasts, natural disasters, magick that no witch or vampire could compete with were described in various ancient texts.

Evie stirred, and I could almost sense her eagerness to speak. But she didn't.

"We made great progress in eliminating Servants of Lillian who'd infiltrated the city before the born took over," Commander Brooks said. "We never came across power like this."

A newer inner circle member, a woman rich in magicks of poison and illusion, spoke. "Do we even have records of magick that can turn water to blood? Make blood rain from the sky? Outside of myths about Lillian?" Nala's gaze moved to Evie cautiously. "Could *you* do something like that?"

My fingers traced soothing circles on Evie's shoulder.

"Maybe," Evie said honestly. "Bending nature requires sacrifice, as well as a great deal of energy and effort. It's hard to imagine that a single person is doing all of this—that they have enough power and access, let alone permission and allies from the otherworld."

"I know this fits in perfectly with the borns' propaganda," Nala said, slightly cutting Evie off in a way that irritated me. "But could they have somehow opened a portal? Could the gods truly be involved?"

"Princeton and Evie are rare," Blade added. "There's one chaos witch like them in every what? A hundred thousand?"

"Way more," I murmured.

"If this deity, Hekate, is involved..." Commander Lachlan said, letting his words trail off.

"She's not involved. Not like *that*," Evie said. "This isn't Lillian either. Lillian might be lending her influence and magick, but only through a witch."

The room was focused on her now, and no one interrupted.

"The gods are not at war. We didn't rip open the cosmos. No one conjured a portal to the underworld." She kept her chin lifted as she surveyed the room. "This is a witch's doing. The same witch who killed Princeton."

I tried not to flinch. Evie didn't know this for certain, and I wouldn't have advised her to state it without further proof.

The silence was intense, eyes darting from her to me and back again.

"The born know who I am, and I have a feeling that witch knows as well."

At this, I gripped Evie tighter. There was no going back now, not for her.

"All of this is calculated. Even the way they mimicked shadows to destroy that building. They may not succeed in turning us against each other..." Evie said.

I stroked her hair.

"... but they might sow confusion among the mortals who are on the fence. Or the mortals who feel we've abandoned them."

Evie was right—while the full picture wasn't entirely clear yet, it was obvious that sowing chaos, confusion, and in-fighting among the clan and our mortal allies was one of the key objectives. Two of my clan had already been influenced to accuse Evie after the attack, though they'd written numerous formal apologies the past few hours. Regardless of their shame, they'd face sharp consequences for their actions, including demotions.

I didn't want us to be backed into a corner. Nor could I stand the idea of this city being ruled by those who wanted Evie dead.

"I wish the timeline could be expedited, but it can't," I said. "We need more resources, and all clans need to be war-ready, *especially* the Serpent Clan. Evie needs to complete and recover from the next turning. We are less than two months away from war. It's time to tie up all loose ends."

Evie exhaled. "I'm going to find that fucking witch."

Now she'd truly gone off script. My jaw tightened, a shadow curling around her thighs.

Harmony spoke next, thankfully drawing attention away from me. "Our allies in the north have reported increased military activity. They're gathering more forces. As soon as we give the word, turned clans on the army's path will rope fleets into battles to disrupt their route south."

Evie turned her head to look up at me, stroking my cheek. An unspoken conversation played out between us, a play of protectiveness, bravery, and fear.

"There's no going back," Evie whispered. "They know who I am. They're already trying to destroy me. I can't let them."

"*We* can't let them, angel," I hissed. "*We.*"

She nodded. "Of course."

It didn't satisfy me, her small assurance that we were a team. Evie was only beginning to wield her shadows, to use her magick in ways she'd never been able to allow herself before. She was still so young. She had learning and growing to do, and she sure as hell didn't deserve to be at the epicenter of the greatest war this realm has seen in nearly a thousand years.

I inhaled her floral shampoo as I kissed the top of her head. I needed to see Evie read again, to stretch out on a blanket in her garden and kick those adorable feet as she consumed a smutty fantasy novel. I needed to watch her make flower arrangements and herbal teas, to sell them at her own shop as she laughed and chatted with her adoring customers.

If the only way to get to that reality was through violence that would inevitably risk her life, then I had to learn to accept that.

Even if the most unhealed part of me would much rather keep her collared and in a safe location until the war was over.

"Why now?" Phineas asked suddenly, cutting off Commander Lachlan's report.

His consistently severe and cold expression held the table in rapt attention. Phineas only spoke when he had something important to say, in as few words as possible. It made his speech that much more impactful.

"If the born had this secret weapon hidden all this time, an alleged chaos witch just like the ones they've been hunting down the entire summer, why use them *now?*"

Evie's thigh nervously vibrated as she thought. "They were hoping to prey on our weakness after Princeton's assassination. That's why they took the city when they did."

Phineas's scowl and irritated gaze didn't escape me. He was unconvinced by the obvious explanation, clearly.

"How do they know who you are?" he asked.

Evie hesitated. I opened my mouth to help, but she beat me to it. She explained to this room her darkest, most well-kept secret as her heart raced.

"After discovering a vampire harmed my younger brother a decade ago, I killed my entire coven and a few born during a celebration. It was the same kind of explosion I unleashed in Etherdale's forest. Just before I escaped with Idris, I'd been promised as a child bride to Lord Aster."

Our inner circle needed to know these facts. Even if my tattoos burned at the mention of Lord Aster's role.

Evie released a breath. "Now, Aster knows not only that I'm alive but also that I'm responsible for what happened in Isolde all those years ago."

Harmony regarded Evie with shock and with tender compassion, and Blade's eyes softened as his own tattoos trembled with rage.

Phineas was the only person in the room who remained entirely unchanged. He was a brutal beast, but he was also the most effective and invaluable eye in the clan.

"I would say something was missing here, but that would be an understatement," he said curtly. Then he merely closed his mouth and looked away, as if he was done with this conversation and refused to elaborate more.

Temperamental, ornery creature. I sighed. "Well, that was helpful as always, Phineas. Anyway," I said, earning a snicker from Blade. "We'll turn every qualified recruit in the queue this new moon. We'll send them through basic training, which will overlap with our grand unmasking. We will finalize plans, continue gathering supplies, countering propaganda, and bolstering alliances. Born will be systematically captured or slaughtered as we gather as much intel as possible on the lords and their motivations, tactics, and weaknesses. In two months, we will rise and take Etherdale. And Earle will officially declare war."

Evie's heart was hammering now, but she didn't protest. No one did. I kept my voice level, strong, unfazed. Even if my perfectionist brain was already parsing through my master plan and fine-tuning variables.

Too many wheels were spinning at once as I analyzed. Phineas's words had dug under my skin, worsened by Evie's bold declaration that she would find the witch who can turn water into blood and destroy a building in a matter of seconds.

This was most likely the same witch who carved Princeton's eyes from his skull, impaled each of his limbs, and sliced his mouth into a demented smile.

My spine tensed as I considered that this same witch had taunted Evie and called her eyes *beautiful*.

"Ow, Kylo," Evie gasped.

She squirmed in my arms, and I immediately released my bruising grip on her. I hadn't realized how tight it had become.

"Sorry, baby," I murmured close to her ear. "I got cute aggression and forgot my own strength."

She glared up at me, an unconvinced brow lifted as her lips curved.

I was still getting used to Evie's acceptance, and even thirst for, violence and war. The darkness in her soul had overtaken the fear in her blood, and it was a mesmerizing transformation to behold.

Blade and the men at the other end of the table were discussing the finer details of our presence on campus.

Harmony put her chin in her hands as she noticed Evie and I staring at each other. "You two are so adorable! My *heart!*"

Phineas rolled his eyes violently before slipping beneath a shadow glamour and leaving the table. As we watched the door open and slam shut seemingly on its own, Evie broke into a fit of giggles.

She turned back to an equally amused Harmony. "Maybe that's his problem. Phineas needs a lover."

Blade snorted, and the rest of the table paused to share in the moment of comedic reprieve.

Harmony nodded. "You're absolutely right. But what's he into? Any guesses?"

"Oh, that man is a sub if I've ever seen one," Lachlan drawled with a charming, easy grin.

This drew a bark of laughter from my own lips. "Agreed. He needs a Domme scarier than he is to finally get that overburdened mind to chill the fuck out."

"Full gimp suit," Harmony said. "Plus a human furniture kink. That's my final answer." She lifted her hands up and sat back in her seat.

"No, no, no." Brooks shook his head. "He's a repressed Daddy Dom. All bark and no bite. Underneath all that rage and melancholy is a big teddy bear who just wants to love and be loved."

The entire room was silent for one beat before erupting in howls and guffaws.

"Princeton would *love* this conversation," Blade said through fits of laughter.

Evie smiled. At all the kink talk, her cheeks were adorably rosy. "He does."

The use of present tense made my stomach flip and my face soften. For a moment, the grief in the room was light and connective, something we all carried together. Smiles didn't drop at the mention of our maker; they only widened.

"To Princeton," Lachlan said, lifting a chalice of blood.

The warm witch lights glimmered above. The room was rich with power and anticipation. The born didn't understand the bonds we had. They never would.

They would never break us.

Not like we were going to break them.

I looked at Evie in a silent request for permission. She nodded, her eyes fluttering as she tilted her head and gave me access to her throat.

"To Princeton," I echoed.

The room clinked glasses. My lips met Evie's neck, kissing softly before my fangs pierced through skin.

24

EVIE

The moment my eyes locked on his, my resolve not to cry immediately shattered. The sob was inevitable, my chest in a tight ball of emotion.

Idris rolled his eyes.

And the sight of it melted me, my grin just as instant. He stood from the couch, but he didn't move closer.

"Don't roll your eyes at me, punk. The last time I saw you, you were *dead*," I growled as I wiped at my eyes.

He laughed. "And leave it to you to declare to the gods that my death was simply unacceptable."

We both beamed. I moved closer and decided to sit down in the opposite chair and let Idris fall back on the couch. We were still underground, though this cozy nook did an excellent job masquerading as a normal living room.

It was the anniversary of the night we ran, the climax of our embodied trauma. Kylo remained by the door, attempting not to intrude on our moment. Idris was far more stable now, especially after feeding. He was unlikely to lose control unless deprived of blood, and even less likely to lose it around his own family. Still, we were both being careful this first visit.

Idris scratched his head. "Sorry about, um, you know."

His cheeks flushed a shameful shade of red.

"Trying to eat me?" I offered, taking full advantage of a good opportunity to tease him the way he usually teased *me*. "Yeah, it was pretty ungrateful of you given the circumstances."

Idris glowered. "I knew all this power would go to your head." He looked past me to Kylo. "You've created a monster."

"I was already a monster." I smiled. "Kylo just reminded me."

Kylo chuckled from behind me.

"Nightmares?" I asked gently.

Idris shrugged. "To be honest, struggling to remember who I was for a few days reset my brain. My dreams revolve around blood now more than anything else," he said sheepishly. "And I finally have power. Purpose. It's making it easier to deal with the other stuff."

We were both accustomed to talking in riddles and vague language. And that avoidance had only hurt us both.

"I stopped running," I said.

He smiled. "I know."

The pride in Idris's eyes warmed my heart. I suppressed the urge to cry again, remembering how close I'd been to losing him forever.

"We don't have to talk about it now, but I need you to know that you can always talk to me about our childhood, from here on out. I won't shut down or escape. I'm sorry for ever making you feel like any of what happened was something to be ashamed of or repressed. I just didn't know—"

"I know, Evie," Idris interrupted gently. "You were a kid too. You've always done your best. Don't be so hard on yourself, okay?"

I nodded. "Okay. Thank you."

"We can talk about it all eventually," he said, moving his gaze from the floor to my eyes after a steadying breath. "But first I want to know how the *fuck* you went from hating the clan to becoming one of its most valuable members. I was fully convinced for a paranoid forty-eight hours that it was all mind control."

"Oh how I wish I had that ability," Kylo mused.

I shot him a feral look that didn't remotely frighten him. His arms were crossed, his blue eyes intense as always.

Idris was watching me carefully when I turned back to him, in his usual thoughtful, intuitive way.

"I love you so much, Idris," I said.

"That's been made very clear."

Every time he opened his mouth, my stomach twisted at the sight of his fangs.

"I love you so much too, Evie," he said. "I'm glad I'm not dead."

Stupid laughter spilled from my lips before I launched into a broad overview of the past few months, with a few obvious edits to make the story safe for a family member's ears.

I told him about my healing—my growth with Princeton and Hekate, and within myself. I also filled him in about Mena's decision, and how I couldn't help but worry for her now more than ever.

"Wow," Idris said. "And I thought *I'd* had a rough couple weeks." Disbelief marred his soft brown eyes as he regarded Kylo. "I can't believe you killed Jacob."

I crossed my arms with a huff. "Yeah, you aren't the only one."

To my surprise, he only laughed. Though perhaps it shouldn't have been much of a surprise, considering Idris had never been a fan of Jacob's.

When he regained composure, he continued, glancing back to me. "And you stabbed the leader of the Masked Order with a poisoned needle?"

Idris's laughter was contagious, and I couldn't help but glance back at Kylo, who was trying hard not to smile.

"Mistakes were made on all sides," Kylo said with a nod.

"That was *not* a mistake," I snapped. "You fucked up, and I merely retaliated in a way that seemed extremely reasonable at the time."

"You can come sit down," Idris offered to Kylo with a smirk. "You're already a part of the conversation."

Kylo nodded, an adorable hesitancy in his features before taking a seat in the plush chair next to me.

"Mena's decision doesn't surprise me," Idris sighed. "I'm glad she has protection, but I can't help but worry the born will use her to get to us if they know who you are."

"I know," I said. "I said that to Mena too, but she still won't budge, and I don't blame her. That's her home. She knows the risk, and she told me that we could never sacrifice ourselves for her either, as impossible of an ask as that is."

Idris nodded. "I'm glad she has a choice. She deserves to live exactly how she wishes."

"Do you feel like I robbed you of that?" I asked softly.

Idris shook a finger. "Don't go searching for more self-punishment ammunition. It hasn't been easy, but I'm *here*. Because of *you*." His gaze was fierce, and I could see the distinct difference vampirism made in his mannerisms—the lethality, the power.

I smiled bashfully. "Old habits." One of his tattoos peeked out from under his green shirtsleeve. "How has it been to wield your shadows? Any new magick discoveries?"

At this, Idris grinned broadly. "It's been fucking awesome. Not all of my magick has come in yet, but I don't even care. The speed and strength alone are the *best*. Most of the progress I've made with my bloodlust has been because I want to be able to fight, literally all the time." He paused. "And because I wanted to see you, Evie, obviously..."

Kylo laughed, and I bit down on a smile. The room suddenly had far too much masculine energy.

Kylo lifted a brow as he took in my expression of judgment. "Are you really not going to tell him about the decapitation?"

One of my shadows shot out to serve as an elbow to his side, but his own shadow was quick to deflect and subdue.

Idris's eyes widened, and he was slow to peel his gaze from my shadow. "The *what?*"

I tucked a strand of hair behind my ear. "So... I may have killed the Whitfields because they killed *you.*" I shrugged. "The decapitation was an accident," I quickly added.

Idris's mouth dropped open. He stared at Kylo. "Like I said, a *monster.*"

The instinctive shame I'd cultivated for the past decade fell away, and in this moment, I was only grateful to be seen in my entirety by those I loved most.

"The *cutest* little monster," Kylo said, leaning back in the chair as he gazed at me adoringly.

"Ew," Idris said. "I think I'm entering bloodlust," he said flatly, his lips a thin line. "You two should probably leave."

"You better get used to it," Kylo drawled. "I plan on being nauseatingly in love with Evie for an eternity. Whether she ever forgives me for murdering the whiny man-child or not."

Idris squinted at me. "Evie is horrible at pretending. No matter what she says, her forgiveness is obvious."

"You don't know anything!" I grumbled.

Kylo chuckled. "She just wants me groveling for as long as possible. As if I was ever able to say *no* to her before."

"You two make me feel incredibly single," Idris muttered.

That was the first time I'd ever heard him mention romance, as he was usually cagey and private about these matters.

"Any vampires catch your eye?" I fished. I twirled a strand of hair around my finger and pretended to examine its end, feigning nonchalance.

"As previously stated, the bulk of my thoughts have revolved around blood and violence." He sighed, his features softening. "But *I guess* you will be the first to know if that changes."

My whole face lit up, and I couldn't help but grin.

Idris looked away. "I already regret saying that."

Kylo laughed. "Too late now."

The conversation continued to weave through every mood as we discussed what happened yesterday on campus and the reality of war on our doorstep. Higher than the grief and rage and fear for each other was the love—the reason we were here, the reason we would fight.

It was a privilege to have so much to lose.

25

EVIE

I paced back and forth in my new garden space Kylo had created for me in one of his countless romantic gestures these past few weeks. This morning was spent crafting more poison, planning for the turning ritual, and fortifying my spiritual allies with offerings and prayer. Unfortunately, creating the new vampire poison—I called it violet bane, due to its nature and ingredients—was a time-consuming and laborious process. It had the potential to be mass produced, which the clan desperately needed for war, but I would need more witches for that.

Kylo told me Princeton was well-connected in the witch communities of Etherdale, and I was beginning to see why. Powerful chaos witch or not, I couldn't do all of this myself.

The afternoon consisted of instruction and training from Kylo on both strategy and combat. We still hadn't decided what my role would be in battle, as I was now the backbone of the clan. There was a reason that in the centuries since Rune's war for Valentin, no one outside of his clan had a clue how they'd been made or by whom. They'd kept their chaos witch entirely concealed and out of the public eye.

The born were either entirely aware or reasonably suspected that I'd taken Princeton's place, and that put me at a stark disadvantage. Not to mention I lacked vampire speed and strength, which meant all of my magick was most effective from a protected area or at a distance. But no matter what my role would be, I knew I would inevitably end up drawn into violence in one fashion or another. I had to be prepared for anything.

Kylo obviously wanted me nowhere near combat, but he taught me everything he knew, regardless.

Because that was the man he was.

Now, I paced. I put my overthinking brain to good use. I was learning that most character defects could be wielded as strengths under the right circumstances.

A tiny spirit moved in the corner of my eye, a wisp of light that clung to a pink rose bush.

"Not now, thank you," I whispered.

Kylo appeared with a glass of water. "Talking to the nature spirits, baby?"

I nodded, and he grinned. I accepted his offering of water, sipping before handing it back and continuing my pacing along the cobblestone path.

Kylo watched with his chiseled, tattooed arms crossed over his broad body. Sunlight illuminated bluish notes in his thick black hair.

I had to avert my gaze from his beauty so I could focus.

"I think Princeton's murder was more than just a power move by the born," I said finally. "I suspect it was a cruel, baneful ritual."

I stopped walking in front of Kylo, softening my tone. "I need to examine that room and any records that were taken about how Princeton was killed."

Kylo nodded. "Okay, angel. Let's go." He stroked my cheek before pulling me closer to kiss my forehead.

We donned our masks before walking quickly to the sex

dungeon. Using the hidden entrance was sort of comical in the light of day, losing the edge of darkness that nighttime provided.

Yet when we stepped inside, the energy shift was palpable, the entrance hall dimly lit and sensual.

Each set of guards let us through without so much as a word.

Kylo interlocked his hand with mine, and I gave him a squeeze. I knew we were both feeling the impending dread, the traumatic weight on our chests from the night that went so horribly wrong.

There were still patrons inside this early in the evening, but the energy was considerably less electric—or horny.

Even in lingerie and leather, most people in the initial room appeared as though they were merely hanging out. Some were feeding, others were playing some filthier version of spin the bottle on the plush, carpeted floor.

As Mena had declared, it did indeed feel like people were finding an escape here, stealing orgasms and pleasure and laughter in spite of the violence closing in.

I looked up at Kylo. His mask was cut diagonally to reveal his lips, which formed a deep frown. I kissed his arm, holding onto him tighter.

We needed to find this witch. Not only so Kylo could avenge Princeton's death but also because of the obvious, unspoken reality that haunted the clan.

The idea that if the born had a witch on their side who was wielding enough power to appear as a god... we would be entering a war than none of Ravenia's clans were prepared for.

I feared that if we didn't eliminate this enemy, our already arduous revolutionary path to overthrow the born would be next to impossible.

I didn't want to think that way. No one did. But whoever this was, they were doing an excellent job at convincing the world their power was ineffable and never-ending. As attested by today's plague of rats overtaking Etherdale's main commercial district.

Someone was hellbent on destroying the city I adored.

"Talk about adding insult to fucking injury," Kylo growled as we entered a room with several pieces of kinky furniture and countless implements for bondage and pain hanging on the walls or strewn across shelves. "When I look around, I'm too traumatized to imagine all the beautiful ways I could torture you here."

A strangled laugh escaped me, both shocked and relieved Kylo was able to find a twisted form of humor in this horrific mess.

He slowly panned to me, his skull mask intimidating as ever.

"Yep, talk about drying up my creative juices."

I patted his arm. "Your creative juices are *fine*."

He paused in front of a chair with a cutout in the center and some kind of instrument peeking through, a rod with a round leather top.

"Huh," he said. "Maybe you're right. I'll be tucking this idea away for later."

"What *is* that?" I asked. I walked closer, realizing the leather contraption was spelled with an electric magick. I didn't want to touch anything in this room, to be honest, but I outstretched a hand to hover above.

The leather bulb began to vibrate with a steady hum. I jolted back, my heart leaping. Kylo laughed.

"I like to call it a princess throne," he said over the sound of the violent vibrations.

"You've used it?" My glare was deadly, my shadows leaking from my pores. "Nope, do *not* answer that question."

The fact that Kylo had so much as kissed someone else before me pissed me the fuck off. I didn't care if he was eighty years older than me. He should've known I was coming and waited like a godsdamned gentleman.

Kylo laughed again, and with a frustrated snap of my fingers I forced that thing to stop its whorish vibrations. Its purpose had become excruciatingly self-explanatory.

Even as I wiggled and pretended to swat him away, Kylo pulled me close. "See? If I'd had an annoying girlfriend when you'd met me, you would've killed her too. We're the same, baby. That's why we're written in the stars."

My glare broke, and Kylo's hand found my rapidly beating heart.

"Don't pretend your little pussy isn't intrigued by the idea of me tying you to a chair like that and forcing you to come over and over until you're screaming and begging for me to make it stop…"

I forgot it all—why we were here, the mortals and vampires in the surrounding rooms, the impending war. My thighs shifted together; my breath hitched. Kylo's hand didn't move from my heart. In turn, I placed my hand on his.

I cleared my throat. "Like I said. Your *creative juices* are fine." I wrinkled my nose. "Also, I really don't want us to keep saying the word *juices*."

"Fair." Kylo took a step back as he chuckled. "Come on, break over."

I hated the absence of his warmth, so I was quick to loop my arm through his.

"Good girl, baby. Stay close," he whispered.

My stomach fluttered. As we moved closer to the site of such an unspeakable horror, our humor and lust dried up completely.

The expression on Kylo's lips alternated from overwhelming emotion to the unshakable stoicism of a clan leader. I held onto him through it all.

"You don't have to go in with me," I told him. I didn't want to force him to relive something so awful.

Now that we were alone in the private hallway in the back of the dungeon, Kylo dropped his mask, and I followed suit. His brows were drawn incredulously, as if my offer was incomprehensible.

"I just—"

"Hush, angel," he said softly. "We face the darkness together. Always."

My hand found his again. We stepped into the cursed room. A chill crawled down my spine. The air was noticeably colder, and though the room had been cleaned, and a month had passed, the scent of death lingered.

I held my breath as if that might help the barrage of etheric input slamming into my heightened witchy senses. Kylo noticed I'd come to a dead stop. He swallowed, exuding strength for me as his deep blue eyes bled grief.

"You okay?"

I nodded. I'd be strong for him, too.

I forced air into my lungs, inhaling slowly and deeply. The witch lights were dim, and I commanded them to brighten for us. My feet carried me to the wall from which Princeton had been crucified.

A warning blast of magick slammed into me the moment my fingers touched the still-stained wallpaper. I gasped as I skidded back, arms flailing for balance. Kylo caught me as the wind settled.

My wrathful indignation was suddenly stronger than my fear. I shrugged off my pink leather backpack and grabbed my blessed jar of salt. Teeth grinding together, nerves pulsing with the strength of someone else's magick, I salted the doorway first. I gently nudged Kylo into the center of the room, pleased by his wordless compliance.

I sprinkled a circle around us. I lit a bundle of protective, cleansing herbs, letting the smoke disperse through the room.

When I sat, Kylo sat, watching me work as if he were a protective, devoted sentinel.

The energy was lighter, my clarity renewed. I stared at the wall with a curled lip.

"Reveal yourself," I commanded, my voice the harsh crack of a whip.

A ghostly mist seeped from the floor. Kylo combed through my hair.

In the next blink, the mist shot forward in silky tendrils, bouncing off our protective circle with a high-pitched screech. I flinched, the back of my head thumping against Kylo's chest.

"Excellent foresight, baby," he said.

I nodded, my gaze still fixed on the wall in wait.

It didn't surprise me that I was meeting resistance. It only confirmed what I already knew. And when faint outlines of sigils began to bleed from the wall—white chalky paint that only I could see—the satisfaction of being right paled in comparison to the heavy weight of dread compounding the longer I stared.

The sigils were in a formation around where each of Princeton's limbs had been impaled. They weren't recognizable, most likely the original creations of a chaos witch.

Still, the answer seemed obvious to me in the context of all that had occurred. The reason why this chaos witch had only recently flexed their power, the purpose of Princeton's missing eyes and meticulously orchestrated death.

"I fucking knew it," I hissed.

"What is it, baby?" Kylo's exhale was shaky, but he continued to rub soothing circles on my back.

Angry tears pricked my eyes. Rage crawled up and down my spine in a familiar heat.

I leaped to my feet and screamed at the top of my lungs, arms spread wide, one hand holding a small key totem for Hekate and another holding the smoldering herb bundle. *"Get the fuck out of this room!"*

The mist multiplied and screeched in a final death march.

My shadows broke the circle, overpowering the pale smoke and driving it back from whence it came. The room went dark for a few beats before clearing completely.

The scent of death released. The air was quiet and still. The witch lights flickered back to their warm stillness.

I was lightheaded for a moment, leaning against Kylo as I caught my breath. I slowly turned to face him.

"This was the work of a death witch, a particular brand of chaos magick," I explained. "They're harnessing power through ritualized murder of powerful beings. This isn't their own power we're witnessing. It's stolen."

Kylo became a mirror of my wrath, piecing together the gravity of this injustice. They'd not only taken Princeton's life, they also had harvested from his corpse and spirit like a foul vulture.

"Maybe Lillian is involved, or other beings of the underworld. It doesn't matter. This witch is making sacrifices and bargains with forces likely beyond their control, and Princeton catapulted them to levels they'd never been able to access before."

"My oldest friend is dead because someone wanted enough power to play god and torment the city," Kylo hissed. He shook his head, bleeding shadow as the floor shook. "And now his soul can't even find peace in the afterlife, because his death is being used to attack everything he built, everything he believed in and devoted himself to."

I watched Kylo fight his own urge to explode, lips in a disgusted sneer.

"We can spend nearly a century constructing a vast underground city, carefully assassinating born elites, rescuing and protecting mortals from the slave trade and senseless murders. Eighty years of education, resistance, community-building, and more fucking *restraint* than anyone will ever know... But the evil we're fighting can kill a few hundred innocents on a weekday afternoon because they *felt like it*, using *our fucking power* to do it."

Kylo's tattoos trembled, his fists clenched. He closed his eyes as a muscle in his jaw feathered.

"It's a lot easier to destroy than to create," I whispered. I reached for one of his fists, bracing against the magick that instantly rattled my bones. "What this witch is doing isn't Princeton's legacy. Princeton isn't a part of them, only his death. Princeton is a part of *us*. He's lives on in this city we love and the magick in our skin and every move we will make against the born and for the good of Ravenia."

I sensed him here with us now, a gentle hand on our shoulders, a mischievous, knowing smile.

Kylo relaxed an inch as my words washed over him.

"Feel the anger," I said. "We're going to use every drop."

"Exactly what that fucker would say to me right now." He opened his eyes. He looked down at the hand I'd unraveled from a fist to rest in mine.

I melted into his chest, and he held me tight, still racked with fury.

"I miss him so much. Like an ache that never ends," Kylo said into my hair.

I nuzzled closer, inhaling his comforting Kylo scent. "I'm so sorry, Kylo. The ache might never fully fade, but it'll get easier. It'll be different. This is still so fresh. Grief is love's shadow, and your love for Princeton was powerful."

"I love when my adorable little monster speaks like a wise elder," he whispered, his waves of anger and heartbreak coming to a gentle lull.

"I have my moments. Or maybe Princeton is possessing me."

"He *wishes*. That fucking pervert."

My nose wrinkled, and I giggled. Pulling away, I stroked Kylo's soft strands of dark hair. Those blue eyes never failed to make my stomach drop like I was falling.

"We need to take that witch out before the first battle," I said.

Kylo sighed. "And we will. But tonight, we both need time off. We've been going nonstop for weeks, and we might not have this luxury for a while." He kissed my temple. "Huge progress was made today because of *you*."

"It's a small first step," I said with a shrug.

"Stop downplaying your beautiful mind and magick or I'll take you into one of these rooms and turn that perfect ass red."

I smirked. "And we're back."

26

KYLO

"What if we're spotted?"

My lips curved. "Thrilling, isn't it?"

Evie's wide gray eyes narrowed.

We walked down a cobblestone street that had once been lively and filled with energetic university students, longtime residents, and merchants mingling and dipping in and out of shops and restaurants.

Now, only a handful of mortals milled about. A heaviness hung in the air, and several establishments were boarded up completely.

"I'm glamoured as a human, and you made your hair dark. Not every born will instantly know who you are, baby. The only person who might is Lord Aster, and if we see him, I will *not* be able to hold back a second time."

"Me neither," she growled.

"We will not hide, angel. No one is going to stop me from spoiling you the way you have always deserved to be spoiled."

At this, my cautious good girl stopped her paranoid scans of our surroundings. Her cheeks flushed my favorite shade of pink.

I was so in love with her it was absurd.

She made a soft noise of surprise when I grabbed her and captured her lips with mine in the middle of the street. I stole her breath the way she stole my sanity. It didn't seem nearly a fair enough trade.

I tugged at her bottom lip with my fangs before begrudgingly releasing her. My smile was unavoidable as I watched her chest rise and fall under her light blue corset. Her pupils were dilated, yearning.

"I miss your pretty blonde hair," I sighed, twirling a deceptively dark strand around my finger.

Evie laughed. "It hasn't even been thirty minutes."

I traced her jugular with my thumb. "Fuck. I'm getting cute aggression again."

She rolled her eyes.

I gripped her throat. "You're the one who allowed me to become addicted to you. Encouraged it, even."

She shuddered, her arousal palpable as her breathing slowed. I loved that every time I had my hand around her throat, Evie merely relaxed.

"Good girl."

I released her, and she looked as bummed about it as I was. I pulled her into one of my favorite clothing shops, where I'd bought her countless gifts over the summer.

The owner, a short man with warm brown skin and a finely sculpted black mustache, lit up the moment he saw us.

"Oh my gods. Is this *her*?" He clapped his hands together in delight.

Evie stilled, and I carefully guided her forward with a hand on her lower back.

I chuckled at Nolan's predictably exuberant reaction. "Yes, this is the witch who stole my heart."

Nolan clutched his chest, brows drawn and lips pouted. "She's *perfect*."

Evie was shell-shocked, her avoidance of strangers and her distrusting, wounded heart likely making her wish she could teleport away.

I enjoyed her embarrassment. It made my cock hard as usual.

"Stole the words right out of my mouth," I said.

A bored-looking and chronically unimpressed man walked gracefully from the back of the store, carrying items to hang or display.

He ignored Evie, but he paused to scan me up and down. He lifted his brows and nodded, as if he approved of my form. Then he was back to his tasks without a word.

At this, Evie finally broke into a small giggle.

"Come, come," Nolan said. "I have new pieces you're both going to die over. I was saving them just for you."

"So you really did all of that shopping for me yourself?" Evie asked, her eyes rounded as we followed Nolan's quick stride to the back of the shop.

"Of course I did. Did you think I made my *henchmen* shop for you?"

Her features were pensive, lips quirking up. "No, that doesn't sound like you. I just never envisioned you picking out each gift."

Her eyes welled with emotion, and for a moment, Evie was the same frightened, uncertain girl I first met. The one who believed that grand gestures and romance would remain a fantasy forever.

"He has exceptional taste, darling," Nolan said, nodding his head.

Evie smiled. "In all things," she agreed. "It's sort of ridiculous."

She made me feel so human and raw. I had the urge to grab that pretty little throat again as my tongue tasted all of her hidden depths.

Nolan began retrieving pieces from a back room to hang up for us. He left us in a tasteful, brightly lit space with tall mirrors and a seating area.

I admired one of the art pieces on a far wall, trying to place its vague familiarity. While I studied the abstract art, Evie studied me.

"What do you think?" I asked her softly.

She tore her eyes from me to the painting. The canvas shone with a warm peachy orange, a perfectly captured sunset over a cliff. Before the precipice's edge was a crumbling archway with intricately painted vines wrapping around the structure and squeezing through cracks in the stone.

"It's beautiful," she said. "Very Helianic."

"You think it's religious?"

Evie nodded. "I do."

"You're right," Nolan chirped from behind us. "Painted by a monk."

I grinned and kissed the side of Evie's head.

Nolan excitedly showed us each article of clothing he'd designed specifically for Evie. Evie complimented them excessively as if that might shift the focus away from her and those blushing cheeks.

"I'll give you some privacy, but let me know if you need anything," Nolan said with a wink.

I thanked him, reaching into my pocket to pay him.

Evie gawked at the heavy coin purse I slipped into Nolan's palm.

She quickly closed her gaping mouth, only speaking after he'd left. "Kylo—"

"Don't even start, baby," I said as I grabbed her waist. "Gifts, romance, time, energy—you deserve to be spoiled at every opportunity, in every way imaginable."

Plus, that was less than a drop of my resources. Not that I

wouldn't bankrupt myself just to make Evie feel like the luckiest witch in the realm.

Her eyes were glassy. "You're the one who's perfect," she said, uneasy and staring at the rack of one-of-a-kind dresses. "I'm going to pass out."

"Of course you're uncomfortable, Evie. Your whole life, people have tried to make you smaller, to convince you that you're not even deserving of basic empathy and consideration. Like I told you in the art installation, you'll get used to being loved by me. One day it'll be as easy as breathing."

She considered, shifting on her feet.

"No more thinking. You can reciprocate by letting me dress you like the perfect little doll that you are."

"That's it?" she asked, as if begging me to give her a way to earn all of this adoration.

I tongued my fangs, my cock hardening at the sight of her so eager to please me. "I think we can figure out additional methods of repayment when we're alone, angel."

When I made a circular motion with my fingers, she obeyed easily. The moment her dress fell to the floor around her feet, I couldn't help my low groan. I squeezed her perfect, perky ass, pressing against her as my cock twitched in my pants.

My lips glided along the shell of her ear, and she shuddered.

"You don't have to earn my love, Evie," I reminded her. "*You* are all I've ever needed."

Her nipples were hardened peaks beneath her thin white bra. Her little pussy was already dripping from the barest of touch.

"My little doll was made for me," I praised as I reached for a classically Evie-pink dress off the rack.

Evie's soft eyes and slowed heart rate alerted me that she was already in some level of subspace, her mind flooded with pleasure.

I fucking loved putting her in this headspace, not only

because it was sexy, but because I knew how much she needed it. Evie craved moments of reprieve from her compulsive, worry-prone mind. She yearned for the safety of being able to let go and trust me to care for her and protect her in the way past authority figures had failed.

And nothing brought me greater fulfillment than being everything Evie had ever wanted and needed.

I dressed her in the soft pink dress with a sweetheart neckline, grinning when she found hidden pockets perfect for carrying witchy little trinkets and collected herbs or flowers.

I lifted one of her arms, satisfied when Evie left it suspended midair after I removed my touch. I pushed it back down to her side and repeated the move with the other, getting off on her sexy obedience.

She was allowing herself to truly become a doll. Her arousal was potent in her blood, and my fangs pulsed in my gums.

"Good girl," I praised, guiding her further into this new role.

I gently pulled her to the mirrors, so she could see how breathtaking she looked. She frowned at her dark hair, as if she'd forgotten she was glamoured.

But as soon as she focused on the dress, her whole face lit up. It was the look that made all of this more than worth it.

She'd always wanted to wear pretty dresses when she was a child, forced by her mother to wear dull, conservative black gowns instead. After her escape, it was no wonder she'd gone for soft pastels and florals, intricate corsets and flowing skirts. Evie had always bravely reached for her freedom—her beautiful soul in full bloom.

The last dress was darker than she was used to, but her eyes were quick to fill with gratitude. It was a deep purple, Hekate's color, a shade of the expansive cosmos. It was also more revealing than Evie typically chose—with a high slit, a deep neckline and a fit that accentuated her curves.

She shivered when I clasped a gold serpent necklace around her neck, my lips skimming the tip of her spine.

"You're going to wear this to dinner, baby," I said, waiting for her to nod before continuing. "Then we're going dancing. And maybe a few other surprises along the way, if you behave."

My lips met her shoulder next.

"I need to suck your cock," Evie whispered. *"Please."*

I straightened, eyes nearly rolling to the back of my skull. I glanced over my shoulder at the closed door that hadn't opened since we'd been given privacy.

With a shrug, I unclasped my pants. "We're already being naughty tonight. Might as well see how far we can take it."

I guided my perfect little doll to her knees.

"Mouth open. Eyes on me."

27

EVIE

I wanted to suck Kylo's beautiful cock all over again when I tasted our first bites of food.

Whenever Jacob took me to a nice restaurant, the act was meaningless, devoid of warmth. His romantic efforts were mechanical, merely a necessary task to check off a list or a way to indicate his wealth and influence. If he'd had it his way, I'm not sure we would've done much of anything but lie around at home and talk about his business plans as I stroked his overinflated ego.

Where Kylo took me wasn't showy. It was small, cozy and candlelit, a place I'd never heard of—as if it were a well-kept secret. The servers weren't even nice to us, answering only in grunts and mumbles.

But the *food?*

"Oh my gods," I moaned for the twentieth time since we'd arrived.

Kylo laughed. "Try this," he said. He made me a fork of octopus on a bed of the airiest mashed potatoes I'd ever seen.

I opened my mouth. As soon as the food melded with my

tastebuds, I made a sound not unlike the ones I made when coming.

Kylo's eyes darkened. "Fuck, Evie," he hissed. "What did I say about behaving?"

I swallowed a sip of water and batted my eyelashes. "That we weren't going to do that tonight?"

Kylo ate too, though not as much as I did. Vampires could still enjoy the act if they worked to preserve their taste for human food. But they didn't need food to survive.

I didn't mind the disparity. I would've gratefully eaten these culinary masterpieces from Kylo's palms if I had to. I bet he'd like that.

"What do you think of that one?" Kylo asked, pointing to the painting next to us that I hadn't noticed until now.

I'd been far too concerned with the insane array of food Kylo had been feeding me.

"Oh wow," I murmured, taking in the brushstrokes of darkness and despair. I squinted. Flecks of paint with an almost opalescent quality were splattered across the canvas. My finger hovered above, careful not to touch. "Like tiny pops of light and meaning in a confusing, dark world."

"Met the artist at a gallery once. He said it was a self-portrait," Kylo said. "What do you see now?"

I applied this new information to the piece, brows furrowed.

"A vampire," I said. "The outline in the top left almost looks like a swing on a tree, a representation of nostalgia, or a loss of innocence. And the solid blocks in the center could be walls—a barrier. I'm guessing self-imposed. Perhaps someone grappling with the grief of becoming turned?"

Kylo smiled. "He was born."

My jaw dropped, head snapping to stare at him in disbelief. "Really?"

He nodded. "He was one of the last of his kind. A mystifying, bizarre artistic movement that came into fashion here in

Etherdale about a century ago. It was tiny, and its adherents were persecuted and hunted down until most had been killed off by their fellow born. Can you guess what they stood for and explored through their art?"

I turned back to the painting—the haunting darkness, the light forever out of reach. A surprising emotion arose, akin to sympathy.

"Humanity," I said. "A rejection of their own nature."

"Fucking sad, isn't it?" Kylo said. "A barren night sky that covets the stars."

I'm not sure what I felt as I pondered this. It was too complex to put into words.

"Do you think it was authentic?" I asked.

"Which part?"

I shook my head. "I don't know. Any of it. We talk about the born as if they're a monolith, but here's one who can create art that's actually *good*—with depth and complexity—a vampire who supposedly detests his own nature in favor of humanity. Are they all capable of thinking or behaving differently? Can they change?"

Kylo watched me with those thoughtful, imploring eyes. "You've added different questions to the mix, angel," he said with a small smile. "I do believe it was authentic. I've always said that most born secretly envy us, deep down in the caverns of their psychic shadows. They're not a monolith, but they behave as one because of the long-standing political, social, and religious structures that keep the elites in ultimate positions of power and luxury. The less powerful born hold the illusion that they too could be a powerful lord one day, and if not, at least they're better off than the mortals forever at the bottom of the hierarchy. Every facet of King Earle's empire was designed to keep mortals from fighting for better and the born from ever thinking differently than how they've been taught. Some will

MAGGIE SUNSERI

inevitably escape these bounds—like you, angel. Perhaps the seed is planted by a lover, a friend, a teacher. Maybe a subversive book, or a traumatic experience, or a piece of art created by the enemy."

Listening to Kylo speak, his impassioned features warmly lit by candlelight, was a religious experience.

"But that doesn't change anything, does it? If only a few born ever choose mercy over cruelty. And if they start to think differently, they're persecuted and killed off by their fellow born."

"Exactly." Kylo fed me another bite of risotto. "We can't make decisions based on another's potential. We have to take them as they are—the person they choose to show us. There have been epochs in which mortals have lived in harmony with the born. Just as there were times the mortals themselves were at war, covens and shifter packs were at each other's throats. This is the nature of history. It's a cycle that repeats. Darkness grows and festers and reaches its breaking point. Power shifts. The new overtakes the old."

I looked back at the painting, and this time, I saw flashes of anger. "I think the artist felt betrayed. The figures dancing, the lovers embracing, the tree swing, the walls. He was robbed of those experiences and emotions, taught instead not to feel anything at all. He hates his brothers and sisters for raising him to hate the world."

Kylo's eyes were warm and enraptured in a way that made my stomach flutter. "That's why your tears have always been a gift, angel. The world is lucky to have you." He kissed my knuckles. "Ready to dance?"

I opened my mouth to say I was a bad dancer, but I chose to smile and nod instead. Because it didn't matter. I would be with Kylo.

And he was right. I didn't want to take any of this for granted.

THE CLUB we entered was mortal-run, with live music and witchy technology amplifying and distorting the instruments in electrifying, captivating ways. The singer was equally enthralling, the lyrics fearlessly attacking the born and everything they stood for with a smooth, rich anger.

Kylo held me close, moving and guiding my body. The room was packed. The swell of energy and power created by bodies in synchronized movement led by defiant music was a different kind of magick but a potent ritual all the same.

Most of the people here were mortals, overwhelmingly human. My tattoo only burned in recognition a few times.

Kylo grinned down at me, gripping the back of my head as he devoured my smile. I was warm and floating, my nerves alight with sensation. I tasted revolution in the air and in Kylo's lips and in my body so close to everyone else's—a tapestry of interconnected fates.

When my friends at Celeste's had dragged me to clubs and bars, I'd often felt overwhelmed and disconnected, unable to sink into my body and out of my overworked, fearful mind. I was awkward and clunky, unable to relate to anyone else.

But now?

I looped my arms around Kylo's neck and moved my hips freely, finding the beat that vibrated up from the floor. A part of a whole, like the web of mycelium beneath the forest floor.

I wasn't different from anyone else, and that was a relief.

When we left the club, I had no idea what time it was, and I didn't care.

"One more stop," Kylo said, his hand in mine as he led me down the street.

My legs were jelly, and my ears rang. My lips tugged into a smile. This felt like another victory, another measure of my healing and growth.

When a group of born turned a corner in the distance, laughing and speaking loudly and arrogantly, I didn't let them kill my mood. Kylo paused. He pulled me closer as we let the born pass from our line of sight.

We continued our walk, and my body was delighted by its own aliveness. It took me longer than it should've to realize what street we were on.

I looked from Celeste's storefront to Kylo.

He did a quick double-check of our surroundings. "Come on."

The store was dark as we approached. "It's closed," I said, stating the obvious.

Kylo led me in anyway, and as soon as we'd taken a few steps inside, a woman popped her head out from the basement.

"Marietta!" I squealed.

She lifted a finger to her smiling lips. "Shhh." She made a beckoning motion.

Most of the witchy supplies had been replaced by flowers, plants, and unassuming teas, oils, and creams. My heart squeezed as Kylo and I followed Marietta down the stairs.

The door eased shut behind us, and with it, clearly some kind of sound dampening ward. The basement that was once merely a storage room was now similarly abuzz with mortals talking under warm witch lights. Couches and chairs were arranged against the walls, and stacks of books and candles were strewn about.

"Evie!" one of my clients exclaimed. Amy was a teenage witch who'd recently developed divinatory powers, and she'd been obsessed with my goods. "Finally!"

All heads turned toward me. Marietta, Celeste's co-owner, folded me into a hug. She was human, but most of the room were clearly witches.

Kylo fed me strength with his strong, silent presence. My fellow witches had not typically been kind to me, and I'd learned to distance myself from them in order to avoid rejection. However, in hindsight, perhaps I hadn't always given them a chance.

Trauma was a murky lens over reality.

"Hi," I said awkwardly, glancing around.

A group of witches to my right sat in a circle, hands intertwined, heads down, and meditative. The sight of it made me sad, a feeling akin to yearning. Another group was reading tarot and oracle cards together, and a huddle of humans played some sort of game that involved swatting each other's hands.

"Welcome to our little corner of the resistance," Marietta said with a wink. "I wanted to invite you sooner, but you disappeared on us, and it didn't seem like you wanted to be found. I've been worried about you."

"Me too," Amy said. "I lit a candle for you the other day, and I've been praying for your safety."

My throat tightened with emotion. "I stayed away because I was worried about all of *you*," I said. "You protected me, and I had to return the favor. You weren't safe with me around."

Another of my coworkers, Quill, broke away from his huddle to approach us with a warm wave.

"Have we finally moved from pretty faery magick to the *good stuff*?" he teased, waggling a brow.

My shoulders relaxed. "Yes, Quill." My smile was tentative under the weight of so many stares. "We're dabbling with the *good stuff* now."

Quill's eyes widened with surprise, really looking at me now, as if for the first time. His smile returned. "Excellent."

A willowy, pale blonde approached from behind Quill. She'd been one of the witches who was holding hands in the circle. She nodded at Kylo. "We're so sorry for your loss." Her gaze swept to me. "And yours. I'm glad you came, Evie. Welcome."

I shot Kylo an accusatory expression, realizing this was more than merely a thoughtful reunion and underground party. This was an introduction to Princeton's witch connections.

He shrugged. "What can I say? I was a workaholic first," he whispered in my ear. "Before I became addicted to you. Now, I multitask." He pulled back.

"Thank you," I said to the witch.

"We're terribly sorry for you and everyone else who knew Princeton," Kylo added graciously.

She nodded, panning back to me. "My name is Gwendolyn. Come sit with us," she said, tilting her head toward the group of witches on the floral rug. "*We* don't bite." She smiled conspiratorially, sticking her hands in the pockets of her colorfully embroidered overalls.

She turned, and Kylo all but pushed me forward with a low chuckle.

The group made room for me, and I was quick to scan each of their faces for looks of disdain. I felt like an outsider, and my skin crawled from the discomfort of it. I wanted to bolt.

No one regarded me with any cruelty. Only excitement, curiosity, or their own nervousness. More witches from the other areas of the basement trickled toward us to join the circle. Amy was one of them, tucking her long black bangs behind her ears as she grinned at me.

At first, I thought they were expecting me to give some kind of speech, and my palms were already clammy in anticipation of holding hands with these strangers.

Instead, everyone focused on Amy. Witches sat back, their postures easy and relaxed now. A few bounced with anticipation. I followed their gazes, my own shoulders relaxing as I realized no one was looking at me anymore.

"Okay, here they are," Amy said. Her blue eyes were wide; her body vibrated with energy. She delicately removed a stack of cards from a small silk pouch. She flipped them over and slid them out onto the carpet. Everyone tilted forward, clamoring to see the breathtaking, iridescent artwork.

I squinted. They were tarot cards, a deck I'd never seen before. The interpretations were gorgeous, filled to the brim with occult symbols. They not only depicted classical interpretations, but I also realized that there were landmarks from Etherdale baked into the cards.

"Oh my gods, Amy!" a male witch exclaimed.

Gasps and awed murmurs rolled through the space as everyone stopped what they were doing to come look.

"You made these?" I asked.

Amy beamed. "Your inspiration candle helped me tremendously. You have no idea."

My chest was tight with emotion all over again. I wanted to study the cards closer, to read the story Amy had artfully drawn over every inch. Some of the cards depicted witches and shifters, while others showed masked turned with fangs and tattoos proudly displayed. I grinned with pure delight when I realized The Tower card was a drawing of King Earle's castle, born nobility falling to their deaths following the lightning strike.

Amy's friends praised her work. Several conversations sparked about tarot and the revolution.

I glanced around. They had no idea how lucky they were to be able to discuss and practice magick together. That familiar sadness, or perhaps loneliness, rooted in my stomach as my gaze returned to the cards.

My breath caught the moment I saw the figure on the Justice card—the dark-haired deity cloaked in purple, a snake on her arm.

"Hekate," I murmured. "You know her?"

Amy studied my serpent necklace and deep purple gown. Her eyes sparked.

Gwendolyn turned toward me. "We all do."

213

28

EVIE

The more I listened to the surrounding mortals speak, the more I understood how intelligent, creative, kind, witty, and unique they all were. They moved gracefully from banter to gossip to intellectual, philosophical debates and then ended with silliness.

I also realized how much we had in common.

A shifter woman took a gulp of her glass of wine, then said, "My ex told me that he disappeared for two weeks after my cat died because he was, *'like, really stressed and overwhelmed with his own stuff right now.'*" She put dramatic air quotes around the last part and imitated a whiny male voice.

Several women groaned and rolled their eyes.

I nearly spoke up, but I stopped myself, as I had most of the time I'd sat here. I merely echoed the rest of the group's sentiments, grateful to blend in as I found my footing.

Every once in a while, I tracked Kylo in the room, finding him in a new spot mingling with new people each time. He was so damn charming and extroverted.

Throughout the conversation, I learned that not only had Hekate appeared to this coven of witches, but she'd also been appearing to mortals across the realm. She was a symbol of the revolution, a being to call on just like Selena and Helia.

"How can we help?" Gwendolyn asked finally. "I'm the coven's high priestess, by the way."

I flinched at the title, picturing my mother, and Gwendolyn looked at me quizzically.

"Sorry," I said. I nearly lied, swept my reaction under the rug, and put on a mask. But I stopped myself. "I was born into a Servants of Lillian cult. I'm not used to being around other witches. I haven't been part of a coven since I was a child, and it…"

"Left a bad taste in your mouth," Gwendolyn offered, speaking as low as I had. Her eyes shone with understanding. "Thank you for sharing this with me. I'm so sorry you went through that. You're incredibly strong for having left."

I blinked. The world didn't crash down. No one had stopped speaking to gawk at me. Maybe a few people overheard us, but they didn't make a show of it. Gwendolyn's warmth didn't drain.

Amy sat next to us before I could speak again.

"Are we scheming?" she said with a grin.

I hesitated. "I don't want to put anyone in danger."

Gwendolyn's gaze was firm. "We're already in danger, Evie. And we're breaking the borns' new laws just by gathering here. We're *already* preparing for war."

I glanced at Kylo, wishing we'd discussed this ahead of time. The bastard had made it a surprise so that I wouldn't have to deal with anticipatory anxiety.

"We know Kylo is turned," Gwendolyn said. "We're all allies here."

I figured as much, but stating it out loud reassured me. Marietta joined us next, squeezing in next to Amy.

I took a deep breath, seeing clearly the path of fate Hekate had artfully woven for all of us. "Marietta, how comfortable are you with contributing herbs from your suppliers for—"

"Done," Marietta said immediately.

Chills swept over my skin. I straightened, my chin lifting an inch.

I cleared my throat. "Good. I'll write you a list of ingredients," I said, my newfound strength overtaking previous hesitations.

Marietta looked at me the way Quill had, as if she didn't recognize me, but she was delighted by who she saw now.

"What are we making?" Amy asked, clasping her hands together.

"A vampire poison," I said. "It's like blood onyx, but stronger and longer-lasting. I've named it violet bane. I found the idea in a chaos witch's grimoire, one who was devoted to Hekate."

Now I knew the people around us were eavesdropping. Eyes lit up with excitement, with righteous hunger for retribution. Hekate as the Justice card was ripe in my mind.

"Some of the tools and ingredients will need to be consecrated for Hekate, which of course can only be performed by her devotees."

"Done," Gwendolyn said with a crooked smile.

The group of young humans playing a card game erupted into sudden laughter across the room, and I thought of Idris.

"What else can we do? We have an entire network of covens, you know," Gwendolyn added.

"And shifter packs," added the woman who'd been telling us about her shitty ex.

An embarrassing tear escaped my eye, and Amy reached for my hand. I let her hold it, but I didn't explain.

How could I explain to them that I'd robbed myself of connection for an entire decade, believing without a fraction of a doubt that I would be rejected?

But I'd been wrong.

I remembered the thought I'd had when I'd fought my way back to the realm of the living. I'd been in that deep dark pit, reaching for the sliver of sunlight above.

Death had been comforting. It taught me I hadn't experienced nearly enough love, not yet.

I want to live, I'd begged. *I promise not to waste it.*

I want to live!

Instead of making me feel weird for crying, Marietta hugged me. After taking time to discuss what was coming, I was pulled into more silliness and games, and Kylo joined us too. Even with the dark context looming over us, we were able to enjoy being normal together. It was a long, beautiful exhale.

THE SUN WAS out as Kylo and I slipped into bed at long last. My limbs were weighted from dancing, my stomach full of decadent food, my mind both exhausted and stimulated by the fun and conversations at Celeste's.

Kylo traced soothing circles on my back and kissed my hair. We didn't speak. Our hearts beat as one as we drifted off to sleep.

I slept soundly knowing I was loved.

Safe.

Held.

"ONE MORE WEEK until your first turning," Harmony said. "How are you feeling?"

She sat with Blade on one side of Kylo's dining table, and Kylo and I sat on the other. Idris took the head. Idris was noticeably less tense today, and he seemed grateful to finally be back above ground.

It still freaked me the fuck out to see him casually drinking blood with his chicken sandwich.

"Prepared but nervous," I answered honestly. "It feels good to be useful. We'll need all the numbers we can get."

"You're more than just useful," Harmony said with a warm smile. "Idris, have—"

A knock sounded from the foyer, cutting off Harmony's question. Kylo's hand halted its gentle trail down my back before he stood.

I couldn't make out the hushed voices from the front door. But everyone could sense the resounding rumble of power through the space.

When Kylo returned, his eyes were pure wrath, his lips in a deep frown. In his hands, a white envelope with a golden wax stamp.

He hesitated before lifting it into the air, revealing the elegant black script on the front. The script that was addressed to *me*.

"It was delivered to Mena's address," Kylo said.

"Who is it from?" I asked, my heart pounding.

The seal had already been broken. Kylo made no move to hand me the letter, even as I stared at him expectantly.

Shadows circled his feet, one of them crawling across the floor to wrap around a chair leg.

All I could envision was the letter that had been left at Idris's apartment, the one that told me the born had taken Idris. At the first haunting vision of Idris's corpse, my breathing became shallower. I calmed myself by looking at Idris now, alive.

"Enough with the suspense, gods," Idris said, holding my gaze.

The ground trembled, and still Kylo refused to pass the letter to me.

He placed the envelope on the table and sat back down. "If I read it aloud, I'm quite certain I will pull an Evie and accidentally kill all of you," he said dryly.

"Hey," I said, glaring at him. I did not like his use of *pulling an Evie.*

Kylo was past the point of humor. His shadow was curled around my ankle now.

My hand was unsteady as I pulled the letter from its envelope.

I scanned the note in record speed as the whole table stared at me in wait.

Evelynn,

From the moment I learned you might be alive, I have been plagued by thoughts of you. Your beauty, your mysteries, your feisty spirit. Your dark appetites may ward off weaker suitors, but rest assured your promised husband does not scare easily. I yearn to know you. I request your presence for dinner at the Nighswander Estate this Wednesday evening. You will not be harmed, and you will be free to leave as you wish. You have my solemn word. Allow me to show you the truth of Lillian's chosen and your lavish destiny, my dearest lost bride.

Oh, and no plus ones.

With warmth and intrigue,

Lord Aster

Nausea sickened my gut, a mix of rage and panic burning through my blood. It was hard to think, my brain moving swiftly into fight-or-flight.

"That's tomorrow," I heard myself say. It felt like I was suddenly floating above the table, no longer a part of my own body.

"It doesn't matter what fucking day it is," Kylo growled.

"Will someone *please* fill in the rest of us?" Idris snapped.

I locked eyes with my brother as our shared trauma rose

from the grave. The color drained from his face. He rose from the table and snatched the letter from my hands.

After scanning the words, he tossed it back down for Blade and Harmony to read next. Idris sank into his chair. My hands trembled, rested in my lap as I wrestled with my mind to stay sharp and clear.

Kylo pulled my hand into his. "I'm sorry for raising my voice," he said softly. "Look at me please, angel."

I met his fierce blue eyes. His face was calm now, steady. An anchor to reach for in the eye of a storm.

"You're safe," he said. "And that isn't changing."

"He can go fuck himself," Idris bit out. "I wish he'd been rotted away with the rest of them."

"I don't understand," Harmony said. "What do these lords think Evie's role is? Is he playing dumb, or does he not know that Evie is Princeton's successor? Are they that arrogant about their own positions?"

"Doesn't matter," Kylo said again, straining against his rage.

Pieces on an invisible board shifted, a new path taking shape before me.

My hand tightened its grip around Kylo's.

"I think it does matter." I took a deep breath, feeling around for my own intuition, ignoring the instinct to disappear into Kylo's authoritative finality. "Stolen or not, that witch's power is devastating. And they're clearly on the borns' side. Lord Conrad and Lord Aster were there immediately after the attack to see how the turned would respond. Perhaps to see *who* showed up."

Kylo's glare burned into the side of my head as I fought to look anywhere but at him.

I studied Idris instead. I didn't want him in battle with the born while that witch still lived. I didn't want that for any of the turned or our mortal allies. They could kill everyone I'd met last night—the club full of dancing mortals, the secret gathering in the basement of Celeste's—instantaneously.

"Evie…" Idris said, shaking his head.

"The born are evil, tricky, and manipulative, but they're not ones to sever oaths. When they make a clear vow, they don't break tradition," I continued.

Kylo's laugh was cold, incredulous.

"This could be my opportunity to get close enough to take out the witch," I said. "Or gather more intel."

I waited for Kylo to get loud and growly again. I slowly met his eyes, where fear finally peeked through the upper layer of anger.

He peered down at me, scanning. "Evie, you're shaking," he whispered.

"No. Fuck no," Idris hissed.

Yes, I was shaking a bit. So what? I was also *right*.

Harmony and Blade exchanged a glance, an entire unspoken conversation occurring in the air between them.

Blade shook his head. "It's unthinkable. We can't send you into the lion's den, unguarded and blind to what awaits."

"Especially not to kill a witch who annihilated an entire building in a matter of seconds," Harmony added. "Who is conjuring plagues and birthing demon hounds from gods know where."

Kylo let go of my hand as he stood from the table. "We will not entertain his disgusting advances," he spat. He grasped the table's edge as he trembled with raw power and wrath.

I stood too, a spark of defiance heating my blood. Once again it felt like no one was listening to me. No matter how many times I proved my strength, my power, and my intuition, I still found myself unheard.

"You said you wouldn't hold me back," I accused. "You said I would always have agency."

"You cannot be serious," Kylo said through a clenched jaw. "You're fighting for your right to walk willingly into a deathtrap set by someone who wanted to abuse you as a *child*."

Harmony stepped in, her powers of empathy soothing the room with notes of warmth. "She's fighting for *us*, Kylo. It might not be the right move, but it's a move Evie is bravely offering to make for *us*."

I looked at Harmony gratefully, the lump in my throat dissolving.

Kylo didn't budge. The room darkened. Idris only shook his head, his eyes haunted by the ghosts of our past.

Kylo slowly loosened his hold on the table's edge. He turned toward me, jaw feathering, arm veins pulsing.

"No."

29

EVIE

Kylo's sharp *no* rang through the air, and I refused to acknowledge it. Not after all his promises that I was free to make my own decisions. My tongue tasted bitter, my own shadows awakening.

"They sent that letter to *Mena*," I said, turning to my brother now for support.

Idris shook his head. "Evie, we said we wouldn't make decisions based on Mena's choice to remain in her home. Was it a threat? Maybe. But that's also your only known place of residence. They know Mena is there, and they didn't harm her. Your protective wards weren't even triggered."

"Which is more evidence that they're at least pretending to play nice. This is an opportunity."

"You don't know that," Idris said.

"True. We don't know what they're thinking," I said. I was growing stronger, more focused. "And that's the entire point I'm making."

It wasn't fair that so many mortals were risking their lives every day to resist born tyranny, but here I was, hiding.

"We don't know who the witch is, so how can we avenge

Princeton? Or take them out before war begins? We don't know what the born believe about us or what their next moves are. Etherdale is suffering. The born don't reveal much of anything during torture. They clearly underestimate me, and I'm not without my own defenses. Let me find us answers. Making myself vulnerable is strategic—it will undermine their potential assumptions about me, and it will lower their guard. If you could just help me plan—"

Kylo took a step back, cloaked in darkness now. "*No.*"

"But—"

"Evie, that man still refers to you as his *bride*. I think it's clear what he wants, no matter what he believes about your role with the clan. Are you not familiar with how their slave trade works? Trafficked girls are drugged, sometimes even enchanted. He. Wants. *You.*"

I'd never seen Kylo strain this hard against his own urges. I could see it now, the woundedness in his eyes, the terror of history repeating. First Aisling, then Princeton, now me.

I wanted to comfort him like he did me. But I also didn't want to bend to his control when I was still fighting to be heard.

"Would you go?" I asked Kylo. "If the roles were reversed, and you had an opportunity to avenge Princeton, would you go?"

Kylo closed his eyes for a moment. "I need to be alone with Evie."

Idris crossed his arms. At first, I thought he was going to question Kylo, but he sighed and stood with Blade and Harmony. "Evie, I know you're all strong and badass now, but please remember that we need you. *I* need you."

Frustration burned through my chest. I didn't respond.

"Once everyone's cooled off, we can discuss alternative strategies," Blade said, his ruthless features tinged with a hint of concern as he glanced from Kylo to me.

They were placating me. I still didn't speak as they filed out of the room.

As soon as the front door closed, I focused on Kylo. I didn't bend, and neither did he. We stared at each other, our intensity illuminated by the warm afternoon glow from the opposite windows.

His lips were turned down, his eyes ruthlessly vampiric. His shoulders were back, his chiseled body resembling a poised weapon now more than ever.

I resisted the urge to shift or make myself smaller. My palms warmed, a tingling sensation crawling up and down my spine as power flowed through.

"You're not being a good listener, baby," he whispered.

The tone instantly made my stomach flutter, the space between my thighs recognizing it immediately.

It was deceptive, the cool confidence, the softness wielded as a slippery poison.

"You're not being a good listener either," I snapped.

Kylo grinned, but it didn't match the darkness in his eyes. The moment his pupils dilated, my instincts kicked in.

He let me run. Through the foyer, then into the main drawing room. There, I halted, realizing I didn't want to play chase and capture with Kylo. I wanted him to treat me as an equal like he promised he would.

I spun around, and in a flash of vampire speed Kylo had his hand around my throat and fangs bared.

My glare was sharp, and I shocked the fuck out of his palm with a jolt of magick. He released me, that cold grin spreading once more.

"Don't you dare," I hissed. "You can't feed and fuck me into submission."

He laughed, a shadow already all the way up my thigh. "Want to bet?"

"You promised me you *wouldn't*," I accused.

Kylo's smile slid into another deep frown. He looked torn, raw. Like I'd peeled off his mask and cracked him wide open. The shadow paused just before it met my pussy that already ached for him.

"Yes, I promised you open discussion and agency and respect. But you are asking me to let you get raped, kidnapped, murdered, or harmed in one hundred different creative ways."

I flinched at his explicit language.

Kylo's eyes held me in their depths tighter than his shadows. "And that is an *impossible* thing to ask of me."

I shook my head. "I'm not asking that. I'm asking for you to believe in my ability to protect myself. To be cunning and strong and powerful just like you."

Kylo gripped my waist. "This isn't about my belief in you. This is about my love for you and my belief in the borns' capacity for evil."

Angry tears finally broke through as I gripped his forearms. "I feel it, Kylo."

The sharp intuition that curled around my vertebrae, the deep knowing in my gut, the way the fates were weaving a clear path for me.

"I'm meant to do this."

The tattoo on my hip pulsed. Then it burned, and I hissed in pain.

I pulled up my dress to reveal the intricate design surging with power. The blooming flowers were pink and unfurled, a glint of light reflecting from the brass key. The serpent coiled, staring at us.

Kylo gripped me harder, his gaze pinned on my bare skin.

"I'm strong enough."

He pushed me up against the nearest wall. His jaw trembled, his black hair dipping onto his forehead as his eyes roamed my face. His hands rested on the wall on either side of me and his thigh pushed roughly between mine.

I gasped, closing my eyes. "I'm strong enough," I repeated.

Too many shadows to count swarmed me, roaming my breasts, then tightening around my torso and my throat and even my mouth.

"Well, angel, I'm *not*," Kylo whispered. "I'm *not* strong enough."

"I love you, and I'm going," I said, though my words were jumbled by the darkness that held me in its grip.

I knew he heard them through our mysterious shadow bond.

He didn't answer. And I had nothing more to say.

Kylo waited, his form trembling with rage and heartbreak.

He waited until I started to grind against his thigh, ceding my power and granting him permission to unleash his darkness however he needed to.

It wouldn't change my mind.

His shadows released me, replaced by his hands. My breath hitched when he began to grope me roughly, capturing a nipple between his fingers and tugging as he stared deep into my eyes. Still, I ground against his leg, chasing pleasure as a balm against the pain and discomfort. The discomfort of displeasing Kylo when every cell in my body yearned to do the exact opposite.

"Strong enough to survive the born, yet too helpless and needy to resist grinding on my leg, hmm?" His lips curled, the condescension taking a deadly turn. "How fucking dare he think he can so much as *think* about you and still breathe."

The shadows whispered Kylo's thoughts, the contents of the letter on repeat.

Plagued by thoughts of you, I heard, the sound tickling my ear as Kylo pinned me harder against the wall.

Kylo's kiss was rough and demanding, leaving my lips bruised.

Your beauty, your mysteries, your feisty spirit.

He bit my lower lip as I gasped in pain. I tasted copper, and Kylo's tongue followed the trail of blood he'd spilled. He sucked now, and my eyes rolled back, his venomous saliva entering my bloodstream.

Your promised husband.

I knew I was leaving a wet spot on Kylo's pants now, and the moment I flooded with hot embarrassment, Kylo chuckled and pulled back.

Lavish destiny.

He gripped my face. "Yes, angel. You did make a mess on my leg with your greedy little pussy."

I whimpered, and he pressed harder against me.

My dearest lost bride.

Kylo's thread of control snapped. He pulled his leg back and plunged two of his long fingers inside me.

"Whose pussy is this?" he growled, voice trembling with fury.

"Yours. Forever."

My own words shook as they left my lips because his fingers now fucked me violently, arching against a spot that left me breathless and overwhelmed with sensation.

"Pathetically wet as always," he said, mocking me with fake pity. "Tell me how much you love being my messy little toy."

"I love it," I cried, an orgasm already threatening to tear through me.

As soon as I took a step off the precipice, Kylo yanked his fingers out.

When I collapsed into a betrayed, frustrated cry, he only smiled at me.

Kylo reached behind me, unclasping my dress and pulling it off me as he ignored all of my whines.

A shadow wrapped around my wrists and yanked them above my head.

He left me there, nude and deprived, as I wiggled and attempted to rub my thighs together. I was desperate, the orgasm running farther away.

CLAIMED BY FANGS AND DARKNESS

Another set of shadows yanked my legs apart and rooted them to the floor.

"I don't want you to come, angel," Kylo hissed. "So you won't. Do you understand?"

I nodded, and I stopped wiggling. The coldness in his voice triggered my instinctive need to please and the terror of feeling like I was in trouble.

Kylo saw the shift in my face and immediately softened. "Who is in control?"

"You," I answered.

He needed this. He needed this as badly as I did, both of us healing the deepest, wounded parts of ourselves within this game of power.

"Good girl," he praised.

I let go of a tense exhale, his affirmation soothing me as intended.

And this was why I ceded to Kylo in this way, why I trusted him with this authority over me even when we were in disagreement. Because I knew he would *never* take anger or malice out on me. He would treat me with love and dignity even when it took the form of sexy violence.

His gaze raked over my body.

"I own you, angel," he said. "If you're anyone's destined bride, it's fucking mine."

He didn't give me a chance to react, though my pussy was quick to throb instinctively at such a declaration.

Kylo pulled one of my nipples into his mouth and sucked. I melted, my nerves coursing with pleasure.

Fangs pierced. I screamed. The sharp bite of pain exploded into ecstasy just as quickly. Kylo whispered soothing praise against my flesh before drinking from me.

I stopped fighting the binding around my wrists.

Kylo pulled away, and I realized he hadn't completely clotted the wound. My blood was warm as it dripped down my torso.

His fingers plunged inside me again, soothing me with slow, coaxing movements. He sank his fangs into my second breast, and I came immediately.

Kylo fed, still pumping his fingers as I convulsed around him.

When he released me, he looked up at me with lips stained crimson. "Bad girl, angel. I told you I didn't want you to come."

"I couldn't help it," I slurred, boneless and still bound against the wall.

Kylo dropped to his knees, following the trails of blood dripping from both breasts with his tongue as he gripped my thighs.

He was playing with his food.

And it only made me drift further under his spell.

He straightened and sucked my abused lip into his mouth, moaning as I shuddered against him, only attempting to get closer as his shadows rooted me in place.

Suddenly, they released me. Kylo threw me over his shoulder. My world tilted. His hand came down hard on my ass, and my yelp was breathy and disoriented.

"Disobedient little angels get punished," he scolded.

He carried me into one of his studies, a dim witch light flickering on above. I couldn't see where he was setting me down. My bare ass hit smooth wood, and shadows were quick to bind my arms to the armrests and legs to the chair's feet.

Between my thighs, something leather and bulbous was poking out. I looked down. My eyes blew wide.

Kylo moved behind me. His hand covered my mouth before I could speak. A spark of magick triggered the enchanted, deviant device.

Vibrations poured through the round head as it rested against my center. I jolted, squirming at the overwhelming sensation.

Incomprehensible noises burst from my lips as the shadows

only tightened. I couldn't move. I couldn't shift away from the intensity that was already too much.

I cried into Kylo's hand.

"Shhh, baby," he soothed. "Be a good girl and take it. You wanted to come so badly, remember?"

The intensity made my pussy ache and surge with heat. The more I resigned to my fate, the easier it was for the vibrations to shift from unbearable to pleasurable. My moans were chaotic against Kylo's palm.

Kylo laughed at me, and his unabashed sadism had my eyes closing and core tightening. I was helpless, out of control. His venom coursed through me, and I was delicately painted with my own blood.

And my demented, romantic mind was still caught on Kylo telling me he wanted to marry me.

"Let go, angel," Kylo whispered.

The softness triggered a violent orgasm, a high-pitched moan racking against his palm still over my mouth.

He stroked my hair as I rode wave after wave.

But the vibrations didn't stop. Not when I squirmed and bucked and screamed against his hand.

Please, I cried through our bond next.

Shadows only roamed my body tauntingly, holding me still as my sensitive, over-stimulated clit was mercilessly tortured.

"Do that again, baby," Kylo groaned. "I love knowing how deeply we've buried ourselves inside each other."

Heat moved violently through my veins. My body grew slick with sweat. I became lightheaded as I tried to suck in enough air through my nose.

"Try passing out," Kylo taunted. "See if that will save you."

I didn't even know *what* kind of noise left my mouth as I exploded again, in a burst of heat and pleasure and aching, tormented nerve endings.

Now I really was on the verge of losing consciousness.

Kylo removed his hand. He kneeled in front of me, grinning wildly with my every cry and plead for relief.

"Sorry, angel. Your God isn't feeling very merciful this afternoon," he said. He stared between my thighs.

My lips trembled, my body tight and aching from tensing so hard.

He met my eyes. "Aw, yes, so sad." His head dropped, his lips on my upper thigh. "I think I know what could help you relax."

His whisper skated across my skin before he feasted from my flesh, fangs buried deep.

I came. Again and again. As Kylo bit my thighs. He pushed the cruel and unusual device harder against my pussy, licking his blood-soaked lips as I screamed again.

I reached a breaking point after perhaps the fifth bite and seventh orgasm. My head fell forward. The shadows released me. I barely noticed where my body was being moved, only that the vibrations had stopped and my dewy skin was against Kylo's.

I melted against him. My eyes fluttered. He sat back in a desk chair, sliding me down onto his cock.

The fullness was a different flavor of intensity, one I welcomed now. I mewled, my head resting against his chest as he bounced me up and down to meet his thrusts.

Kylo let out a rasp of curses as I clenched around him, soaking wet and barely able to move.

"Good girl," he praised, stroking my hair and kissing my damp forehead. "Manners, angel."

"Thank you, Kylo," I somehow managed, my voice raw.

"For what?"

His touch was soothing, but his thrusts were anything but. They were deep, merciless, claiming.

"For letting me come."

Kylo's soft chuckle rumbled through his chest.

My moan was faint, my lightheadedness reaching a peak.

But Kylo didn't relent. He filled me with all of him, and when that wasn't enough, he picked me up, cleared off his desk, and pushed me to lay my torso against the flat surface as he took me from behind.

I could barely touch the ground with the tips of my toes. My eyelids fluttered again. Kylo's broad hand was on my back as he drove into me.

A feral growl tore through him, possessive and tortured. Between states of consciousness, I could feel his emotions, the intensity of his love and worry and obsession.

When I stilled, Kylo scooped me into his arms to face him. He impaled me with his cock and gripped my face. I blinked slowly, each time locking on to those intense pools of blue.

In his arms, his cock twitched as it found my cervix. His eyes darkened. He fed from my throat as my eyes closed, and his warm seed spilled inside me.

The last thing I heard before I passed out was a strong, unwavering voice in my ear. "You'll wear a discreet collar. I will be as close to the estate as possible the entire duration. I will listen for every change in your heart rate and rhythm. You'll be sent with a method to communicate with me in case of emergency. And you will have a hard time limit. I will not negotiate these terms further."

30

KYLO

I held Evie close in my arms as I fed her blood replenishing potion. I stroked her soft blonde hair, and I praised her for being so good for me. When she finished, I carried her to the bathtub.

She curled against my chest in the soothing, warm water, and seeing her this sweet and docile only shattered my heart all over again.

I hadn't wanted to give in. Those words had left my lips against my will. But Evie's mind was made up. And my only choices were to break her trust all over again, tell her I didn't believe in her beautiful magick and resiliency, or to trust that the same gods who had bound us together would protect Evie until the end.

I could see it in those vengeful gray eyes. Evie saw this as an opportunity, and she was going to seize it one way or another. This was the only way I maintained any sense of control in protecting her.

I held her tighter, washing her depleted body with immense care.

Emotion after emotion rolled through me, but I didn't show

it. I'd already unleashed as much as was safe for her. I'd never hurt her again.

Even if I destroyed myself in the process.

"I promise, Kylo," she whispered, her small hand wrapping around my fingers. "I promise I can do this. Just like I rose Idris from the dead."

"Shhh. Relax and let me take care of you."

After our bath, I scowled as I applied enchanted ointment to Evie's throat, erasing all visible evidence of my ownership. It might provoke her targets and put her in greater danger.

She wore one of my shirts as she sat on the edge of the bed. I enjoyed how my clothing swallowed her whole, and I could tell she loved being wrapped in my scent just as much.

"Would you, angel?" I asked, unable to stop myself.

She cocked her head in question.

"Marry me?"

Her cheeks turned my favorite shade of pink. It wasn't fair to ask such a thing when she was venom drunk and barely on this plane of existence, but nothing felt fair right now, so I did it anyway.

"That's so traditional for a vampire clan leader," she teased, biting her lower lip. She winced, realizing how bruised and wounded I'd left it.

I rubbed the healing salve there next.

She looked up at me with those big, adoring gray eyes. My thumb was gentle as it skated across her lip.

When I retracted my touch, she rubbed her soft pink lips together.

I pretended not to be waiting with bated breath, but I wasn't sure how convincing it was.

Her silence squeezed my chest. Only Evie could make me feel this damn human and vulnerable.

She placed her hand over my heart. Her eyes widened, deepening with beautiful, complex emotions. She knew how hard my heart was beating. And even after all of this, she still seemed surprised. That was how deeply Evie's sense of unworthiness had been ingrained.

Like soulmate love was for other people and not for her.

Her own heart picked up its pace, leaping to meet mine.

She finally opened her mouth. "It's too soon..." she said softly, staring at her hands in her lap.

My heart panged. Everything inside me suddenly felt heavy and crushing, not to be dramatic or anything. Still, I nodded in understanding. I'd hurt her, and that had set us back. Maybe she didn't feel as strongly about us anymore. Or maybe she'd always been a step behind.

She slowly moved her gaze back up to my eyes.

"But maybe if you ask properly, next time."

My exhale was slow. Evie ran a hand through my hair, her smile a blend of earnest and devious.

I lifted her by the waist and threw her higher onto the bed. She squealed as she landed back on the pillows.

"Angel, do you delight in torturing my exposed, hopelessly captured heart?"

She giggled.

"You really are a monster."

I'D NEVER BEEN MORE tense in my entire century of existence. Evie and I had spent the day in deliberations with my most powerful, keen men and women of my inner circle.

Idris was livid, and I could tell he blamed me on some level for not talking Evie out of this. Which was reasonable. I hated myself right now too.

I regretted all of it. I didn't want to do what was right. I wanted to lock Evie inside my estate until Lord Aster, Lord Conrad, and their pet witch were already dead.

"Kylo, I promise," Evie assured me for the hundredth time as she got ready, making herself look enticing for born predators. "I won't attempt an assassination except to save my own life. Not this time."

The words *this time* were a different kind of dagger to my guts.

I glared at myself in the mirror, watching my cloud of darkness gather around us as Evie applied blush to her cheeks.

Phineas had been the only one who was entirely on Evie's side, agreeing that it was too enticing of an opportunity for information-gathering to pass up.

I'd hated him in that moment. I hated everyone who'd been won over by Evie over the course of discussions, who'd helped her craft a solid plan and false identity to assume. They treated her like a clan member, an asset, a weapon.

They didn't treat her like *my Evie*.

"It's only dinner," she said.

My fists clenched.

"This is what the born do. They hide their darkness under a façade of civility and decorum. If they wanted to take me by force, they would've attempted to endanger Mena. This is all just politics, arrogance, and greed."

I'd heard it all before. I still didn't care.

"It thrills me that the best-case scenario here is that Lord Aster is attempting to seduce you," I said dryly.

"The born want what they can't have," she said with a shrug. "Their predictability is good for us."

I clamped my mouth shut and turned away. I was unable to watch Evie accentuate her devastating beauty for a second longer.

The knowledge that another man would be enjoying her company tonight was more than enough to make me lose all semblance of control I'd carefully maintained for eighty years. But the fact that it was a born lord?

I closed my eyes, finding my center using one of Princeton's breathing techniques. I felt like a newborn all over again, knocked back to square one as I fought the urge to declare war myself with a brutal rampage.

Every time I was plagued by visions of the born mutilating Aisling's body, I had to restart the exercise. And when the accursed memories morphed into visions of Evie, I couldn't breathe at all.

"Kylo."

Evie wrapped both hands around my arm. Her lips met my biceps. "I'm here."

I slowly pried my eyes open. Evie was no longer trembling. She wore a shield of strength atop her terror, her own uncovered traumas.

"I'm strong enough," she said.

Believe in me, was the message beneath.

I nodded. "I'll be in the old library across from the estate."

"I know."

"You have the paper?"

Evie put a hand over her heart, signaling she'd tucked the enchanted method of communication into her bra.

Great.

She wore a conservative summery dress, sky blue with tulle sleeves and a high neckline. She was covering most of her skin and it still wasn't enough for me.

I didn't want any of those demons to see even an inch of her.

The last piece was in a box on the dresser. It was a choker necklace with a clasp that doubled as a tiny ink pen.

It was also a discreet collar, a reminder for Evie that she was safe, protected, and *owned*.

I placed it on her neck in front of the mirror, and my frown didn't ease. Not even when Evie's lips curved slightly, thumbing the familiar moonstone, and the crescent moon, star, and heart charms.

"This is beautiful, Kylo," she said softly. "Very *me*."

I released a sigh. "I wanted my name front and center, but that's for next month. When all of this *civility* and *politics* and *decorum* have been overtaken by good ole fashioned violence."

"It's unlike you to be so tacky. What happened to subtlety?"

I snorted, irritated with Evie's ability to make me laugh at a time like this. "My undying devotion isn't meant to be subtle."

She turned away from the mirror to face me. "We can workshop it. Surely there must be a classier alternative to your name on my neck."

"Looking forward to those negotiations," I forced out.

I grabbed her waist. She stroked my cheekbone and traced my tense jaw.

"Will you read to me before bed?" she asked.

I swallowed, basking in the hopeful, determined, unkillable light of Evie's eyes. She was reinforcing the inevitability of her safe return to me. "Of course, angel."

31

EVIE

The last stubborn remnants of my anger and distrust over Kylo's betrayal died off completely the moment I stepped into born territory.

I'd already all but forgiven him. But now? When he was choosing *me* so selflessly, giving me my ultimate freedom despite how much it was killing him inside...

I fucking loved that man.

As born guards led me through the grand front gates of the Nighswander Estate in the heart of Etherdale, I pushed all of my true self to the side.

I blocked out the image of Idris yelling. The way my stomach sank as he begged me not to go. Kylo's heartbroken face the moment he said goodbye, the wounded emotions he concealed before everyone but me.

Tonight, I was a witch without allegiance. I killed my coven for mistreating me. I killed the group of born who kidnapped my brother. The turned were protecting me, but these lords could only guess why. They didn't know for certain that I had taken Princeton's place.

And Lord Aster thought he could win me over, regardless.

Perhaps the ruthless, naive girl who escaped the Servants of Lillian to take refuge in Etherdale *could* be swayed. Maybe the reason she was surrounded by the turned was merely the promise of protection after a life spent looking over her shoulder.

I didn't hide my fear as two born men escorted me up the path to the small castle. They'd each smirked at me, one of them unabashedly flashing his fangs as his nostrils flared. But neither of them touched me.

The gardens here were rich with spirits, and some of them were not so friendly. I fortified my psychic shields, maintaining my clarity as I paid careful attention to my surroundings.

"Lord Aster will be pleased you've made it, Miss Lockwood," the more stoic, dignified born man said without glancing back at me.

I flinched. "I don't use that name anymore," I said. I'd meant for my voice to come out stronger, but the nervousness was ripe and unavoidable.

The other vampire snickered. "I'd imagine not."

Okay, so either the born didn't care about telling my unsavory origin story to anyone, or these two vampires were more than mere low-level guards.

I studied their clothing. They weren't in plain uniform like the vampires who stood watch at the gates. They were in archaic, flashy suits. On their fingers were chunky gold rings, likely imprinted with family crests.

Nausea churned in my gut. I forced myself to focus on the present.

I wasn't a helpless child anymore. I was a powerful adult witch with people who loved and protected me.

Even in the lion's den, I was *safe*.

My body struggled to believe this completely, but I was at

least able to keep walking. All the way up the grand staircase to the heavy front doors. They opened with a dramatic boom. Beyond, war relics were displayed—uniforms, armor, and ancient weapons.

Because of course the born chose decor that signified violence rather than actual art.

The wallpaper was nauseatingly blood red. The gold detailing on every piece of furniture and molding was classless.

The vampire who had unabashedly sneered at me caught the look on my face and barked a laugh.

"Not to your taste?" he asked.

Lord Conrad appeared above us at the top of the staircase, his cold expression somehow becoming even colder.

Oops.

"Is that her?" a shrill, feminine voice squealed before bursting into a fit of maniacal laughter.

My breathing became shallow as I strained to listen for more. I allowed my witchy senses to expand, to wander around the space.

I met an overpowering, foreign power immediately.

The witch was *here*.

Harsh voices sounded from beyond the foyer, like the source of the unhinged laughter was being scolded and shushed.

Lord Conrad stood unmoving, staring down at me. He lifted a single dark brow. "I suppose I shall be attending this dinner, after all." His light, ghostly eyes revealed nothing; his voice was bland with only a drop of surprise.

I knew it was coming, but still I shuddered the moment Lord Aster stepped into the space to greet me. His smile was broad and cocky, his posture relaxed.

Strangely, a faint red line trailed from his jaw down his neck, as if he'd been scratched by a cat. His cool blond hair was slightly disheveled.

"Welcome, Evelynn, I'm so pleased you accepted my

invitation," he said smoothly, his gaze flitting across my form. "Blue suits you much better than black."

Disgust surged in my blood. He was comparing me to how I looked when I was thirteen years old.

"It's Evie," I said, unable to hide my instinctive scorn.

Lord Aster's pupils dilated ever-so-slightly, but he didn't react to my tone. I was tightly wound, a part of me regressing back to that farming commune in the hills of Isolde. It was baked into me to behave, to treat elders and the born with the utmost respect, to be pleasant and agreeable even when I was uncomfortable. To smile even when I was rotting away inside.

"Very well, Evie," he said, homed in on my neck now.

I held my breath. Was he staring at my necklace, Kylo's covert marker of ownership? Or at my fluttering jugular?

Either way, I was soothed by Kylo's presence here, even if in the form of jewelry and our blood bond.

"Come. The party is getting started. Dinner will be served shortly," he said. His grin was easy, but his eyes flashed with pleasure, and worse...

Hunger.

I forced myself to follow Lord Aster into the next room, a grand drawing room where close to twenty guests stood in far dressier attire than I currently wore.

It was silly to suddenly feel embarrassed or out of place when I obviously didn't *want* to fit in. But still, my casual, youthful summer dress stood in noticeable contrast to the lavish, sensual gowns and suits around me. And the elites in the room were not shy in showing me that they noticed our differences too.

One born woman nearly spilled her flute of alcohol laughing. She lifted a brow and whispered loudly to the man next to her as they stared.

"Don't mind them," Lord Aster said, far too close to me now as he led me deeper into the glittering, opulent space.

"You're as perfect as I remembered. Your innocence is a gift, my dear."

The nausea grew thicker, and I had to make a conscious effort to keep my power at bay.

We stood in a corner of the room by a bar cart, and I noticed the men from before hovering nearby. Lord Aster handed me a flute of what I now recognized to be elixir.

I stared at its shimmering, golden depths and then into his nearly red, amber eyes.

Maybe he really did think I was a fucking idiot.

I made no move to drink, and I waited for Aster to speak first. That was one of the main things we'd hammered home in deliberations. I was to speak as little as I could get away with, letting the born guide the conversations.

"Your eyes are piercing," he said, pretending to be mesmerized.

Oh, you have got to be joking.

Before I could find something to say that didn't get me into trouble, the lights flickered, and furniture rattled. I frowned, reining in my power before I realized it hadn't been my power that surged.

Lord Aster sighed. "We talked about this, kitten."

Confusion overtook my nausea. I followed his gaze with a turn of my head.

Behind me, a tiny woman my height but thinner stood in white lace that appeared to be more of a nightdress than an evening gown. She had wide gray eyes like mine, but dark brown hair that fell just past her shoulders. We seemed to be close in age.

She wore *white*.

Horror knocked me off my axis as everything fell into place all at once.

The girl smiled. Lord Aster stepped closer to me.

"We finally get to play," she said as she slowly stepped forward.

She was referencing the note a figure in white had left for me after Etherdale University's massacre. At the time, I'd been so sure the attacker was a man. Clearly, I'd been wrong.

Her smile was giddy. Her voice matched the squeal of excitement and cackle I'd heard earlier. But in her eyes was a haunting, churning darkness I knew all too well.

The witch who killed Princeton was a born vampire's bride. Or slave, to be more precise. A girl who'd been born to a cult and auctioned off as livestock, *just like me.*

My gaze swept from her to Aster and the fading pink scratches on his skin.

"Quite the conundrum, isn't it?" Aster said, watching my face carefully. "I may have had my suspicions, but how was I to know my dearest Evelynn had been alive all this time?" He raised a hand, lightly placing it on my shoulder as I went stock-still. "Apologies. *Evie*, I should say," he corrected.

I slowly panned back to the brunette version of *me.*

She covered a giggle with a hand over her mouth. "You look terrified! Don't worry, I'm not the jealous type." She beamed at the born at my side, her eyes filled with adoration and…

Insanity, if I had to put my finger on it.

"Wait, but… " The words tumbled out of my mouth as my mind spun. I shrugged out of Aster's revolting touch. "That means you were here in the city before I—"

The girl giggled again. "She's so cute!" She extended a hand. "My name is Juliette, by the way."

When I refused to shake her hand, she scowled.

I ran through the events of the past few months, dread growing heavier in my gut.

"I never forgot about you, Evie," Aster said, delighting in my confusion. He fed off my terror as his eyes lit up. "You conjured storms as a child too."

What? My traumatized brain was forced further backward through time, a vague sense of recollection arising from the abyss. I remembered my power as a child, the way I'd been punished for it. The way I cried when it rained, the terror of each lightning strike. I'd been scared of storms, yes, but...

Had I been causing them?

No one spoke to me about my magick, only how I could serve the coven. How I could be a good daughter of Lillian and wife to a vampire.

I'd known instinctively to hide my connection to the shadows, the friends who whispered things I wasn't supposed to know. I knew to hide. I knew to make myself small.

"Everyone said you were dead, that the atrocity must have been the work of one of Lillian's heretical bastards, but I had my own intuitions," Aster continued. His thumb caressed my shoulder. "I always knew you were powerful, despite assurances from your mother that you were ever-so-sweet and harmless." He chuckled.

At the mention of my mother, I felt the color drain from my face.

"The moment I heard about the witch-conjured storm over Etherdale, I had my lead. It was easy to connect the dots from there, given you'd made enemies of some exceedingly vocal and well-connected humans. They were more than willing to blabber on and on about the mysterious girl who showed up with her brother on a woman's front porch a decade ago. The country accent she'd erased, the frightening nature of her magick."

Now I was sure I was white as a ghost. The music, lights, and laughter were all suddenly too much. I felt exposed. Or maybe like I was on trial.

"They were going to take me to *you*," I whispered, forcing the words from my lips. I ran through the incident in the woods, the site of my magickal explosion. I thought my identity was safe—neither the born nor the Servant of Lillian seemed to know anything about my past. They treated me like just another chaos witch with clan ties. I studied Aster's smirk. "You already knew who I was."

Aster sighed, glancing at the born around us. "You made things rather difficult for me—for *us*—when you killed some highly esteemed friends of ours. But perhaps I should've known better than to let them involve your brother. You were just so untraceable…"

But I was hardly paying attention to him anymore, my gaze now locked on the girl who watched me with crazed, assessing eyes.

She'd been here in Etherdale because of *me*. She'd killed Princeton because of *me*.

It was *my* fault Princeton was dead.

"Why would you do that?" I asked, a tremor racking through my voice as I glared at her. "Were you trying to kill me? Is that why you killed him?"

She balked, shaking her head. "I would never kill you, Evie."

Her voice was sickly sweet, and my intuition slammed into me in a cacophony of warning bells. Something was terribly wrong with all of this, more than I could've ever imagined.

"Oh, you just wanted to pluck out my fucking eyeballs?" I asked. Candle flames grew taller, the air turned colder.

A hush fell over the room, and Aster straightened.

The girl's lower lip trembled, as if *I* were terrifying *her*.

She looked to Aster as she spoke to me. "I was only trying to protect you, Evie."

"You did a very good job, pet," Aster consoled. He shot me a scolding look, as if I were bringing down the vibes of his tasteful dinner party.

My fists clenched. But still my mind ran in impossible circles, trying to make sense of this twisted web.

What. The. *Fuck.*

"Just like you protected your brother, right? Was that why you killed your parents?" she asked, her big doe eyes imploring me intently.

"You massacred an entire building full of people," I spat, horrified. I scanned her for answers the same way she did me.

Juliette reached out a dainty hand as her lips curved. She managed to barely stroke my arm with her long, pink fingernails before I jerked backward and out of her reach.

"It's not a competition," she said with a pout. She crossed her arms. "We're *both* special."

"That's right, kitten," Aster said. "You're both *very* special girls."

His deceptively handsome, charming features were trained on me now. The urge to puke arose.

Worse than the devastating guilt was the strange, sickly anger that I didn't know how to put into words. I felt violated, as if a part of my soul had been consumed without my consent.

Juliette was watching me so intensely that it made me want to gouge out *her* eyes.

"She doesn't like me." She feigned sadness that I could see straight through to the emptiness beneath.

Aster stroked her cheek. "Miss Evie is still stuck in survivor mode. You remember what that's like."

I took a step away from them. Aster was strangely tender toward his unhinged, psychotic slave-wife.

They both stared at me now, and I could nearly taste the thirst on their tongues. I fought the urge to bolt, instead choosing to endure this overwhelming discomfort.

Juliette needed to die. Yet as strongly as I seethed with hatred, there was a part of me that now hesitated.

For some reason, I'd been envisioning someone older—a man. Not a girl who looked like me.

Not a girl who'd likely been married off as a child.

Was she evil? Or was she traumatized?

No. *Fuck that.* She killed Princeton brutally, harvested his eyeballs and used his death to make herself more powerful.

She was a mass murderer. She'd massacred innocent students...

Juliette stared at me as she leaned into Aster's gentle touch, his hand cradling her face.

... and *she thought that made us the same.*

32

EVIE

Inhale. Hold. Exhale. Hold. Inhale...

The more I practiced my breathing to soothe my shattered nervous system, the more I thought of the witch who'd taught me the technique in the first place. *I* led the born to Princeton.

"There's no need to worry, dearest Evie," Aster said.

His tone might've been soothing if it weren't from a disgusting predator.

"You're not in trouble," Juliette added with a nod as Aster continued to gently pet her.

"We know this city has poisoned you against us, your true family," Aster drawled. "You took refuge with the turned when those humans came after you. That was a very smart move for such a lost, wounded little girl."

Yep, the urge to vomit was back.

I gripped the flute of elixir far too tightly now.

My lips formed a tight line. I'd come in strong, poised, prepared. Now I felt turned around, confused, even ashamed by what I'd inadvertently revealed.

"You came here with a plan, no?" Aster asked, those amber

eyes roaming my form. His smile was relaxed, as if I'd already given him everything he wanted. "To spy? To scheme?"

"She came here to kill me," Juliette said, fake emotion in her childlike voice.

"Shhh," Aster hushed before focusing back on me. "She will do no such thing. But you may ask anything you want, Evie. Unlike the turned, we have nothing to hide."

The born were tricky, manipulative. I had to clear my mind and refocus. Even as the walls were closing in.

"Go ahead," Aster dared. "Ask."

I glanced around. Not a single decadently dressed born was fazed by my presence. No one was concerned. No one was strapping me down to torture or interrogate me about the turned.

"What possible reason would I have to join you? I know that's why you invited me here," I said. "Are you going to kill my adoptive grandmother if I don't?"

Aster lifted a brow. "I have no reason to do that."

Lord Conrad appeared, joining us with a handsome, dark-haired, shirtless man. He appeared to be human.

Was he trafficked? Or a hired courtesan? Rage infected me, even as the human wore a content, satisfied smirk.

Aster sighed. "But to answer your first question... you don't have a choice, my long-lost bride."

The hairs on the back of my neck stood in high alert.

"The turned can't win," Conrad said plainly.

He cleanly cut into the human man's wrist, letting blood trickle into his golden chalice. He took a swig of fresh blood, his ghostly eyes sparking with the faintest hint of life. The shirtless man kissed Conrad's shoulder.

"We're not playing chess, girl," Conrad continued. He paused to kiss the man's wrist, closing his wound and feeding him a dose of venom. He licked his lips. "You fool no one. You're merely a fool."

The words were a sharp, icy slap. Words dried up on my tongue. I moved my gaze back to Aster, studying him almost desperately.

As I watched him, tracing the confidence and hunger that was accented by pity, Juliette studied *me*.

"Forgive my oldest friend's callousness. He lost his tact a century ago," Aster said softly. He lifted his hand, as if to touch me, but thought better of it when I took a small step back. "He is, however, correct. You were sold a beautiful lie, Evie. You're a darling for believing it. I don't blame you. Mortals will always find comfort in sweet delusions over bitter truths."

The weight in my stomach was heavier now. It infected my chest, squeezing against my ribcage.

"This is why I will never marry again," Conrad grumbled. "You've become infected with nonsensical, flowery language, brother."

Aster shrugged. "Mortals fascinate me. I enjoy their literature. That doesn't mean I've forgotten Lillian's natural order."

The ire slipped into my gaze immediately.

"What gorgeous fire," Aster whispered, peering into my eyes.

Juliette hung onto his arm and continued her unyielding stare in my direction.

"Nevertheless, I brought you here to warn you as much as I did to woo you," Aster continued. "We know the turned are in hiding, that they wear human disguises and disappear into glamoured neighborhoods. It doesn't matter their true size or strength. Not here in Etherdale, not in the rest of the realm. They don't have the resources to last even a battle or two against our armies. Let alone the organization, the experience, the sheer numbers. When they finally emerge, they will be crushed like every other failed uprising."

It wasn't true. Kylo knew what he was doing. He had allies all over the realm. Our witch friends were crafting poisons as we spoke. He had a plan for securing resources from Valentin. We had enough to take Etherdale—there was no doubt in Kylo's mind about that.

My stomach was in knots. The born men were watching me, and I knew I was bad at hiding my emotions. When they both smiled, I knew I'd let it slip that they'd struck a chord.

"Earle didn't cede Valentin to Rune and the turned because they won a war," Conrad said. "He did it to *end* a war. Huge difference."

"What do you mean by that?" I asked. I knew the basics of Valentin history thanks to Kylo's obsession. What he said sort of mirrored Kylo's version of the story, but I wanted to hear the borns' official spin.

Conrad smirked. "Don't you know what happens during a mortal uprising or, gods forbid, a full-blown war?"

Aster stepped closer to me, encroaching on the distance I'd put between us. "Forget weapons and potions shortages. What do you think happens to the blood supply with so many vampires relying upon increased blood to fuel their power?"

This was what blood replenishing potions were for, and why it was crucially important to secure them from Valentin. Unfortunately, key ingredients must be sourced from the mortal lands there.

"Mortals suffer the most during war," Juliette said.

Her sweet, soft voice made me want to punch her in the face. If only so she'd stop studying me like she wanted to wear my skin as a suit.

"That's right, kitten," Aster said. "Earle signed the treaty and allowed Rune to rule Aristelle because if he hadn't, every last mortal would've perished along with the born and turned. And if a war like that were to happen here in Ravenia?" Aster shook his head. "It would be a bloodbath. Futile for the turned, and downright devastating for the poor mortals caught in the middle. If you actually care about your fellow children of Selena and Helia, then you should know that *nothing* would be worse for them than war. Nothing at all."

"So we're just supposed to roll over and take it then?" I hissed. "The sacrifice of children, the murder, the rape?"

Conrad wrinkled his nose as if in distaste. "It would seem time with the thugs has ruined all semblance of your former manners, witch."

My skin was hot, my mouth dry.

Juliette shook her head as if she were admonishing me.

They cared more about my tone of voice and respectful language than they ever would about mortal life.

"There are proper channels for meaningful change. Local governments, open dialogue between mortal representatives and their lords, and petitions to the king's council," Aster said gently. "Have your turned friends tried any of those?"

The condescension oozed from Aster's every pore, and I couldn't tell whether he believed his own bullshit anymore.

"Because if they continue down this path, they will be responsible for the deaths of thousands of mortals and the destruction of the world as we know it. The gods are already displeased. If the turned don't stand down, Lillian will eat the whole world with her wrath."

My eyes flitted to Juliette, who was now smiling smugly as she stretched and wrapped her arms around Aster. She snuggled closer to him, pretending she had nothing to do with the so-called *acts of Lillian.*

"Enough politics," Conrad said with a shooing motion. "Dinner is almost served, and I plan on enjoying myself."

"Agreed," Aster said, still focused on me instead of the girl in his arms. He flashed a confident grin. "I only want you to thrive, lovely Evie. There's still hope for you. For your brother and *grandmother.* For all your little friends in the city. All is not lost, not yet."

It felt like I had both nothing and everything to say. I wanted to ask them why they'd been rounding up witches, kidnapping or murdering them, yet they weren't bothering to harm *me*. A chaos witch who actually fit their description.

They didn't see me as a legitimate threat. Not like they had Princeton.

After all that I'd escaped, the destructive powers I'd displayed, these born still viewed me as nothing more than lost property. I was another piece to add to Aster's collection of traumatized girls.

Juliette grinned now, still watching me. I ignored her completely, which finally succeeded in making her frown in genuine displeasure.

Women and men in glittering, feathered outfits gracefully entered the space. Their attire left little to the imagination as they performed at the front of the room. A magickal device was set up by the windows to play recorded music. A male witch layered in all black switched out small orbs in the sound bowl as each recording ended.

I locked eyes with him, and a chill shot down my spine. My teeth ground together.

On either side of me was a lord. The room had all turned to watch the immersive dancing, the humans that delicately teased with feathery scarves and sensual movements. Born licked their lips.

The performers didn't seem drugged or enslaved. It blew my mind that there were still mortals who willingly entertained the born, merely because they were paid handsomely for it. I'd heard the born were lavish spenders, if you survived your time with them.

I didn't want to judge anyone desperate for money, but surely there were safer alternatives.

Yet here they were, mortals wrapped in shimmering jewels, offering themselves up to the born with a smile.

So much of this world had never made sense to me. The way

people behaved, their justifications, their cruelty. Kylo and the turned had helped me find meaning amid the orderless chaos.

Now Aster and Conrad's arrogant rhetoric was bouncing off the walls of my mind, a loop of doom that repeated.

A hand slipped into mine, and the moment I tried to yank away, Juliette gripped me tighter.

I winced in pain, surprised by such a tiny person's strength.

Aster and Conrad were distracted by dancers who'd immediately approached them for personalized attention.

Juliette leaned in close, her haunted gray eyes suddenly alert and focused.

"Don't worry, I won't tell him about the man you love. The one with the black hair and dreamy blue eyes," she whispered. "*I don't get jealous, but Sir does. He gets very jealous.*"

I went still. Was she a mind-reader? A psychic of some sort? Had she been watching me?

She said she didn't get jealous, yet I didn't have a better word for the desperate energy radiating off her in waves. Like she wanted to be close to me, so inseparable that we became *one*.

"Let go," I hissed with a glare.

Juliette pouted dramatically. "You're on a dark path, Evie. Come back to Lillian's light. Lillian may be scary, but she's also forgiving. All you need to do is repent."

I gave Juliette a warning burst of heat, and her eyes fluttered as if with pleasure. She let go of my hand.

For a moment, I debated killing her. It was hard not to when Juliette was channeling the words of my abusive mother.

I calculated how many born were in the room.

Killing her would be easy, so long as she didn't expect it. A shadow straight through the heart, the neck, or the head. Escaping the born would be harder, but not impossible, assuming I could command enough shadow with enough precision before anyone used their super speed to subdue me.

But then I'd kick off the war. Before the new recruits had

been turned. Before the Serpent Clan could join us. Before Kylo's pieces were perfectly in place. The clan was already disadvantaged, and I'd be making everything much harder.

I wasn't an idiot—I hadn't been swayed so easily by the borns' so-called *warnings*. Yet they were ripe in my mind, nonetheless.

The unflinching confidence that they would prevail.

And worse, the guarantee that we'd be sentencing thousands of mortals to death by daring to fight back against their oppressive systems.

Juliette smiled, like she knew exactly what I was thinking. "It's not playtime yet, sister."

I envisioned it. My hands around her throat. Her mouth filled with blood.

The way Princeton hung there from the wall, motionless and desecrated.

"This was why I recommended a slow introduction," Conrad said, breaking the spell between me and my doppelgänger.

Aster sighed. "Evie, the use of magick is not permitted. To do so would be to forfeit my promised terms."

In other words, it would give him an excuse to detain me.

I noticed the small shadow that was curling around my feet, and I instantly absorbed it back inside me. But not before catching Juliette's delighted eyes.

Covetous eyes.

Aster nodded at Conrad, who pulled Juliette away from me and to the other side of the vast space. Juliette whined and protested, but she didn't fight him. Aster took my untouched flute of elixir. Many born in the room were staring at us, assessing, even as the dancers continued their performance.

If anything, the room merely appeared amused.

As if we were quarreling house pets.

"I have a gift for you," Aster said. "Come with me."

He reached for me, swallowed, and thought better of it. His hand fell back to his side.

"It'll only be a moment. Then we will enjoy a beautiful dinner, and you can head back to your *friends*."

I considered my options. Stay in the room with a couple dozen predators or follow one of them into an undisclosed location.

Remember what you came here to do, a voice broke through the noise, a comforting, maternal reminder of my purpose.

I followed Aster.

33

EVIE

Aster led me to a library.

The born might burn *our* books, but it appeared as though theirs were safe and abundant.

It was an admittedly gorgeous space, quiet and kissed by candlelight. Rows and rows of books surrounded us, all the way up to the ceiling. Ladders were positioned for easy access to the top shelves.

"There she is," Aster said, a triumphant smile skating across his lips when he caught me gawking at the space. He handed me an ornately wrapped present with a golden bow.

I hesitated before untying the bow and sliding off the wrapping paper. I stared at the book beneath—an ancient, beautifully covered text with gold edges. It was an old book of fairy tales.

A spark of recognition made my eyes go wide, and Aster's smile broadened.

It was a special edition of the book I'd taken from a market in Florimell. I'd slipped it into my backpack when Mama wasn't looking. I spent the next afternoon reading about faeries in secret, out in the field after lessons were over. Mama found me, and after grabbing me and shaking me in pure outrage, she burned the book to ashes. She accused me of being on a dark path. Screamed that I was ungrateful and disrespectful to Lillian and her word.

Staring down at the embossed lettering on that very same book, my throat tightened. It wasn't safe to be this raw and triggered, not in the den of my enemies.

"How did you know?" I demanded.

"There, there," Aster said softly, still resisting the urge to reach for me. "You can read whatever you want around me. I was raised to be a gentleman, to all the gods' creatures. So long as the natural order of Lillian is obeyed, I do not believe in harming Helia's children for cruelty's sake."

Deep, molten anger scraped up from the very core of me. Every word out of this man's mouth was a careful manipulation. As if he was any different from the monsters who'd raised me for tithing.

"You may not remember, but I came to visit a handful of times as the region's lord. I wasn't always pleased with what I found. Piousness to the extreme is indulgent," he said.

I stared at him, digging through my memories as they became hazier and less accessible. I thought I'd only met him once, right before Lillian had declared through my mother that we were to be married. I remembered vampires floating through at other times, like phantoms, omens of death that haunted the tall grass and rolling hills.

"I was there that day, for other reasons. But I heard yelling as I was heading to the firebird stables. Your mother hadn't wanted to tell me about the incident with the book, but I demanded to know why you were being punished. I asked what book it had been, and it stuck with me."

How old had I been? Seven? Eight?

My body felt exposed, my insides revolting against this conversation. The idea that Aster had set his sights on me so young. The fact that I could hardly remember anything from those times except in jagged pieces and snapshots in a haze.

"You're wrong about me, Evie," he said. "I didn't consummate my marriage with Juliette until she was of age."

"How noble of you," I spat, unable to stop myself.

Aster's eyes darkened, but he still made no move to hurt me. I held the book in a death grip, trying and failing to calm my racing heart.

Kylo told me he'd be monitoring my heart, listening for changes. He'd be able to tell if someone had drugged or fed from me.

The idea that he was likely worried out of his godsdamned mind was what kept me from exploding. I took a deep breath, working to soothe my heart that longed to be back with Kylo's.

"I didn't mean to upset you," Aster said. "Juliette was the same at first. Skittish and prone to melancholy. Did she look harmed to you? Even when she's aggressive, she is never mistreated." He gestured to the nearly faded scratch marks on his neck.

I glanced back down at the book. He was telling me a story about himself, but more than that—he was selling me on a future with him, a future with the born.

If only he could see the tattoos beneath my glamour. He'd likely kill me on the spot.

I was *impure* and *ruined* in ways Aster could hardly imagine.

It was this defiant, smug thought that kept me rooted in place. I didn't back down. I didn't run. I held the book to my chest. I locked my tears away for later, for when I was far away from these hungry sadists.

"Are you ever frightened of Juliette?" I asked.

Aster's lip twitched. His eyes narrowed, his features shifting into something less readable. "How could I be scared of such a tiny, lovable creature? She may be temperamental at times, but she's a very obedient girl for me."

I processed his words, attempting to keep my features as neutral as possible. I stored every admission and piece of body language away in my mind for later. For when Kylo and I could strategize and scheme.

"You two half-humans have far more commonalities than differences. You both crave a protector—a strong, powerful man who can handle your beautiful darkness." Aster's amber eyes sparkled. "You're special, Evie. I've always known it."

My body was still. I absorbed every slip of information, ignoring the sickness in my gut and the shame lodged in my throat.

Would I have fallen for this if I'd never killed my coven? If I'd been sent to live with Aster instead? What about if I'd met Aster before Kylo, before I'd learned what true love was? At what point in my life would I have been too vulnerable and unable to resist Aster's meticulous, predatory methods of control?

I felt the weight of my collar, the reminder of Kylo's devotion. His unselfish, steady, nurturing love. And beneath the glamour, I connected with the mark of the clan and my connection to Hekate.

The magick that had protected me before I'd ever known the protection of a man.

"Do you still read?" Aster asked.

I nodded. "Of course."

He smiled as if he were winning. Like he'd already won.

He continued to make small talk, never once mentioning the turned. I attempted two more careful attempts to discuss Juliette and what was happening in Etherdale, but Aster shut the conversations down and swiftly redirected to more questions about *me*.

At dinner, I sat with him on one side of the long dining table while Juliette and Conrad sat on the other. For a moment, it appeared as though Juliette was on the verge of tears. Her hands

CLAIMED BY FANGS AND DARKNESS

were in her lap, her eyes empty. But in the next blink, she was smiling and staring creepily at me once more.

The born were on their best behavior as delicacies were served and blood was poured. Not a single human looked less than happy and radiant as they served the vampires.

I'd seen the born when they weren't civilized. The way they fed recklessly, tossing dead humans to the side once drained.

That was what my brother's assaulter Vernon had done the night we ran. He'd laughed and cursed, as if it were a harmless mistake to kill the woman in his arms. A witch elder had said she was a whore, anyway.

I wondered if this table thought *I* was a whore.

Every once in a while, I'd catch a vampire staring my way, and the answer was obvious. The downturn of their lips, the smugness in their eyes. The disdain mixed with tinges of curiosity and hunger.

Aster wouldn't even be interested in me nor Juliette if we had been full-blooded witches. It was our humanity that made our blood so unique and special to the born. They wanted to suck out our innocence until we were just as empty as they were inside.

I managed to eat, still refusing to touch any liquid other than water. I nibbled on the small plates of artfully arranged meats and vegetables drizzled with rich sauce.

"Do you enjoy dessert, Evie?" Aster asked.

Juliette watched me from across the table. Every time Aster asked me a question, she stopped whatever she was doing to listen, to absorb.

"As much as the next person, I suppose," I said, refusing to give a genuine answer.

Aster twirled one of my strands of hair around his fingers, testing me. I fought the urge to pull away. "I've always loved your blonde hair. It's even prettier now, more complex. Just like you, dear."

I stared at him. Then I raised my gaze toward the clock over his shoulder. I only had thirty more minutes until I needed to be out of here and back with Kylo.

Otherwise, he'd come for me no matter the consequences.

"Stay for dessert," Aster said, his voice a low caress as he leaned closer. "Then I can walk you out."

I nodded and sipped from my glass of water.

On the other side of the table, the born were laughing about some elite sporting tournament I'd never heard of. They were discussing betting strategy, throwing out monetary sums most mortals couldn't even conceptualize.

Music danced through the space. Elixir and alcohol flowed freely. Everyone was relaxed in their warm bath of hedonism and apathy. No one mentioned war.

A human girl fell into a vampire woman's lap. The vampire locked eyes with me as she fed from the young woman's neck. She winked.

Aster frowned at the exchange, shifting closer to me. He asked again about what I liked to read, and I begrudgingly offered a few titles.

He smiled. "I've read that series."

I couldn't help the flash of surprise in my features. "Really?"

"I love romance," he said.

Lord Conrad rolled his eyes.

Juliette watched us with a deepening frown.

"The subplot with the coup, led by the incubus fellow—what was his name?"

"Andrew," I said.

Aster's face was weirdly genuine and animated. "Loved it. Spectacular. Though I didn't enjoy the protagonist's ultimate decision."

"Of course you didn't. What would you know about martyrdom?" I asked softly, unthinking, before I closed my mouth tight.

Aster paused. Then he chuckled. He glanced down at my lips, only amused by my provocation. "I find your brain very attractive, Evie. I like that you're well-read, that you can keep up."

Juliette was glowering now, her lip curling. When she noticed me looking at her, she was quick to wipe the expression from her face entirely.

"Sir, can we read together tonight?" she asked, resting her chin on her folded hands. "I love fantasy books," she said, her voice an octave higher and softer when she spoke to Aster than when she'd spoken to me during our confrontation.

"Of course, kitten," Aster said, peeling his eyes off me to answer her.

When he turned back to me, his features almost appeared conspiratorial—as if to signal to me that he, too, saw Juliette's pathetic jealousy. Juliette didn't miss it, this subtle shift, the sway of Aster's attention and fascination. His placation of her childishness.

I lifted the glass of water to my mouth, and Aster tracked the movement. Yearning swam in his eyes, once again focused on my lips.

"I had a dream last night," Juliette said loudly. "Of a man with pretty black hair and blue eyes."

I stiffened, but I didn't take the bait.

Aster appeared irritated by Juliette's outburst. "What happened in your dream, sweetheart?"

Conrad took a swig of his chalice of blood. At first he looked bored, but then his eyes focused on me. Something shifted, a slight cock of his head.

"His head fell off," Juliette giggled.

The glass in my hand shattered.

A hush fell over the room. Aster stared at my hand, the gashes across my palm that now oozed blood. Juliette stopped laughing.

"Fuck, that smells *heavenly*," a vampire across the table groaned.

Aster's pupils dilated. He inhaled deeply, and I held my breath.

His mouth opened, and I prepared to fight, to run, to wield my power.

"Fetch a bandage," he commanded to one of the attendants. He then glared at Juliette. "Bad girl," he hissed.

"I didn't do anything!" she yelled.

Annoyed born glared her way, while others were far more focused on my hand dramatically oozing blood on the chocolate cake below as if it were a rich, fudge topping being drizzled especially for each of them.

Conrad's nostrils flared, but his eyes were trained on my face. Assessing. Curious.

I was so deep in fight-or-flight that I let Aster take my hand into his. He carefully pulled shards of glass from my palm as I winced.

"It's just the one that's deep," he murmured, inspecting my wounds.

He pulled my palm closer as he craned his head.

I barely had time to register what was happening until it was too late.

Aster's tongue followed the trail of blood. He sucked.

"No," I said, tears burning my eyes.

The saliva entered my bloodstream, dulling my senses. Aster pulled back, his mouth stained with my blood.

"Just clotting your wounds, dear," he said. His voice was strained, his eyes ravenous. He swallowed. His lips formed a faint smile. He dabbed at his mouth with a napkin.

The attendant came back with a bandage and salve.

It had only been a small amount of saliva. He hadn't fully fed.

I was fine. Everything was fine.

Aster cleaned and bandaged my hand. He slowly pulled the bloody chocolate cake toward him.

My stomach soured.

"I've never tasted blood like yours in my six hundred years of existence," he whispered, his gaze fixated on me.

Juliette's glare burned into the side of my head.

"Unique. Perfect," he whispered.

I wanted to sink into the floor. An unwanted, sickening pleasure spread from my palm in gentle waves.

The moment a bloody bite of chocolate melted on Aster's tongue, I felt a deep, unyielding hatred slam into me in the etheric plane. The lights flickered.

Juliette smiled. She batted her eyelashes. Her eyes were pure venom, a splash of darkness against her lacy white exterior.

Dread and panic and shame coated my skin. On the old clock, the arms were two minutes past my time limit.

"It's time for me to leave," I said.

Vampires stared at me. They looked to Aster, as if not even they knew what was going to happen next.

I resisted the urge to scan the doorways, to listen closely for any sign of Kylo breaking down the front door.

Aster nodded in disappointment. He set down the fork. "I'll escort you out."

A breath released from my lungs.

"I hope next time we get to play, Evie." Juliette's ire had completely disappeared. She smiled cheerfully as Aster led me past the powerful, wealthy monsters eyeing me with controlled fervor.

One of the born women twirled a hand in a wave, her lips forming a taunting smirk.

They were all fucking with me. They showed me exactly what they'd wanted me to see, nothing more and nothing less.

Tears welled in my eyes, my palm still radiating decadent warmth.

Aster had fed from me. I felt violated, uncertain, and frightened of Kylo's reaction. And worse, my anger and hurt were both muted, like they were trapped behind a gentle stream of ecstasy.

"I hope I didn't cross a boundary," Aster said, glancing over at me. "I'd love to see you again soon."

The lump in my throat returned with a vengeance as we descended the steps at the front of the property. My freedom was within reach.

My mother's scolding voice was loud in my ear, telling me to be quiet and agreeable. I was being too sensitive and dramatic; it really wasn't a big deal.

I shut my eyes for a moment. A tear slid down my cheek.

"You did," I whispered. "You did cross a boundary."

Aster stopped walking. He held my blurry gaze, brows drawn. He cleared his throat. "You were losing a lot of blood. Venom is a healing agent. I wanted to help, not to feed. I appreciate you saying *no* to me. I only want to bring you pleasure. You're too special for anything less."

It wasn't an apology. It was an excuse wrapped in a disorienting, manipulative package. If not for Kylo and my healing after dating someone like Jacob, maybe I wouldn't have noticed. Maybe the pretty words would've been enough. Maybe I would've brushed it off.

Instead, I kept the violation ripe in my mind as I nodded and stared up into his eyes. "I'm open to seeing you again."

Aster smiled. His eyes faded back into warmth after I showed him my compliance.

He wanted us *obedient*, after all.

Aster's thumb stroked the top of my wounded hand before he let me go. In my other hand, I carried his gift. I walked past the guards, through the grand black gate. I crossed the street, where I knew Kylo could see me from his post in an old medical library. I kept walking, all the way until I reached a side street a block over.

That was where I finally gave in.

I let the tears fall down my cheeks as I took off running. Kylo let me do it.

He let me run until I couldn't breathe anymore.

He appeared like a prince of the underworld, birthed from a shadowed mist. In the middle of an alley, he stood, masked and cloaked in beautiful darkness.

I ran straight into his arms.

34

KYLO

Each change in Evie's heart was maddening. I staked out on the upper level of the library, in a dusty archival room that had a clear view of Conrad's front gate. The property itself was obscured by tall trees, but I could just make out a spire and tower.

I could be inside in three minutes, tops.

That was my only comfort as I stood in the stuffy room, listening to Evie's heart hammer and then settle. Over and over, her fear was a palpable force, driving me to the brink of utter insanity.

Why the fuck had I let her do this?

I knew why. But it didn't soothe me. I wouldn't be soothed until Evie was in my lap as I read to her and inhaled her comforting, floral scent.

I let Evie do this because I loved her. And loving someone meant letting them make their own decisions, even if those decisions wrecked me.

It had been less than thirty minutes, and Evie's heart had already communicated four different moments of increased distress.

But there was no evidence of blood loss or drugging. Her heart was within its normal range of Evie anxiety.

I hated to admit this. I downright refused to do so out loud. But if Evie were anyone else, I would've been on board. She was going to sit at a table with Etherdale's greatest threats, our most prized kills in our fight to take back the city. And they were going to underestimate her, merely because she was half-human, small, pretty, and female. I hated to admit that beneath my rage and terror, I did in fact believe that the born were arrogant enough to attempt to steal Evie without force.

If she were merely a soldier, everything would be different. I might've even found joy and satisfaction in these power games, the idea of manipulating and employing methods of subterfuge upon the born.

I would've relished the idea of getting close enough to Princeton's murderer to avenge him.

But Evie was Evie. Not only my soulmate but also the backbone of the clan. Not a single cell in my body was relaxed nor satisfied.

All I felt was the overwhelming urge to drag her back to me and away from the man who saw her as his bride.

A low rumble rattled the shelves of old books. I closed my eyes and steadied. But I couldn't shut out the sudden erraticism of Evie's heart.

She was still deeply traumatized. Yet she had willingly entered a castle full of monsters who would hurt her at the first opportunity. She did so merely to serve the clan, to not allow an opportunity like this to pass us by.

She'd always been miraculous, brave, cunning. Ever since she escaped her fate at thirteen years old, carrying a young Idris all the way to Etherdale from Isolde.

Imagining Evie at thirteen wasn't helpful. Because then the vision transformed into what would've happened to her if she *hadn't* escaped. If she'd become Lord Aster's locked-away slave instead.

A flicker of magick lightly shocked my hip. I reached into my pants pocket, opening my main journal to find a note from Harmony.

Update? Keep breathing, friend. We love you, and we're ready for anything.

Harmony, Blade, and a group of skilled fighters were also nearby, in case things went south. We were prepared for anything, even if it meant declaring war earlier than I'd hoped.

Consequences meant nothing to me when it came to Evie. And I didn't care how great of a liability that was for me nor the clan. If the gods hadn't wanted our souls tied as one, they should've kept us apart.

But they didn't. And now there was no going back.

Love you too. Even Blade.

I wrote back, imagining my closest friends' smiles.

No updates yet.

I slipped the journal back into my pocket. Not even the scent of ancient books soothed me, which meant I was truly in peril.

Evie had argued against the duration of her time limit, and she'd only agreed on two hours and thirty minutes after she vocalized that it was enough for an *initial* meet. Just like she'd agreed to wait to kill the witch or anyone else in Conrad's residence.

She agreed to these things because Evie believed she would have another opportunity in the future.

And I wished I could find that admirable or fierce or sexy but all I felt was all-consuming wrath instead.

If a born so much as laid a hand on Evie, all bets were off. The way I killed Evie's useless ex would look merciful compared to what I would do to a born man.

My muscles spasmed from how hard I was tensing and for how long. Two hours passed, and it could've been two weeks.

Her heart had settled at the ninety-minute mark, and for whatever reason, that pissed me off more than her anxiety.

How had Aster attempted to seduce her? With food and gifts and conversation? Would they tell her that war was unwinnable, and she had a safe place to land if she decided to jump ship?

It was the reasonable assumption. My skin was hot, my mind consumed with volatility. But how did their witch play into all of this?

The witch who wanted to remove Evie's eyes from her skull.

I believed in Evie. I swore I did. Underneath the visions of my angel being harmed were the memories of her raising her brother from the dead. It hadn't mattered what anyone said, Evie had defied the laws of reality that night.

She could make the sky weep and the earth rot. She stood beside gods and forged alliances with spirits from all corners of the otherworld.

Evie wasn't helpless. Far from it.

Yet, four minutes away from her deadline, a shift in Evie's heart had me forgetting everything—her power, my belief in her, the threat of war.

Her heart sped up and then slowed. She was losing blood.

Three minutes. Three minutes until her time was up.

It would take three minutes for me to get to her.

Unless it was a trap. Unless they were prepared for me. I yanked out my journal, scribbling Harmony's correspondence code. My pen hovered over the page as my mind raced.

Evie's heart was erratic, but the blood loss stopped. She

wasn't being drained. If a vampire were feeding, her heart would beat far slower, and the blood loss would be dramatic.

Had she been wounded somehow?

Fuck.

Time was up. My usually sharp mind was scrambled when I needed it most.

Storming the place would put Evie in danger. I would only pull that move if it were obvious she was already in peril.

And it *wasn't* obvious. What had happened wasn't clear at all.

I stared at the front gate, glamoured by shadow. It was three minutes past her deadline. At five, I'd write to Harmony.

I said every prayer and curse in my vocabulary.

A shaky breath left my lungs.

Evie was moving closer. I could feel it through the bond, even if I couldn't see her yet.

I slipped the journal and pen back into my pocket.

The gate opened, and I finally saw her. Aster touched her hand, and darkness bled from my shaking form. Evie frowned as she pulled away from him, her body language clearly indicating discomfort. Not that Aster gave a fuck.

A bandage was wrapped around one hand, a book of some sort in the other.

The guards let her pass through the gate. The moment she left my line of sight, I moved quickly to meet her.

When Evie took off running, my heart ached with hers, knowing it was a clear response to resurfaced trauma. I let her move the way her body needed to move as I tracked her.

I let her crumble and flood the earth with her tears.

And when I could sense that she was out of air, heaving and hurting and needing to return to safety, I appeared before her.

My glamour dropped. I stood, masked, as shadows circled.

Evie immediately ran into my arms. Worse than the scent of her fear was the lingering scent of fresh blood.

I pulled back even as Evie clung to me. I scanned her body quickly.

"I—broke a glass," Evie gasped. Her face was streaked with tears, and her lower lip trembled. "I'm okay. But I broke a glass, and I cut myself."

She was okay. My angel was okay.

I studied her again. But when she melted back into my chest and clung there, I gave up entirely. I held her tight and kissed the top of her head.

The book she was holding pressed up against my back. When we finally parted again, I reached for it.

Evie shrunk, as if with shame.

"*Tales of Aracynthia,*" I read.

It was an ancient book of bedtime stories. They were a touch dark, recommended for older kids. Most involved stories of faeries and portals to other realms, the unseen becoming seen, myth bleeding into reality. Classic Evie themes.

I looked down at her red, tear-stricken cheeks.

"It was a book I stole when Mama took me into Florimell to help her shop," Evie said, her voice quivering. "*He* was there, apparently, when I was seven or maybe eight. Mama destroyed the book and punished me for taking it. I didn't know that he'd seen me so young, that he knew much about me at all."

Anger was its own current, and I was grateful for my mask now as I stared down at Evie. It concealed the curl of my lip and monstrous rage in my eyes from her.

"I don't remember much of anything," she said softly. "I didn't know I conjured storms as a child. I didn't know that they were—"

The words melted away as Evie grew less and less rooted to reality. She shuddered, and I sensed her immediate blood pressure drop.

I scooped her into my arms before she could protest. We took the route with the least amount of foot traffic back to the glamoured turned neighborhood. As soon as we crossed the border, I let my mask fall so Evie could stare up into my familiar eyes.

My pace slowed. She relaxed deeper as she held my gaze.

"Good angel," I praised. "Is there anything I need to know now that cannot wait until tomorrow morning?"

Evie's eyes flashed. Fear, mostly, and something akin to doubt.

"Anything that puts you or the clan in immediate danger?"

She shook her head.

"Then let go, Evie. Tomorrow we will go over every detail. The turning ritual is in only a handful of days. You need to take care of yourself now, understood?"

"Okay," she said with a frown. "But—" She cut herself off, merely nodding instead.

"Good girl," I said. "I only care about *you* right now. The rest can wait until you've come back to yourself."

Inside the house, I wrote to Harmony, letting them know Evie was safe, and we were back in turned territory.

I took the book from Evie, the gift that had let her know Aster had been paying attention to her since she was a young child. The knowledge was eating away at her, and it killed me to see. I resisted the urge to pull a born move and burn the gift. Instead, I tucked it into a desk drawer to donate to a school. I'd buy Evie a new copy one day.

Aster had also revealed that he'd known about Evie's *power* since she was young. I wanted to hear everything, to connect more of these harrowing puzzle pieces. But that wouldn't be good for either us, not when we were both so triggered by the past and her demons.

"Come on, baby," I murmured, taking her hand in mine and led her to the bedroom. I undressed her and pulled one of my oversized shirts over her head.

I was rigid as I undid the bandage on her hand, paranoid I might find fang marks staring back.

Instead, it did indeed look like she'd sliced herself on glass.

"Did someone hurt you?" I asked, unable to keep that question at bay.

She stared at the floor when she shook her head. "I broke the glass I was holding. I lost control of my emotions."

I inspected the cuts. She didn't need stitches, and her witchy healing was working faster than the average mortal's. I cleaned her hand and wrapped a fresh bandage around it to be safe.

Or maybe because I didn't trust nor enjoy the idea of Aster taking care of her. Not like I could.

I kissed her forehead, grateful she was exactly where she belonged.

"You're going to be the death of me," I said.

"I'm sorry." Her solemn gray eyes met mine. "It's a good thing you're immortal."

"Don't apologize. Tell me your mantra, Evie."

She hesitated for only a moment to remember the declaration I'd been making her repeat ever since I tattooed her.

"I'm not sorry," she whispered.

"Again."

That sacred fire finally graced her irises, the fire that had so bravely led her into the lion's den.

"I'm not sorry," she hissed.

"That's it, baby." I stroked her cheek.

Shadows poured from her, holy smoke that submerged us both into darkness.

"One more time. Make it count."

Evie's voice was raw and aching, the most beautiful mix of strength, grief, and vengefulness.

"*I'm not sorry!*"

I held her in the center of the whirling, bloodthirsty

shadows. When I noticed she was releasing too much, I let my own shadows find hers.

"Shhh," I soothed. "This isn't over, angel. We're going to give them exactly what they deserve."

Thankfully, Evie settled her power before I was forced to subdue her in a more decisive manner.

The darkness ceded. I stared down at this perfect creature of starlight and wrath. Too fucking adorable to exist.

If Aster had resisted feeding from her potent blood—if he had truly managed to put on a mask of decency and chivalry to vie for Evie's trust and affection—then he wanted her desperately.

And I had a feeling that desire extended far beyond sex and matrimony.

He wanted Evie's magick. He always had.

35

EVIE

I was a liar.

And after everything I put Kylo through for his betrayal, I felt the truth on the tip of my tongue with every breath.

I needed to tell him that Aster tasted my blood. I didn't want to say he fed from me, when it had been so brief. No fangs breached skin.

I also didn't want to be a victim.

I wanted to be strong instead.

Maybe that was another reason the truth dried up every time I opened my mouth. I wasn't in any true danger.

Aster crossed the line and then stopped as soon as I said *no*.

Plus, I needed to go back. After I'd recovered and hashed out strategy with Kylo and my new family, I needed to finish what I'd started.

I needed to avenge Princeton's death, or I didn't deserve to take his place. Not when I was the reason he'd been murdered.

Kylo's fingers were at my mouth again, feeding me a grape from the nearby platter of snacks. He read to me as promised, and I lay my head against his chest while curled in his lap.

Guilt tore up my insides. I felt blemished. Ruined. Like Aster had sneakily rooted himself inside of me.

What if Kylo wouldn't look at me the same? If he knew that someone else had touched me, when he was supposed to be the first and only person to taste me forever?

No, I knew that wasn't the man I loved.

Yet I chose to lie all the same. Because Juliette and I had unfinished business.

She killed Princeton because she wanted to be like *me*. It was insane. Even if it was also to hurt the clan and take out our chaos witch, I couldn't deny the intuition that Juliette was making these moves with this secondary motivation in mind. She wasn't just a puppet, though the born might see her as one.

I knew the truth: She was pulling her own unhinged, psychotic strings when no one was watching.

"You okay, angel?" Kylo asked.

I nodded, letting the anger recede back into the shadows. It would be there waiting for me in the morning.

Every time my stupid, empathetic brain reminded me she was traumatized like me, that she was a child bride who was now a slave, I remembered the way she stared at me, threatened me. The hundreds of innocents she murdered.

The knowledge she would only continue to kill unless stopped.

"Are you?" I asked, kissing his arm.

She'd only been trying to provoke me, and it had obviously worked. But Juliette's threat on Kylo's life had me snuggling closer to him than I already was.

We were nothing alike. She was going to die soon, for starters.

"I'm okay because you're okay," he said. He buried his hand in my hair, inhaling deeply. "My brave, sweet girl."

I settled back into our aftercare rhythm. Turned out it was

just as healing for us to engage in these rituals after getting psychologically fucked by the born as it was after violent sex.

Once I was more stable, I told Kylo the bare facts ahead of our meeting tomorrow. I told him about Juliette and her strange obsession with me. The complexity of her being both evil and also a traumatized slave. I glossed over Juliette and Aster's insinuations that I was going to join them in some weird throuple situation, and Kylo seethed with hatred as deep as mine. Then we melted back into our self-care, knowing each moment of softness was a luxury with war pressing against us from all sides.

Kylo spent an hour before bed writing in his journals. He answered correspondences, scribbled down thoughts, and planned out tomorrow. I'd already written to Idris, who was grateful to hear from me directly despite his anger at my decision.

I was half watching Kylo, half resting my eyes.

"If I don't do this, I have no hope of sleeping," he explained. "I have to get my thoughts out at night, or they'll eat away at me until morning."

"You are the only thing that has successfully given me a break from my obsessive, ruminating mind," I said sleepily. "That's probably why I love you so much."

Kylo snorted. "I'm glad my angel finds me useful," he said, gripping my thigh. "Speaking of my talents..."

He closed his final journal and placed it on the bedside table before gently tugging me down onto my back. He dipped between my legs, his mouth finding my clit.

I gasped.

"Shhh," Kylo said. "I'm not trying to wake you up. Stay your cute, relaxed self while I suck out those last remaining thoughts of yours. You'll be doing the same for me, I assure you."

I enjoyed the thought that I was helping Kylo, so I did

exactly as I was told. I sank into the pillow and soft bedding beneath me.

The orgasm he drew from me was warm, gentle, and dreamlike.

In the next slow exhale, my body was curled perfectly against Kylo's.

"After it's all over, let's go somewhere where it snows," I said with my eyes closed and my body weighted.

Kylo's chest rumbled at my back, his arms and shadows snug around me. "Okay, baby. We can go anywhere you want. We'll travel the world, you and I."

If I wasn't so exhausted, I would've smiled. I imagined I was smiling between states of consciousness.

I wasn't even sure why I said that—why I was thinking about the snow, or being tangled up with Kylo by the fire, surrounded by wilderness. Maybe because I wanted to be truly alone with him for the first time, with no responsibilities weighing us down or threats looming overhead.

I didn't want war. I wanted to watch the snow fall.

I wanted to taste a snowflake on my tongue as Kylo grinned, maskless.

Free.

THE AIR SMELLED of flowers and death. I was in my garden, staring up at gentle rays of morning sun.

At first, I smiled, but then I realized the air was too still and quiet. Where were my helper spirits? My protectors? My garden faerie allies and tricksters?

Someone giggled next to me on the picnic blanket. I joined in her laughter, but it felt wrong, as if I were reading a script. An actor in a play I didn't write.

Eclipsing the sun, a young woman's face hovered over mine.

Her features were innocent, a small nose and wide gray eyes and soft pink lips. Her dark hair was glossy, her skin just barely kissed by the sunlight.

"Isn't this nice?" she asked me.

She wore a summery, floral dress with a corset top. While hers was white and blue, mine was white and pink.

For a moment, I caught a glimpse of us from above—we looked like lovers, a perfect mirror image.

I nodded and smiled. I'd never had a sister. I'd never known how it felt to be loved by a girlish best friend, to trade dresses and secrets. How it felt to wear whatever I wanted, to lay in gardens and kiss beautiful boys and girls.

I frowned, and the woman leaned closer, her lips inches from mine.

These weren't my thoughts.

Soft, warm lips brushed mine. They were eager, demanding, and—

I shoved Juliette off me.

"What the fuck is wrong with you!" I screamed.

Juliette's face flickered from hurt to wrathful to impassive and back again, like she couldn't decide who or what she was.

She needed someone else to decide for her.

I scrambled to my feet, and she did the same. In matching dresses, we stood in this poor imitation of the gardens I had tended to with care for a decade.

"You don't know me!" I hissed, voice trembling like the ground beneath our feet. I gestured around. "This isn't right. You will *never* get it right."

The woman of many faces settled on one. Her eyes were infernos, her chest heaving, her palms twitching at her sides.

"You want to take my place!" she screamed back. "You don't want to be with *us*. You want me gone so you can have him all to yourself. You think you're the special one. You can't share."

I opened my mouth to tell her I'd rather die than be with her predator husband, but I didn't want to reveal anything about my motives.

"There's a deep, frightening darkness inside of you, Evie," Juliette said, her lower lip trembling as if from fear. "I told Aster about how you threatened me during the performance, to hex me with your dark blood magick. I can see you, the *real* you."

"You threatened *me*," I said incredulously. She was the one hexing all of Etherdale.

In the dreamworld, my subconscious was stronger than my conscious mind. It was harder to stay grounded, harder not to let Juliette's words affect me at my core. To remind me of my mother's last words, saying I was a plague on this world.

My throat tightened, and Juliette's eyes flashed with satisfaction.

"You want to sever the tie between two souls meant to be together forever," she said, a manipulative tear sliding down her cheek. "Sir and I have known each other in every lifetime, since the beginning of time. We've been lovers, friends, brother and sister, father and daughter..."

"Um, *ew?*"

I made a face of disgust, and Juliette fucking lost it.

"It's romantic!" she shrieked as she tackled me to the ground.

Her long fingernails raked across my cheek, and I hissed in pain. We rolled, flailing limbs and bloodthirsty eyes.

On top of her, my hands finally closed around her throat. I'd been fantasizing about this since the moment we met.

I squeezed and pressed. Her face grew red.

Juliette began to laugh. "I want to smile when I die," she said, straining to speak. "Like Princeton. He smiled."

The yell that tore through me was inhuman. She had carved a smile into Princeton's face with a knife.

"You are fucking crazy!" I yelled.

She stopped fighting. She let me squeeze and squeeze until the body beneath me wasn't her anymore—it was Kylo, eyeless.

Such a beautiful shade of blue.

36

EVIE

I woke up screaming. Kylo was on top of me, wrestling my hands to my sides.

"Shhh, angel," he said. "You were dreaming. You're safe."

The scream evaporated, and the sight of his eyes still in his skull soothed me back to reality.

"I have to kill her," I said, jaw clenched and body vibrating with rage.

Kylo stroked my face with a frown. "You scratched yourself," he murmured.

I winced at the sting, seething even stronger now. That woman was a demon in the truest sense of the word. She belonged in the pits of Lillian's hells with the rest of them.

It took me several long seconds to calm my heart and steady my breathing.

Kylo kissed my forehead. "Let's get coffee first before we do any killing."

When my frown evaporated, he shook his head and laughed. "The depth of your addiction frightens me."

AT THE DELIBERATION TABLE, Blade lifted a brow at my brown and gold ceramic mug.

"I don't think I've ever seen a mug of that size," he said.

Kylo's lips turned down. "That's how Evie evades her two-coffee limit. She started using a bigger cup."

Harmony laughed.

"I respect the fuck out of a loophole," Blade said with a nod.

It seemed we all needed laughter today. I welcomed the brief reprieve from my nervous, restless jitters. Commanders and other inner circle members took their seats, all eyeing me with equal parts relief and anticipation.

I swallowed, returning my attention to Harmony and Blade.

"How are things with Abby?" I asked Harmony. Abby was a turned woman Harmony had been seeing.

Harmony winced. "I found out she only saw me as a steppingstone to climb the ranks."

Blade grumbled an insult under his breath and crossed his arms.

It irritated me to think someone would ever take advantage of someone as bright, warm, and genuine as Harmony. But it didn't surprise me. It seemed those traits were the exact qualities shitty people looked for.

"I'm sorry, Harmony," I said. "You deserve better."

"Thank you, friend." She waved a hand. "I'm too busy with clan responsibilities, anyway."

"We'll get you a war fling," Blade said. "We all need one."

Kylo lifted a brow. "A fucking *what*, Blade?"

Blade grinned impishly. "You know, a lover to distract from all the death. Someone to squeeze at night after a gruesome battle."

Commander Lachlan's smile was equally devilish. "Kylo

wants to tell us to focus on our devotion to the clan, not on war flings, but he can't say *shit* anymore." His eyes flickered to me.

Kylo's glare was deadly, and I giggled as I sipped my coffee next to him. We both sat at the head of the table in matching high-back chairs.

He looked at me and softened. "You are all limited to *one* war fling. No exceptions."

"Seems discriminatory," said a woman with sharp green eyes and a shaved head.

She was shockingly gorgeous, and I recognized her as Bexley, a new member of Kylo's most trusted advisors. Apparently, she came from old money, a family that was loyalist to their core. I bet she had a lot in common with someone born in a Servants of Lillian cult; it was why she sat with us here today.

"Not all of us have monogamous hearts," she said with a devastating smile.

Harmony's eyes widened, shifting in her seat. Blade was watching Harmony's reaction too, mischief ripe in the curve of his lips.

Kylo sighed. "The plight of being in a position of power. I simply can't account for the varied proclivities of you insatiable deviants."

"Is that a day collar, boss?" Bexley shot back, eyeing my neck.

My face burned, and I glared up at Kylo.

He smiled slowly, enjoying every second of my humiliation. His hand tightened its grip on my thigh. I willed my pussy not to react the way I knew she wanted to.

"All right," Kylo said. "Everyone's here. Let's begin before my girlfriend catches another stray."

Kylo intentionally kept today's gathering to the smallest number possible. I'd grown closer to most everyone at the table, save Phineas, but even still, I squirmed under the weight of so many eyes on me. Especially when discussing things that still felt raw and personal.

But I opened my mouth, because I had to get back to Juliette.

"The witch who killed Princeton is Aster's child bride," I said.

Surprise echoed through the room. Horrified faces looked at each other and then back at me.

"Well, she *was* a child. Now she's an adult woman, another half-witch."

I pulled a slip of paper from the pocket of my dress. It was stamped with Lord Aster's family crest.

I'd found it in the *Tales of Aracynthia* this morning.

Kylo glared down at the paper. I had to block out his anger to continue.

"I now have a direct line of communication to Aster."

Kylo's scowl deepened.

"He told me he had a suspicion I was still alive, and when he heard about the storm I'd conjured here in Etherdale, he followed the lead. I don't know how long he's been here, but obviously since before Princeton was killed. I believe Juliette can sense power, as a chaos witch, which was how she set her sights on Princeton and decided he was an important kill."

I hesitated, shame and guilt eating away at me since the link to me was obvious and unspoken. A power-hungry witch who coveted my shadows wouldn't have been in Etherdale if it weren't for me.

"She harvested from his death and the power it generated to fuel her own. She's a death witch. A vulture. She's mimicking power by stealing it, and she's working with dark forces in order to do so. The more power she has, the easier it is for her to generate more from the atrocities she commits. She's turned murder into a ritual."

"Why didn't she kill *you*?" Phineas asked, earning a look of pure ice from Kylo.

"It's not an exact science. Magick requires exchange, sacrifice, balance. I think her power is limited. It needs sustenance in order to continue, just as vampires need blood. It's not self-generating like magick that works with the universe's natural ebbs and flows."

I was trying to focus on the facts, to resist telling the room how insane Juliette was. How *revolting*. It didn't matter. It felt personal to me, but none of them would understand the violation the way I did. I needed them to trust me to get back inside the Nighswander Estate and finish what I'd started.

"She didn't steal Princeton's magick exactly. She only harvested what she could from his ritualized death. This conversion comes at a loss, and she will need to keep refueling to maintain her strength."

"Evie is more valuable alive than dead," Kylo summarized. "They don't wish to kill her; they want her to join them."

"But if she doesn't switch sides, I reckon they'd still opt for her dead rather than alive and working for us," Phineas pointed out.

A shadow wrapped around my calf.

Kylo nodded, the movement forced. "I would say that's a fair assumption."

"Did you get to speak to Conrad?" Commander Lachlan asked.

"Yes."

The room waited, and I started from the beginning. I told them exactly what the lords said—that they knew about our glamoured neighborhoods and hidden numbers, but that we'd be crushed no matter what we were hiding. How war was unwinnable, and Rune only prevailed in Valentin because war would've destroyed everyone on the island if it had continued.

As I spoke, I studied the faces of each turned.

Not a single person blinked in surprise. No one showed even a shred of doubt or worry.

It soothed me. Yet, I couldn't help but compare the unflinching confidence of both clans of vampires.

Both sets of conviction couldn't be true.

One clan had to be wrong.

Terribly wrong.

"The bit about Valentin was half-true. That's the useful born spin on reality," Kylo muttered. "The turned and mortals were the decisive victors. They pushed the born out of all previous strongholds. But the born were humiliated, and they refused to play by any fair code of ethics. They went on vengeful rampages, destroying entire villages of innocent mortal civilians. And King Earle still needed mortals to produce Valentin's most valuable exports. He signed the treaty that named Rune and the turned as the rightful leaders of Aristelle to preserve what was left of the born and the mortal populations. But it wasn't a draw—far from it. No one got precisely what they wanted, considering the born still exist in Valentin."

"And they're pushing for round two, if the rumors are to be believed," Blade added.

"That would *not* be good for us," Harmony said.

"Well, I don't know," Bexley said. "It would weaken Earle, spreading his army thinner if they were to be drawn into Valentin's conflict. Not to mention, Rune might look to Ravenia for allies."

"We'd have to rewrite the master plan," Blade said, lifting a brow at Kylo.

Kylo shook his head. "Valentin doesn't concern us yet unless we hear something definitive."

I saw the spark in his eyes, and under different circumstances, it would've made me smile. I wondered if Kylo would marry Rune instead if he had the option.

"And what they said about the toll on mortals?" I asked.

I shifted in my seat amid the sudden silence. I didn't want to seem like I was doubtful of the clan I'd pledged my soul to. I looked down at my forearm, the inky black sigil that shimmered slightly purple under my scrutiny.

Kylo traced the marking gently, making me shudder.

"War *will* hurt mortals. This is inevitable," Kylo said. "It's one of the loyalists' main talking points, along with the nonsense Aster bolstered about Lillian's wrath. These are fear tactics designed to preserve the status quo, to keep us from fighting back. Local governments, the council, and Earle himself do not care what is happening to mortals *now*. They only care when their own interests and quality of life are impacted. Their systems are designed to oppress, placate, patronize, and confuse. They want us exhausted. They want us weak."

"And they're using Juliette to accomplish that," I said. Anger coiled around my spine. "They're blaming us for every attack on Etherdale, claiming it's our resistance that's causing their violence. It's the same method of control I was taught as a young girl. Keep the born happy at all costs, and if they harmed me, it was *my* fault. Never theirs. Because that was Lillian's natural order."

Kylo kissed my temple. "Mortals are already fighting with us. They're willingly donating blood. Many more will join. Others will be caught in the crossfire, or they will even side with the born. Mortals have been suffering for a while now, facing death and abuse and slavery. War is not romantic. But sometimes, it is the only choice we have to build a better world. Violent oppressors cannot be fought with peaceful tactics."

I released a breath. A calmness washed over me from the otherworld, like I was in alignment with truth again.

"You said Aster kept calling you and the other girl *special*," Phineas cut in, his face a mixture of stoicism and impatience. "His draw to powerful witches and his friendship with Lord Conrad are quite curious. Did Aster seem close to the courtiers in attendance?"

I paused, reflecting on the night. The respect between the two men, the way others in the room insinuated they knew about what I'd done to my family, as if Aster had shared that information.

"Yes," I said. "They all seemed close. You're right—it didn't appear as though they were all united only because of me."

Wait. If that was true... would Aster have been in Etherdale regardless of his obsession with finding me?

"Well, all born nobility are against the turned," Blade said, his face twisted in confusion. "Of course they're going to unite when it serves them."

"But why the preoccupation with her magick?" Phineas asked. "Especially as far back as sixteen years ago? How long have Conrad and Aster been close friends?"

It reminded me of when Phineas had told us something was missing. He had questioned why a chaos witch allied with the born only now wielded their godlike magick.

Phineas had asked the right questions. His intuition was sharp—that was undeniable—like that of a witch. I could see now why Kylo tolerated his prickliness and rudeness.

"All lords may be against the turned, but are all lords loyal to King Earle?" Phineas asked. He leaned back, crossed his arms, and stared at the far wall with a look of vague pensiveness. He twirled a hand, oblivious to the way he held our interest. "And how does this tie in with what is occurring in Valentin? The growth of oppressive, Lillian-centered religiosity, the Servants, and the ever-expanding slave trade? The shadows have whispered all manner of peculiarities. In Earle's council. In Aristelle..."

Kylo was literally on the edge of his seat, leaning forward, almost as if holding his breath. He caught me staring, and that adorable little dimple formed with a crooked half-smile.

Phineas continued his stare at no one, brows drawn. He

tilted his head slightly, sighed, then nodded to himself as if engaged in a lively internal dialogue.

"Phineas! Enough with the drama," Blade grumbled. "Out with it."

Phineas slowly panned to Blade, lips turned down. "I suspect an attempted coup may be in the cards. The dissent in King Earle's council grows stronger as unrest permeates through the realm. Earle is said to be afflicted with madness, more than mere obsession with preserving his legacy. There is talk that a millennium under his rule has been *plenty*."

"Dissenters in the council," Kylo murmured. "That's rare. And the connection to Valentin?"

Phineas nodded, eyes glued on the table as he steepled his fingers in a pose of deep thought. "I'm still investigating. A leader has risen on the born side of Aristelle, a man named Durian. He's a religious fanatic, pushing a holy book called the *Book of Lillian* that contains the so-called word of the Dark Mother. He claims it's an ancient book that predicts his own rise to power and declares Valentin as rightfully belonging to Lillian's children. It's a political propaganda device, obviously."

"Are you familiar?" Kylo asked me.

The conversation made me tense, the past's phantom limbs trailing down my spine. I shook my head. "Not with those names. We read similar texts, though. Detailing how mortals were born to serve vampires."

"What you've heard is true," Phineas said, nodding toward Blade. "I predict a larger conflict in Valentin than their ongoing skirmishes. As Kylo said, we don't know enough to factor that into our current trajectory." He paused. "*However*, it does mean a perfect storm of instability is brewing for the crown. Durian will not be the only born leader who rises from this Lillianic revivalist fervor. Earle may have let protections for mortals continue to slip over the past century, but he has never officially condoned slavery or the Servants of Lillian cult. These institutions undermine traditional customs of seduction, courtesans, and mortal-vampire interdependence. Yet if more and more elites are turning to taboo methods of satisfying vampiric urges, I would imagine these born might grow tired of needing to conceal their lifestyles. They'd prefer to practice their lawlessness out in the open like the commoners."

"And with Earle's alleged madness, they have the perfect surface-level reason for staging a coup," Blade said.

Phineas nodded. He appeared to be done speaking, which allowed my mind to finally whirl and spin.

I knew Kylo and I had similarly obsessive brains, always searching for the connections and patterns in any set of information. For better or for worse.

He looked at me, and I scanned those thoughtful blue eyes.

"The bulk of the Servants of Lillian cults are in rural lands, away from Prospyrus," Kylo said, words leaving his lips rapidly. "Isolde, obviously, but also in the lands surrounding Etherdale— lands under Conrad's control. Etherdale has always pissed off Conrad because it's a stain on his rule, something he's never been able to control the way he's ultimately desired. Earle is a problem because of what he has allowed to fester under his reign, but I cannot deny that mortals are treated the best in his capital city. It would make sense that an ambitious born, or group of born, may be looking to capitalize on instability to take Ravenia for themselves."

"To instate an even worse ruler than *Earle?*" I said, horrified.

"Oppression disguised as religion would be the end of this realm as we know it," Blade said. "There would no longer be protections or mortal-run anything. What Conrad is doing to Etherdale would be a microcosm of an authoritarian Ravenia, far more disastrous than the monarchy. Witch hunts would become widespread, erasing any coven or shifter pack that doesn't submit to the born. Slavery would be the norm, not an underground practice. Mortal loyalists have no idea what they're welcoming when they open the door to vampires like Conrad."

"Hold on," I said. "So the connection to Aster, his preoccupation with powerful witches, their apparent disregard of the turned altogether..." I studied Kylo. "*Their* sights are set on overthrowing Earle too?"

Kylo released a breath. He calculated. The room stared at him, waiting. "Potentially. We need proof. But it makes sense."

"Proof means possible leverage," Blade agreed. "We could use this to our advantage."

I was trying to keep up, but I was also computing where the hell *I* fit into all of this. Aster was undeniably a creep.

But was he also a usurper?

It didn't seem like that was the basis of his interest in me, but if it were, then he obviously wouldn't show it.

I hadn't consumed nearly enough coffee for this.

My stomach twisted into knots, my heart panging. Originally, I'd been so certain that I'd led Juliette to Princeton. But now I wondered how much of Aster's narrative was true, and how much was a cover-up for an intertwining of fates that existed before he even knew I was still alive.

When he'd visited me as a child, he'd come with other frightening vampires. But I couldn't remember their faces, nor were they ever introduced to me. Could one of them have been Conrad? And Conrad had said he'd *never marry again*. Had he been married to another vampire, or a mortal? Was he just as involved with the Servants as Aster was?

I looked down. The enchanted correspondence letter stared back at me. I didn't know how much blame was mine to carry, but it wouldn't change my future either way.

Responsibility rested on my shoulders, and the tattoos on my arm, hip, and back provided a steady supply of momentum.

The conversation had been sidetracked to strategy for Etherdale border patrol, but I knew it would eventually return to the next phase of my subterfuge.

As much as Kylo hated it, what lay bound in the center of this twisted, tangled web of power, secrets, and violence was *me*.

37

KYLO

"What are we going to do about *that?*" Harmony asked, nodding to Aster's official letter in front of Evie.

"Has he written to you yet?" Bexley asked.

Evie nodded, and I stiffened. She hadn't mentioned that to me. And the idea that she would keep something like that to herself poked at my deepest fears and wounds.

She quickly met my gaze. "Just to say he enjoyed our time together, essentially. He asked when he could see me next, and I haven't responded yet."

My mind snagged on the word *essentially*, the paraphrasing triggering an instinctive need to know exactly what the fuck Aster had written to Evie, word for word.

I enjoyed strategizing. Solving problems. Exploiting weaknesses and executing plans. But now that Evie was involved, there was this massive block in the center of the chessboard. An Evie-sized obstacle I wanted to avoid despite its inevitability.

"How does it make you feel to know that Juliette is like you?"

Blade asked, his features tinged with softness as he asked Evie something so sensitive.

The table looked equally curious. Besides Phineas, my innermost comrades were highly empathetic creatures. The best revolutionaries were.

"Conflicted on some deep level," Evie admitted. "But trauma isn't an excuse. Traumatized people choose to fight for goodness every day—that's the entire foundation of turned clans, right?" Her next exhale was heavier. "I don't know how much of Juliette's behavior is clever puppeteering or the result of years of manipulation. And I'm not sure it's productive to figure that out. She's violent, she's riding on a sudden influx of power, and she is capable of killing masses of people. She needs to be eliminated."

"Agreed," Phineas said. His eyes were closed, hands clasped in his lap, lips in a perpetual frown.

He was one of the most amusing creatures in the realm, entirely unintentionally. Sometimes I wondered if he was the way he was because he'd seen far too much from behind his veil of shadows.

"That makes sense," Harmony said to Evie. "I'm sure it must've been difficult being around the born. You did exactly what you were supposed to do, though, *flawlessly.*"

Evie smiled slightly and nodded, but she looked uncomfortable under this blanket of praise. As if she didn't think she deserved it. I worried she might blame herself on some level for Juliette's proximity to Princeton. She needed to understand that however Juliette entered that space, she would've done so regardless of Evie's presence there. That mission had nothing to do with her, especially if Conrad and Aster were *already* in some shady alliance.

"Okay. Take out Juliette. Find proof that Aster and Conrad are involved in this potential coup—or their own separate power play, perhaps—and use it to destabilize and split born forces," Blade summarized.

"Unless it proves easier to merely destroy them and crush their little dreams before they even have a chance to chase them," Harmony muttered.

"Destabilization might benefit us in ways we can't yet fathom," Phineas said, voice as calm as a stoic sage. "Even after Etherdale is ours, a mad, paranoid king makes the prospect of hidden enemies excellent fodder for psychological warfare."

Every once in a while, someone glanced my way, expecting me to speak up the way they were accustomed to. But I couldn't say it—I refused.

I let Blade do it instead.

Blade's eyes flickered from mine to Evie's. "You can't return to the born until after you've recovered from the turning ritual. Princeton needed three days minimum, sometimes longer, before he could wield any amount of his power again. And you need to gather your strength starting, well, *today*."

Evie frowned. "That's so much wasted time," she said.

I gripped the armrest, irritated that she was already fighting against taking care of herself. And worse, she wanted to harm herself in order to be with Aster again as soon as possible.

My tattoos burned, and a sudden charge of dark power in the air had all attention turning toward me.

I still didn't speak. Evie reached for my hand where it gripped her thigh.

"Juliette needs to be taken out before the turned of Ravenia unmask and rise from the underground. That's only a month away," Blade said. "If you think you can do this, then we need to craft a plan."

"I can," Evie said, squeezing my hand. She perked up, her back straightening, her own power a current that traveled through her skin to mine.

It was the power that strengthened me every time her blood slid down my throat.

I hated how much I loved her fire, her violence. When it was also what ripped my fearful heart to shreds.

"The window for gathering information and exercising potential psychological warfare from within is *before* you assassinate Juliette, of course," Blade continued.

Evie seemed troubled by this, even as she nodded. "That has to be the finale."

"Right. Once you break character in Aster's manipulative narrative, all bets will be off. They will seek to capture or kill you by any means necessary," Blade said.

I couldn't even look at Evie. I glowered at the table instead.

"It's a tricky game," Harmony sighed. "Like Evie said, the born appeared surprised by her acceptance of Aster's invitation. It's as dangerous as it is advantageous to send the backbone of the clan into a den of enemies. It makes it easier to underestimate her and also introduces doubt about Evie's loyalties or role here. Still, we must assume that anything they tell Evie, the born may *want* to get back to us. They could see Evie as their own avenue to mental warfare."

"The born know virtually nothing about us," I said, breaking my silence. The words felt raw and scratchy as they left my throat. "We don't know what *they* know, and they don't know our true capacities, intelligence, and connections across the realm. Maybe it's a bluff that they hold zero concern for our magnitude, maybe it's not. They *do* underestimate us. They have no idea about the underground, and they think we are posturing, angsty adolescents. We've been concealing our true nature for eighty years. They're even hungrier for information than we are."

Phineas's eyes opened. They locked on Evie. "Are you psychologically fit to be a double agent?"

Evie bristled. Her eyes widened before becoming bold and narrow.

He only continued. "Can you control your emotions? Can you lie with ease? Can you withstand potential traumatic experiences and still complete your mission? Do you understand that they will be monitoring your every word and facial expression for intel, and any *truth* you uncover from them may have been slipped on purpose?"

The love of my life didn't back down. Even as my gaze caught on the bandage around her hand, the admission that she'd *lost control of her emotions* once already.

I wanted to tell the room Evie was unfit. That she struggled to lie, that she wasn't healed enough, that she was too empathetic and prone to manipulation.

But I didn't. Because when Evie was backed into a corner, she was able to do the unthinkable. She was able to let go of all of her limitations if it meant protecting herself and her family.

I felt that poisoned needle in my gut as if she'd done it all over again.

"I will let nothing get in the way of avenging Princeton and the clan."

A current of anger and grief bound the room together before it was swiftly alchemized into hunger. For vengeance, retribution, and a righting of justice's scales.

"I know it isn't fair for me to take this kill, when you all knew Princeton for far longer. But if this is how I can be of service, let me," she said. She looked around the room, and her humility and genuine spirit melted my comrades.

Lachlan nodded. "Shall we begin?"

He said it to the table, but he was really asking me. As soon as I nodded, my dearest friends peppered Evie with their generosity. They gave wisdom, helped outline potential obstacles and solutions, and they answered her questions about born customs and political intricacies.

CLAIMED BY FANGS AND DARKNESS

And I started advising too, because I had no other choice. My love needed to outweigh my fear.

For her, always for her.

∾

A DATE HAD BEEN SET for my soulmate to see the man who called her his bride. Again.

"We'll meet you there," I said to Blade and Harmony. They were going to accompany us to meet Idris for lunch.

"He's good, you know," Blade said, stopping just before the door. He smiled at Evie. "Idris. He's been downplaying his skills to you, I think. He was at the top of his class in all his fighting courses at Etherdale. For a newborn, he's killing it."

Evie released a relieved breath. "I had no idea—about being top of his classes. But of course, I didn't. He knew how much I hated that he was in them to begin with. Thank you, Blade. I'm glad he's doing well."

"Evie, he is thriving," Harmony said. "The bloodlust is painful, but it's temporary. What happened wasn't ideal, but Idris was always going to choose this path."

Some buried guilt lessened, I could see it in the sudden drop of Evie's shoulders, the surprise in her eyes.

After they both slipped through the door, I let go of my own buried emotions.

Alone with Evie, my shadows bled. I stepped closer and stared down at her as she assessed me with those big, gray eyes.

"Why didn't you tell me?" I demanded. "About Aster writing to you?"

Evie blinked. Her past trauma made her sensitive to criticism and displeasure from authority figures. But I *was* displeased. I softened myself the best I could, and our shadows grew tangled at our feet.

MAGGIE SUNSERI

I tasted her fear through the bond. Her guilt. Her drive to make things right again.

"It was just a polite follow-up," she said. "And you were already hurting. I don't like to cause you pain or… anger."

I cursed, running a hand through my hair. "Angel, I am not angry at *you*. Please understand that."

She analyzed my features, which were likely doing little to prove my point.

"I'm doing everything I can to give you your freedom," I said. "Even if it's fucking killing me to put you into such a dangerous position, unable to fight by your side. But keeping things from me isn't helping. It would hurt me far more to think you're hiding the truth, even if you think you're protecting me."

Her lower lip wobbled. She took a steadying breath. "What if someone hurts me in some way? What if the born cross a boundary before I've killed Juliette? Would you still allow me to fight?"

Power rattled against my bones. Deep, icy hatred fought to bleed from my pores. A muscle in my jaw feathered. I couldn't look at Evie anymore—I closed my eyes instead.

"If the born break their word and hurt you, I will declare war myself," I said.

There were three long beats of silence.

"Even if it ruins the plan you've been building for a century?"

I gripped her waist and tugged. Evie exhaled shakily. I needed to know she was still within reach, that I hadn't lost her.

"I've always accepted that the born may throw a wrench into every aspect of my plan," I said. "War is never perfect; war is war."

Evie was silent. And I could feel it through the shadows: her hesitation, her worry, her fear for mortals caught in the crossfire.

I was being split in two. The side of me who was married to

cosmic justice, devoted to the clan and Ravenia's mortals was at odds with the part of me whose highest purpose was to protect Evie and the light of her beautiful soul.

"We *are* fighting side by side," Evie said. "Always."

When I opened my eyes, she was thumbing her collar. The heart that bled for her skipped a beat. The deep, enduring intimacy of a simple piece of jewelry couldn't be understood by just anyone. But Evie understood. She'd always seen me as reverently as I'd seen her.

"You're mine to protect and cherish, do you remember that, sweet girl?" I asked, my throat tight with intensity.

"I want to protect you too," Evie said. "And our family."

I didn't want to nod, but I did it anyway. "I know you do. My love isn't sane. Never has been. I'm not a holy man, angel. I'm your jealous, vengeful God. You have your freedom, and I have mine."

In other words, I made no promises on what would happen if the born laid a hand on her. That was who I was, and Evie knew it. I wouldn't apologize for killing the human boy, and I sure as fuck wouldn't apologize for storming Conrad's tasteless estate and ripping each vampire apart, skin from bone.

Evie sighed. "I understand. I love you, Kylo."

"I love you too, my innocent, harmless little flower petal who wouldn't decapitate a fly," I teased. My chest was still tight, my anger a poison rotting me from within.

But I teased Evie if only to see that adorable glare and half-smile.

She melted into my chest, and as I held her, I cursed the world for putting her in a position to be hurt again.

If Evie thought my handling of her ex was extreme, she had no idea what I was truly capable of.

I shuddered at her soft touch against my back, the love that poured from her palms. I could see so clearly the future we deserved. Evie's cabin in the woods, travel and adventure, a sprawling garden and shop for her to sell witchy goods. Her head in my lap as I read her philosophy, laughing at her witty, scathing criticisms of nihilism.

"I see it too," Evie whispered.

I held her tighter.

38

EVIE

"They're here early," Blade said. "Can they join us?" He was nearly bouncing with excitement as he looked up from his journal.

Kylo glanced at me and Idris and made a quick calculation.

Nervousness and curiosity wove through my spirit, and I could tell my brother felt similarly as he straightened in his seat. Idris sat across from me as I ate.

"Bring them in," Kylo said.

They were talking about the leaders of the Serpent Clan, our strongest allies.

Blade beamed. Blade, Harmony, and Kylo were in their own conversation, standing off to the side of the table as Idris and I chatted.

I set down my sandwich, the only one in the room doing more than merely nibbling at mortal food.

Seeing Idris drink blood was jarring, to say the least. "You didn't tell me you were top of your class in your fighting courses."

Idris cocked his head. "Can't imagine why." He shrugged. "I surprised myself. I thought my insomnia was hurting my potential, but I don't know—it came naturally to me, I guess. It was healing to feel like I had at least some amount of power."

I smiled. "I'm sorry I ever held you back. I just wanted to keep you safe."

"I know, Evie," he said. "I've started seeing an emotional healer. A witch allied with the clan."

I grinned. "Good, Idris. That makes me really happy to hear."

"You should see one too," he said pointedly. "Now more than ever." He frowned.

Similar to Kylo, Idris was *not* enthused about my sudden role as a double agent. But Idris and I were both learning how to care for each other in healthier ways. To support each other without falling back on old fear-based scripts.

We were learning together.

I nodded. "You're right. I'll see what Kylo recommends." Anyone I divulged personal information to would need to be carefully vetted. "What about architecture? Do you miss it?"

Idris shrugged. "I don't miss all the reading and homework."

I rolled my eyes. Fanged or not, Idris was clearly still his age.

"But yeah, I do. I can't do it all, not right now. I have plenty of time to circle back." His lips curved.

His smile was quick to fade, and I couldn't help the creep of guilt. I wasn't used to being the one *causing* the worry.

"I'm going to be okay," I said. "We all are. Mena's protective wards are strong. I'll know if anyone threatening crosses her path. And I—I have all of you." I nodded toward the skilled, century-old vampires to our right. "I couldn't outrun my fate."

Idris tentatively reached for my hand, and my chest warmed. "I think I've always been waiting for you to remember who you are." His soft brown eyes oozed with emotion before they shifted into something more reserved.

I squeezed his hand.

He let go and leaned back in his chair. "And now we get to be frightening, shadow-wielding, vampire killers together. Still pretty stoked that I'm not dead."

I smiled in spite of myself, shaking my head at him.

"Did you tell her about yesterday?" Harmony asked Idris.

Idris's eyes lit up. "Well, it's not that big of a deal yet. But my shadows did something new."

For the first time in our relationship, I leaned into Idris's excitement for violence. It was selfish and hypocritical not to. We all chose our paths.

And his death had been the harshest wake-up call of all.

"Spill."

Idris mirrored my excitement, relaxing in his seat. "I don't know how useful this is, but um, they sort of allowed me to speak to the vines on the walls. And then I could command the vines themselves, getting them to wrap my sparring partner."

"Earth magick," Harmony said. "Just like his sister."

Idris groaned the moment tears sprung to my eyes.

"Hey!" I wiped at my eyes. "You got to be mushy, now it's my turn."

"If you must."

I laughed. "I must."

Kylo chuckled, and I hadn't realized he'd refocused on me and Idris. But at the sound of the door opening in the underground dining room, all five of us were quick to redirect our attention.

In walked Allie, and behind her, a set of turned vampires.

I was vaguely aware of my lips parting and eyes widening. I wasn't sure what I was expecting, but those expectations had been blown out of the water.

The man's hair was ash blond, cut shorter on the sides and long and spiky at the center. His eyes were uniquely green. His walk was powerful, hands in his dark trouser pockets, and his green shoes appeared to be made from reptile skin.

The woman was equally striking, with light blue eyes that

were electric, magnetizing. Her full, wavy brown hair came down to her chest. Her smile was relaxed, confident. A scar across her cheekbone blemished her fair skin, only adding to her undeniable allure. Her clothing—a silk navy blouse and sleek black pants that showed off her lethal, feminine build—was as fashionable as her male counterpart's.

Kylo caught the look on my face and lifted a brow. A mix of possessiveness and amusement crossed his features before he stepped forward.

He extended his hand. "Clarke and Vesper of the Serpent Clan," he announced to the room. "Welcome. I'm Kylo."

The man shook his hand first with a warm smile, and the woman followed. My own possessiveness rose to the surface, even if it was a little irrational. I couldn't help but compare Vesper's unique, mature beauty to my own for the briefest of moments.

They both appeared to be turned in their thirties, a tad older than the rest of us. But it was unclear their true age, underneath the mask of immortality.

"Thank you for your hospitality," Clarke drawled. He scanned the room as Kylo introduced the rest of us.

"Blade and Harmony share the second-in-command position," he said.

"Clarke and I are co-leaders. Best friends, not lovers, for those curious," Vesper said with a seductive smile. She gazed at Clarke adoringly. "Our forces are on track to complete the final port raid in three weeks tops, maybe sooner. As soon as they have a chance to land, regroup, and organize, we'll be ready."

Kylo nodded. "Perfect. By then we'll have our own poisons to contribute."

He glanced my way. I was grateful to have met the group of allied mortals for many reasons, but especially now that they were helping me craft Hekatean goods for war.

I'd learned that the Serpent Clan was chiefly responsible for intercepting and stealing Valentin imports on their way to the born. It was an increasingly dangerous business these days, but a necessary one with Earle doing everything in his power to hoard potions and poisons.

They were stationed on Ravenia's Western coast, closest to Valentin and just outside our biggest port city. Their numbers and power rivaled ours, which made them crucial to our plan to take back the city and secure this region for the turned.

"It was a tough decision, but we knew this was where we were most needed," Clarke said. His cool confidence blended with a gentle empathy as he regarded his comrade.

Vesper nodded. "It was time I return. I've been incubating long enough." Fire sparked in her piercing blue eyes, and when she looked at me, her smile was nearly conspiratorial. "He'll be surprised to see what I've become. He'll be surprised I'm alive at all."

My witchy senses felt the magnitude of her next words before they were spoken.

"I've come to kill my husband, Conrad Nighswander."

I was slow to scan the room, to recognize that Kylo, Blade, and Harmony were as shocked by this admission as I was.

Clarke again reached for Vesper's hand with tenderness. And the touch melted some of Vesper's hardened edges.

Beneath the heat of her rage, it was grief that marred Vesper's soul.

"We may have similar stories to share. I'd love to tell you mine, when you're ready," I said, the first to speak. "I'm sure it was a long journey."

Idris and Kylo exchanged a shocked look that irritated me. As if they were aghast by my volunteering to socialize. Yes, I was stranger-averse. But it was different when I knew someone might understand me on a fundamental level.

I was still learning how to be close to others, but deep

connection was the reason I'd chosen life over the gentle release of death.

And in studying Vesper's complex, vivid aura barely visible from her physical form—I could tell she'd made a similar choice, once.

"I'd love that, Evie," Vesper said. "How about we all reconvene tomorrow evening, somewhere above ground?" She glanced up at the bright, decorative ceiling and the warm lights that mimicked an early afternoon sun. "As lovely as you've made this space, I must admit I'm hungry for a dazzling view of the city. If you would be so kind as to indulge me."

Vesper transformed again, a seductive air about her that lit up the room with electricity.

"Done," Blade said. He appeared spellbound, trying to absorb as much of Vesper as possible with his unflinching gaze. All of his imposing body was angled toward her, his chest open and muscles flexed.

Now Harmony and I exchanged a look. We both quickly glanced away, but it was too late. We both burst into giggles, covered up by throat clearing noises.

A grin spread across Clarke's face. Kylo shot us a glare as if to say *knock it off,* but his eyes couldn't help but melt when they met mine.

"Please excuse them," Kylo said. "We'll escort you back to your rooms and let you rest. If you need anything, don't hesitate to alert your assigned attendants or message us directly."

"Much appreciated, friend," Clarke said. "It's a pleasure to finally put such elegant, moving letters to a face."

"Likewise," Kylo said, his adorable dimple peeking through.

Kylo's charm was completely dialed up, and it turned me on to see him this way—a respected leader, even to those he'd never met before.

Kylo caught my hooded stare, his eyes flashing equal intensity, before he turned back to our guests. "We can talk shop soon, but rest assured, nothing would bring me greater pleasure than allowing you to dispose of Conrad as you see fit, Vesper."

Vesper nodded, something in her features relaxing. She gave a gracious nod, though it was clear she wouldn't have taken any other answer.

As they left, the reality of her admission sank in.

My leg bounced with nervousness and excitement. There was this undeniable energy Vesper and Clarke left in their wake. It felt like The Tower, in the best way possible.

An inevitable change. A crumbling of the old to make way for the new.

There were two—nearly three—victims of born-mortal marriages on the board, and two of them had clearly fought for their own freedom and the protection of their fellow mortals.

While Juliette had chosen the exact opposite.

39

EVIE

We gathered on a rooftop in a turned-dominated part of the city. The building was on the flashier side, complementing the stylish energy of Clarke and Vesper. Kylo certainly knew how to dazzle. Lights were strung above us, and a few attendants meandered about. Food and drinks were on several tall circular tables.

Kylo had dressed me in another sexy gown, a beautiful shade of dark plum. We were all dressed up tonight. I had to make a concerted effort to stop staring at Kylo's sleek, devastatingly dark and powerful outfit. The dress pants, black jacket, and deep green button-down, the powerful leather shoes that he'd made me kiss before we left the house. I imagined those shoes pinning me to the ground...

I gave my head a little shake to reboot my sinful thoughts.

While Kylo, Idris, Blade, and Harmony stopped to chat with Clarke, I joined Vesper to look out over the city.

She was in a striking black dress with a slit up to her hips on either side. Her arms were folded over the railing. In the distance, we could make out a group of born in burgundy

CLAIMED BY FANGS AND DARKNESS

walking in a military formation down one of Etherdale's main streets.

She glanced at me. "Your clan is doing the right thing by waiting for the right time to strike. But I know it must be difficult to watch."

"Incredibly. My heart breaks for our city."

Vesper nodded. "Sometimes collective heartbreak is the necessary catalyst for real change." She returned her gaze to the born patrolling the streets—streets that were once lively but now lay barren.

The spirit of the city still prevailed. It shone in the glittering lights, the sprawling gardens, regal libraries and academic buildings, the resiliency of mortals still living and loving and fighting.

Somewhere, right now, mortals were breaking ordinances to dance together. A human was reading a forbidden text. A witch was breathing life into a defiant candle spell.

Vesper looked at me again, and this time, she seemed to see right through to my deepest thoughts. Light entered her eyes, a warmth I craved as much as I cowered from.

"The stories we're swapping tonight are similar, aren't they?" Vesper asked. Her scar was nearly luminescent under the witch lights.

"Yes, and no," I said. "I escaped before I was forced to marry."

Vesper's eyes softened, relief washing over her features. "Praise be to Selena... and Helia?"

I affirmed her intuition about my parentage with a nod.

Her raw empathy touched me. It was unusual for me to feel so instantly comfortable with someone.

But I'd been changing for a while now.

"Looking out over Etherdale..." Vesper faltered and cleared her throat, as if overcome with some deep, unknowable emotion. "... it feels like I've found something. I always feel that way when I see a cityscape."

She smiled, and for a moment, I saw through her maturity gleaned through trauma to the human beneath.

I smiled too. We walked together to the others, and after a few more moments catching each other up to speed on clan happenings, we sat in a cozy nook in the corner of the roof.

Blade and Clarke drank whiskey. Kylo and I shared a fruity seltzer. The passing of our glass back and forth made Idris roll his eyes. Vesper smiled.

Idris nodded at me before I began, giving me the burst of strength that I needed to tell our story.

When I revealed the identity of my promised husband, Vesper's eyes flashed. Clarke lifted his brows.

None of us had any idea how interconnected our fates had been woven. But it didn't surprise a witch like me.

"Thank you for sharing this with us," Vesper said. She glanced from me to Idris. "You are both so young to be this wise, strong, and purposeful. What a gift. I'm sorry you endured such grief to get here."

"Thank you," Idris said, as I parroted the same.

Clarke reached for Vesper's hand, squeezing it once as if transferring strength through touch. It was her turn now.

"I was not born to the Servants of Lillian," she said. "I was a human courtesan in King Earle's court."

Oh. *Oh.*

Kylo's hand paused its gentle stroke just above my knee.

From what I'd heard and read in novels, only the best made it to such a cut-throat position. And one needed to be a masterful seducer to maintain their place at court, especially when incubi and succubi dominated the profession. Humans didn't have the luxury of sex magick on their side.

I had to admit I'd always looked down on courtesans who served the born, not because of the sex work, but because of *whom* they were entertaining.

"It was as brutal and exciting as you could imagine," Vesper said, her eyes alight. "Ever since I was a child, I was blessed and cursed with the insatiable desire to eat the whole world."

I could see it now—the evidence of Vesper's magnetism, the way she reeled us all in with ease. Her voice was smooth, loud enough to be heard but low enough to keep us leaning forward. Confidence bled from her every pore, giving her an ethereal glow.

"I've always wanted it all. Novelty, adventure, sex, and indulgence of all shades and colors. I was raised in a tiny, conservative, mortal-centric town in the rural north. My family did everything in their power to keep me away from the city. But I couldn't be denied."

"Still can't, some might say," Clarke drawled. His eyes danced with teasing adoration.

She batted her eyes at him before refocusing on us. "I loved my time as a courtesan in Prospyrus. I could spend hours talking about the people I met and the conversations I had. The art and the food. The performances, exhibitions, and music. Working my way up to King Earle's court was everything I'd ever wanted. All the luxury and stimulation in the world was at my fingertips. I saw myself as a student of life. I wanted to learn and experience everything I could." She paused, her smile slowly fading. "Insatiability casts a nasty shadow, however. The net I cast brought in more than beauty. Evil is drawn to the light just as strongly."

The hairs on the back of my neck tingled. I was hanging on Vesper's every word. We *all* were.

"Courtesans are respected in King Earle's court. They are treated with dignity and spoiled lavishly. Why else would intelligent, beautiful mortals flock to serve the born?" She sighed. "I was naive. My upbringing had sheltered me. Because my town was protected from the born, it was hard for me to understand the darkness festering in the realm. I thought my family was overprotective, their thinking old-fashioned or repressive. And to be fair, it is true that mortals are treated best in Prospyrus. Of course, I witnessed and experienced born violence, but I also knew born who were protective and virtuous, at least on some level. My worldview divided the born into bad apples versus the noble, those who abided by traditions and treated me well and those who were lost to cruel hedonism. I was lured easily into my line of work, and my patrons enjoyed keeping me happy. I also reveled in the freedom my lifestyle provided me. I belonged only to myself, or so it seemed. I could do or be anything I wanted. Money and access were never a problem. I believed I was living out my ultimate dreams."

I could see it now—why someone like Vesper would be drawn to such a life. While I'd hid from the world, she'd bathed in the world's depths with reckless abandon.

"The first time I met Conrad, I found his enigmatic presence seductive." Fire consumed Vesper's entrancing blue eyes. "He set his sights on me immediately, paying attention to no one else during his diplomatic stays at court. He was cold, unreadable, except when he allowed me to see these brief glimpses of something *more* underneath. He spoke to me about science, astronomy, and logic. He remembered everything I ever told him with an intensity I thought charming. He brought me gifts that were meaningful to me, unique and specific. His visits became more frequent, his stays longer. His possessiveness was apparent early on, but he wasn't violent or controlling. Not at first. He was patient. His advances were flattering. His manipulation was expertly crafted, doled out slowly over time."

Clarke's eyes mirrored his friend's fire, his hand finding hers again. The tenderness made my heart warm as I braced for what came next.

"In the beginning, he pretended to respect my freedoms and passions. He told me he only wanted to add to the beautiful life

I'd cultivated. In reality, there was nothing he hated more than my independence and self-reliance. My friends at court tried to warn me about Conrad's conservative, religious leanings, the things he espoused behind closed doors. But I didn't listen. I was too far gone, and Conrad convinced me that the attacks were born of jealousy. He slowly isolated me from everyone but him. He poisoned me against people, activities, and places I'd once loved. He staged attacks against me from all angles, forcing me to recognize him as my protector and only true confidant. He knew I had no interest in marriage or rigid institutions of any kind. So he—"

Vesper shut her eyes, chest suddenly rising and falling. Clarke put his arm around her, rubbing her shoulder. He whispered something, but she shook her head. She slowly opened her eyes.

When they met mine, my heart already shattered for her.

"He tampered with my birth control," she said. "And I fell pregnant."

I couldn't stop my mouth from falling open. My chest tightened with grief for Vesper. Kylo swallowed, squeezing my hand as darkness churned in his eyes. Idris shook his head, empathy pooling in his features the same as Blade and Harmony.

"He told me I was notoriously forgetful, that I clearly hadn't taken my last dose as I should've. He let me feel so guilty and distraught, and then he promised to take care of me. But when I told him I'd be visiting a healer to terminate the pregnancy, the mask finally dropped. He'd been slowly infecting my mind with confusion, isolation, and doubts about my own perceptions and views of the world. He shamed me for making such a choice, ignoring all of my protests that most babies conceived to vampire-human pairings were sick and unviable. Those that survived, of course, were succubi and incubi. He told me it would devastate him if I were to murder his child; he said his bloodline was strong, and me and the baby were divinely protected. I was only twenty-five at the time, and it felt like my life had only just begun—before I met *him*."

I was sick to my stomach. All that had once been bright and infectious about Vesper had dimmed, as if mirroring the transformation Conrad had thrust upon her. The youth he'd stolen.

"He somehow got me fired from my dream position at court, and my entire world crashed down around me. I had only him, by his design. He convinced me to come back with him to his estate, to take a break and clear my mind. He promised me I could still see a healer to terminate the pregnancy if I chose, which was a lie, of course. The mask had already slipped before, but now it was obliterated. The man I met in Prospyrus was not the same lord who brought me to his country estate. He allowed me to believe we were going to his residence in the city, but that had been another lie—even as he convinced me that it was my fault I had *misunderstood* him. Now I was in a small, born-ruled town, completely alone, pregnant, and trapped. He was controlling and volatile, his coldness wielded as a weapon. Now that he had me, all pretenses were gone. He was cruel. Nothing I did was ever good enough for him. He told me he detested my impurity and my past. He hated everything about me, really."

Vesper took a break to sip her water.

"Why? Why choose *you* if he clearly wanted the exact opposite?" I asked.

Vesper's laugh was bitter and humorless. "That's the thing about men like him. They want a challenge. They don't want someone who is already pliable and easy to control. They want someone who shines, someone free and independent and powerful. They want to *break* you. Like it's an art form. And he did break me. While his healers ensured my baby was healthy, Conrad meticulously destroyed every ounce of my self-worth and sense of reality. By the time he first struck me, we were already married, and I was three months away from giving birth. It was in that moment that I made a vow." Vesper's palms glowed, a tiny flame escaping her fingertip. It danced for a moment before she pulled the magick back inside. "I didn't care what happened to me anymore. But my baby girl would never know the violence of her father. I would do anything I had to do to get her away from him. I would stay alive and healthy for *her*. Everything I did from that moment forward was for my daughter. She was the only thing that kept me sane from within my gilded cage. In the rare moments I was allowed to be alone, I sang to her. She responded to my voice, but she caused a damn racket when I sang. At one point I feared her excitement may break one of my ribs."

Tears slid down Vesper's cheeks. She smiled ever-so-briefly.

"I told her about all the things I loved. The music, the art, the people. I wanted her to experience everything that had been stolen from me." Vesper recentered herself, swallowing down a sob. She stared at the table between all of us. "Sorry, I know this has been a long story. I'll wrap things up."

"Don't apologize," Kylo said, and we all murmured the same sentiment.

"We're honored to listen," I said.

She stared off into the distance now. "I did manage to escape, after my daughter was born. Conrad was away, and I seized an opportunity to implement the plan I'd been crafting for months. I'd been blood marked, so I knew my time was limited, and soon Conrad would be alerted to my scheme and hunt me down. That was why I gave my baby to a merchant leaving for Valentin. I told her not to tell me exactly where she was going, nor did I tell her anything about myself. Only that I was an abused woman on the run. It was the hardest and best thing I've ever done, saying goodbye to my sweet girl forever." Her voice cracked, features twisting with anguish and strength.

"All my life, I'd been chasing beauty. And nothing I'd ever

experienced in my twenty-five years of indulgence had prepared me for the awe-inspiring sublimity of holding her in my arms. I know her nature makes her a target, even if her glamour gives her a human appearance. Some of my dearest friends from my old life were succubi and incubi. So I equally know how special, kind, and lovable she is." She wiped her tears and leaned into Clarke's hold as he continued to rub her shoulder. "Wherever she may be."

I'd never met a sex demon before, at least not to my knowledge, given their glamours. General sentiment wasn't favorable, as they were descended from Lillian the same as the born. Sometimes the born even used them as spies. But they were also half-human, and they hadn't chosen their lineage. I imagined there were good and bad uses of their powers the same as with witches. And like a half-witch, they appeared human and had stronger, more desirable blood.

Vesper swallowed. "He found me soon after I said goodbye to my daughter. I didn't escape him for another two years."

My stomach lurched.

Vesper had regained a semblance of composure, her face changing into something more wrathful now instead. "You could imagine how he treated me during that time. He couldn't torture my baby's location out of me, because not even I knew where she was. Only that Valentin's vampire-free dry lands were the safest place in this world for her. Once I escaped for good, I had a witch obliterate the blood bond so Conrad could never find me again. I almost died during the procedure, and I entered a fugue state soon after. I somehow found myself on the West Coast, in Juniper, where I'd given my daughter to a fellow mother. I was the closest to Valentin I could get in Ravenia, and that was where I decided to stay. I met Clarke, and he saved me from this haze of dissociated numbness. He helped me heal and find my purpose again. After years of stability, I became turned.

I gave myself a new name, and I dedicated myself to a new mission."

She smiled, cheeks stricken with tears. This time she let the flame in her palm dance wildly.

"To destroy my husband, his friends, and everything his cold, soulless heart holds dear."

40

EVIE

"I once believed that the monarchy protected us from born tyranny," Vesper said. "If only the born followed the rules and acted with class and sensibility like those in Prospyrus, then all would be well. But as I said, I was naive. I see the truth now. After all, Earle and the council never denied Lord Conrad a seat at the table or rescinded his title. To be complacent is to be complicit. Monsters who know how to play the game might be the worst monsters of all."

I was in awe of Vesper. She didn't shy away from her story or her emotions, and now she fell back into a position of strength. The scar across her cheek took on a new light.

"I'm so sorry," I said. "You're incredible. I'm glad you're both here."

"And you as well," Vesper said. "I wasn't always so spiritually attuned. But I feel it now—the web of connection that has bound us all together. I do not think it a coincidence we named ourselves the Serpent Clan, when that is a symbol of Hekate."

Powerful chills swept over my skin. I'd told them a bit about Hekate already, as they were curious about the name switch.

"I had a vision of snakes when I turned," Clarke said, his eyes dancing. "Snakes and fire. The fire was clearly Vesper."

Vesper's lips curved.

"I, too, was not always as spiritually aware," Kylo said. "I was open and well-read, but I was more focused on philosophy and tangible, corporeal action and affairs. I've always had a higher power, and I encouraged that in my clan as well. But Evie showed me how crucial the otherworld has always been, how important the ethereal to a life well-lived and a revolution well-fought. Now I see it everywhere—the connections, the serendipitous twists of fate, the wisdom, blessings, and lessons from beyond." He grinned, and I blushed furiously. "*Magick is falling in love*, Evie once told me. *With the unseen world and its inhabitants.* I can feel that now more than ever before."

My eyes rounded. My body swelled with emotion.

Idris didn't roll his eyes or make a face as he watched us.

This time, he smiled.

Vesper shook her head and sighed. "I love *love*," she murmured wistfully.

"Aren't they so cute you could die?" Harmony asked.

"Absolutely," Clarke said with a heavy nod. "Speaking of intertwining fates, we have officially made contact with someone close to Rune in Aristelle."

And just like that, Kylo forgot all about me.

"Too soon for either party to reveal much, as tensions are peaking in Aristelle, and we have yet to rise from the underground. Rune won't want to jeopardize relations with the crown at a time like this. But we now have an open line of communication."

"Perfect," Kylo said. Excitement bled through the cracks of his clan leader mask. "That's all we need for now. I will make my bid for a diplomatic meeting after we secure Etherdale."

Vesper frowned as she stared off into the distance. I wondered if she was thinking about her daughter. Had she ever thought about trying to find her, now that her blood bond with Conrad had been broken? Or did she still think it too big of a risk? Maybe by the time Vesper was stable and turned, she figured her daughter was better off without such a huge disruption to her life. I knew it wasn't my place. I couldn't imagine the emotional complexity of a situation like this, but I wondered all the same.

Kylo decided it was time to bring them in on our mission with Conrad and Aster, as difficult as it was for him to talk about. I leaned in close as he explained.

Vesper's eyes widened and then narrowed. Clarke straightened.

"Do you have any insights into the nature of their relationship?" Kylo asked. "Or a potential play for the crown? I know this must be difficult—"

Vesper cut him off. "This is war. I know what I signed up for, and I've done my healing. This is why I'm here." She regarded me fiercely, almost protectively. "I don't like that you're doing this either, but I would do the same in your shoes."

I nodded, relieved and soothed by her presence.

"Aster absolutely visited Conrad at his estate while I was being abused, and I saw them together at court a few times as well. One of the more palatable born men, a councilman named Kole Tefar, hated their guts. He was one of the people who tried to warn me about Conrad's religiosity. Kole is as loyal to the crown as they come, and he would often speak of Conrad and Aster's arrogance. He felt as though Earle and other council members weren't seeing some of the southern lords for who they really were."

Kylo's powerful mind churned. Blade made similar calculations. They both exchanged a look, an unspoken conversation unfolding as Vesper continued.

"Whether they want to take Earle's place, or help someone else do so, I can't say. It's possible this idea was conceived after

I'd already escaped. If Aster was intrigued by your power when you were a child, perhaps that marks the start of their treasonous ambitions. They certainly have the motive. Conrad's religiosity was rooted in the same framework of the Servants of Lillian, even if he preferred an unwilling mortal to a willing, groomed tithing."

I swallowed, and Vesper's face softened.

"Or they just want to take over this region and turn it into a prosperous, slave-trade-centered playground for the born," Clarke said.

Blade nodded, weighing these ideas as a crease formed between his brows.

"We don't have much time now," Vesper said. "I think if you can't make headway in your next two visits with Aster, you must transition into luring the witch away for a kill. I don't want you making that strike when you're on their turf."

"Agreed," Kylo said, his features relaxing as he found an ally in Vesper. "This was our thinking as well."

Vesper sipped her drink. "I want to be able to help."

"And kill Conrad," I said.

Her smile was all charm. "Yes." She pinned me with something more serious. "But I also don't want you taking unnecessary risks. We're in this together, okay? Don't forget that. Let's get them to play by *our* rules for a change."

Some amount of weight lifted off my shoulders. I couldn't help but nod, and I watched as the movement lessened Kylo and Idris's tension too.

It had recently felt like it was all up to me, despite clan support. I was grateful for the opportunity to be a part of something so much greater.

War talk faded, but its heavy cloud never fully dissipated.

For the rest of the evening, we enjoyed each other's company, and more of the clan slowly trickled up to join us.

Turned musicians played live music, and soon it was a full-on party.

I'd never seen so many turned above ground, not like this. And for a moment, I imagined how it would feel if we could exist like this forever.

From Kylo's arms I watched Idris talk to a couple of his friends. He laughed and clinked glasses with them before disappearing into the crowd of dancers.

Vesper had an entire crowd of people gathered around her, as if she were holding court. She lounged on a velvet couch and spoke animatedly, her smile warm and eyes hooded. I was quite sure she was seducing them all at once.

Kylo kissed the top of my head. "You really like her, don't you?"

I smiled. "Who wouldn't?"

"Good," he said. "I want your life to be full of love. Not just from me. You deserve your own world outside of me, too. You know that, right?"

I stared into his earnest pools of blue. "I know. The assumptions I made in the wake of your murder-coverup couldn't have been more wrong. I know you were never trying to control me—not like *that*." I released a breath, thinking about Vesper's horrific story. "I think intimacy is hard for me. But I'm learning. Maybe I would've been more insatiable if I hadn't been born so afraid."

Kylo gripped me tighter. "Everyone who has ever truly known you has loved you. Take your time, baby. But believe that you'll be rewarded for your brave vulnerability."

"You are unrealistically emotionally advanced for a man," I muttered.

Kylo grinned. "Thank you, angel." He stared at my lips. "Like you said, I simply needed those extra eighty years to approach maturity."

I laughed before snuggling into his hold. The music washed

over us. And after a few more blissful moments in our bubble, I pulled away.

"I am ready to socialize again," I declared with a serious expression.

Kylo mirrored my faux severity. "Let us socialize, then."

He shook his head with a chuckle as I grabbed his hand and waited for him to steer me in a new direction.

Parties were too daunting. Approach a pre-formed huddle of people and insert myself into their conservation? I would rather be shot with a crossbow.

So, I let Kylo do it for me.

Bexley flirted with Harmony off to the side. A few turned I didn't know were in the mix, along with a handful I'd crossed paths with before.

"Do you read romance novels?" one of the women asked me. After I nodded, she squealed. "You must join our new book club!"

Lachlan lifted a brow. "Absolutely insane time to start a book club."

A few vampires laughed, but the woman put a hand on her hip. "We need stories now more than ever."

"True," Kylo said.

The woman beamed at Kylo's approval. Her smile was beautiful, her teeth impossibly white. She'd brushed shimmering makeup across her cheeks and eyelids, shades of red and dark pink that blended perfectly with her dark brown skin.

"I'm Darcy," she said to me. "Have you read the new Rielly book?"

"Evie," I said, though I knew my introduction wasn't necessary. "No, I've been a bit busy," I said. "I hope I can soon."

"You'll have it by tomorrow morning," Kylo interjected before turning back to the men he'd been talking to.

I blushed, and Darcy stared at me with round eyes.

"You are living every book girl's dream. I hope you know that."

I sighed. "Do I ever."

We both laughed, launching quickly into a dialogue about the author's previous books. It was funny to me that before I'd met Kylo, I'd assumed the turned were all a bunch of bloodthirsty brutes who'd never stepped foot in a library not once in their lives.

It was a blessing to have been proven wrong. Over and over again.

"I'm going to use the restroom," I whispered to Kylo.

"Down one flight of stairs," he said. "There will be an attendant to help if you get lost."

"Such little faith in me."

He kissed my temple, and I told Darcy I'd be right back.

"I need a sweet treat," she said with a nod. "You want one?"

"Always."

My smile was easy and my belly warm as I made my way to the stairs. Socializing could be fun. Rewarding, even. Who knew?

I slipped past the guards and through the door. I was giddy and laughing softly at my own witty internal dialogue, war's oppressive loom sinking further into the back of my mind.

The stairwell was quiet. No attendants to be found. I shrugged and reached for the first door on the level just below the roof. Behind me, the door to the roof opened and shut again, and someone hummed gleefully.

I stepped through the door and into an empty restaurant space. I peered around the darkness for the bathroom. Maybe the woman behind me would know?

Whoever it was hadn't followed me inside. I conjured a small witch light and found it on my own.

After, I studied myself in the ornate mirror over the sink. It was strange how much more blissful and radiant I appeared these days, when my life was objectively more precarious. Was it because I'd finally freed myself and awakened my power? Was it my dedication to the clan? Kylo's love?

It was a combination of all of it, I decided.

The empty restaurant was different as I walked back toward the stairs. It was eerier, the energetic environment more chaotic. A creeping sensation crawled up my spine, a familiar burn on my skin. The witchy warning bells went off too late.

A body slammed into me, knocking me flat on my back. A kitchen knife pressed against my throat. I went still.

"Hi, sister," a familiar, creepy voice whispered above me.

41

EVIE

J uliette straddled me, staring hungrily into my eyes. She was in a light blue dress that looked suspiciously like one that I owned.

In one movement, she could slit my throat. Adrenaline coursed through my blood, and I allowed my heart to hammer and pound. Surely, Kylo would hear it through the bond and come help me.

Several thoughts moved through my brain at once. One, Juliette had followed me *from* the roof. Which made absolutely no sense. She wasn't turned. How the fuck was she here?

Second, I wasn't supposed to be using my power. Not so close to the turning ritual. I needed all of my strength.

Not that I had a choice, with a knife against my throat. Juliette could kill me the moment she sensed me draw power.

Juliette inhaled deeply, and my face twisted in disgust.

"My creature was right. You do smell really nice," she said cheerfully.

Her *what?* A flash of memory flitted through—of the demon beast that had attacked me in the street. It had stopped just before chomping my face, staring at me in recognition as it inhaled.

Juliette must've had some kind of psychic link with her hellish creations.

"Does Aster know you're here?" I choked out beneath the pressure against my throat.

Her big gray eyes didn't falter.

I was curious, but I also needed to stall. My heart was leaping now. Kylo must've felt it. At the very least, he would check the bond once he realized I'd been gone for too long.

I couldn't tell if I was already bleeding or if the coldness of the blade was causing illusory sensations.

Juliette studied my face and my chest, soaking me up in a way that was more than violating. It wasn't sexual... it was something creepier that I didn't have words for.

She wet her bottom lip. "I've decided you can be with Sir, Evie. Our bond is too strong to be shaken. He will love you and guide you into being the best version of yourself—I can see this clearly. It was written in the stars from the beginning. You have a karmic soul tie. We *all* do."

I wanted to scream at her again, to tell her she was a fucking lunatic. But I wanted my throat to be intact even more.

"How generous of you," I spat.

She nodded, either unable to read my true feelings or uninterested in them. "Yes, I do try very hard to be good. It's difficult though, because being good means something different to each person. Have you noticed that?"

I stared at her blankly, breaths leaving me in shallow gasps.

With her knife-free hand, her finger slowly traced my discreet collar that hung just below the blade. Something strangely sad entered those empty gray depths.

"You won't tell Sir about tonight, and I won't tell him about Kylo or your tattoos or anything else that he would consider *bad*," she said, nodding her head.

What exactly did she know? And *how*? Panic was a volatile force in my guts.

The knife pressed harder. She scowled as she continued nodding, waiting for a response.

"Okay," I rasped. "Fine. I won't tell Aster."

Juliette stared hungrily at my neck, and now I knew for sure I was bleeding.

"How could I possibly believe you haven't already told him, or that you won't in the future?" I asked. Nothing about this deranged person made sense. She could ruin me. Easily.

Her brows drew close. She stroked my cheek. "I told you I would never kill you, Evie. I want you alive. Which means Sir cannot know the true depths of your darkness. We can fix all of this, okay? Once I help you back onto the path of light, you'll understand."

She smiled, and I fought the urge to recoil from her sickening touch.

"Understand what?" I croaked.

"That we're *one*, silly!"

Multiple things happened at once. First, Juliette grabbed a vial from her pocket and scooped my blood inside. Second, the door flew open.

Third, I attempted to move but couldn't—the knife must've been dipped in paralytic poison.

I watched as Kylo shouted. Juliette stared at him with a beaming smile and wide eyes for the briefest moment before launching herself out of a tall, open window.

A firebird cawed, followed by the flapping of strong wings and Juliette's maniacal giggle.

The sound that left my lips was pure, scalding frustration.

Without the knife against me, my limbs began to wake up. My hands twitched. My power stirred.

Kylo kneeled and assessed me quickly. Shadows bled from him. His voice boomed. *"What did she do?"*

"She took a vial of my blood," I spat, angry tears burning my eyes. "Temporary paralysis and a cut on my neck. Physically, I'm fine."

My tattoos emitted heat, and shadows whispered pure hunger.

"Don't, Evie. You need your strength," Kylo said as he scooped me into his arms and bent lower.

His tongue traced the wound, and the venom dulled my intensity against my will.

"She has my fucking blood," I said through a clenched jaw. "I am so *fucked*."

"Why wouldn't she have used the blood you spilled at dinner?" Kylo asked.

"It needed to have been taken. Ritualized. Harvested." I closed my eyes, listening to the sound of more people coming down the stairwell with dread. "That was my opportunity. She was alone. Aster didn't even know she was here. And now she's gone. With *my* blood. To do gods know what with it."

I remembered that Juliette had told Aster I threatened her with blood magick. That was the thing about people like her— their lies and accusations were always a reflection of their own motives and actions.

"Angel, she shouldn't have been here at all. You did not fail," Kylo hissed. "This is not on you. This building is glamoured and warded. The only mortals here were vetted and escorted, and we know them intimately."

My breath was ragged. "Just like the fucking sex dungeon. How does she keep getting into turned spaces? She wasn't only here—she was on the roof!"

Idris and Blade burst through the door. I could move a bit better now, still resting against Kylo.

"Ollie was found in a pool of his own blood in the stairwell. He's dead," Blade said. "What the hell is going on?"

Kylo's face dropped. "That witch was here, at the party, and we don't know how. She took some of Evie's blood and ran. What of the guards?"

"No one else was harmed to my knowledge. The guards from downstairs were the ones who smelled blood and alerted me," Blade said.

"You okay?" Idris asked.

I nodded. It was a low dose of venom, but it was still working well to calm my body. My mind was still holding strong to visions of gruesome violence and retribution.

"It doesn't make any sense," Blade continued. "How did she get past everyone else and only kill one attendant?"

"The one who was supposed to be in the stairwell?" I asked.

Kylo nodded.

My head spun. "She is sick in the head."

Vesper slipped into the room. I felt embarrassingly weak, more so than before. Vesper only regarded me with concern.

Idris ran a hand through his hair before rubbing his mouth. He glared out the open window. "What can she do with your blood, Evie?"

I shook my head. I clenched both my fists until my knuckles were white. "A lot of things. But I have no idea her intentions. She made absolutely no sense. She's too volatile. She's acting as a manipulated weapon for the born. But she also has her own dark motives, ones that belong only to her. She—" I choked out the next words as if they were as disgusting as Juliette was. "She has this obsession with me that is terrifying. I *hate* her."

The room was silent for two beats. I felt exposed and hot and useless.

"She is your shadow," Vesper said softly. Her piercing blue eyes slammed into me like an ocean wave.

I blinked in confusion, remembering my healing sessions with Princeton. He'd talked about an internal shadow that needed to be integrated.

"Hatred is a curious thing. It can tell us a lot about ourselves."

42

KYLO

Our investigation into Juliette's presence in a turned-controlled building proved just as fruitless as Princeton's murder investigation.

All we could assume was that she was somehow powerful enough to slip through magickal barriers. But why were the barriers still strong? Did she patch them back up? That seemed unlikely.

Even more confusing was that no one had seen a brunette witch who fit her description. It was as if she floated around the party as a ghost.

There were so many unanswered questions. And worse than the questions was the paranoia about what this unstable witch might do to the love of my life now that she had her blood.

Today was the day. After I locked Evie away from the world for three days, keeping her safe and healthy and well-rested, we were now preparing Princeton's spell room for a turning rite.

"I have a new idea," I said. "What if we—"

Evie looked up at me from her spot on the floor, drawing sigils with enchanted purple paint. "Kylo," she pleaded softly.

I sighed and stared at the wall. "I'm sorry, angel. What do you need from me?"

Evie's face relaxed with gratitude, and I felt guilty for disrupting her flow on such an important day. I was jerky and restless, trying to find any convincing argument against her plans with Aster, or any alternative to subterfuge that Evie might agree to. But now wasn't the time.

I loved her so much that it broke me. Her life was in an enemy's hands. All we could do was hope Evie's protective measures were strong, that Juliette wasn't as all-powerful as she was making herself seem. So far, nothing out of the ordinary had happened since that night.

And none of it was good enough for me. I refused to let Evie out of my sight. My body rebelled at the thought of sending her back to Aster. I'd told her that I wanted to change the plan we'd meticulously perfected, to instead lure Juliette away now rather than wait until after two more meetings with Aster. We'd fought about it until Evie sobbed, and my love splintered into opposite urges.

In the end, I'd given her freedom. Again. And I didn't feel good about it. I didn't feel noble, selfless, or divinely led.

But it wasn't about me. That was what it meant to be a revolutionary. I had to look outside of myself, even when all of me was hopelessly addicted to and possessed by another.

I took comfort in the beautifully mundane. Like that Evie and Vesper had taken to drinking coffee and reading together in the mornings on the front porch. My heart warmed every time I heard them break their comfortable silence to talk and giggle.

We'd been prepping for the ritual the past few days, and now we were doing only what must be done fresh. Final touches.

Evie was equally jittery, for her own reasons. She wanted to serve the clan to the best of her ability, and it touched me to my core.

Candlelight danced around us. Beyond the secret bookcase, initiates were gathered in groups. Evie had four rounds of approximately twenty-five humans each to turn, and I was to give them basic clan tattoos and dose them with blood to complete the rite. She'd crafted her own sigils and ink, followed each step exactly according to Hekate, Princeton, and the otherworld's instruction. If all went well, Evie would be positioned to continue bolstering our numbers as we descended into war.

She was prepared. She'd been studying and communing with her guides for weeks. I kissed her forehead.

Her eyes were wide, her heart jumping like a rabbit.

"You've got this, baby. This isn't like before—with Idris, or with your explosions. This is what you were made for. It's the same as your beautiful herbal and flower magick, just bigger."

She smiled. "Thank you."

"As soon as you enter your trance and open the circle, I'll bring in the first round."

Evie squeezed my hand. She peered over my shoulder, laughing softly. "Warwick looks so pissed."

I grinned and followed her gaze to our born vampire blood bag that was hanging in magickal suspension. I often left him visible during rituals, merely to let him watch us bastards multiply.

"Thanks again, buddy," I called. "Couldn't do it without you."

Warwick's soulless eyes glared back. His blood was in several large jars in the center of the spell circle, some of it in the ornate, ritual bowl.

Something fiery crossed Evie's features as she stared at the blood.

"I'm ready."

She stood in the center of the spell circle. I watched her transform like someone might watch an artist birth a groundbreaking piece of art. I basked in holy awe.

The darkness that bled from Evie as she chanted was that of deep space and starlight. Unfathomable. Sublime.

She called on Hekate, and I could feel it too—the flood of maternal, wise, protective energy. The spark of the revolution called for as much love as violence.

When she invoked her guides, she named Princeton directly, inviting him to be with us.

It was just a flash of curly hair and bone amulets in the corner of my eye. But it was enough to make my eyes glassy and my throat raw.

I didn't know how I was worthy enough to witness such goddess-like power. It seemed wise to fall to my knees before her.

Through my vampiric hearing, I heard awestruck murmurs from beyond the bookcase. I was quite certain Evie's booming, resounding power could be felt across the entirety of the underground.

Suddenly, a shadow wrapped around my arm. I gasped. My eyelids fluttered as thoughts and sensations flooded my mind that didn't belong to me.

Through Evie, I saw The Tower. Born falling from a great, crumbling castle, King Earle's crown struck by righteous lightning.

I saw The Star—Evie's head in my lap as I read to her, her hair adorned with glowing constellations, a gently flowing stream beside us. I drank from the water where love was certain and always enough.

Justice. Idris's head splitting open and the Whitfields' blood splattered across the walls of their basement.

The Hierophant reversed. Religion turned toward ego, a girl with a child in her arms, running. Witches gathering in secret, fingers to their lips.

Judgement. The reckoning. I saw myself on the streets of Etherdale, blood dribbling down my chin. Uniformed born lay lifeless at my feet. Smoke and death and blood swam through the air. War was more brutal than I ever could've imagined. There was no going back.

I ended up at the kitchen table, reading Mena's cards. She was cloaked in leopard print, red lips curved. She smelled like perfume and the ghost of a secret cigarette.

"You're going to be something huge, doll. You know that?"

I shook my head. I could think of nothing worse.

Until the fire scorched through the block in my throat and I hugged my thirteen-year-old self and I learned that darkness melted like chocolate on the tongue and my enemies bet on sports while children were brutalized in their basements and more than all of that—

I wasn't sorry. Mena had been right, and I wasn't sorry.

Back in the spell room, I struggled to separate myself from Evie. It was like we'd been fused. The magick she channeled was a high that surpassed that of my own. It was indescribable the way her brain worked—the ease with which she recognized symbols and connections, flowed through currents of subconscious waters to direct her psychic will.

I was in love with a godsdamned genius.

The circle was alive, sigils glowing as purifying white flames danced.

"Bring them in," Evie said.

I wanted to tell her I would do anything she ever asked of me forever, but I settled on, "Yes, angel," instead.

In a half-trance myself, I brought the first round of humans into the space. Chills swept down my spine, remembering how it felt to be in their shoes. I watched as nervousness melted into devotion near-instantly as they entered Evie's magickal world.

Flowers bloomed from the vines crawling along the ceiling and walls. Forest sounds permeated through the space.

The angel of darkness stood in a powerful purple gown before her main altar. She didn't speak, yet each initiate knew exactly where to lay. Shadows circled and whispered.

"Hekate, anoint these bodies and souls with the spirit of the revolution," Evie said. She carefully traveled through the formation of intertwining bodies, delivering a drop of her blood to each forehead.

Some initiates gasped, their eyes moving rapidly as if plagued by visions.

"Though shadows may belong to each of you, so too shall you belong to the shadows. In exchange for eternal life, you pledge your service, your devotion, and your loyalty to a power greater than yourselves. You will become one part of a whole. You will be brothers and sisters in a family that will always stand with you, whom you will protect and uplift just as they will guide you through this transition. You will be a protector of the realm, of Helia and Selena's mortal children. You may be masked today, but tomorrow, you will wear your clan tattoos proudly in a liberated world."

We shared a mournful silence together. We remembered the grief the born had callously thrust upon us. Dead family members or friends. The choices we lost, the innocence trampled upon by greed and cruelty. One woman began to weep, and Evie pressed her palm lightly over her heart. Evie's lip trembled. A spark of magick passed between them, a warm peach glow from chest to palm and back again. The woman settled.

Evie continued her careful ritual with the grace of an ancient high priestess. The blooming ceiling birthed a field of stars, like the room where I first told Evie I loved her.

I assisted her dutifully. I forgot about my quest for control. My fears and limitations. My mind cleared and made space for service. It felt like I could finally breathe again.

Chests rose and fell in unison. Hands reached for each other as these humans fell deeper under Evie's spell.

Humbled, I remembered at long last that *this* was what it was all about.

Once more sigils had been drawn and protection measures in place, Evie's eyes sharpened. She lifted a ceremonial dagger.

"Thank you for trusting me. It is only through death that we can become reborn."

43

EVIE

I killed all twenty-five humans myself. They were my responsibility. Just before their last breath, they drank born blood. I cried each time the light in their eyes drained. I watched their lives play out behind their eyelids. I saw their homes, their families, their lovers and heartbreaks, their dreams and passions and hopes for the future. I saw the lives the born had stolen from them, the dark cast of oppression across every inch of their world.

Most of all, I felt their powerlessness. The overwhelming frustration of being born so weak in a world ruled by monsters.

I freed each soul from its corporeal cage, but they remained safe within the spell circle. A shimmering mist and gusts of wind whistled through the air. Blood blossomed from each chest, trickling into grooves in the floor to feed my sigils. Power surged, reaching some ineffable peak. I was positioned at the crossroads of The World. Infinite fates spread from me in a beautiful tapestry.

Kylo watched me like he was seeing Selena herself enter a religious temple. When I made my last kill, he kneeled before me and took my hands in his. He brushed his lips against each of my knuckles.

At this moment, our dynamic was upside down. And that felt right. When I was doing magick, *I* had the power.

And it felt so fucking good.

I brushed my thumbs over the tops of his hands before slowly pulling away. "Thank you. You can get the ink now."

Kylo nodded and stood, devoted and wordless.

Unlike last time, the drain on my strength was steady and manageable. I could easily do the next three rounds at this pace.

I took back my position over the most prominent clan sigil in the center of the circle. All candles, crystals, and magickal objects were positioned in their proper places. Everything consecrated, everything blessed. Spirit allies held us in a protective cocoon.

I called to the shadows. I marked myself with born blood and licked my fingers clean.

In its bitterness, I saw The Tower one final time. I saw my father avoiding my eyes, preferring to look at the ground rather than atone for the abuse he allowed. My mother, eaten alive by shadows as she cursed my existence.

"From born blood we rise."

I raised a white pillar candle in my right hand and pointed to the ground with my left. I became The Magician, the conduit, the fate weaver.

A concentration of power entered my crown and my right hand, flowing through my body and down to my pointed fingers.

I blinked, and we were on Etherdale's streets. Fangs were bared, magick flying in all directions. We were maskless, clan tattoos proudly displayed. My chest rapidly rose and fell, a battle cry leaving my lips as I wielded godlike power.

Coveted power.

I blinked again, and I was back in the spell room. A

concentrated stream of shadow magick shot from my left hand. The shimmering gusts of mist combined with the shadow in some holy alchemy, fusing my magick with each spirit's unique signature.

A gasp left my lips, my heart pounding hard. Spirits shot back into bodies. Darkness entered mouths and nostrils.

We all gasped as one. Eyes flew open. Kylo watched me protectively, standing close by.

Hearts began to beat, forever and inevitably changed by the process of death and rebirth. Hekate had them bear witness to the plight of the realm and the truth of themselves, triggering a spiritual awakening that would combat the bloodlust of vampirism.

"Drink," I said.

Kylo moved closer to me, though it wasn't necessary.

This wasn't like the first time, when I turned Idris. I was in perfect control. These vampires were as bound to me as they were to Kylo. They wouldn't harm me.

I was their maker.

Each newly turned had a chalice of blood beside them. The final step in the process. Some hissed in pain. Eyes flashed with hunger. Disoriented bodies jerked up, confused by their own speed. Hands reached for cups.

Blood slid down throats, and I sighed in relief along with them.

Kylo's hand soothingly stroked the back of my neck. I took his hand and kissed his knuckles before giving a nod.

The tattooing portion of the ritual went beautifully. I watched as Kylo whispered reassurances to each initiate, his voice low and soothing. It was like when he helped Idris after his panic attack. Seeing the paternal side of Kylo was not only heart-melting, but it was also ridiculously sexy.

Before the second round was brought in, a strange sensation erupted in my stomach. Almost like a weight or pressure, a slight tinge of nausea. My physical and witchy senses had never been more heightened. I followed the sensation as my eyes rolled back, searching for its source.

I saw myself in a mirror. I was twirling and giggling in a ruffled pink dress.

"Thank you, Kylo!" I said.

I stepped closer to the mirror. Then, I was inside the mirror, and my own hand reached toward me. It slipped right through the glass and grabbed my wrist.

"Evie?"

I opened my physical eyes. Kylo held me upright, concern swimming in his features.

"You swayed," he said. "Are you feeling drained?"

I shook my head. "No, just witchy things," I said, my go-to non-answer. I wasn't really sure how to explain what I had seen.

"Your heart sounds great," he said. "I don't have words for the awe I feel. I'm sorry I ever doubted your fate as Princeton's successor. You're a reckoning, Evie. Judgement herself."

I kissed Kylo. On his lips I tasted star paths and battlefields.

"Thank you for believing in me," I whispered.

It was brief, the sudden flash of guilt—the reminder of the lie I kept to protect the city. As soon as Kylo knew that Aster had tasted my blood, he would launch into war before we had the help of the Serpent Clan. Before all necessary parts were in motion.

I was doing what was right. Even if I felt like the shittiest hypocrite in the world.

"You sure you're okay?" Kylo asked.

I nodded. I had to stop thinking about this—this distraction from what needed to be accomplished. There was no room for error, not now.

Tuck it away for later, Evie. For after the ritual is complete, Princeton said, loud and clear. *And tell Kylo, hi.*

It was a testament to the power we'd channeled that he was speaking so clearly.

"Princeton says hi," I said.

Kylo's face shifted, his darkly beautiful features slipping into vulnerability. He smiled, his little dimple appearing. "Tell him I say hi back."

"He can hear you."

"I miss you, brother," Kylo whispered. "Thank you for helping Evie. I know you saw her fate from the beginning. We're going to make you so fucking proud."

I took a steadying breath and rooted myself in Kylo's love.

"Let me take a moment to recenter, and I'll be ready for the next round."

Kylo kissed my forehead. "Bloodier than the floral arrangements and teas, but just as beautiful."

His lips brushed against my smile, and I stepped back into the magick of the revolution.

You're going to find what you need. Watch carefully where authority flows...

The voice slammed into me from nowhere and left just as quickly. In a brief glimpse, I saw the inside of the Nighswander Estate. A door with a bright white light emanating from the cracks around its frame.

AFTER THE LAST ROUND, I finally understood what everyone had been talking about. The moment the spell circle collapsed, so too did I, and with it, all of my strength.

As we walked back through the underground, turned spilled out of rooms to cheer. And for the first time, I didn't cower from the spotlight. I caught sight of Clarke and Vesper in the crowd. Clarke nodded deeply, and Vesper smiled. I basked in warm pride.

I wouldn't have been able to use a drop of magick if I tried. Not even a candle spell. It was like I'd given birth psychically.

Approximately one-hundred-and-nine times.

My emotions crashed as well, the nagging sense of guilt encroaching on my celebratory spirit. But each time the feeling clenched my heart, I saw the vision of the door again. The promise that I was on the right path. I would tell Kylo the moment we'd succeeded in digging up dirt on the born and killing Juliette.

Kylo sighed, stroking my cheek as I lay curled in his lap in the living room.

"I'm so evil," he said with a shake of his head.

I quirked a brow. "True, but why do you say so?"

His cock hardened beneath me, and my eyes widened in surprise.

"Don't get me wrong, seeing you in your element was immensely satisfying," he said. "But something about you being this weak, vulnerable, and needy…" He groaned. "It's so fucking sexy."

I faked a glare, knowing full well his words were traveling right down to the apex of my thighs. "That's fucked-up, Kylo."

He pouted. "I know." His hand dipped, kneading one of my breasts as I sharply inhaled. "And yet, it is true."

It was true for me too. The idea that I could no longer fight Kylo off, that I was entirely at his mercy…

He continued groping me, releasing another low groan. He could scent my arousal, hear every beat of my heart. We were more connected, inextricably intertwined, than ever before.

"Do you know how many times I've wanted to use you while you were sleeping?" he whispered, his warm breath tickling my ear.

I shuddered, shifting to straddle him. His dark eyes roamed me just as his hands did.

"To slip inside your warm, perfect little pussy or mouth,

taking advantage of my beautiful mortal doll while she lay vulnerable."

Fuck. Why was that so hot? I let out a small moan, grinding against his lap. I welcomed the filthy darkness. I bathed in all that I once denied.

My fingers traced Kylo's deadly, sharp jaw. "Do it. You have my permission," I whispered.

His eyes rolled back. He cursed, gripping me tightly as his muscles flexed. "This is why we're soulmates."

A surprised laugh burst from me. "Really, Kylo? That, specifically, is why we are soulmates?"

His grin was arrogant, devastating in a way that reached the very core of me. My grinding against the swell of his cock became needier.

"Shhh, no more thoughts for you. Only, *yes, Kylo.* Or *you're right, Kylo, just as you are correct about all other things.*"

He stole my laugh with a bruising kiss. He sucked on my lower lip, fangs teasing my plump flesh. Sensations were electric and melty under the heavy blanket of my exhaustion.

His hands slipped under the oversized shirt, trailing up and down my body in soothing, gentle strokes.

He pulled back an inch. "I don't think you will ever understand how lucky I feel," he said with a sudden earnestness. "There was a moment I wasn't sure you'd let me do life with you, not like this. I'd lost everything. Yet I knew I would be content to see you be free and loved like you'd always deserved, even if it wasn't by me."

His blue depths held me in captivation, and I struggled to breathe.

"I don't believe that," I said. "You knew I could never be free of you, no matter how hard I tried."

"You underestimate the self-hatred I harbored for breaking your trust, angel," he whispered. "All I've ever wanted was to prove to you that you were safe with me. That you would never be harmed or used or betrayed by a caregiver again."

Guilt reached for me, and it felt like a monumental step back to squash it down the way I used to deny my true self and all of that buried shame.

"I love you so much. Thank you for caring for me."

"You don't have to thank me, sweet girl."

I couldn't regress. I wanted to continue healing, being better than I once was. He deserved to know the truth.

I opened my mouth to tell Kylo what had happened, to beg him not to stop me from completing my mission. But he spoke first.

"It is equally toxic that I enjoy being the only vampire to ever taste this sweet pussy and," he leaned in close, lips skating across my jugular, "your addictive blood."

The truth once again dried up on my tongue.

It wasn't fair. Aster had violated *me*. It hadn't even been an actual feeding. I refused to let it ruin me, to cast a dark stain on my body and my relationship. I refused to suffer for the sins of another all over again.

I melted back into the safety of Kylo's obsessive certainty. Guilt slipped away as Kylo undid his pants and freed his cock.

"Be a good girl and sit in my lap, angel," Kylo said, the perfect mix of cool authority and doting gentleness.

I slipped him inside me, groaning in satisfied pleasure. I was depleted, and Kylo filled me up completely until there was nothing left but him.

"Needy and pathetically wet as always," he said sadistically, pinching a nipple until I squealed in pain. He moved me up and down as he thrust to meet me. "Good little witch. This is your purpose now, understood?"

I nodded. "Yes, Kylo."

He plunged his fingers inside my mouth. I sucked, relaxing deeper and deeper under his spell.

"Good girl. No magick this time. Just us," he said.

I traced his chest, and he rubbed my clit with his slick fingers.

"As much as I enjoyed being melded together during the ritual and seeing inside that twisted, beautiful little mind of yours."

I gasped. "What?"

He grinned. "Does that scare you, baby?"

"Yes." Now more than ever.

"Good. It's fucking sexy when you're scared of me, too. I want to be deep inside you in all ways, but your mind most of all."

He thrust hard, and I cried out.

"Shhh, you can take me. We've been practicing, remember?"

My body acted like it did *not* remember at all, actually. Yet, tiredness made it easier to let go, to relax enough to accommodate Kylo's monstrous appendage.

"That's a perfect, docile angel," he whispered. "Feel free to fall asleep at any time."

His grin was wicked, and I wondered if I really was drained enough to fall asleep with him inside me. It seemed unlikely.

He lifted me into his arms, carrying me to bed. On my side with my back to Kylo's chest, I relaxed into his hold.

Kylo reached around to grip my throat, and I nestled in even deeper.

Warm and floaty, I gasped when he entered me from behind, his strokes slow. He whispered praise in my ear, telling me how well I did today, how safe and loved I was.

All the while, he used my pussy, feeling my body beneath his shirt.

No magick. Kylo's shadows rested with mine. It was just me and him, two puzzle pieces that had always fit perfectly together. Since I first told him nihilism was intellectually lazy, and he encouraged me to stop hiding from the world.

The sick bastard coaxed me to a blissful half-asleep state, pumping in and out, lips skating across my ear.

"You've been mine since the beginning of it all, baby," he whispered. "Since we were stars, and the world was a quiet landscape of darkness and light."

Warmth spilled deep inside me, and I fell blissfully into the light.

44

EVIE

Tomorrow I would see Aster. My new recruits were successfully beginning basic training, and more prospective recruits were already moving into the queue for the next turning, whenever that may be. So much depended on the battle for Etherdale—how quickly we'd be able to take back the city and push the born out.

Aster continued to write to me, a few times a day. Or at least, that was how often I responded. I showed or told Kylo about every message.

This morning, the enchanted paper was tucked under a book on the outdoor coffee table, where Vesper and I enjoyed our coffee and reading ritual.

"I hate his guts," I said with a sip of my coffee.

"What did he say today?" Vesper asked.

"He asked me what I was reading, so I told him. And now he's mansplaining and rambling on and on about the author and the historical period he came from. It's painful to keep acting impressed and intrigued, but he eats it up every time." I rolled my eyes.

Vesper made a gagging gesture, drawing out a laugh from

me. "I love when men are pathetically desperate for us to see how very worldly and intelligent they are. None worse than the narcissistic born."

"This author would quite literally spit in Aster's face," I added.

"The truly wise and insightful people I've met in my life did not have to say so," Vesper murmured. "It was something that was felt. Intellect without empathy and awareness is useless."

"When I write back, it's like he's not even reading what I'm saying—he's just searching for the parts that are relevant to *him*. It's exactly how my ex used to communicate. We'd have these conversations where it felt like every time I spoke, he was merely waiting for me to stop so it could be his turn. Then when he did speak, it was often in these long, self-absorbed monologues."

"He only wanted to see himself reflected back in you. Men like him desire a beautiful ego-stroker with enough intelligence to understand his mind, but far too little self-respect to dare question it," Vesper said. "I know that type well."

"You must understand a lot about human nature and psychology after your time as a courtesan."

I hoped I wasn't overstepping. I found Vesper's life fascinating, especially the time before Conrad entered the scene.

Instead of closing herself off, Vesper's eyes lit up like they had when she'd first began telling her story.

"I hope this is okay to ask, but… do you miss it?"

Vesper smiled. "Yes, I do. I think a part of me will always miss the life I had. Before my sense of reality was forever changed. I'm not sure I could go back to the profession, even in a free world, not as the woman I am now. But I miss it, still, I really do. The glamour, the excitement, the endless adventure and exploration. The art of a successful seduction and the thrill of keeping the spark of desire alive. It was a life that required a certain level of naivety and ignorance in some ways. But it was also a time of immense growth, deep self-knowledge, and learning about the world and the varied people who inhabit it. I read widely, was able to speak to esteemed philosophers, playwrights, authors, artists, and politicians. A life rich in ideas was just as valuable to me as a life surrounded by luxury."

"I can see it in your aura," I said. "You come alive when you talk about that side of yourself."

Vesper's smile was tinged with sadness now. "You can't pull back the veil of ignorance. Once it's gone, it's gone. I hold no shame, not for any of it. But I know now that the structures that built the life of my dreams were the same oppressive entities that stifled so many others. Courtesans will always exist, no matter who's in power. As long as I'm alive, I will always fight for my brothers and sisters to work not only safely but also damn joyously if they so choose."

I smiled. "I will too."

Vesper's smile was crooked, the sunlight illuminating the golden undertones of her skin. She asked me more about my ex, and how Kylo and I met.

I finally worked up enough courage to say what I really wanted to say.

"If you ever want me to read your cards or anything else, I'm happy to," I offered. I didn't feel comfortable enough yet to bring up her daughter explicitly, but I hoped she knew my offer extended into that realm as well.

"Thank you, Evie. I'd love to get a reading sometime."

I exhaled. I asked her more about the people she'd met and her favorite experiences. I enjoyed watching the way it lit up her entire etheric field in shades of orange, pink, green, indigo, and purple.

In a burst of wind and shadow, Idris suddenly appeared, scaring the shit out of me and almost making me spill my coffee.

I glowered, and he grinned back.

"That never gets old," he said wistfully. He'd been staying in one of the apartment units in the turned neighborhood since he'd gained clearance to venture above ground. He and Vesper were neighbors. "What are you all talking about?"

"Sex work," I said.

Idris blushed furiously. He scratched the back of his head. "Oh, um, I can come back later."

Vesper and I laughed, which didn't help Idris's discomfort.

"Sit down, punk," I said. "What's in your hand?"

Idris took a seat and waved what appeared to be some sort of invitation. "Mena is hosting a soiree tonight. She told me she'd off herself if we didn't come."

I rolled my eyes. "Oh, the drama." I soon melted, remembering that we'd hardly seen her in weeks. And that wasn't going to get any better. "Then we'll be there."

"She also told us to bring all of our new friends," he said, lifting a brow. "Does she *know*?"

I shrugged. "Probably. Mena is crafty that way. She's like an unpaid private investigator. She definitely suspects something, but I'm not sure how far those suspicions reach."

"True," Idris murmured. "She doesn't know I'm a vampire though, and I'm not ready to tell her, okay?"

I nodded. "Of course. Take your time. Let's just have fun tonight, and you know, invite all of our friends." I shot Vesper a conspiratorial look.

"I'm not one to turn down a party. Especially not when I know the guest list will be this immaculate," she drawled.

"Oh, just you wait," Idris said. "You and Mena are going to *love* each other."

I nodded. "I hope you usurp Kylo for top spot in Mena's favorite people list, personally."

"God, me too," Idris laughed.

Vesper's smile was sly. "Challenge accepted."

For a moment, I forgot how to act normally. I'd returned to my true childhood home, kissed my grandmother on each cheek, and then watched as everyone I loved gathered in one space.

Not only Kylo, Blade, Harmony, Vesper, and Clarke—but also Amy, Marietta, Gwendolyn and the other witches. They all stepped through my protective barriers and into Mena's soiree.

"What if she shows up, somehow?" I whispered to Kylo.

"Then we'll kill her." He smiled and kissed the side of my head. "You're safe, baby. Enjoy it."

Mena was a radiant beam of pure light. She wore a burnt orange tent dress, layers of turquoise and gold necklaces, and big hoop earrings. Her gray hair was in a messy bun, wavy strands escaping to frame her face and leopard print glasses.

She was freedom embodied.

"Kylo, doll, you simply must give me your honest opinions on the pieces I'm working on!" she exclaimed as we gathered in the main drawing room.

I smirked.

"It would be my pleasure."

Mena clapped her hands together and blew us all a kiss before leading Kylo up to her art studio on the second floor.

"Be right back, I vow it!" she called over her shoulder.

Idris shook his head.

"Should I be worried?" I asked, sending everyone around me into a fit of laughter.

The revolutionary spirit was potent. I caught sight of Vesper holding court in the corner of the room, already surrounded by a new group of mortal fans. One of the men brought her a plate of grapes, as if in offering. Vesper accepted the gift with a warm, infectious smile.

All turned were glamoured, of course. But I had a feeling the mortals here were well-aware of their presence.

Clarke was chatting up a shifter man, and Blade, Harmony, and Idris joined in on a competitive, loud game of cards.

I was content to meander through the space, more comfortable in my own skin than I ever thought possible.

"Evie," Amy called, waving me over.

I joined the group of witches on the ground. They were giggling and clinking glasses, poring over a book of astrology together.

"I'm so glad you all made it," I told them. I scanned their faces, relaxing when they regarded me with kindness.

Gwendolyn pulled me into a side hug. "Thanks for inviting us. Mena is wonderful," she said.

"She's the best." I released a breath. "How have things been going?"

"Second batch will be ready soon. We're getting quicker and more efficient," Gwendolyn said. "Hekate's presence in our lives has never been stronger. Dreams have become more vivid, some hopeful, and others quite dark. Sometimes they spill into the waking world."

I nodded. "I know exactly what you mean. How are things in the city?"

"Most loyalists have only hardened their positions. They think the turned are the cause of everything wrong in Etherdale, that the born are only trying to help make things right," Amy hissed.

"But," Gwendolyn said, swallowing a piece of pastry. "People on the right side of history have only become more radicalized. Etherdale is preparing for war, that is for certain."

"I know it feels wrong to say," Amy said. "But there's this surge of excitement and freedom in the air that's electrifying. Like it's all crashing down, but that's exactly what we need. We know it's going to be bloody and devastating, but it's the only way to get to the other side. I've never seen the people of

Etherdale so united, so kind and gracious and generous with each other—the ones capable of it, anyway."

"It's not wrong to say," I said. "I feel it too. The light beyond the shadow."

"Pluto entered Aquarius today," a thin male witch said, pointing at a colorful chart of astrological signs. "That's why we were toasting. We've entered an era of intense community-building, collective transformation, change, advancement, and *duh, revolution.*"

Amy grinned, clinking glasses with me.

Astrology was out of my wheelhouse, on my list of things to explore, eventually. It was nice to know I had people to learn and practice with.

After ten minutes of chatting, Mena re-entered the space and clinked her glass with a small spoon.

"Thank you all for being here tonight. I know it was not without risk. Nothing worth doing ever is." She winked.

Kylo was quick to find me as he scanned the room, his features warming when he did.

"Tonight, the theme is *change.* Talk to strangers about the way you have transformed. See my new, lovely friend Antoine for an astrological reading." She gestured to the male witch sitting with us. "Enjoy. Indulge. And remember that change is inevitable. Resisting its pull is futile. Let yourselves be changed by each other. By music and literature and art. By the city herself."

I smiled when Mena locked eyes with me. I felt seen, and I did not cower from the sensation. She nodded.

"My home is open to all of you. You will always be welcome here. No questions asked, for as long as you need. We need each other, now more than ever."

Love oozed from my every pore, gathering into pools that slid down my cheeks. I wiped the tears away, my smile never faltering.

When Mena was finished, she did a little curtsy and threw her head back with a laugh. "Get back to it!"

Idris and I moved at the exact same time. I pulled Mena into a long, deep hug.

"The world doesn't deserve you, Mena," I whispered.

"Oh, she might. She'll just have to earn it," Mena said. "By protecting my two favorite souls in the vast cosmos."

Idris hugged her next. His soft brown eyes shone with appreciation. "You saved me, Mena."

I rubbed Idris's shoulder. "You saved *us*."

Mena waved a hand. "Oh, pshhh. You saved yourselves, you silly eggs." She rubbed Idris's hair in that way he hated, and he half-heartedly rolled his eyes. "I merely provided you with a well-rounded education in culture and worldly affairs."

"Such as proper orgy etiquette," Idris joked.

"And what to do if your harem of boyfriends don't get along," I added.

"Ah yes, essential life skills. You're welcome." Mena patted our heads. "I'm glad you're both here. And happy?"

She watched us both nod in confirmation with beaming relief.

"Shoo. Enjoy. Make memories."

I found Vesper next, who was now chatting with Gwendolyn.

Clarke appeared, sporting a rakish grin. "It's no Juniper, but I'm quite charmed by this city already."

He and Vesper unapologetically stood out in their chic, futuristic outfits of leather and sleek fabrics.

"I'm going to go steal Mena from Kylo," Vesper whispered with a wink.

Kylo appeared by my side, and we watched Vesper approach Mena. Within five minutes they were whispering and laughing together like young girls.

"She just might accomplish that," Kylo said.

"She will," Clarke said confidently. "The conniving, lethal little creature." His smile was full of pride as he watched his best friend work her magic.

I was gooey beyond words to see the web of community and care spread out before me, linking us all together.

"Because of *you*, Evie," Kylo whispered.

He needed to stop reading my mind. I bit his arm, and he yanked me back by the hair before locking his lips with mine.

"Kylo, please, I need you over here," Blade called, interrupting us. "You're the only one who truly *gets* me."

They were playing some version of charades across the room, and Kylo reluctantly pulled away to glare at Blade.

"Go," I said. "We spend entirely too much time together."

Kylo laughed. "She's already sick of me," he said, clutching his chest as I gave him a little shove.

Gwendolyn and Clarke were talking about magickal theory. I decided to capitalize off the opportunity to take the tiniest of socialization breaks.

I slipped through the rooms of guests, overhearing a mix of small talk, flirting, jokes, and revolutionary rhetoric. The aura of the gathering was a bright golden hue with flecks of red, purple, and green.

Upstairs in my second childhood bedroom, where I stayed before I moved into the cottage, I sat on the edge of my bed. On the dresser in front of me, a vase of fresh pink tulips sat.

The sight of it made another silly little tear form in my eye. What a simple, devotional act of love.

I studied myself in the full-length mirror to the left of the dresser, my golden party dress accented with embroidered purple flowers. My gray eyes were shiny, my features accented with shimmery blush.

I sighed contentedly.

Before I turned away, something bizarre happened.

My reflection smiled at me. Dread pooled in my stomach. I

reached a hand up to my face, feeling my lips that were most definitely *not smiling.*

My reflection then mirrored me perfectly, her lips forming a deep frown. I stepped closer, heart beating hard, hairs on the back of my neck standing straight up.

I turned my head right than left. Blinked. I nearly convinced myself I'd imagined the whole thing.

Until she smiled again.

45

EVIE

Was Juliette hexing me? Making me slowly go insane? Or had the visions about mirrors been some sort of witchy message?

I wasn't sure. But perhaps I'd find out tonight on my second visit to Nighswander Estate.

The image I held in my mind as three born guards led me to Aster on the back lawn was that of my loved ones laughing together. Witches, humans, and turned. The deepening of Kylo's dimple. The cadence of Idris's laugh. Vesper charming the fuck out of Mena and swapping seductress conquest stories. Blade consistently losing every game of charades without Kylo's help to interpret his *unique* way of thinking. Harmony's sweet energy lightening every room. The dancing and stolen kisses and plotting and toasting to the stars.

"Hello, dearest Evie," Aster said, turning to me.

The men at my back left us. I glanced around searching for Juliette.

"Don't worry. Juliette won't be joining us yet," Aster assured me as if reading my mind.

I was simultaneously relieved and unnerved. It was hard to concentrate when I was consumed by the desire to throttle her.

"She really looks up to you, you know," Aster said, his tone scolding. "I know she can come on a bit strong, but that's because her heart is so full of love."

Fucking doubtful. "Is that so?"

Aster sighed. "She's broken, in many ways, from her upbringing. Can't you relate to that, at least?"

Broken seemed apt. But I resented yet another insinuation that Juliette and I were the same.

"It's hard to believe she looks up to me when she's doing everything in her power to hurt me," I said.

Aster crossed his arms. "Funny thing is, she says the same about *you*."

"Does she now?"

Aster lifted a hand. "Let's drop this. I only want to enjoy our time together." He scanned the length of me. "What a darling dress. I love your sense of style."

I forced the words, *thank you* from my lips. The sound of a gentle, flowing bird bath came from our left. The falling evening sun peeked through a lush green canopy of trees. By all appearances, we were alone.

"How are you doing? I'm glad to see you look healthy."

Lovely. As if I were a prized mare he was seeking to repossess.

"As well as I can be," I said, slipping into my role with ease. "I've been thinking a lot about what you said. About the war being unwinnable for the turned."

"Ah," Aster said, waiting for me to elaborate as we slowly strolled.

"I'm scared," I whispered, as if it were a secret. I channeled authentic fear, the wounded parts of me that Aster had no idea I'd healed and integrated. "I don't know who to trust. After what happened with my coven, I certainly don't trust people like you."

I waited, watching Aster's face for clues on how my words were landing. It was one of my most practiced skills. He was unreadable at first, sharp and assessing, before falling into a show of empathy that didn't quite meet his eyes.

"I can feel your distrust, precious Evie. It must've been terribly difficult to take care of yourself for so many years," he said softly. "Often, when we are afraid—especially from childhood hurts—we turn to comforting savior fantasies. Fierce protectors, white knights, grand battles of good versus evil. But reality exists in shades of gray, not in absolutes. There is always more to a story and its characters than our first clouded initial assumptions."

I clocked the manipulation immediately, but I furrowed my brow, pretending to be confused and deep in thought.

"Why did you have Juliette kill all of those innocent mortals?" I asked point-blank.

"Prime example of an assumption."

"So she's wreaking havoc on the city entirely of her own accord?"

"We protect the people we love, don't we, Evie?" Aster sat on a wooden bench, handing me a small bunch of wildflowers that I couldn't imagine him collecting himself. "Juliette's magick is protective. She heard a group of students talking about my assassination, and she lost her temper. She's blessed by Lillian— her magick is divine wrath. Not always easily contained or predictable, but her heart is in the right place. She's a wound that bleeds."

Aster looked bizarrely genuine as he stared out into the trees, tall grass, and blooming flowers.

She's a wound that bleeds.

"When we first met, all she did was cry. I hadn't planned to take another bride, but I couldn't just leave her with those *people*. It took months to get her to speak to me. A year to get her to talk in full sentences. Her magick was slow to develop as well. It came alive as she did." He smiled. "She's trying to protect me the way I protected her. That's all."

That was absolutely not *all*. "There were hundreds of innocent people in that build—"

"And a great many of them were actively planning their lords' demises," Aster snapped. "I am being honest with you, so please do me the courtesy of giving me the same respect. Hundreds more mortals would be sacrificed to war. Both sides are enacting violence upon the other. You cannot pretend the mortals and turned freaks of nature are these poor, nonviolent innocents when they are actively plotting against us and slaughtering our kind in the streets. We didn't enforce harsher laws in this city to destroy it. We did so to preserve *order*. We do not want war. *No sane person wants war.*"

His words landed heavily, a sharp contrast to the gentle summer air.

I extended my witchy senses, confirming what I could see plainly in Aster's features. By all appearances, his convictions were honestly held. Even if his aura was otherwise disgusting, evil, and horny.

There was something interesting in the way he emphasized the avoidance of war. I thought about our hunch that Aster was vying for the throne, and how he might achieve that with minimal bloodshed.

Dissenters in the council. A coalition of southern born elites. The ties to the burgeoning slave trade.

You're going to find what you need. Watch carefully where authority flows...

"I find you to be contradictory," I said. "You speak as though you don't have any control over the Servants of Lillian and the abuse these cults foster. Like taking us as brides was the only way to save us from the institutions you allow under your rule."

CLAIMED BY FANGS AND DARKNESS

Aster stared forward, blond hair bathed in the golden light of a falling sun. His lip twitched, his amber eyes a cool mask. "The hawk eats the snake. The snake eats the bird. The bird eats the insect. The insect eats the grass. Death, brutality, decay, senselessness... it's all a part of the cosmic design, wouldn't you say?"

I frowned deeply. Was I the snake or the bird? Either answer pissed me off. "A convenient perspective."

"The Servants have been around for centuries. They fall in and out of fashion, like bloodlines fall in and out of power. Everything serves its purpose. Cut off the head of a snake, and two heads may grow back in its place. Some may believe themselves to be, but we vampires are not gods. If witches wish to abandon Selena and serve our Dark Mother instead, who am I to stop them? It is not my place to exert control over the world; that is a futile and misguided urge that only leads to suffering. I merely exist within its natural order just like everyone else."

I was beginning to understand how much manipulators loved to evade basic questions and answer with long, pretentious monologues. I asked Selena for patience.

"I am a man, Evie," Aster said, his amber eyes molten now. "I will not apologize for my natural desires for female companionship. For sex and beauty and romance. I am also a vampire, which particularizes my desires of the flesh. This does not mean I have no values or ethical codes. I pursued brides from the Servants for a reason. If I hadn't stepped in, someone worse would've."

I almost laughed at the absurdity of his logic. Anger boiled my blood until I was afraid I was close to leaking shadow. I took a deep breath to calm my magick.

Aster truly did think of us as rescue pets.

Rescue pets with magickal gifts that may prove useful to his political agenda.

"I gave Juliette an education. I have been a faithful partner, mentor, and guide. She has never once asked to leave me. I give her everything she needs and more. Our roles are mutually fulfilling, and I will not apologize for taking care of her the way she innately desires."

It was so sick. The grooming, the justifications, the rejection of criticism or accountability. My stomach turned over. The haze of trauma reached for me, blurring the edges of my mind, while I fought to stay present and sharp.

"I don't need anything from you," I said. "Why would I agree to marry you rather than remain free?"

Aster pinned me with a hard stare. "Are you free, Evie?"

No. Not entirely—not anymore. But true freedom was a myth. Loving and serving others meant a loss of personal freedom, but the trade-off was well worth the fulfillment, community, and justice.

"Stealing your freedom is not my objective, dear," Aster said. "I want to keep you safe. Your magick makes you a target for the rest of your life. Every power in the realm will seek to kill you or use you, or use you and then kill you."

I swallowed. He wasn't exactly wrong.

"When the turned are squashed like every other mortal rebellion in the past millennium, where will that leave you?" Aster paused. "Don't misunderstand me. I also want your precious heart—I've wanted it since the moment I learned you were still alive."

No, since I was a fucking *child*.

"How does Juliette feel about that?"

Aster smiled softly. "Juliette has always desired sisterly love. She isn't the jealous type. She believes love can and should be given freely; she doesn't subscribe to archaic models of monogamy. She's told me from the start that she believes I'll always know what is best for us. That if I want to love you, I should."

I fought the urge to snort. Once again, the dark thought passed through my mind: At what point would this level of love bombing have worked on me?

I shuddered.

"And what about Conrad?"

Aster looked stunned, jolted out of his dreamy romantic bullshit. "What about him?"

I caught a note of anger in his eyes. It was interesting how much he and Juliette talked about this incestuous poly lovefest when they both showed such blatant possessiveness beneath the surface.

"You seem close," I said, pretending to look more nervous than inquisitive.

"We're old friends, yes. Not many of my brothers and sisters understand my lifestyle. But Conrad is a romantic too, believe it or not. His coldness is a reflection of deep heartbreak, the death of his wife a couple of decades ago that still torments him."

There it was. A blatant twisting of the truth. I already knew Aster was full of shit, but catching him in the lies was soothing in this sea of careful, consistent manipulation. I saw Vesper's story clearly in my mind, the scar that cut across her cheek.

"Conrad and I are building something beautiful, together," Aster continued, oblivious to the fire building in my chest. "Etherdale is not the only city that has lost her way. The realm needs gentle guidance from strong, measured rulers, not *war*."

My heart skipped a beat. I closed my mouth, playing dumb. I couldn't be heavy-handed, not when Aster was flirting with treason.

"I hated the turned too, you know," I said, lowering my voice. "I hated what they'd done to the city that had always protected me. The circular violence, the provocation of Conrad and his men. But then the born started rounding up witches like me. They attacked me and my brother. I did what I had to do."

371

I let a degree of pleading and uncertainty enter my eyes and voice, channeling the current as if I were practicing magick.

And the more it worked, the easier it became.

Aster pulled my hand into his, and I let him. "I know you did, Evie. And now they want you to spy on us, to give them anything that might level the scales. But I have nothing to offer —we will preserve order merely because we have more power and numbers. That is the truth."

I stared at our hands. "I'm afraid if I don't give them something, they won't let me keep coming back."

"Is it a jealous lover? Is that who you report to?" Aster asked. His jaw feathered, a low hum of power coloring the air.

I shook my head, pretending to be offended. I channeled the old Evie, the one who would sooner die than be with a vampire.

"I've never been fed from before," I said quietly.

Aster's eyes flashed intensity, hunger. For a moment, it felt like I was channeling Vesper now—the wisdom I'd gleaned from her over the past week, the lessons from her stories and the way she held everyone under her spell.

He was distracted and vulnerable. I played innocent as I claimed power. It was a risky move, a test of Aster's commitment to his show of chivalry.

His throat bobbed. His pupils moved rapidly.

"I told you what I am," he said, voice gravelly. "A *man*. A vampire."

He stood, lording over me before his hand slowly reached for my face. I fought the urge to recoil from the cool brush of his fingers.

"You know exactly what you're doing, don't you?" he asked.

My stomach twisted. Aster pulled me to my feet, his warm breath fanning over my face. I homed in on the tips of his fangs as I went still.

"You're teasing me." His lips curved. "Bad girl."

Was this... working? I could stomach the nausea so long as Aster didn't harm me. So long as he kept his word.

"I was the first to taste your blood..." he continued, sucking in a deep breath as his gaze drank in every inch of my body. "Blood unlike any other. Pure sunshine and flowers and decadence. Something dark and rich hidden beneath the surface. Tell me, Evie. Are your true desires as dark as your magick?"

I was disgusted, and I knew I had a hard time hiding my emotions, so I channeled the discomfort into fear. Vampires loved fear.

"Aster," a voice called in the distance.

Conrad walked out from the shadows of the estate. His eyes tracked our closeness before landing heavily on me.

His body was cloaked in expensive clothing. His face was unblemished. He carried not an ounce of remorse for the brutal torture of his mortal wife. The wife he'd forced to carry his child.

Aster smiled, looking at Conrad with admiration.

46

EVIE

Conrad spoke to Aster in a hushed tone as we entered the estate. A few born women gathered in the back foyer. They assessed me with snakelike eyes, expressions cold even as their lips curved.

"This will only take a moment, dear. I'll have you wait for me in the library," Aster said.

He gestured for my familiar babysitters to take their positions. Upstairs, I watched as Aster followed Conrad into a study. The door closed, and I swallowed a gasp.

A witchy wind danced around us. The outline of light, the ornate carvings on the door—it all lined up with my premonition.

I needed to listen to the conversation happening inside that room.

Instead, I was ushered down the hall and into the library. I couldn't leave empty-handed. Not today.

I pretended to study the books on a nearby bookshelf while my guards stood by the door.

"Are you from here? Or Isolde?" I asked them.

"Why?" one fired back snottily.

"Just trying to make small talk," I muttered.

"Isolde," the other said. "Ignore my brother. He's in a mood."

I had one shot. What I was about to do was as crazy as when I stabbed Kylo with a poisoned needle. Maybe crazier, considering I was surrounded by bloodthirsty demons, and I was going to use one of my only emergency measures.

Glancing over my shoulder, I locked eyes with the nicer born brother. "Could you help me reach this book?" I asked.

The irritated one rolled his eyes.

"Sure, miss," said his dark-haired brother. Country manners. I wondered if that was how they both knew about what I'd done. They were clearly Aster's men, from the same region I was born.

The vampire reached for the book I'd pointed to. My hand slipped inside my hidden dress pocket, fingering the satchel of freshly made herbal powder.

At the same time, I concentrated, a chant rolling through my mind as I forced a book across the room to fly off a shelf.

I glanced in that direction, quickly making sure the ornery vampire brother had done the same. At the same time, with my heart hammering against my ribs, I flicked powder into the closest vampire's face.

With a small gust of wind, he inhaled. He dropped the book and stood stock-still, frozen in place.

"Are you okay?" I asked. "Something's wrong," I said, girlish and confused.

His brother rushed toward us, right into the lingering, faint cloud of shimmering powder. He inhaled and joined his brother in a peaceful waking dream state.

"Okay, cool, be right back," I said.

Had I just done that?

I couldn't help my grin. So far tonight I'd lied, seduced, and incapacitated... and it wasn't even seven o'clock. Maybe I was actually fantastic at subterfuge, and everyone who'd doubted me should feel pretty fucking embarrassed right now.

These were my triumphant thoughts as I slipped into the vacant hall and toward the illuminated door. My steps were careful, testing the floor for creaks before extending any amount of weight.

The powder wouldn't do any harm. The vampires would recover and have no recollection of what had happened, as if they'd merely lost time. I'd snap them out of their spell as soon as I returned.

Ear pressed against the door, I said a silent prayer to Hekate that no one else decided to wander upstairs while I eavesdropped.

"Just because we have Hemsworth doesn't mean we have Godfrey by default," Aster said.

"I know that," Conrad snapped, irritated. "We need Kole gone. *He* will be the one they send to Valentin."

"Why would Kole go for that?"

"The little weasel craves validation. He'll bend with the right push. We don't need him sniffing around for breadcrumbs. Spineless ass-kisser that he is. I have a feeling we can focus on this group next..."

The floor creaked. I stifled a scream as cold fingers suddenly brushed through my hair.

Juliette placed her head on the door next to mine. Her dark wavy hair was damp, her white dress thin and revealing.

I waited for her to blow my cover, but once again, she didn't. She just put a finger to her lips with a big, childlike smile, her gray eyes dancing with mischief.

I realized in my panic I'd missed parts of the conversation, tuning back in when I heard my name.

"She's perfect," Aster said.

Juliette's eyes drained of light, but her smile remained.

"She's the perfect missing piece."

Conrad grumbled something I couldn't discern. "I've kept word of her from reaching Prospyrus. No easy feat after that little temper tantrum."

"Did you have to take him out?"

"No. Bribery was less messy this time."

I memorized the names they'd mentioned, repeating them over and over again in my head. They'd been discussing council members. I was sure of it. Because I recognized Kole as the loyalist Vesper said had it out for Conrad and Asper.

"What are they waiting for? The bastard children? It doesn't make sense," Aster spat. "I tire of this. The sooner it's done, the sooner we can leave. I hate that *my* bride is stained by her association with the vermin."

My lips formed a thin line. Juliette stroked my hair. I fought the urge to tackle her to the ground and blow my own cover as I squeezed the everlasting fuck out of her neck.

"Would taking her now help?" Conrad asked.

A pause. "I made vows. I want her to choose it. And she will. She's warming to me."

"But not to your mental patient," Conrad muttered.

Juliette's face soured. Smug satisfaction warmed my gut.

"Enough. Don't speak about my wife that way," Aster said, but not nearly as strongly as Conrad had been speaking to *him*.

Aster may have been collecting powerful witches. But it wasn't hard to tell who had more power in that room—who had been subtly bowing to the other and making commands and jabs.

If they were making a play, it was Conrad who held the greatest authority.

Suddenly Juliette began to wail.

You have got to be fucking kidding me.

She cried like a toddler, slumping against the door. I left her there as I ran down the hall, hoping her cries covered up my movement.

As long as I made it back to my guards in time, nothing could be proven.

The door to the study opened the moment I slipped back inside the library.

"Kitten, you know what happens when we eavesdrop," Aster scolded. "Come with me. *Now.*"

I almost hesitated. *Almost.*

Juliette wasn't my concern. Instead, I inhaled deeply and snapped my fingers. I whispered a loosening chant. The men coughed. I watched them innocently as I cracked open the book the nicer brother had fetched for me.

"Goodness! Are you all right?" I asked sweetly.

In a daze, they looked at each other and then at me. The lighter-haired, testy brother made a sound of derision and stalked off.

The dark-haired vampire blinked, staring at the book I now held on flesh-eating bacterial diseases.

"Need anything else?" he asked, handsome features twisted in utter confusion.

"Nope, all set!" I closed the book and moved toward a nearby reading chair.

The sound of the library door opening halted me in place.

Conrad stood in the frame. His cool blue eyes landed on me. All I saw when I looked at him was Vesper. It was as though I could hear the inhuman sound that had left her lips the moment she'd handed her baby away. The way her heart hemorrhaged, her soul in agony, soon to be dragged back to hell and tortured by the vampire before me.

His dark hair had a slight wave to it; his face was frozen in time. But the ancientness was apparent in the way he carried himself, the ghostly quality of his aura as if he were the walking undead.

"Aster is attending to personal matters. Care to join me for a drink?" Conrad asked.

"Of course," I said softly. I imagined how his head would look severed from his body, rolling across the library floor.

I followed Conrad down the hall into the same room he and Aster had emerged from. I listened for any sign of Juliette, but Aster must've taken her somewhere out of earshot.

Conrad gestured to a set of leather chairs. On the other side of the room, papers and notebooks spread about on the dark finish of a grand mahogany desk.

"I'm not going to drink an intoxicant," I said as Conrad poured two glasses of whiskey. I fought the urge to scan more of the room, to search for any crumb of tangible evidence that might be useful.

Conrad smirked as he lounged back in the adjacent chair, posture wide and cocky. "Very well."

I was on edge, fighting the instinctive fear of being this close to someone capable of such evil. Above the fear was the slowly simmering rage, the utter hatred.

"You have a very expressive face, even when you're trying hard to conceal it," Conrad said with a sip of his whiskey. He swirled the sphere of ice around, lifting a brow as he assessed me with cool apathy.

When humor leaked into his eyes, I knew for certain he was able to spot my anxiety.

"What do you want, Evie?" he asked.

"What do I want?" I repeated.

"You're a smart girl. Smarter than you act, I bet."

Um, rude? What a strange insult.

"It's a compliment," he said with a sigh. "I am asking you what you desire out of life. What fuels you?"

"Justice."

Conrad laughed. "I didn't expect you to be honest. How charming," he murmured.

He leaned forward, and for a moment, I could see it—the hint of charisma beneath so many layers of immortal indifference.

I could understand how a naive immortal might chase those glimpses of warmth and humor, believing themselves to be oh-so-special for making someone this hard reveal a hidden softness.

It was a trap.

"Justice is a mortal delusion. There is no justice in an indifferent world. The past is dead, and there is no resurrecting it."

I sighed. Another convenient take. "What *should* I want?"

Conrad's eyes widened. For the first time, he smiled. "I like this question."

I felt the weight of my discreet collar, grounding myself.

"You should want the protection of the strongest power in the realm," he said boldly.

"And that's *you?*"

Conrad's smile widened. "I can tell you that it's *not* your ragtag group of angsty adolescents begging to sit at the adult table."

They had no fucking idea. At first, I thought they were overplaying how much they underestimated us. Perhaps in order to dig for information. Kylo's eighty-year plan of concealing the clan's true capacities had worked.

They had no idea who they were up against.

"You've never been outside of Etherdale, have you? Besides your nowhere village in Isolde, of course."

I shook my head. "Not yet."

Conrad sipped his whiskey, leaning back again. His pale blue eyes snagged on my lips, and I wondered how well I'd concealed my smugness.

"Etherdale is sleepy and utterly dull compared to vampire-run cities such as Prospyrus," he said.

"Then why are you here and not *there?*"

"Mouthy little thing," Conrad drawled. "Believe me, I would be there if I could. I hate this godsforsaken city."

Well, that was bloody apparent. It filled me with such instinctive rage that Conrad thought himself better than the city he was currently destroying—the city supposedly under his custodianship—if only to prevent the turned and mortals from having it for ourselves.

"You would too if you'd ever traveled."

"You don't know me."

Conrad shrugged. "You're a frightened young woman who reads, dreams, and believes in fairy tales. You love pretty dresses, jewelry, and art, and you fill your mind with ideals of justice and mysticism and meaning because you can't accept the possibility that you exist in an apathetic universe of meaningless chaos. A place where fairness is merely a construct, the strong prevail, and the wise understand that everyone is out for themselves."

I wanted to tell him how wrong he was. I wanted to tell him about the hidden clubs of dancing humans and the covens who met by candlelight and the family I'd joined by blood and shadow. But he'd never understand.

"Choosing to suffer won't win you favor with the gods." He gestured to my untouched glass of whiskey. "There is a path where you are safe, well-traveled, well-read, and spoiled with all the luxury this world has to offer. There is a path where you no longer have to deny yourself."

All the born understood was power and pleasure. They could speak on an intellectual level about morality and existentialism, but they couldn't truly feel what mortals felt. They were too self-absorbed to step out of their own perspectives and into the mind of another.

So, I let Conrad misunderstand me. I pretended once again

to be conflicted, confused. Just a poor little lamb in need of a shepherd who knew so much more than she.

Conrad swirled his whiskey. "Who is the man with black hair and blue eyes?"

47

EVIE

M y heart tumbled. I opened my mouth, but Conrad spoke again.

"Juliette provoked you at dinner. That girl tends to know things she shouldn't..."

I didn't say anything. It was safer that way. I focused on my irritation with Juliette instead of my fear of being caught in a lie.

One more visit. I had one more visit to gather just a shred of evidence that could be used against these sick fucks. I lifted my gaze above Conrad's shoulder briefly, toward the desk with loose papers strewn about.

When it was clear I wasn't going to answer him, Conrad spoke again. "Did it feel good to kill your parents, Evie?" he asked. "To murder your entire coven?"

I frowned, my fists tightening.

"Is that why you're so high-strung? Are you terrified of revealing that underneath the innocent exterior you're as bloodthirsty and vengeful as the rest of us?" Conrad flashed his fangs, a shudder of pleasure rolling through him. "Whatever happened to the Whitfield family, I wonder? Did that feel good too?"

Both Conrad's and Aster's questions and self-indulgent monologues were designed to make me doubt myself and my family. They wanted me to see the world as they did: a place where morality was relative and the born were its natural rulers and nothing any mortal did could ever truly matter. We were nothing, and they were everything.

The only life in which I was free and protected was with *them*.

"There you are."

Aster entered the space, gaze darting between Conrad and me rapidly. He didn't hide the slight downturn of his lips.

"Come, Evie. I have more dazzling on the agenda," Aster said.

He beckoned me like I was a dog. Conrad smirked as I stood. He twirled a hand. "Nice chatting with you."

Aster's fingers brushed the small of my back. He regarded me possessively, relaxing once we were out of Conrad's sight.

What strange primal urges from men pretending to be gods.

Juliette was nowhere to be seen.

Aster showed me books he'd found for me, gifts that corresponded with information I'd let slip about myself. He took me to a room with a telescope, where he guided me to look at the stars. He named them, and he spoke of mysticism and astrological correspondences.

He overwhelmed me with depth and philosophy and literature and cosmology. He dug for information, imbued his words with humor until he finally succeeded in making me laugh. When I did, his entire face lit up.

As I laughed, I imagined how it would feel to bathe in Aster's blood while Vesper tortured Conrad nearby. Kylo by my side, showing Aster who the fuck already owned my body and soul.

It was nearly time for me to leave when a party formed

downstairs. Music and dark magick echoed off the castle walls. I could sense a sickly, powerful energy nearby as Aster walked me back down.

Before we joined the bodies cloaked in fineries, clinking flutes of elixir and feeding from beautiful mortals, Aster stopped me.

"Stay with us. Don't go back," he said, twirling me to face him. "This will all be over soon. And if you want to build a better world, we can together. I will value and honor your input; you have my word."

He read the hesitation in my features before I could voice it.

"I'm scared of Juliette," I said, the most convenient and realistic excuse at my disposal.

Aster shook his head in frustration. "Give her a chance. You two have more in common than you think. But I will *not* choose between you, nor will I allow either of you to hurt each other. Is that understood?"

I forced myself not to react to Aster's sternness, the utter insanity of the life he thought he could manipulate me into accepting. I nodded.

"I need more time to think. Could we meet again Friday?"

I threw out an earlier date to appease Aster, but mostly because I wanted to kill Juliette as soon as possible. Next visit, I'd need to plant the seed to lure her away, to meet her on my terms for once.

"I'm willing to spend time with Juliette too," I added, as if begrudgingly.

Aster's face softened. He stroked my shoulder, delighted when I didn't pull away. "Very well. Then tell your handlers you overheard guards mention a new shipment arriving tomorrow. They'll see it arrive, perhaps attempt to intercept it, all thanks to you. Blood replenishing potions and the like. To ensure your return."

I offered a demure *thank you*. I let him whisk me through the maze of bodies. I swallowed my nausea as Aster danced with me, his amber eyes locked on mine. He inhaled deeply. His eyes were tinged with vampiric desire.

Sequined girls in my periphery were performing burlesque amid multicolored lanterns that dropped from the ceiling. Thirsty born men and women circled them, perhaps waiting patiently for the show to end so they could feed off their most desired performer.

Everything in this space radiated a delicious, chaotic form of magick. Lillian's magick. I was caught between the sick feeling in my stomach and the unavoidable influence of wave after wave of energetic pleasure and power.

Intoxicating darkness, violence, sex, and wealth flaunted without shame or restraint. Here in this cocoon of mindless hedonism, there was no guilt, terror, or fear of death.

No one here knew what it felt like to be mortal. To be in love for the first time with a vulnerable, open heart. To fight powers greater than themselves. To bravely believe in something more than what can be known from flesh and ego. To hope or dream or sacrifice for the good of people they will never know or meet.

As I looked around the room, I wondered if any of these vampires had known Vernon, the man who traumatized my brother when he was only seven years old. How many of these vampires had hurt children themselves?

"May I?" a voice asked sweetly.

Juliette was in a new dress, a white gown with floral detailing that was sickeningly familiar. I wasn't sure why her copying my wardrobe bothered me as much as it did.

I took a deep breath. Here was my chance to ask Juliette what the fuck she was doing with my blood, and then I could leave and shower this night away.

Aster grinned when I willingly let go of him and moved

toward Juliette. Even if every fiber of my being protested the action.

The witch who killed Princeton smiled warmly. She looped her arm around my waist and pulled me close.

"You look really pretty today," she whispered in my ear.

All around us, vampires had stopped what they were doing to stare at us. Their eyes lit up, auras flushed red. Aster didn't move, watching us as if he were straining against his own dark desire.

Juliette and I were being fetishized. My skin crawled, wanting to be anywhere but here. I heard my mother's voice in my ear, telling me to behave. To take it. To be grateful I was pleasing my born masters.

"Why did you take my blood?" I hissed with a smile. The music and revelry were loud enough to cover up our whispers.

Juliette frowned.

As much as it hurt, I finally switched tactics.

"You look pretty today too," I forced out.

Juliette glowed as if I'd given her the whole world. "I'm not going to hurt you, Evie—not unless you try to hurt *us*."

"So you took it as insurance?"

She cocked her head. "What does that mean?"

Oh, good gods.

"Isn't this nice?" Juliette asked. "We don't have to be alone anymore."

I studied Juliette, and I hated the way my mind let even a drop of pity bleed through the cracks.

"Oh," she murmured, reaching for her nose.

Blood trickled from her left nostril. Juliette stared at her finger. Her eyelids fluttered. She collapsed.

Aster rushed to catch her with vampiric speed. Her small body spasmed in his hold.

"I didn't do anything—I swear," I said quickly.

Aster shook his head. "It's been happening more frequently.

It's a side-effect of her magick. It's too strong for her body to handle."

Conrad appeared. I noticed the born who'd once been watching us with oozing lust suddenly lost all interest, as if Juliette's seizure was a buzzkill.

I couldn't stop the words from leaving my lips, not considering the consequences.

"No, it's not," I said.

Both men looked at me.

"This is a consequence of using *stolen* power."

Aster frowned, and Conrad stared at me similarly to how he had at the dinner table when I'd broken the glass.

I'd let something slip that was not in my best interest.

I shut my mouth tight.

Juliette gasped, staring at me with sudden clarity. Her speech was slurred, her eyes welling with tears as she glared my way.

All she did was point and shake her head. Conrad escorted me out through the labyrinth of beautiful, soulless monsters.

"How? How is she stealing power?"

I stared at him on the front porch, incredulous. "You don't know?"

Understanding was almost within my grasp, all of these strange, jagged pieces that must fit together somehow.

All I knew for certain was that it was in my best interest to *stop fucking talking*.

Conrad squinted at me. His mind churned, and he slowly led me down the winding path. Freedom was within sight. I could already smell Kylo's familiar scent, feel his strong, protective arms around me.

"I already asked you what you wanted once today, but now I will ask something more specific. Do you want Juliette out of the picture?"

His voice was low. It was just us. At first, I grew defensive until I realized Conrad wasn't accusing me—he was making an offer. He thought I could be bought. If only he found the right price.

He saw the answer on my face, a smirk forming.

"We aren't rewarded for self-denial," he repeated. "We'll all be bones together one day. You mortals quicker than the rest of us."

Conrad paused at the gate, scanning the street as if he were looking for someone.

As if he were looking for Kylo.

He slowly turned his attention back to me. "Goodnight, Evie." His hand brushed mine.

Through his touch, I felt a cavernous, hollow darkness that spread on for an eternity.

48

KYLO

s soon as she was in my sight, I could breathe again.

Tonight, we were more careful, waiting until we were back in our glamoured neighborhood before I pulled Evie into my arms with a firm grip on her head. She nuzzled into my chest.

"I'm safe. No one hurt me," she said.

"Fuck," was all I could manage for now.

She burrowed deeper, warm and yielding in my hold. The fact that this precious girl had been in a house full of vampires who wanted to harm her drove me to the brink of utter insanity.

Crickets chirped, the warmth of a summer night holding us in an embrace. Voices carried from down the streets, comrades hanging out on porches or stoops.

Evie finally pulled away to meet my eyes. "We were right. About their play for more power. I don't know how far they're willing to go—but they said that they've won over a councilman named Hemsworth, and they have an eye on another named Godfrey. They want Kole to be the one to go to Valentin, I guess for a diplomatic meeting, so that he doesn't interfere with whatever they're up to."

I was slow to transition to political talk when I was this hyper-focused on the rhythm of Evie's heart, just as I had the past three and a half hours of agony.

"It's been almost one thousand years," I murmured. "How psychologically unwell must Earle be for dissent like this to bloom for the first time? Even if Conrad and Aster had been craving power for a while, they would never attempt a coup unless they saw undeniable vulnerability."

Evie nodded. "They both mentioned a desire to improve Ravenia, as if the current regime is failing. Also, Conrad is clearly pulling the strings. My witchy intuition is strong on that."

I paused. "Hmm. Yet Aster is the one hunting for powerful chaos witches to groom."

"I know. This feels strange to say, but it seems like Aster is wrapped up in all of this for more than just power. In his own sick and twisted way, he thinks he's doing *good*."

I snorted. "Or that's what he wants *you* to think."

She frowned. "I know he's not *actually* doing good. But I think he does believe his own bullshit. Aster thinks they're maintaining order and preventing mass mortal death. And yes, that position also includes a strong conviction of born supremacy and a natural hierarchy. It's contradictory—the way he can talk about mortal literature and spirituality, notions of virtue and chivalry, yet also admire someone like Conrad and take child brides. He sees Juliette and me as rescue pets. As if he hadn't saved us, we would've been in much worse hands. He wants me to join their weird polyamorous relationship. Juliette is copying my wardrobe, and she's also suffering physical health effects from using stolen power."

The more words that tumbled out of Evie's mouth, the more irate I became.

Evie studied my face, her small hand reaching for my tense jaw. I didn't lean into her touch.

After a pause, I spoke. "You didn't come home with a gift?" The irritation was evident in my voice.

She hesitated. "They're back at the estate."

I laughed humorlessly. "Ah. Because Aster thinks you'll be switching sides soon enough."

Staring at our feet, Evie released a small exhale. "I did everything right. I gained more of their trust. I subdued two guards with my homemade stun powder so I could eavesdrop on an important conversation. I've confirmed how greatly Aster and Conrad underestimate the turned, because they think they can handle this quickly and fly north soon after. I know where to look for concrete evidence of treason next time, confirmed by my spirit allies. I played the part we discussed—"

I closed my eyes. "Stun powder?" I asked. The fact that she'd casually employed something so risky set my skin on fire. One wrong move and they would've taken her into their custody without a second thought.

"I'm confused," Evie said, her voice shaking slightly as if with sudden emotion. "Why aren't you proud of me? I'm here, unharmed, and triumphant—I brought you a name of a dissenter in Earle's council, at the very least."

I pulled her back to my chest. I felt raw and on display, the worst parts of me eclipsing the rest. She had no idea of the torment of letting the love of my life be offered on a silver platter to the man who still calls her his bride.

"I am endlessly proud of you, angel," I said. "I swear to the gods I am."

My shadows could no longer be contained. They coiled protectively around her in various degrees of solidity and smoke.

When one of her own shadows escaped, I quickly

intertwined my shadow with hers. Evie tensed in my arms, her heart beating rapidly.

"You okay?" I asked her. I pulled back, studying her fearful features. I could taste her sudden panic through our bond. "Let's get you some tea, and then we can read together. Unless you want to chat with the others and—"

Evie pulled her shadow away from mine and back inside herself. "Tea sounds good."

She attempted to pull away from me, but I held her in place with my hands on either shoulder. "What don't you want me to know?"

The slight wince in her features, covered up by faux confusion, soured my stomach.

"Not with me, Evie," I whispered, my chest tightening. "Don't start being dishonest with *me*."

At my unavoidable hurt expression, Evie's lower lip trembled, her brows drawn in.

When she still didn't speak, I closed my hand around her throat and let a shadow limb skate over her pounding heart. It rested there, waiting.

I didn't hurt her, but I let my power vibrate through the air. That, combined with my hand on her throat and wrath in my eyes, was enough to provoke Evie's power.

Our darkness melded. I saw a piece of bloody chocolate cake.

I felt Evie's terror and disgust. A spoon met Aster's lips. He called her blood *perfect*.

"Kylo," Evie gasped, coughing.

I realized in horror I'd applied pressure to her neck. I quickly yanked back my hand.

"I'm sorry," I said, the words as strangled as hers had been.

For the first time in decades, I felt something akin to real bloodlust threaten my perfect control. All I could do was stare at her. The reality of what I'd seen was slow to reach the analytical side of my brain.

"He clotted my wound and tasted my spilled blood. I told him to stop, and he did, and I wanted to tell you so many times but you said you would declare war early and—"

"This didn't happen today." My voice was rough, harsh. My power trembled beneath my skin.

A tear slid down Evie's cheek as she shook her head. I could taste her shame and panic on my tongue, and the caregiver side of me wanted to pull her close and give her comfort.

But the animalistic side was too strong, old wounds reawakening as the truth came into clearer focus.

"This happened the first time you met with him. You lied to me."

"I didn't want to," she said. "You said if Aster touched me, you would—"

I backed away from her. My veins were pulsing, darkness clouding the corners of my eyes.

"I need you to get away from me," I barked.

Evie flinched. Her eyes widened, and another tear fell. More darkness spilled from me, and she didn't move.

"Now!"

The sight of her flinching again at the sound of my yell was a stab to my stunned heart. She took off running, and I had to fight every vampiric cell in my body to stay rooted to the ground instead of chasing after her.

My breathing was ragged. I hissed when my fangs suddenly ached with all the intensity of a newborn. Several competing urges flooded my body: the urge to hunt Evie down and bury myself inside her until she screamed, to soothe myself with the taste of her blood, and to find Aster and peel off his skin inch by inch.

The least enticing urge was to calm myself the fuck down

before I entered bloodlust and accidentally killed the other half of my soul.

I forced myself to my knees. Shadows swirled around me in deathly gusts as I dug my hands into the earth, grounding myself.

"Princeton, please," I managed, the words leaving my lips as if from down a dark tunnel.

Over and over, I saw Evie's frightened features as she told Aster *no*, tears blooming in her wounded gray eyes.

"Kylo!" someone yelled.

The sound could hardly reach me over the sound of blood rushing to my head, the gusts of wind, the whispers of starving, vengeful shadows.

I called to Princeton again through Evie's blood in my veins and her lingering magick in the earth, grasping for a lifeline.

Voices reached me as I fought to stay grounded. To breathe. To not let myself cross the point of no return.

You're not going to like what I have to say...

It was just a whisper that tickled my ear, maybe even wishful thinking I could mistake for something more.

"Say it," I hissed. My muscles trembled, my mind consumed by thoughts of her.

Her blood on Aster's tongue. The sight of her running from me, how easy it would be to catch her. To wrap her blonde hair around my fist and pull her small body back against mine. To push her head to the side and—

Remember your why, Kylo. *Back to basics.*

Princeton's voice might've been soothing if his words weren't making everything so much worse. Because now I was thinking about that primordial wound, Aisling tortured and killed as I was forced to watch. I felt the same helplessness then as I felt now letting Evie spy on the born without my protection.

That is not *your* why...

A body slammed into mine. My back hit the earth, my teeth rattled together. Blade held me down with his massive size and strength. His magick was potent and sharp, making my skin prickle and mind more alert.

I thrashed and snapped my jaw. I was aware that I looked like a beast gone mad, but my fangs were burning, my every instinct telling me to *chase Evie and destroy Aster.*

"She's fine—she's with Idris and Vesper," I heard Harmony say from behind Blade.

"Use your words, brother," Blade said, straining against my power. "What the fuck is going on?"

I pulled my shadows back, so I didn't hurt my friends. And in that moment, I remembered my *why.*

Frustration and shame and rage battled it out. My human and monster sides were at war. But like I had countless times before when being trained out of bloodlust by my mentor, I held onto my love for Blade and Harmony and the clan. I held tightly to my duty to protect Etherdale and mortals across the realm. And to my adoration for Evie that transcended blood and flesh.

The darkness receded from the corners of my eyes. I didn't want to let go of my wrath. But bloodlust was out of the question—especially not with so many eyes on me. I had to put my leadership role ahead of my ego.

"Fuck," I hissed through gritted teeth.

Harmony dropped down next to us. "What's got you feeling so operatic?"

Blade snorted, and the humorless laugh that left my lips sounded like more of a warning than anything else.

My body was heaving, magick straining against my tattooed skin. "*Operatic* seems light compared to what I am feeling right now."

Blade cautiously moved off me. "I saw it in your eyes," he said, voice low. "Were you about to—"

I swallowed, ashamed to admit the answer to Blade's unspoken question aloud.

"Aster stole a taste of Evie's blood." It didn't look like feeding, exactly, but I didn't fucking care.

"Helia's heavens," Harmony said.

She and Blade assessed me with new eyes, fully aware of how intensely possessive and unhinged Evie made me. The drive to protect her had already been driving me mad. But now?

I couldn't breathe right.

We were in a community garden space, a quiet nook in this mostly residential neighborhood. I glared toward the faintly visible border, the glamour and defensive magick that kept us protected.

I pushed to my feet. I needed movement. I needed action. This wrath had to go somewhere, or it would eat me alive.

"Where is she," I hissed.

Harmony and Blade exchanged a concerned glance.

"You sure that's a good idea right now, mate?" Blade asked.

I paced as if I truly had gone insane. My thoughts moved rapidly, body lit up from within.

"Fuck it all, I can't think straight until I kill some born," I said.

Harmony released a breath. "Okay. Let's go."

THEY WEREN'T who I wanted to kill. Masked and lustful for violence and bloodshed, Blade and Harmony helped me find a group of born to slaughter.

They were lowlifes hanging out near the university who had taken over a once-popular restaurant. They were an unspoken threat to progressive students and faculty—a reminder that Conrad had the city under born control.

A reminder that they were *powerless*.

This group wasn't who I wanted to kill, but that didn't matter once I barged into the restaurant and saw them lounging back in chairs or leaning over the bar. They were all cocky smiles, spread arms, and archaic clothing with blood red accents.

Not a care in the fucking world.

Until they saw me.

I rampaged. I didn't care if I showed my godlike power, the strength I'd been carefully concealing for eighty years. What did it matter if they knew?

They were about to be dead.

The sigh that left my lungs was a pleasurable relief. Blade stood in front of the exit. Harmony stood a few steps behind me, channeling her defensive shields as backup.

With deathly speed and precision, I grabbed the nearest born with a shadow limb and tore open his neck. I ignored the shouts and orders as born leaped to their feet. Magick deflected off Harmony's shields. I tore heads from bodies. Now the only person in this room smiling was *me*.

I groaned at the sensation of blood dribbling down my face, coating my hands. I savored the rawness of a kill using only a dagger and my bare hands. The feel of broken flesh under my fingers, the crunch of bones as shadows squeezed, eternal life reduced to corpses.

I did to the born what they did to us with no remorse. What they had always done and what they would continue to do if left unchecked.

Blade annihilated the first coward to approach the doors, using his favorite short swords to skewer them through the chest.

A dagger flew at my head, and I caught it midair with a smoky tendril. My predator's gaze found the born woman who'd thrown the weapon immediately.

I threw it right back, letting it strike her between the eyes as a swarm of shadow consumed her.

The primal release of magick and rage was a scalding snake that slithered through me. Every time I heard Aster's voice calling Evie's blood unique and perfect, I made my next kill that much more brutal. It was as if I were trying to fill a bottomless pit of hunger that could never be sated. Not even doused in blood, born power fueling more of my own as I drank their putrid essence.

"I think he's dead, buddy," Harmony said softly, patting my shoulder.

I was currently standing over a born man, letting my shadows impale him over and over as blood sprayed.

I felt nothing at all.

"In fact, I believe they are all dead." Blade slowly approached us. "That wasn't exactly quiet. We may want to get out of here before more show up and this turns into something bigger."

"Let more show up," I hissed.

Before my comrades could attempt to talk me down from my admittedly unhinged behavior, I scented something different in the air.

"Wait," I said. "Do you…"

"Human blood?" Harmony finished. "I think I hear something too."

I took a breath, attempting to bring myself down from this peak of madness by at least an inch.

"If they killed Alfie to take over his restaurant I'm going to go on my own killing spree," Blade growled. "I loved that guy. Also, there weren't any human servers when we came in."

The three of us had the same thought at the same time.

Once we found the basement door, we braced ourselves for the worst. Yellowish witch lights lit our path as we descended the dinky wooden stairs.

Someone whimpered. Blade cursed.

"Fucking hells," Harmony gasped.

Restaurant storage items had been shoved up against the walls to make room for one of the most nauseating sights I'd seen in the past decade.

Young human men and women were in various states of bondage and undress. Two demented, Lillianic altars stood in the center of the space. A girl, likely no older than eighteen, lay on one altar with bites all over her small body. She was deathly pale and unmoving.

"Blade, write to the closest care center," I said.

Harmony had already begun to soothe the room with her energy and speech, gingerly cutting away bindings and removing gags.

The animal side of me shut off, the human one taking its place. My *why* became painfully apparent.

Them.

We were doing all of this for *them.*

I moved to the girl on the altar, checking for a pulse. A relieved sound escaped me when I found one, however faint.

"You're going to be okay. You just need blood replenishing potion. You're going to be okay," I whispered.

Her short dark hair framed a youthful face. I felt sick with grief, disgust, and outrage that any being could be so cruel. I thought of the girl's family and friends. I thought of Evie.

I untied someone's daughter from one of the born's many sadistic feeding toys.

Once I knew backup was on the way and our path was clear, I scooped her into my arms and delivered her to the nearest care center myself.

49

EVIE

"Gods, Evie," Idris said.

I sat with him and Vesper on the roof of their apartment building. Idris had seen me running, and now I was explaining what happened. Even though I really didn't want to.

Kylo had never yelled at me like that before. His words rattled around in my brain—telling me to get away from him.

There was a choked feeling in my throat I couldn't swallow.

"I fucked up. I'm the worst hypocrite in the world," I said. I was trembling slightly. I saw it in Kylo's eyes—the shift, the fury. And I knew on a logical level that his wrath had been directed toward Aster.

But I'd lied to him. I'd hurt him just like he'd hurt me. And it was me he'd yelled at to *get away*.

I was sick to my stomach. The look of pity and conflict written into Vesper and Idris's features made me want to crawl out of my skin. Especially Idris's. It was an old habit to want to protect him from my pain.

"It's more complicated than that," Vesper said with a shake of her head. "This was different. You didn't lie to him to shield *him*.

You did it because he had made it clear that he would declare war before the Serpent Clan was ready to fight with you. It wasn't a fair position to put you in. You lied to shield your family and city. To give us the best fighting chance."

"I don't know how to feel," Idris said. He glared at the closed fists in his lap. "I still don't get why you have to do this. Why can't you let the vampires who have been building this revolution for decades handle killing Juliette and destabilizing the born? Why does it have to be *you*?"

More hurt flooded my chest as I stared at Idris. He once told me he believed in me. That the whole reason he wanted to be turned in the first place was to be as strong as I was.

"Why can't it be me, Idris?"

He stood, running a hand through his dirty blond hair.

"Juliette killed Princeton because of me," I said. "Maybe they would've been in the city, regardless. But she's obsessed with *me.* That's why she's doing all of this—creating hellish beasts, terrorizing Etherdale, killing hundreds of students."

Idris stared at me in disbelief. "She's doing those things because she's a psychopath!"

My heart tumbled, and Idris lowered his voice.

"Trauma or not, she's with the born and that's that. None of this is your fault. These things have been in motion since before you were born," Idris said.

"He's right about that part," Vesper said with a sip of tea. "But you're your own person. I know that your brother and your partner are both trying to protect you. But this is your fight as much as it's theirs." She looked at Idris gently, a comforting maternal air radiating from her striking appearance.

"Exactly," I said, grateful Vesper was here. I fought the urge to make myself smaller, to cower in the face of my loved ones' displeasure and anger. "I'm not doing all of this only out of guilt. Yes, it's not fair that Aster has had his sights set on me since I was a child. It's disgusting, but it gives me an advantage. I'm only trying to help everyone win a war against a king who has ruled for a *millennium* and his powerful army that covers the entire fucking realm. We need all the advantage we can get. Why can't you see that? Why can't either of you see that?"

Idris blinked, his face twisting with conflicted emotions. The nearly full moon illuminated us with her soothing silvery rays.

"You're bleeding nighttime, Evie," he whispered, a sad smile on his lips.

It's what he said to me before I killed our coven.

Darkness bloomed from me like ink underwater. A sob was forming from deep within me. I wanted to be saying these things to Kylo too. He hadn't given me a chance.

I pulled my shadows back inside. When the sob finally broke free, Vesper sat next to me on the bench and rubbed my back. I clumsily accepted her affection, stifling more tears as painful vulnerability reared its head.

"We can't see it because we love you and we don't want you to risk your life or the healing you've only just begun," Idris said. He kneeled and squeezed my hand. "That we both have only just begun."

"War is going to risk everything anyway," I said. "I don't want to be treated with kid gloves. Same as you."

Understanding washed over Idris's features, and he didn't look too happy about it.

"Mirrors are a curious thing," Vesper murmured, staring off into the distance.

My head snapped toward her. "What?"

"The way you're being treated now is how you once treated your little brother, I'm assuming?" Vesper said as she glanced between us.

"You could say that," Idris said with a sigh. He sat back down.

"You said the same thing about hatred—that it was a curious thing. You said it could tell us a lot about ourselves," I said slowly. I remembered all the imagery and dreams of mirrors the last few weeks.

"Both *are* curious, this is true. Mirrors and hatred tend to go hand-in-hand. Why do you hate that Juliette is mimicking you, Evie?"

I frowned. I wanted to say because it was irritating and psychotic, but that felt too obvious. To be honest, I wasn't really in the mood for cosmic lessons.

Where was Kylo? All of me was on high alert, paranoid about what he was doing right now. Could he not stand to look at me anymore? Or was he going to do something stupid like storm Conrad's estate?

I just wanted to make things right. But every time I had the urge to get up and go look for him, I remembered him yelling at me to get away.

I slowly refocused on Vesper. I allowed my spiritual paradigm to take back its shape, focusing on the lump in my throat and the visions of mirrors. Princeton and Hekate's presence bled through the cracks in my defenses.

"Because I'm scared of her being right," I admitted. "Terrified of it."

"Right about you being the same?"

I nodded. "I'm afraid that if I admit she's traumatized the same as I was, perhaps even worse, then I can no longer purely hate her and want her dead."

It wasn't the whole truth, and I knew it. Something far deeper was triggered by Juliette's fixation and mirroring, a rumination I was scared to say out loud.

Vesper saw it in my face. I know she did.

"You said she was my shadow."

Vesper moved her gaze to focus on the city in the distance. "You are not the same, Evie. But the people I've hated the most have often had a quality within them that I detested about myself. A quality I denied, a quality I didn't like seeing mirrored back to me. It's good you're still feeling empathetic toward her. Doesn't mean her fate needs to change."

"It doesn't," Idris affirmed. "My classmates in that building are gone, and they're never coming back. Because of *her*."

"No one forced her to do that," I added, shaking my head. The heat of anger was a welcome relief to the guilt and worry eating away at me. "She did it to prove she was as powerful as I was. But who knows, she might end up killing herself before we can. Whatever she's doing is destroying her from within."

At this, a smug smile formed. I tucked thoughts of psychological shadows and mirrors away for later.

"I can't sit here anymore. I need to go find Kylo," I said. "I'm scared of what he might do."

"His friends will calm him down. He's going to feel what he feels, and then he needs to deal with it like the rest of us. We cannot jeopardize the realm over a piece of bloody cake."

My stomach sank. I hoped Vesper was right about that.

"Do you want me to go with you?" she asked.

"I'll come too," Idris said, which wasn't really a question.

"No. I'll be fine. I want to talk to him alone."

MY DRIVE TO go to Kylo was beyond instinctual. It was baked into every cell of my body. Cemented there through the intensity of our love, our kinky games, the power play and a bond that brushed the cosmos. Kylo had seen all of me. My spiritual inner world, my wounded heart, my dreams and my buried desires. Just as I'd seen all of his.

When Allie told me he'd left with Blade and Harmony, my anxiety spiked. She told me they were rescuing a cell of trafficked humans and would return shortly.

So he hadn't gone straight to Aster. He hadn't declared war. At least not yet.

I waited for him in his—our—home. I pulled my knees to my chest as I sat on the couch in the living room. My legs bounced. My lower lip was sore from compulsive biting.

The word *hypocrite* was a mantra I couldn't shake, replacing the one Kylo had instilled in me. The mantra of *I'm not sorry.*

Because tonight, I was absolutely fucking sorry. At least, that was how I felt. But honestly, Vesper's assessment was more aligned with the truth than my current state of shame. I hadn't wanted to lie to Kylo. I didn't do it out of selfishness or even to protect him. I did it for everyone else.

That logic fell away the moment Kylo stepped through the front door. I was a wound that bled, desperate to earn back his love.

My feet took me to the foyer. Kylo's form was rigid, his eyes burning into me with intensity. Everything about him made me want to fall to my knees.

"I'm sorry I yelled," he said. "And for squeezing your throat—that was not intentional, and I'm deeply ashamed of losing control. I would *never* consciously hurt you out of anger."

"I know," I said.

"I don't want to admit this," he said softly. A muscle feathered in his jaw. His dark blue sleeves were rolled up, revealing his many sigil tattoos. Veins in his forearms pulsed. "But I sensed true bloodlust taking over in a way I haven't felt in eighty years. It wasn't just a small slip. I was on the very edge. If I had lost complete control, I would've killed you."

That was why he had yelled at me to get away. Not because he couldn't look at me anymore.

I stared at his feet. "I'm sorry for hurting you. I withheld information for the sake of our clan," I said. "I didn't want to be dishonest with you. It was tearing me up inside. But you told me what would happen if Aster hurt me, and it didn't feel like enough trauma to justify triggering a war we aren't ready for. The Serpent Clan will be here in a few weeks. I don't care if you're the one who kills Aster, but please Kylo, don't put anyone in danger because of me."

"Not enough trauma," Kylo scoffed with a dry laugh.

I raked my gaze from his eyes down to his boots again. My body moved beyond my conscious awareness. I sank to my knees before his rigid form. When I began to untie his laces, I heard the faintest hitch of his breath.

"Evie, what are you doing?"

"Being submissive and adorable because I love you and I'm sorry," I said.

Kylo's next chuckle was less cold, even as I felt his power rattle the air around us.

I paused. My eyes moved back up his form. "You're covered in blood." In my heightened emotions, my brain had skipped right over it.

"I may have gone on a born killing spree," he said, voice gravelly as he stared down at me.

"You didn't answer my apology speech."

Kylo moved his glare forward, keeping his hands at his side. I was so used to him touching me that the absence of it was like a slap.

The choked feeling was worse than ever. I diligently finished unlacing his scary combat boots, waiting for his next words.

"I love you too, angel. Like I've said on numerous occasions, I love you so much that it should terrify the entire world."

The words soothed me, even if he still hadn't answered my desperate plea.

"Kiss them."

The words rooted deep inside me, blending with the intensity of power and emotion engulfing us.

I bent forward and kissed each of Kylo's boots. My lips became soft and malleable against leather.

Kylo released a sigh as he stepped out of his shoes. He finally touched me, tangling his hand in my hair and pulling me up to stare into his deep pools of blue. Staring into his eyes felt cosmic, eternal. Like two halves who were always meant to return to wholeness.

"I won't declare war over his disgusting violation. I will wait to artfully torture him to the point of insanity and watch the life drain from his eyes. I will do what is best for you and what is best for the clan."

Now it was my turn to release a breath.

"But you are not to return to him," he growled. "Do you understand me, angel? Never. Again."

50

EVIE

He was using his Dom voice as a weapon. I wanted to lean in, to nod my head and melt into his chest and feel his hands running through my hair. I wanted his praise so badly that I felt real hatred for the part of me that had become so strong.

The part of me that knew it wasn't right of Kylo to make this order. And it wouldn't be right of me to blindly follow it.

"It's done," he hissed. "We have what we need, and I *am* proud of you for getting us a name we can use. The born can investigate for more proof themselves. It will have to be enough. It's not worth the risk anymore."

I hadn't affirmed him. Kylo pinned me with a look that was unquestionable. The angles of his face appeared sharper, the size of him more imposing. The secret collar around my neck felt tighter than before.

I saw a vision of mirrors. Juliette, Aster, the sickness of their bond. I wanted to shut my eyes tight.

We weren't them.

Juliette was the unhealed version of what I might've become.

"Do you hear me, angel?" Kylo asked, a balance of gentleness and authority. "It's *done*."

I forced the words out of my mouth. "But I have something in motion to lure Juliette away. I can be quick—"

"Evie, it is my duty to protect you. My intuition is never wrong, and I know in my bones that if you return to that place, he will not let you come back," Kylo said, holding my face in his strong hands.

"That's not an intuition. That's a fear."

Kylo frowned deeply. "I have never once questioned your instincts, Evie."

No, he hadn't. Kylo always took me seriously, even when so many others had cast doubts or told me I worried too much or found excess meaning in the fabric of reality. He believed in me even when no one else was capable of it.

"I have no way to communicate with Juliette outside of seeing her in person. I'm so close to something huge. With all of them. With Aster. And even with Conrad, who warmed up to me—"

Kylo retracted his touch and turned away from me. I could feel his rage like a red, scalding fire close to my face.

"Damnit, Evie," he cursed. It was as though he were struggling not to raise his voice or perhaps not destroy the wall he was now facing. "You are talking about a man who forcibly impregnated a woman and abused her for years. And another man who calls that abuser his *friend*. These demons want to do the same thing to *you*. Please tell me you see that."

He whipped around on me, shadows pulsing and eyes dilated.

"After we slaughtered the born who'd infested a human family's restaurant, we smelled mortal blood below. Do you know what we found in the basement?"

I shuddered to guess. Dread pooled in my stomach as I waited for another brutal truth.

"Trafficked mortals, some of them teenagers. They were in sexual bondage, in various states of nudity—all to make them as appealing of a meal as possible. One of them was nearly dead, strapped to an altar where she'd been fed from and tortured and left to die. I carried her to a care center as she fought to stay alive."

Nausea was swift. My heart hammered as my face fell.

"The born want free rein to treat mortals as playthings. To torture, rape, and kill under the guise of religion. *That* is the world Conrad and Aster are building. Not one of *order*."

"I know that," I said, fisting Kylo's shirt as I steadied myself. The fabric was still slightly damp with blood. "Of course I know who Conrad and Aster are. I know what they want for me and the rest of the realm." I searched his eyes. "Is the girl okay?"

Kylo nodded, gripping the back of my neck as he stared down at me. "She was stable when I left. She's in good hands now."

A shaky exhale rolled through me. "I know, Kylo. I *know*."

"Then fight *with* me," he whispered, urgent and intense. He gripped my chin between his thumb and forefinger, using more of his dominance as a weapon of persuasion. "You've been extraordinarily brave. You've uncovered so much more about Conrad and Aster's positions than we ever would've known without your help. And we now understand more about Juliette too. Let it be enough. We can take them *together*."

I didn't know what was right anymore. The visions, the competing intuitions and goals. The tangled web of connections and manipulation I'd found myself in the center of.

Kylo's love was one of the few certainties I had.

His presence was all-consuming, drug-like in its intensity.

"Okay. Together."

Kylo released his hold on my face and kissed my forehead. I didn't miss the tremor that racked through his lethal form.

"I'm sorry," I said again.

He shut his eyes. Our shadows intertwined. I sensed his hurt, his panic, his bottomless wrath. Most of all, his fear that I was capable of making him helpless to protect me.

"I know why you did it, but I feel what I feel," he said.

"What do you feel?"

Our shadows locked tight. Over and over, I saw Kylo rehashing the expression on my face when Aster tasted my blood. The tremble of my lip, the shock of shame and fear in my eyes. It was a reconstruction of the memory he'd felt through our bond. A projection of what I might've looked like when I'd said the word *no*.

His hand moved to my waist. "Tormented."

"I'm sorry." I rested my head on his chest.

"Please stop apologizing. Are *you* okay, angel?" he asked, peeling me off him to assess my face. "I'm not merely upset for my sake—I'm mostly upset because you didn't let me care for you after someone hurt you. I can't imagine how triggering that was, and you carried it alone."

"Oh," I said with a frown. "I don't want to think of it like that. As I said, it wasn't that bad. I don't want his behavior to ruin anything about me or *us*."

Anger flashed in Kylo's eyes. "You have to take care of yourself, too, Evie. I fucking demand it."

My shoulders sank. "I'm fine," I said quietly, even as tears burned my eyes.

"He hurt *you*, angel. That's the most egregious part of all of this." Kylo shook his head. "He is incapable of ruining anything about us. And certainly nothing about *you*. You are perfect because you were born perfect, with a soul that humbles me with its radiance and capacity for love. That will never change."

My mind spun. I was struggling to stay grounded. "This is a lot."

Kylo sighed, stroking my face. "It's war." He dropped his hand and moved away from me.

The words fell over us as he peeled off his bloody clothing, first his shirt and then his pants. I swallowed a gasp as he towered over me, rippling muscles painted with crimson. The sight of his semi-hard cock made my mouth water, one of the few parts of him without splatters of blood.

Our shadows' whispers coalesced into a focal point of clarity.

From born blood we rise.

Kylo returned to me. His forehead touched mine. We shared the same breath, the same thirst for vengeance, the same wounds and fears. Mirrors and shadows.

"You need to feed," I said, because I could feel it. He'd expended power on his killing spree.

"Not from you."

I pulled away like he'd struck me.

He yanked me back toward him, his hand cradling my face. "I don't want to hurt you."

My lips met his jaw, tasting salt and blood on my tongue. He shuddered.

"Emotions are too high. I was so close to endangering you tonight, and that's inexcusable."

"Then we'll be gentle," I said. "I want it to be *my* blood."

Kylo groaned. In one swift movement he had me in his arms, my back against the wall. His breath was warm as he sucked at the skin over my collarbone. "Gods, angel, *please*. Did I not just say I was tormented?"

"I don't recall."

His laugh tickled my skin, leaving goosebumps in its wake. "How am I to be gentle with you when all I want to do is march you down to the Nighswander Estate by your collar—the pretty pink one with a bow on it—and claim you as I brutally torture every born who watched you bleed?"

"Do you have enough limbs to do all of those things simultaneously?"

Shadows leaped from him, coiling around my wrists and pinning them to the wall above my head. I panted, burning with my own aliveness and desire to be as close to Kylo as possible.

"I guess we'll soon find out," he whispered in my ear.

He studied my eyes again, searching.

"I'm not a wounded baby bird," I growled. "I want you. I belong to *you*."

He hardened beneath me, grinding against my sensitive core. Only the fabric of my panties and dress stood between us.

"I've missed when my wounded baby bird gets growly with me."

I rolled my eyes, and Kylo retaliated with a kiss that shook the house's foundation. Like a dam had broken, he consumed me, naked and bloody. My bindings fell away, and I trailed my hands down his chiseled form as Kylo sucked and teased my lips with his fangs. His tongue tasted all of me, body and soul.

It was as though we were trying to prove with our bodies that everything was settled and we were both fine. But no matter what I'd agreed to and how badly I wanted Kylo to forgive me and not be upset with me, I couldn't shake the cascade of doubts rushing into the foreground.

I'd already told Aster I would return to him at the end of the week. How was I going to explain my sudden change of heart? How were we going to lure Juliette away now? Before she hurt anyone else? What about my own intuition, the vision that something we needed was inside Conrad's study?

Kylo read my thoughts—the warring desires to please him and to be useful to the clan.

A feral noise escaped him as he pinned me harder against the wall. He pulled out his dagger, its energetic field radiating the energy of fresh kills. I could hear the sound of shadows feasting, born choking on blood, shouts that faded swiftly into silence.

Kylo sliced off my panties. The violence, the blood, the

weapons, the looming threat of war—it was all a drug, a balm to ward against the crack in our foundation.

The fissure we both wanted to ignore.

He pushed me up higher so that my legs fell over his shoulders and his shadows held me in place. His lips skated across my core before he devoured that too. He cursed as I moaned and writhed against him.

He gripped my ass as he fed on my flesh, sucking, pulsing, easily bringing me to the brink of release with his mouth alone.

He plunged two fingers inside me. "So wet and needy for me, aren't you, angel?"

"Yes, Kylo."

He angled to hit the spot that had me unraveling against him.

"May I please come?"

Kylo kissed my bud. "Yes."

I came hard, riding against his ridiculously skilled tongue, legs trembling.

He lowered me back into his arms, carrying me to one of the high-back chairs in the living room. On the side table, one of the books we read together and a stack of tarot cards sat.

We both glanced there at the same time—the evidence of our connection written in the stars, our inner worlds that had blended together when we hadn't been looking.

"Pull a card for me, baby," Kylo said as he helped me out of my dress. His caress of my breasts was gentle, the thumb over my nipple drawing a needy moan from my lips.

As I reached for the deck, he buried himself inside me. I gasped, my fingernails digging into his shoulder.

"We're going to be gentle," he said, voice strained as he glared at my jugular. "We *have* to be gentle."

I gingerly shuffled the deck as Kylo slowly rocked his hips. "If it helps, I, too, love you so much it should terrify the world."

He smiled, but it didn't reach his haunted eyes. It twisted my guts to know I'd hurt him. I'd hurt him more than he would say aloud. Because Kylo would always choose to protect my heart over his own.

"What do you want to know?" I whispered, looking from the cards to Kylo's eyes.

"Whatever you think is best, angel. I just want to hear you talk about magick," he whispered.

His breath hitched as he went deeper inside me. I mewled, grinding slightly as I struggled to settle on a question for the cards. It was a new deck, beautiful faerie and forest themed illustrations that Kylo knew I'd adore.

"I want to know what you and I look like after the war, when The Tower has been replaced by The Star."

The light finally touched Kylo's eyes.

I drew a card. I smiled at the unique depiction of The Sun. Fiery reds, oranges, and yellows that reminded me of Mena's cake at her hope-themed soiree.

I showed Kylo the card, and he kissed my cheek with a grin.

"You're remembering when I forced you to dance with me at the party and then charmed the fuck out of Mena and Idris while we ate sun cake."

I sweetly kissed his lips in affirmation. "The Sun is the card of pure, unbridled joy and happiness."

"Another," Kylo rasped, gripping my hips as he fucked me with slightly more intensity.

Spirit energy enlivened the surrounding air, lightening the heavy weight on both of our shoulders.

I pulled The Empress. A woman wore a crown of blooming flowers as she sat on a throne. One of her hands was placed on her round stomach, while the other held a bunch of grapes.

I blushed furiously, and Kylo halted deep inside me.

"Show me that card," he commanded with a smirk.

Why was I feeling this way? The card's imagery wasn't literal—it had many meanings and complexities, like all the cards. This was just one representation of the classical interpretation.

I showed him. And Kylo's eyes turned molten.

"Are the spirits fucking with us?" he said with a groan, cupping a breast and making me cry out with a violent thrust.

"Most certainly," I panted. "They enjoy doing that."

"Now is not the time to conjure images of you carrying my seed."

"It's not just a fertility card in a corporeal sense," I said quickly, cheeks still burning. "It's also a card of luxury, creativity, and abundance. Or like, maybe you'll feed me lots of grapes once we live in a free world."

Kylo's chuckle was dark as his grip on me tightened.

I set down the cards. I melted against Kylo's chest, soothed by the sun-kissed imagery.

"Our future looks bright," I whispered. "We just have to get there."

Kylo stroked my back. "I'm dragging you there whether you want it or not, my vulnerable little meadow nymph." He kissed my temple.

"I want it."

It was the strongest yearning I'd ever held. To be in a world where everyone I loved was safe.

I pulled back and tilted my head, giving him access. "Don't kill me, pretty please."

Kylo plunged his fangs into my throat as his arms wrapped around me, his cock buried as close to my womb as he could manage.

Never, I heard through our bond.

My eyes fluttered as Kylo fed from me. As I was relaxing into a state of pure bliss, the Seven of Swords, the familiar card of betrayal, flashed in my mind. My stomach sank and my body tensed briefly at the vision. But just as quickly, pain transformed into pleasure and the imagery washed away.

Kylo made soothing touches across my skin. He held me close.

Through the bond, visions of violence leaked through—Kylo pinning me down, taking me roughly and brutally, showing my collared, fang-marked body off to the born.

Mine.

Though his fantasies were dark, all he showed me tonight was tenderness. After we finished, he took care of me as he always did, and I fell asleep in his arms.

When I woke in the middle of the night, he was gone.

51

EVIE

The next time I drifted to sleep, I was semi-lucid.

I was aware I was in a dream, but I wasn't sure exactly what had happened before I arrived there. I stood in a forest of tall trees and plentiful wildflowers. Insects chirped, and I could barely make out the hissing of a snake.

"You can't have it all."

I turned to see Juliette, dressed in Evie-pink.

"It's not fair," she said. "You can't have them all."

I closed the distance between us. The forest morphed into a desert wasteland, nothing but barren earth as far as the eye could see.

"Which is it, Juliette? Do you want to be me? Or do you want to kill me?"

She smiled. Blood poured from her nose. She looked down at her pink dress, frilly socks, and platform Mary Jane shoes.

"I would never kill you, Evie."

A single tear slid down her cheek. The front of her dress was now stained with two crimson lines.

"Why do you want to be sisters?" I asked her. More and more lucid consciousness spilled inside me. This was my chance to make everything right. To lure her away so I could take her out before we launched into war.

Before she could try to kill one hundred turned in the blink of an eye. Or perform another death magick ritual and conjure a new race of demon creatures.

As soon as I had the thought, one of them appeared before us —an apparition of the rabid undead beast with slits for a nose. I leaped back, but it soon disappeared into a cloud of white mist.

"They died," she whispered. "All of my dogs died."

"That is an extremely liberal use of the word *dog*."

Juliette's lip trembled. "Do you not feel alone anymore because of *him*? The man with the blue eyes?"

I ignored her question like she had ignored mine. I didn't want her talking about Kylo. Even *thinking* about Kylo. "You want to be sisters because you feel alone."

I had dreamed of sisterhood when I was a girl. On days Mama was particularly cruel, I wondered what it would be like to have a sister. I loved caring for Idris. But this was a different fantasy, one where I didn't have to be the lone eldest daughter. Perhaps I'd wanted my pain to be shared, or to see myself reflected in another so I didn't feel as painfully different from everyone else.

Juliette's shoulders dropped. She gazed into the distance. "You were promised to Sir by Lillian. He never forgot you, even when he was giving me all of his heart."

"That's touching," I said. "Anyway, I think you were right."

Juliette's gray eyes suddenly beamed with hope.

"I'm on a path of darkness," I said, voice low and eyes frenzied. I played up the drama just like she had—a perfect mirror. I oozed false fear. "I've abandoned Lillian's plan for me, and I feel trapped."

Her eyes flashed, unable to hide her emotions. "I understand completely."

Behind her, I saw a mirror. And that mirror reflected a

mirror behind me, creating a loop of Juliette and me facing each other that spanned an eternity.

I swallowed, focusing back on her. "Can we meet?"

"We're meeting right now, silly!"

I smiled, forcing my body to reflect ease. "I mean, in the flesh."

Juliette rocked back on her feet. Her forehead creased. "Aren't you coming back Friday? Sir says we're going to have a tea party—the three of us. Maybe Conrad too..."

She watched my face, clearly searching for something. Was that what her accusation was about? Was she afraid I had feelings for both Conrad and Aster?

"Yes, I'm coming back Friday. But I was hoping you and I could hang out, just us."

A smile slowly crept across her face. "Okay. We can *hang out,* Evie."

I smiled back. This was almost a normal interaction. Shocking.

She cocked her head. "How about we meet at Celeste's?"

My smile dropped.

Juliette batted her eyes innocently. "What's wrong? You love Celeste's."

"Is that a threat? How long have you been watching me?"

"Nooo, it's *insurance.*" She winked.

Great. Glad I'd taught the psychopath a new term.

Juliette took a step back with a shrug, the infinite mirror images shifting as she moved. "We're going to fix all of this. You just have to remember that you *can't have it all,* okay?" She nodded and smiled. "Since you don't want me to meet your *friends,* I'll see you Friday, Evie. Don't be late... or I'll have to go looking for you at all your favorite places!"

"No, wait—"

She disappeared in a fit of white smoke and screams. Demon dogs roamed in the distance. The mirrors shattered.

I woke up.

Kylo was still gone.

I TOLD VESPER EVERYTHING.

We were enjoying our usual morning coffee ritual, this time on the back patio of our home where it was more private. The yard was lush, my new garden already thriving under my care and magick. In the distance was the small grove of trees where Kylo liked to read—where he tattooed me under the stars.

Vesper wore a deep burgundy corset and sleek black skirt. It was a sharp contrast to my pastels and florals. She had styled her hair in a slicked-back ponytail.

"What do you want to do?" she asked me when I finished. She set down her coffee on the table between us and leaned back in her chair.

"I don't know. She knows where my grandmother lives. She knows I'm friends with the humans and witches who frequent Celeste's. She knows about Kylo. I'm not certain of how much she knows about the clan—but we still don't understand how she was able to enter a glamoured location. I think she's been watching me for months now."

"I'm glad you felt comfortable talking to me about this," she said. "I don't want to step on any toes as we approach war, especially as a guest in Kylo's domain, but you're my friend too. You deserve to control your own destiny."

The words healed something deep inside me, hearing Vesper call herself my friend.

"It sounds like you're already defending your choice—you know exactly what you want to do."

I gripped my coffee tight, as if it were an emotional support pet. "It's not even about wanting to—it's about *needing* to. I'm terrified of what will happen if I don't. But I promised Kylo I wouldn't return. I can't lie to him, not again. I don't even know where he is right now."

"Your love runs deep," Vesper said, tilting her head slightly as a small smile formed. "Believe it or not, I'm still a romantic. I'm just unfortunately attracted to men, and I don't find the vast majority of them to be redeemable characters."

My lips curved in spite of myself. "That doesn't surprise me —either admission. And yes, our love runs so deep that I don't think either of us knows how to balance it with our duty to the clan. Our devotion to Hekate and the world we're building together. Is it inevitable for love to be so blinding?"

Vesper nodded. "I think that's one of its natural functions. We weren't born to be self-contained, pious ascetics. We were born to love each other. And a cost of love is freedom, which is perhaps why I find it hard to engage with romance these days. Other forms of love—friend love, community love—tend to leave more wiggle room."

Vesper never wanted to feel trapped or controlled again. How she was able to maintain this position of maternal wisdom after everything she's been through, even when discussing Conrad himself—it was a testament to the incredible, miraculous woman she was.

"Then what's the right answer?" I asked, self-aware enough to hear the pleading tone in my voice but too desperate to care. I searched Vesper's face frantically, as if I might find the decisiveness that I needed.

"There isn't one. Sometimes the correct choice is the one we make."

I leaned back in my chair. "No offense, but that is not helpful."

Vesper laughed. "The truth isn't always," she sighed. "I don't want you to put yourself in a dangerous position either. If I'm being completely honest with you, I feel as though waiting to strike as a greater unit is the best decision. We've already learned so much from your visits. There has to be a way to lure Juliette without making you vulnerable. She clearly sneaks off when the lords aren't aware. We just have to catch her at it."

I could see it now: the fear that Vesper had been carefully concealing from me. I remembered Kylo's emotional words, reminding me that Aster and Conrad wanted to abuse me the same way they had Vesper if I gave them the opportunity. Vesper cared for me, even as she respected my autonomy.

"But what about Conrad's offer?" I asked quietly, hyperempathetic to the slight wince in Vesper's features. "He all but admitted he was willing to remove Juliette from the picture if that was what I wanted."

"You can't trust him," Vesper said firmly. "They want *you*, Evie. Especially if Juliette is taken out. Then they will *need* you."

"I wonder how they envision using us after they're done with Etherdale," I said.

"It sounds like they want to move out of the South entirely. They want Prospyrus; they want the crown. Conrad is violently ambitious. That was why he'd bred enemies at court, like Kole. He was always resistant to bowing to seniority and respecting chains of command. Especially when those customs interfered with his own aims. It doesn't surprise me he grew tired of being blocked and thwarted. Men like him need to be at the top or they will die trying."

"So they'd use me as a weapon," I surmised. "A pretty, fuckable weapon. And that's why when I was eavesdropping, I heard them say they paid a bribe to keep my power a secret. I don't know how they can honestly believe I'll just go along with their plans."

Vesper's eyes darkened. She tongued a fang, a habit I'd seen her do a few times—as if she found comfort in reminding herself how powerful she'd become.

"The born have many methods at their disposal to

psychologically break a person. Especially with Conrad's pain magick. If you don't comply, they have ways to force you."

"It won't get that far," I said.

I stared sadly into my empty coffee mug before admitting defeat and setting it back down. I averted my gaze to my new garden. Herbs and flowers with faintly glowing auras gently called to me in singsong notes that carried in the wind.

"Kylo has taken care of me since the day we met. We belong to each other. Yet I also pledged my soul and its vessel to Hekate and the revolution." My eyes pricked with frustrated tears. "I didn't think it was possible to respect a man as deeply as I respect him. I owe him honesty. But I'm afraid that if I give him that, he will make my choice for me."

Vesper listened and held me with a gentle gaze. She didn't shame me or try to influence my decision either way.

"Juliette said if I didn't show up Friday, she would go looking for me at *all my favorite places*. Which means defenseless mortals would be endangered—our allied coven, or maybe even Mena and the mortals she's harboring in her home. Either way, I'm at a disadvantage. But at least if I go to them, *I'm* the only one at risk."

"I wish I could come with you," Vesper said.

"Me too."

"Have you prayed about this, Evie? Spoken to Hekate and your spirit allies?"

I looked back over my garden. I felt the warmth of the sun on my face. I imagined sitting on a porch with Vesper when this was all over, with Kylo inside showing off his culinary prowess while being terrorized by Blade and Harmony's teasing, and Idris and his friends sparring in the distance.

Who knows? Maybe by then Vesper will have had a change of heart about looking for her daughter. Maybe after the war was won and Conrad was dead, she'd feel differently.

"Yes, I've prayed," I finally answered. "They tend to go silent when paths split. They want me to make my own decisions, so long as I'm grounded in something higher than myself. Again, not very helpful."

Vesper nodded. "Such is the unfortunate plight of being alive."

I snorted. "Fuck."

"Enough said, really." Vesper followed my gaze to the garden. "You're going to do the right thing. And if you don't, you can always change course. As long as you understand that some consequences cannot be undone, especially when matters of the heart are involved. Or fragile mortality."

I stared at my hands in my lap. I felt like a trapped and cornered animal, threatened from all angles. Which made me crave Kylo all the more.

Had he changed his mind in the middle of the night? Had he decided he couldn't forgive me for my dishonesty?

"Are you excited for the rest of your clan to join you here?" I asked Vesper, desperate for a distraction.

Her eyes lit up from within, like an eternal flame. "Beyond words. I can't wait for our families to converge. They're going to love you."

I smiled. "If they're anything like you and Clarke, I know the feelings will be mutual."

"The born have no idea what they've conjured through their apathy and abuse. Forget ripping open portals to Lillian's hells. They're about to witness an entire legion of monsters rise from the underground."

A familiar vision flashed in my mind, for only a moment. The same as I'd seen during my first turning ritual.

Unmasked turned fighting in the streets. Shadows feasting. Hearts beating as one.

Kylo, covered in blood and grinning.

52

KYLO

"She made it," Harmony said as she took a seat on the other side of my desk in the study. "She's going to make a full recovery."

I smiled, even if it didn't reach my eyes. Harmony was reporting on the girl I'd saved from the borns' demented altar.

I'd been working underground since I woke up in the middle of the night. Work was my first soothing addiction, before I'd met Evie.

If Princeton were still alive, I would've gone straight to him. He knew how to get my head screwed back on straight. He would know how to help me.

But he was gone. I had to figure my shit out on my own now.

When I'd roused in the middle of the night, Evie had been warm and sweet in my arms. I'd kissed her hair, listened to the steady beat of her heart. She'd become so strong in the past couple of months. And now, asleep in my hold, she looked like that wounded girl I'd first known—the girl who cried and yelled for Idris and her mother in her nightmares.

I couldn't take it. Anxiety was eating me alive. Knowing Evie had agreed so instantly not to return to Aster because she loved me, and not because she truly wanted to stand down.

"I don't know how to make her see that she doesn't have to do this," I said. "Since that first invitation from *him*, I believe she's been operating out of misplaced guilt. She thinks she led Juliette to Princeton, and this is how she can atone for her sins. She can't let it go."

"Hmm, sounds like someone else I know…" Harmony said gently, reaching to rub the top of my hand before retracting her touch.

"I know what that bastard would say. I can hear it so clearly."

I didn't need to say Princeton's name. Harmony knew.

"That this is exposure therapy," I muttered. "Evie is provoking the most destructive part of me. The monster that was created when they killed Aisling."

"That's also the *best* part of you, Kylo," Harmony said. "That's what led you to become a vampire. To study and train and nurture the best version of yourself. You're an obsessive fucker, but that comes with just as many strengths as weaknesses."

I groaned, raking a hand through my hair. "Is it too late to abandon my virtuous principles and merely lock her in a room until we've taken the city and Aster's head has become a lawn ornament?"

Joking wasn't providing its usual relief. Now, I was thinking about Aster, and Evie near Aster. In response, shadows leaked from me in vengeful, harsh whispers.

"We unmask in three weeks," Harmony said. "In three weeks, you won't have to hold back any longer. You will follow through on the plan you've been building for nearly a century. We *all* will."

"My logical brain understands what you're saying. My primal, emotional self wants it all. I want to uphold my duty to the realm and its many turned clan allies. And I also want to storm the Nighswander Estate *today*."

Harmony's gaze was firm, her warm brown eyes glowing with her gentle magick. "We can't have it all. We have to choose."

"I can't lose her, Harmony. I can't fucking lose her. And I don't just mean her life. I also can't bear for her to learn the hard way what Aster and Conrad are capable of. They want to pluck those pretty stars from her eyes, and I would rather die than let them."

Harmony's brows drew in. The room flooded with soft, healing energy. "And I think it's those stars in her eyes that generate Evie's greatest strengths and weaknesses too. Her hopefulness makes her brave and resilient, as much as it leaves her vulnerable and blind to danger."

My heart felt like it was physically cracking behind my ribs. And like a lovesick fool, I still couldn't help but smile at such a beautiful, tragic description of my soulmate.

"I'm glad you see it too."

She smiled. "I adore your and Evie's love. It makes *me* hopeful. I think it makes us all hopeful."

I hadn't felt so human since I first heard Evie tell me she loved me. Or maybe not since the beginning of all of this. The day I died and became reborn.

"On a different note," I said. "Our allies along the route to Prospyrus are stable now and awaiting word. Last week's skirmish was contained. As soon as Earle deploys his numbers, our allies will intercept and buy us time."

Harmony was silent for a moment, assessing my sharp change in conversation topic. I swallowed, looking back to the correspondence before me.

"Can you help me figure out how to handle the shifter rivalry near Morha? It's starting to trickle into clan affairs."

Harmony nodded. "Of course, Kylo."

~

"Good, Idris," I said from behind a sparring mat. I decided to spend the afternoon helping out with combat and magickal instruction. That was another thing Princeton would've reminded me: Being of service liberated me from the bondage of self.

It was irritating how true this simple advice was. The more I made myself useful, brightening younger clan members' days with my praise and insight, the better I felt inside my tormented mind.

I'd written to Evie, telling her I was working underground, but she hadn't responded. And I was having very normal and sane feelings in the wake of her silence.

Idris was battling it out with a fellow newborn. He was agile and precise, exceptionally promising for a young vampire. I tried to keep such comments to a minimum, as I didn't want to alienate him from his class of turned any more than he already was.

My clan was fiercely loyal and grounded. But we were vampires, and emotions and urges ran high. Especially in the young. Idris's status as Evie's brother was both a blessing and a curse to his ability to fit in.

The bearded man he was fighting suddenly took the upper hand, swiping Idris's legs out from under him. He launched on top of Idris and pinned him with a match-ending hold.

Idris looked stunned, glancing from the man to me as his brow furrowed. He shook his head slightly, stood, and congratulated his opponent.

I was helping a woman communicate with her shadows when Idris found me again, sipping fresh donor blood.

"I hope I didn't distract you," I murmured.

The woman before us was using her shadows to move objects around, her forehead creasing in concentration.

"You didn't. Don't say anything, please, but... he used his blinding magick."

Paternal protectiveness flooded me, but I remained outwardly level as I nodded in understanding. Using magick during hand-to-hand was prohibited. It defeated the purpose of honing those particular fighting skills. His opponent had cheated.

"So perhaps I did serve as a distraction," I said with a sigh. "If you experience any real trouble, come to me at once or tell your superiors. We are nothing if we are divided."

Idris looked away, frustration and discomfort souring his features. "I need to handle this myself. That's the only way it ends." At my imploring expression, he elaborated. "It's not everyone, just a disgruntled few. Nothing warrants action from superiors. I need to prove myself. To earn my seat at the table like everyone else." He paused again. "And please, for the love of all that is holy, do not tell Evie."

I smirked, and my heart panged. "Okay, Idris. I hear you. There's no reason to tell Evie—for now."

Idris's face relaxed. "Thanks. I want to make this quick, for obvious reasons, but is she okay?"

I returned my gaze to the cross-legged girl learning to move her shadows. Limbs were shifting from smoke to solidity as she attempted to arrange objects with her eyes closed.

"Yes, she's okay. And I intend to keep her so." There was no reason to worry Idris. He should be concentrating on becoming a stronger fighter.

Idris nodded, releasing a breath. "Good."

I felt a low buzz of power emitting from him, and I side-eyed him to see the jittery anger in his features and the tapping of his fingers against his thigh.

"How are you?"

Idris frowned deeply. He shook his head. "I'm fine. Thanks. I'll see you around."

He took off, and I couldn't help but watch him. His powerful stance, the faint darkness blooming from his palms as he stalked toward a group of his older friends.

Hearing about Evie's violation was probably incredibly triggering for him. But he didn't want to talk about it, and I couldn't make him. So long as he channeled that anger into noble pursuits and clan justice, he really was going to be fine.

I knew from experience.

Speaking of being fine, I needed to soothe myself with a born torture session. I'd earned it.

53

EVIE

Tomorrow was the day. Only Vesper and I were aware of the invisible deadline. The impossible choice that still wasn't entirely clear.

Kylo and I hadn't been the same since the moment he discovered my deception through our bond. He was working nonstop, as if he were avoiding me. And when he was with me, his attentiveness and devotion gave me whiplash—as if I were imagining the distance.

That was how I felt now, lying with Kylo outside as the sun began its lazy descent. The nights were getting cooler, signaling autumn's arrival. I welcomed the change.

We were reading together, every once in a while coming up for air to discuss or laugh or kiss. He told me about each clan in Ravenia: where they were located, how long they'd been hiding, and any special gifts or powers each clan's members held. It soothed me to understand deeply that we weren't alone.

And when Kylo and I finished a lively philosophical debate, which concluded with him pinning me with kisses, my choice was being made for me in a way I hadn't anticipated.

"I love your weird little mind," Kylo said as I giggled underneath him. He teased my lips with his tongue.

I couldn't do it.

Talking to Vesper, I'd been nearly certain that the right choice was to cave to Juliette's threat. That it would be worth it, and I could handle this on my own without endangering anyone else. But Vesper had been right—I was no longer totally free and autonomous, and that was okay. Because the trade-off was the kind of love I'd always dreamed of.

It wasn't a loss to choose Kylo. I wasn't self-sacrificing. I was admitting that we were two distinct trees intertwined, nourishing each other as we grew and reached for the sun.

I would tell Kylo about Juliette's threat. We would fight together, as I promised. And as I sat with this choice in my belly, it didn't feel like a trauma response or people-pleasing. It was a conscious decision rooted in something higher. Faith that we'd be able to succeed on our own terms, in the way we needed. We could protect everyone together. If Juliette tried something, we'd have our opportunity to strike.

My heart warmed, my burden finally light and free. I stroked Kylo's strong jaw, letting my sudden serenity pass through my body and into his.

Kylo exhaled. "I'm making you pasta tonight, baby."

"Sexiest thing you've ever said."

He laughed. "Sad if true."

"Or that's how much I love pasta."

"Precisely the reason you're getting it." He kissed my forehead. "But also because you eat bread in this really cute way."

I blinked. "What? I eat bread strangely? How do I eat bread? Now I'm self-conscious."

"You know how hard I get when you're embarrassed," he groaned. "But I said *cute*, not *strange*. You're just so dainty about it, tearing off pieces like a delicate baby animal."

I scoffed. "I don't even know what that means." I was going to say that I would refuse to eat bread around him from here on out, but that was a level of self-punishment I was far too healed for.

Kylo lowered himself to kiss my stomach, his eyes darkening as he looked up at me. "Stop being so fucking adorable or I will attack you."

"I'm just being me."

I pulled him back up for a kiss, running my hand through his soft black strands of hair. Everything about him was warm and solid, a certainty I'd been chasing since the day I was born.

He pulled back, studying my face as if in reverence.

I smiled. The words were poised on my tongue. *I choose you. I will always choose you.*

"Kylo," a female voice called.

Kylo groaned in irritation. "Not *now*. We're off tonight," he growled.

"I'm sorry. It's an emergency," Allie said, coming into view as Kylo slowly pushed off me.

My heart started beating fast and hard. Allie would never have bothered us in Kylo's private, enclosed backyard unless something was wrong.

Kylo helped me to my feet, and I leaned my back against his chest as we both braced ourselves.

"There's been another killing," Allie said. Her usual stoicism had been shaken, her brunette hair in disarray. "Like Princeton's."

I slumped against Kylo, the air knocked from my lungs.

"No," I whispered. "It's only Thursday."

Allie shot me a confused look, her features tugged down with heaviness.

"Who?" Kylo and I asked at the same time. I gripped his arm as it snaked around me.

"The high priestess of a local coven. Gwendolyn."

My eyes pooled with tears, a broken sound leaving my lips.

"Her friend found her in the woods. Her eyes had been taken, her body desecrated. Sigils had been carved into her skin. It looked like a ritual had been performed."

"Who? Who found her?" I asked, fighting the urge to throw up.

Kylo gripped me tighter, his hand raking through my hair as his chest rose and fell rapidly.

"The younger witch. I believe her name was Amy."

I turned away from Allie and into Kylo's chest, horrified. I vaguely heard Kylo talking with Allie before she took her leave. He rubbed soothing circles on my back.

Juliette had killed my friend, unprovoked. For no fucking reason other than to harvest more power and to hurt me. She'd scarred a teenage girl forever. Amy and Gwendolyn had known each other for years; I couldn't fathom the trauma of Amy finding her friend and spiritual leader's mutilated corpse.

"She just ruined more lives," I said. "Because of *me.*"

Kylo gingerly peeled me off him, staring hard into my eyes. "Baby, I am so sorry," he said, voice cracking as his eyes mirrored my grief. "You are not responsible for this. Why do you think Juliette's actions are on you?"

"Because she's targeting people I love. Because she envies my power and everything else about me. Because *I* haven't killed her yet!"

For the first time since Idris died, I started to feel out of control.

Kylo placed his hands firmly on both of my trembling shoulders. Cloudy onyx began to obscure my vision, and I tasted rain on my tongue.

"*Hey,*" Kylo said firmly, snapping my attention back to his eyes. "Deep breaths. Just like we've been working on."

He looked down at the earth beneath us that was now rotting and turning black with char.

I sucked in breath after breath. *Calm down. Calm down. Calm down.*

"Evie, you are not a god. You haven't taken out Juliette because doing so while surrounded by the born would've ended in your demise. Or maybe if you managed to wield the highest force of your power and kill everyone in the castle, you would've drained yourself in the process and tipped off Earle's armies to your presence. Not to mention Juliette herself is powerful. She might've prevented you from succeeding so easily. You are not a failure for protecting yourself and the city by not acting foolishly." Kylo paused, studying my tear-stricken face. "And I say all of this as someone who has felt responsible for every born atrocity committed in Etherdale since the day I turned. Nothing I do is good enough. It won't be until they're *gone.*"

None of his logic was penetrating my hemorrhaging, guilty heart. Juliette had struck when I was least expecting.

As if she were guaranteeing I show up tomorrow.

"I need to do this," I said, wiping my face. Rage began to trickle through the cracks of my horror, visceral disgust and hatred making it hard to stave off an explosion. "Please don't hold me back."

Kylo bristled.

"Help me instead. *Please.*"

He pulled me back against him, holding me now as if he feared letting me go. My tears soaked through his shirt, reminding me of when it had been drowned in born blood. It was my turn now.

I could feel him thinking as he soothed me and kept me from plunging the world into darkness. His heart was hard and steady beneath my ear, his shadows circling protectively.

"I was going to cancel my meeting with Aster tomorrow," I gasped, finding it difficult to speak as sobs racked through me. "But if I don't show up, Juliette will do this all over again and again. Every death will be on my shoulders. I cannot live with myself if she kills anyone else. I can hardly live with myself now."

Kylo was rigid beneath me. "You had a meeting with Aster tomorrow?"

I winced. "I made it at our last meeting. I wasn't going to keep it. But Juliette threatened me if I failed to show up. I was about to tell you that I choose you, no matter the consequences. But with Gwendolyn…" My voice trailed off.

I took a small step back, facing him as rain poured. I wondered if Juliette could see it through the glamour over the neighborhood. I bet seeing me unravel brought a smile to her face.

Kylo's features were conflicted, emotions warring as his shadows gripped my ankles like tree roots.

"I still choose you," I said. "And I need you to choose me too."

Thunder rumbled, and Kylo's shadows grew louder, more demanding. Our power began to flirt, to meld, to leak into the world as a deadly, ominous force.

Our violent love was on display. I saw the Judgement card— the angel sounding a trumpet for the mortals with arms outstretched below. The clouds surrounding the angel were heavy, the mountain range in the background vast.

A reckoning that was unavoidable, an inner calling that could not be denied.

"I. Can't. Lose. You," Kylo said, low and commanding like thunder itself.

Lightning struck. Winds surged.

"You won't."

He cursed. We both looked up at the sky together. Dark gray clouds grew ever-darker, winds whipping around viciously as shadows screeched.

His hand shot out. It closed around my throat, but it didn't squeeze. His thumb gently stroked my neck. We stared into each other's wrathful eyes. Our shadows fused, becoming tinged with deep purple. We breathed in the same anger. We expelled the same purpose. The faint hissing of a snake broke through the haze.

We communicated wordlessly. Tears falling, bones bracing, muscles flexing. His jaw tightened, and my chin rose. The stench of death was ripe in the air, a reminder and a promise.

"I will always choose you, angel."

He kissed me. In the eye of the storm, we communicated through our bond rather than with words. A dance of betrayal, obsession, yearning, grief, and devotion.

I love you. I have to go. I'm sorry.

I love you. I can't let you go. I'm sorry.

54

EVIE

Maybe it made me a coward, but I chose not to see the coven in the wake of Gwendolyn's death. I didn't want to intrude. I wasn't one of them.

I also felt responsible no matter what Kylo said.

I wrote to them my condolences and promised that I would take care of the killer. I would attend the vigil and death rites. I'd be there for them after I killed Juliette. It wouldn't fix what had already happened, but maybe it would help.

Or maybe it would merely allow me to look into Amy's eyes without shattering into a million jagged pieces.

In front of the mirror where Kylo had first shown me my tattoos, Kylo slipped a dagger into a fabric holster on my upper thigh. The weapon met Hekate's tattoo of a serpent coiled around a key. When Kylo touched me, the snake came alive as always, shining with iridescent magick. Flowers bloomed in shades of pink and violet. His hands skimmed my leg reverently before kissing my hip. He pulled my deceptively sweet skirt back down, a piece of blush satin and tulle with a matching corset.

"You remember what we practiced last week? Where to strike with poison for the quickest paralysis?"

"Yes, Kylo," I said, reaching for his hand. "I remember everything you've ever taught me."

Our training sessions were ripe in my mind. I would never be quicker than a vampire, but my dagger was fused with violet bane—my new-and-improved version of blood onyx. I'd even consecrated the blade itself in the name of Hekate. I'd done several protection rituals, preparing myself for this final mission before war.

Kylo didn't support my plan, yet he'd helped me craft it anyway. He and a team of top fighters would be waiting nearby, more than the first two visits. Kylo held back on making rash decisions after Aster tasted my blood, but I no longer expected him to do so if my life was on the line.

The stakes had never been higher. Guilt had become a second, ill-fitting skin, unshakable no matter what decision I made. I was sleep deprived, plagued by visions of Princeton and Gwendolyn all night. Terrified as they'd taken their last breaths. Eyeless.

Dead.

Sometimes I saw Amy, spreading out her handmade tarot cards as witches gathered around her. The bright defiance of youth in her green irises.

My mission tonight was to kill Juliette and only Juliette. Quickly and quietly. And then to leave or escape by any means necessary. Earle wouldn't declare war over a dead wife. Killing lords, on the other hand, might trigger what we weren't ready for.

I couldn't plan for all possibilities. But I hoped to take care of this in a way that made it look like a disappearance, at least temporarily. Anything to buy the Serpent Clan more time. Plan B was riskier, and it was a plan I'd been dissuaded against.

Plan B was to accept Conrad's offer to remove Juliette from the picture under Aster's nose.

I ran through the plot over and over. Kylo grilled me on defensive techniques. Idris swallowed down his anger to give me his best fighting tips. Vesper told me more about Conrad, and Clarke shared wisdom from his time working in a born feeding club.

Stun powder was loaded into a hollow rose quartz pendant. A tiny pen and note were tucked into a hidden corset pocket.

Kylo thumbed my silver, discreet collar as I said my goodbyes.

"Let me come," Idris blurted. "Let me be a part of the extraction team."

I glanced at Kylo for help, my heart sinking.

"I'm sorry, Idris. Not this time. It's safer for Evie if you stayed back. You would be a distraction."

The harsh words hung in the air between them. At first, Idris looked like he was going to fight Kylo. Surprisingly, he chose to nod instead.

He exhaled, hugging me a second time as he cursed. "Please be careful. I need you."

I hugged him tight. "I love you. I'll see you tomorrow."

When I pulled back, for a moment, I saw the little boy who'd blossomed under Mena's care. The boy who'd gone from cowering in fear to playing with toy knights and sticking up for me when the neighborhood kids made fun of my country accent—the accent we'd both buried with the other ghosts.

"No more running," I whispered. "Thank you for giving me a reason to stay."

He grinned. "I think I share that victory." He angled his head toward Kylo.

Kylo watched me like a devoted sentinel, deceptively stoic before the small crowd that had gathered. It was only after I'd hugged Vesper, Blade, and Harmony that we broke off from the rest of the team.

"You can't walk me all the way there," I said. "Conrad suspects—"

Kylo twirled me around to face him. He gripped my waist, masked and radiating blood-curdling power. "I won't. Give me a block, angel."

It was risky, but I didn't fight him. Not when he was going against his own intuition to give me my freedom.

He never agreed to let me go. He'd only ceded that it wasn't his choice to make.

With every step forward, I hurt him.

My chest was tight. My body surged with adrenaline, the kind of resolute determination that couldn't be denied.

Fate hummed in my ears like the call of Judgement.

"I want The Sun, baby," Kylo said.

I looked over at him as we reached the end of the block. My throat tightened. "I love when you speak magick to me."

His lips twitched below his diagonally cut mask. "I will speak magick to you until the end of our days. In our next life and the one after."

"I can't wait for you to stalk me all over again."

"If I could get hard right now, I would."

My laugh was nervous, an inappropriate release of tension. Kylo drank the sound from my lips like a dying man, gripping me hard as he stole every last drop of my oxygen away. I ran my hands along the smooth skull structure of his mask, remembering the days I pretended not to know who'd been lurking beneath.

He pulled back from my lips, only by an inch. "I need you to walk away from me now, angel. Or I will never let you go."

"You're not letting me go," I said. "We'll still be bonded by blood and ink and shadow." I thumbed my discreet collar, another reminder of our inseverable interconnection. His blood marked me. My blood fueled him. "We will never be free from each other."

"Stop threatening me with beautiful promises and go, angel. I need you to start moving."

I couldn't see his eyes, only the tightness of his jaw and the downturn of his lips. The cobblestone beneath our feet vibrated.

"I love you. I'll be right back." I turned and, with everything in me, I left him in the shadows.

"Evie! You made it to the tea party!"

Juliette's squeal hit me like a dagger to the eardrum.

With dread, I stepped into a small drawing room decorated in soft pastels and florals. Juliette rose from Aster's lap. Aster, who appeared pleased to see me, was seated in an oversized club chair covered in plush velvet.

The round table in front of him was filled with far too much food and drinks for two mortals and a vampire, all artfully plated on fine dishware. An ornate tea set was in the center of the table amid an array of sweets and small sandwiches.

I'd never employed more self-restraint in my life than when I let Juliette pull me in for a hug and I managed not to impale her with shadows.

"Are you okay?" she whispered. "You look a little sad."

Juliette coughing on her own blood. Juliette stabbed through the heart. Juliette begging for mercy and receiving as much mercy as she gave Gwendolyn, Princeton, and those hundreds of university students.

These are the soothing thoughts I meditated on as I pulled back, smiled, and said with way too much enthusiasm, "I'm great! Just hungry!"

Aster smiled as he watched us, blowing out a relieved breath. Behind Juliette's back, he mouthed, *thank you.*

He had no idea what his dress-up doll had done. He thought I was actually here to give her a chance.

Fucking idiot.

"Did you see my flower arrangement? It's spelled for harmonious gatherings," Juliette chirped, gesturing to the colorful bouquet in a yellow ceramic vase.

"How original," I said. There was an unavoidable slip of tightness in my cheery voice.

"Special magick from a special girl," Aster praised, characteristically oblivious.

Juliette had dropped her bridal whites and was instead wearing the same shade of blue I'd worn previously. And her flowers were an exact replica of what I'd sold at Celeste's before the born had pushed me out of business and crushed my dreams of opening my own shop.

It wasn't as if the mimicking was worse than the murdering, but gods above did it inflame my rage in a way I couldn't consciously put words to.

It made me regress to a childish state of pettiness, triggering an urge to expose Juliette and win this game I'd never agreed to play in the first place.

Instead, I sat across from Aster, refusing to show her any reaction other than disinterest, as if I hadn't even noticed her obsessive mirroring.

She tried again to talk in depth about her garden and her love of faeries and trickster spirits. She bathed in Aster's affirmations and praise like a love-deprived child, desperate to be seen and acknowledged.

I swallowed down a sip of tea—after, of course, assessing its magickal properties for poisons.

The lavender and lemon balm made me think of Mena.

I looked straight at Juliette, who settled and stretched in Aster's lap like a cat. Red fang marks dotted her fair neck.

She locked eyes with me. I grinned, and her gray eyes flashed in surprise.

"The tea is lovely." I reached for a macaron and let it melt on my spiteful tongue.

"What about you, Evie? I know you once supplied all manner of witch goods to a local establishment. Have you been crafting anything new lately?" Aster asked.

I studied him, the amusement in his amber eyes, the way Juliette was now playing with his blond hair as she frowned deeply.

What had I been crafting? Oh, you know, vampire poisons and weapons, mostly.

"Candles and teas," I said sweetly.

Juliette made a little huff, biting into a cookie. As usual, her actions and moods made little sense. What had changed between the time she told me she wanted to be sisters and now that had inspired her to kill my friend?

"Those girls at Celeste's aren't good for you, Evie," she said, her eyes swimming with a sudden earnestness.

Aster lifted a brow. "What are you talking about, kitten?"

Heat crawled up my spine. My palms tingled.

"Those girls aren't her friends. They're nothing like Evie," Juliette said, answering Aster's question. "They would never be able to understand her."

Something wounded and subconscious reared its ugly head against my will, a nudge from my deepest fears.

Wait. Had Juliette been trying to hurt me? Or had she been trying to *protect* me? In a demented, jealous sort of way. Just as she'd done for Aster.

"Thanks for looking out for me," I said, watching her closely.

Juliette's face relaxed. "That's what family is for."

Don't you dare, I urged my sickened, thirsty shadows. Aster relaxed in his chair. I bit into another pastry as he started off on one of his monologues.

"Nothing is more important than family, girls," he said. "One of the greatest writers Ravenia has ever seen, Bartholameu Holt, once said that the right chosen family is far stronger than a lineage by blood. That's why it's so important to choose wisely."

"Exactly, Sir," Juliette said. "You're the most intelligent man in the realm."

Aster rattled off his sanctimonious diatribe as I continued to envision his head on a spike and Juliette's blood watering my carnivorous plants.

The sheer insanity of Aster and Juliette thinking I'd be wooed by a fucking tea party and promises of wealth and protection in the midst of bloody authoritarianism was beyond comprehension. But it shouldn't have surprised me. While they tortured children in the basement and burned witches and holy books, they simultaneously held classy dinner parties, ensured proper decorum and appearances, and made bets on sporting events.

Why would Aster think I might choose to sacrifice my own comfort or safety in the name of justice? When he'd never sacrificed his own comfort a day in his life?

I hadn't even been paying attention to whatever Aster said that caused me to laugh. It was as if I was on autopilot, the only mode in which I could reasonably operate without setting everyone in this castle on fire.

"Where's the book you wanted to show Miss Evie?" Aster asked Juliette.

"In my room," she said, her face lighting up. "I'll go fetch it."

"I'd love to see your room," I said casually as I sipped my drink.

Juliette looked from Aster to me and back again. "Okay!"

I started to rise, my sheathed dagger heating in anticipation.

But Aster held up a hand. "Ah-ah. Evie can see your princess chambers after tea," he said.

Juliette didn't bat an eye, only nodding her head in subservience before bouncing out of the room.

Shit. Not exactly who I'd meant to end up alone with, but alas, the night was still young.

"How are things?" Aster asked when Juliette was gone, moving to sit closer to me in the adjacent cushioned chair.

I cleared my throat softly. "Not great. I'm almost ready to leave the protection of the turned," I said. "I just have to gather some of my belongings and make sure people I care about are safe."

Aster's eyes flashed. He inched closer, too close now. His blood red aura crept toward me like a parasite. "How can I help?"

"You must swear to me that you're really trying to improve mortals' lives." I played up the internal conflict for additional believability. "The witch hunt needs to end. You've been burning books that could help witches like *me*. These policies have harmed the innocent. The turned vampires say you and Conrad support the slave trade. Is that true?"

Sipping tea in a puddle of tulle, I made myself look like the most naive, unaware girl in the world.

Aster's eyes softened as he lied to me. "No, pretty girl. As I've told you, I am vehemently against slavery in all its forms. I do not believe in the cheapening of love and sex. I stand for old-fashioned chivalry. A male vampire's purpose is to protect and provide, not harm. I vow to you, Evie, our love story has been written in the stars. I have only ever sought to protect mortals, including from witches who have lost their way and who sow bloodshed. But if you believe our tactics unjust, we will listen. The lords have always listened to our vulnerable, mortal constituents."

I gazed down at the pretty food and sighed. He spoke such beautiful bullshit.

Aster leaned forward again. He moved a blonde strand behind my ear. "I've wanted to do this since the moment I saw you were alive."

55

EVIE

No. I had less than two seconds to think, to figure out a way to dodge without breaking character.

Aster's lips met mine. They were too soft, too demanding, too blood-stained.

I wanted to die. Tears threatened to well in my eyes, but I swallowed them down. Instead, I gently pulled away.

"Sorry, did I misread?" Aster asked.

"No," I whispered. "I'm just feeling emotional. I've had such a difficult few months. Or perhaps a difficult life." I smiled sadly. "The promise of a safe home sounds too good to be true."

At this, Aster's lips curved. His eyes welled with a strangely genuine emotion for a vampire. As if he really did see himself as virtuous and noble—a white knight for all wayward, abused girls.

Or maybe he merely found our wounded nature attractive.

He touched a hand to my face, and I feared he was about to kiss me again when Juliette saved me.

"Oh," she squeaked at the door.

Aster's hand moved to stroke my hair in a way that made me want to slit his throat. I slowly turned my head.

Juliette's face moved from rage to delight and back again like the perfect little psychopath she was.

I wanted to scrub my lips until they bled. And I couldn't even think about Kylo, or I'd lose it. I had to keep it together and complete my objective, or all of this would have been for nothing. Or worse, I would risk the fate of Etherdale and everyone I loved.

No pressure.

"Here's the book," Juliette said, walking slowly toward us. Her smile was warm, but her eyes were manic.

Aster placed a hand on my thigh but thankfully backed out of my personal space.

Juliette showed me my own favorite fantasy novel, one with a main character who reminded me of Kylo.

"Have you read it?" she asked. "It's my *favorite*."

I was quite certain I'd mentioned this one at dinner when Aster and I were talking about books.

"Yes." I fought the urge to grind my teeth together. Instead, I presented an air of pleasantness. My mother had trained me well.

"The man is sooo dreamy, wouldn't you agree?" Juliette asked, staring off into the distance.

Aster's face soured, anger flashing in his eyes. He turned his sharp gaze to me. Could men really be jealous of fictional characters?

"Yes, that's one of the many draws of the book," I said blandly with a nervous laugh.

"The dark hair, the ruthlessness, the charm," Juliette continued. She sighed.

Aster glared between us. When I tensed, impassivity rolled over his features like a veil.

"And look, it's a special edition." Juliette opened the book to hand-drawn illustrations and moved close to show me.

"Only the best for my good girls," Aster said.

Juliette closed the book. I regretted eating, as my nausea was swift.

"Kitten, Evie will be joining us shortly," he said, shifting the conversation back to something that was of interest to *him*.

Juliette's eyes widened. She stared at me so hard I feared she might burn a hole into my head.

"I know you two had your differences when you first met, but I will not tolerate any fighting going forward. You are each too special to me, and I refuse to see either of you hurt. I hope you can both see that there is more than enough love here for all of us."

Juliette nodded enthusiastically. "Yes, Sir, of course."

Aster smiled. "Are you still feeling all right, darling?" he asked Juliette, then turned to me. "She was under the weather for a few days. It worried me greatly. But last night's sleep seemed to have provided the healing she needed."

Juliette's beaming smile widened. "Yes, I'm feeling much better now. Strong and healthy just like Evie."

Rage swept so violently through me it blurred my vision. Not only did she murder my friend to *protect* me. She also killed her for a health and power boost.

Aster watched me carefully, no doubt catching the unavoidable downturn of my lips. I'd told him why Juliette was ill. Either he hadn't been listening, or he didn't care.

Conrad cared. He seemed to care about Juliette's weaknesses quite a bit.

"You're not in competition, Evie," Aster admonished, reading my thoughts and likely remembering what I'd told him the other night. "Juliette's health is a product of her upbringing. I won't tolerate cruel words or vicious lies, either."

Juliette made herself small and wounded, once again crawling into Aster's lap and nuzzling into his neck.

I reached for a strawberry. I let the fruit burst in my mouth as I set the stem on my plate. Aster watched my lips.

I nodded, brows furrowed. "The turned have said a lot of confusing things about all of you," I said, deciding to defuse the tension by pretending I'd been brainwashed.

Aster's face relaxed. "This does not surprise me, dear. Juliette endured the unthinkable at the hands of her caregivers. One day, she may tell you about it. But her newfound power and strength is a blessing, not a curse. She'll protect you as fiercely as she's protected us. Won't you, angel?"

Juliette sighed dreamily, peering over at me with satisfaction. "Always."

As her hand outstretched, our mirrored image was a poltergeist that rattled my bones. Childhood trauma, newfound magick, kink and power dynamics and *angel, angel, angel*.

I lifted my hand.

I interlocked my fingers with Juliette's. Aster's eyes turned molten as he stared at me.

Through our touch, I tasted charred earth on my tongue. Death. Oblivion. The lightning strike against The Tower.

I dropped my hand while listening to comforting whispers of my shadows in the corners of the room. The weight of my dagger pressed against my thigh. Such sounds and symbols of violence used to terrify me.

Now it was a joy to stop running and *fight*.

That was what I channeled to make it through the next conversation about books, stars, fate, and magick. All these things that I loved, bastardized by two people who would never understand any of it. They would never know love or safety or a power greater than themselves. They would never know *me*.

"Can I show Evie my room now?" Juliette asked.

I thought she'd never ask. My smile was steady, calm. The same calm I felt when I decided to stab Kylo with a poisoned needle. The certainty of a path chosen.

"Yes. I'll be in my study. Be good," he said with a wink.

I nearly floated down the opulent hall of tasteless art.

Depictions of born men and women with dead eyes, or soulless constructions of Ravenia's landscape. Bland. Empty.

My senses were heightened; my breathing was measured. I became the fuckable weapon Aster had always dreamed of.

Below us on the first floor, born were lounging, socializing, feeding. I wondered what they were doing in the basement.

Aster kissed Juliette on the forehead. He hesitated only a moment before doing the same to me.

"Behave, girls," he said as he disappeared into his study.

Juliette put her hand in mine as I considered how badly it would hurt to burn off the top layer of skin where Aster's lips had been.

When Juliette led me into her room, we were finally alone. No one had bothered checking me for weapons. They'd never truly seen me as a threat, since the beginning.

Juliette's room mimicked my space in the cottage, only far more dramatically pastel. There was no subtlety, just an explosion of soft colors, florals, cozy knits, and witchy trinkets.

"Do you like it?" she asked, looking around her space before setting her heavy gaze on me.

I nodded. "I do. That's a beautiful bed."

A tall, grand piece of furniture with a canopy, twinkling string lights, and several pillows and blankets. A worn teddy bear sat in the center. Juliette dove onto the bed and sprawled out as she watched me.

The temperamental demon was grinning without a care in the world.

My dagger warmed my skin with every step. I stood before an arched window, looking down at the castle grounds. I made a quick mental note that it was the opposite direction of where Kylo and the team were stationed.

My heart skipped a beat when I lowered my gaze. A sturdy vine connected the outer windowsill to the window below it, woven into a suspiciously ladder-shaped formation.

Juliette had to have a way to sneak out, after all.

"Is that the garden you were talking about?" I asked Juliette without turning.

I wondered if she thought I'd hop in bed with her to kiss and braid each other's hair.

Gods, I bet that was exactly what she expected.

"Hello, Evie," a deeper voice answered.

I whipped around to find Conrad standing just inside the door. My gaze swept to the empty bed.

"She's in the bathroom across the hall. We only have a moment," he said. "Aster wants us all to head downstairs for dinner."

Fuck. I'd had Juliette alone for less than two minutes. The whiplash had me feeling a mix of confusion and impatience. I couldn't fail. I had to see this through, and I didn't want to spend another minute pretending to be charmed by a disgusting predator and his psychopathic child bride.

Why was Conrad here? Why was he emphasizing we only had a moment alone?

You can't trust him.

Vesper's warning was a red, glaring sign in my mind.

Conrad approached me, his features forming an unspoken question. He'd asked me if I wanted to take out Juliette. He'd called her a mental patient. He'd been alarmed by my explanation of her illness and her stolen power.

"Are you well?" he asked.

"Yes." My heart thumped, but I decided it was time to try plan B. "I think I'd be better if you help me with what we discussed the last time I saw you. You asked me what I wanted."

Conrad was stoic as his icy blue eyes watched my lips.

"I think you already know what I want," I said.

It was risky. But it was also destabilizing in multiple helpful ways. Letting Conrad take care of Juliette would keep my hands clean, and it would dirty Conrad's. What if poor Aster found out his best friend killed his wife?

Conrad smiled, such a rarity for him that it startled me. "I'm so glad to hear that, Evie." He stepped closer. Too close.

I took a small step back. "I need it to happen tonight."

A flash of confusion, or maybe pensiveness, crossed his features as he assessed the way I'd backed away from him.

"She sneaks out at night," I continued, voice barely above a whisper. "That's how she's been harvesting power from other witches. Aster must know she does this, the sneaking out, I mean—maybe we could make it look like she left tonight, only this time, she doesn't come back."

Conrad went rigid. A strange expression crossed his face, nearly angry. It was more emotion than I'd ever seen from him before.

Oh, fuck. Panic coursed through me, wondering if I'd somehow misread him. And now I couldn't go back. I'd chosen wrong. I should've stabbed Juliette through the heart and leaped out the window the moment we were alone. If only I'd known…

But Conrad's words had been clear. *He* was the one who asked me if I wanted her out of the picture.

I calculated how many seconds it would take to impale him with shadows against how quickly he could drain me of blood. Or immobilize me with his pain magick. I needed more distance between us—

"Tonight," Conrad said, breaking through my panic. The emotions washed from his features, leaving only calmness behind.

I halted. My magick paused at my fingertips.

"I'll take care of it," Conrad said. "So you've made your choice. You'll stay here."

"Yes."

Conrad smiled again, but it was strange, mechanical. It didn't match the deranged look in his eyes. This was the first time I was seeing a hint of the madness I knew festered beneath the surface.

He backed away from me, and I released a breath. But when he slipped out of Juliette's room, my heart never calmed.

My intuition was glaring. Something was wrong. I should've felt settled, but instead, I was even more frantic to get out of here than I'd been before.

I eyed the window.

I could escape now, if I wanted to. Before Juliette came back.

My eyes closed. I saw Amy and Gwendolyn laughing together. The witches huddled around the book of astrology and clinking sparkling drinks.

Heat crawled up my neck. I was uncomfortable inside my own skin, but I stayed rooted in place. The choice I made would have to be the correct one. I would make everything right again.

When Juliette returned, I took a single step forward.

Juliette screamed. She pulled out a knife from behind her back and stabbed herself in the stomach as she glared at me.

56

EVIE

My jaw fell slack. I stared at the knife sticking out of Juliette's abdomen as she screamed bloody murder. The uneven circle of crimson bloomed from her wound.

A wound that bleeds.

"What have you done?" she asked me, her eyes weeping fat tears. *"What have you done?"*

In a burst of vampiric speed, Conrad, Aster, and three guards entered the room. I backed toward the window. Aster's eyes moved quickly from Juliette to me, rage quickly eclipsing his shocked expression. Conrad merely expressed quiet amusement.

I didn't bother telling Aster the truth.

As soon as he snapped an order at the guards, I conjured my shadows. In quick bursts of movement, I impaled all three of them through the chest. With Juliette slumped against him, Aster conjured a defensive shield. The faintly glowing red magick encased him, Juliette, and Conrad from my screaming shadows.

Kylo's voice was sharp in my mind. He would tell me to let it go and to save myself.

I sent another shadow through the window.

On my third step toward my escape, the most excruciating pain I'd ever experienced slammed into my head. I buckled in agony. My mind was wiped. I screamed. It felt like my head was splitting open, pulled apart over and over again.

The more I fought to use my magick, the sharper the pain became, until I was a puddle of screaming, crying shadow on the pastel pink rug.

The pain only subsided when cool metal closed over my wrists. Through the blur of tears, I tried to stand. Instead, I threw up violently.

"Clean her up," Aster's venomous voice hissed. "I'll be with the healers. I can't stand to look at her right now."

A new set of guards hauled me roughly to my feet. I couldn't wield a drop of my power through the magickal bondage.

Juliette would live. I'd gathered no further proof of treason. And now I was bound and powerless.

I'd failed.

The moment Aster left with Juliette in his arms, Conrad's quiet amusement transformed into a smirk.

"Not your smartest move, girl." He shook his head with a sigh. His movements were slow and measured. He stopped in front of me, his eyes back to their haunting emptiness. "Though, neither was sleeping with the vermin."

I made no outward reaction. My heart thumped harshly.

"Aster is a fool to believe you are untouched," he sneered. *"Pure of blood."* His laugh was as cold as his pale eyes. "Not to worry. Even worthless whores may seek redemption through proper devotion to the Dark Mother."

He gripped my face so hard I winced. At the sight of my pain, he smiled.

"It will be an honor to help you repent and atone."

I fought the urge to throw up a second time. I'd never felt more trapped. Failure was a crushing weight against my ribs. And Kylo—oh gods, what was Kylo going to do?

His intuition had been right. I hadn't listened. And he let me go, anyway.

I'd clearly been set up. But why was Conrad acting so differently now than just moments ago? And how had Juliette known I'd been lying or planning to kill her? That had to be the reason she attacked herself.

Conrad released his grip with a disgusted look on his face. The guards dragged me away. I tried and failed to channel even a crumb of my shadows.

You are not a god.

I'd become so strong that I'd forgotten what it was like to be this helpless. Not since I was a child, at the mercy of my parents who'd meticulously groomed me for abuse and slavery.

Without my magick, I had no protection. I was alone again.

We headed toward the bathroom, where one of the guards yanked me by the hair toward the sink and the other washed the puke from my face. I was manhandled as I flailed, tears burning my eyes, desperate and confused as to how the fuck I'd gotten here.

Back in the hallway, a woman in black slowly walked toward us. Her light brown skin held fine lines, her posture straight, her black hair in a neat bun.

A Servant of Lillian, a witch who'd forsaken her nature to serve the born.

"Get the fuck away from me!" I screeched, finally losing my last thread of composure.

I kicked my legs. My lip curled as I made inhuman sounds of rage I hardly recognized.

Cloth was shoved in my mouth. A hand covered it for good measure. I could hardly breathe as the woman stopped just in front of me.

"Put her on her knees," she said.

The guards shoved me to the ground.

"Lillian, forgive her, for she knows not what she does," the woman began, lording over me like a specter.

I screamed against the cloth in my mouth. I fought to stand, to get off my knees, but strong hands held me in place.

"She has been led astray. But she has mercifully been brought back to your loving care, by your grace. She will once again walk the path of the righteous."

Aster had made it seem like he was above this cult, and yet the first thing he did was hand me over to the source of my greatest traumas.

I knew these lords had been putting on a front, but the sharpness of this sudden shift was disorienting.

I had to get out of here.

The woman continued praying over me.

My body trembled; my throat was clogged. Flashes of my mother and my childhood tore through my mind. Voices that had become quiet in the past weeks were suddenly bone-chillingly loud.

Worthless whore.

My mother had called me names too. I wondered if they would've escalated to crueler sexual remarks as I'd grown older. She called me greedy when I ate too much, obsessively concerned about every aspect of my appearance and behavior. All for the benefit of my future born master.

Was Kylo preparing to storm the castle? He would've felt every shift inside me. He would know something was wrong.

Guards dragged me down the hall again, bringing me into a new room across from Juliette's. The flashes from my childhood clung to me like psychic glue. My knees ached from kneeling on the hard floor. I could nearly feel the hundred pricks from rice digging into my skin, my father downstairs pretending not to hear me scream.

Warm, dim lights illuminated a regal bedroom, a show of wealth painted in wine red and gold.

The bed was huge and ornate, and when the guards dragged me toward it, I bucked and hissed like a rabid beast.

When they unlocked one of my cuffs, I managed to squeeze out a drop of my power, sending one man flying across the room. He yelled and landed roughly against a bookcase. I yanked the cloth gag out of my mouth.

Before I could deal with the other, more bodies rushed into the room. Through the shouts and dark mist blooming from my palm, I struggled against the heavy weight of stifling magick holding me down. Sweat beaded on my forehead, panting and straining to force more power through.

Hot breath tickled my ear. "We've got ourselves a fighter."

Hands were all over me. Lillian's magick boxed me in. With a click, the cuff was secured back into place.

And I was now bound to the bedframe.

I couldn't stand. I could only sit or kneel.

Hands retracted, but I could still feel the violating scorch they left behind. The guards left the room. The one I'd sent flying glared at me with a look of cold death.

"I wish I'd done worse," I hissed.

When the man went rigid, his comrade pulled him forward.

"We can't," he barked. "Come on. Leave her."

Nostrils flared, but the man fell in line. They left me there, bound to a bed, panting and searching my surroundings frantically.

Books had fallen from the bookcase the vampire collided with. It was one of many bookcases. On the center of a coffee table stood a marble vase with a familiar floral arrangement.

I was in Aster's bedroom. I heard creaking and muted voices from around and below. Otherwise, my new reality was quiet and still.

There was nothing to distract me from the shame eating me

alive. The shame I'd inherited from my mother. The shame I'd been learning to release.

My stomach churned with sickening horror. My heart was a tight fist.

I'd failed *everyone*.

57

EVIE

Hours passed.

No one came for me.

Until the door opened, and the Servant returned.

I screamed at the nightmarish sight.

I blinked. Once. Twice. A third time. I convinced myself I was hallucinating. The past and present merged, a grotesque tapestry of the dark pit inside of me.

The hole where my mother's love was supposed to go.

Because in the woman's hand was a bag of rice.

Her black gown skimmed the floor as she approached me with a look of self-righteous ire. She scattered the rice on the floor underneath me.

I refused to cooperate. I swept the rice away with my feet. I crouched instead of kneeling. I pulled against my restraints.

She grabbed my arm and scalded the shit out of my skin. I cried out, unable to move away from her with my hands bound.

"Kneel."

I shook my head. Through the blur of my tears, it was my mother standing over me. The lump in my throat returned, a sob forming deep in my core. I swallowed it down.

She burned me with her touch until tears spilled down my cheeks and onto the floor. She pushed me down, forcing my knees into the pointy grains.

"Every time you try to stand, the time of your punishment increases," Mama said.

Fuck. I closed my eyes. She wasn't my mother.

I wasn't there anymore. That home was gone. *She* was gone.

I was free. Or at least, I used to be.

The pain blurred the edges of my already scrambled mind. I fought to stay sharp, to think my way out of this. I hadn't realized I'd started to sob until something deep and guttural was working its way out of my system. The emotion was violent, as heavy a downpour as the day I'd conjured a storm over Etherdale. The day Kylo had first brushed my hair and told me I was worthy of all the love in the world.

My legs went numb. My head hit the bed frame, cuffs digging into my wrists as I made myself small and limp.

New footsteps approached. "Get out of here," a man hissed.

Through the blur, I saw Aster, sleeves rolled up as he stared down at me. Instead of rage, his features were soft.

In a quick movement, he uncuffed me from the bedframe but kept me bound. He loosened my restraints—not enough to allow me to wiggle free, but so they weren't cutting off my circulation.

He pulled me into his arms and smoothed my hair as I shook violently.

I was tense in his arms, unable to relax. He picked each grain of rice out of my skin.

"There, there," he whispered. "You're safe."

The words were a direct contradiction to everything I felt inside, everything I knew to be true. Nothing made sense.

With a hand stroking my hair, Aster reached for my necklace, my discreet collar. The symbol of mine and Kylo's unending devotion. He unclasped it.

I reached out a hand to stop him, my fingers closing around his wrist.

"I'll keep your pretty necklace somewhere safe. Be a good girl so I can uncuff you."

I let go of him. He removed my necklace as I struggled for air, cheek pressed against his chest. I'd regressed to a vulnerable version of myself—a version I thought I'd overcome.

When he uncuffed me, I needed to act quickly and efficiently.

He set my collar on the floor. But a new piece of metal closed around my throat, one with a familiar magickal signature.

When he removed my cuffs, I knew I was as trapped as I'd been before.

"Behave, or they go back on."

It wasn't a collar. It was more magickal bondage. That didn't stop the next sob from leaving my lips.

I was in another vampire's lap, powerless and triggered, Kylo's symbol of ownership replaced by Aster's.

"Juliette is stable," Aster said. He'd gone back to holding me tight, consoling me with his touch.

The strong part of me knew what was happening. The crafty psychological warfare. He knew how I'd been abused, and he recreated it. He let someone else punish me so he could swoop in and be my savior.

Yet, my body was just happy to be free of pain. And for my mother's voice to have receded back into a haunting whisper.

"I didn't stab her. She stabbed herself," I said, voice shaking.

Aster didn't respond.

My skin was hot with shame and embarrassment. When I attempted to crawl out of his arms, his hold tightened.

"Skittish little thing," he murmured, the inflection of his voice mimicking how one speaks to a child. He inhaled deeply.

My every muscle tensed.

"She was the same when we first met. Attention-seeking outbursts, anxiety, and fear. You were born afraid, weren't you Evie?"

His voice was a dark rumble, his lust leaking out into his faux compassion. It was all so sick and wrong, a perversion and poor imitation of love.

"If you don't believe me, why aren't you angry?" I asked. "Why are you being kind to me?"

It wasn't kindness, but I didn't say that.

Aster lifted me in his arms without answering, off the floor and away from the spilled grains of rice. When he set me on his large bed, I scrambled back, putting as much distance between us as possible.

Would he?

I eyed the door. I reached for my power and came away empty. There was nothing stopping Aster from assaulting me but his own word.

He didn't move, still standing next to the bed. "I don't know what to believe anymore. You and Juliette are being nasty to each other, and I won't stand for it. Not the lying, and certainly not the violence."

"If you're concerned about violence, then you should ask her where she goes when she sneaks out at night," I hissed.

I still had my dagger. I fought the urge to look at the door again.

"Juliette is not a prisoner, dear," Aster said calmly. "She is not being held against her will. You will not poison me against her, nor will *she* poison me against *you*."

That was beside the fucking point. Nothing I said was making it through to Aster because Aster didn't care about the truth.

He just wanted to remain in control of two traumatized girls with dark power.

No better than Conrad. Never was.

Gods, now I remembered my last interaction with Conrad. What did he know? Why was he talking about me sleeping with the enemy? And had he kept this from Aster, or did Aster merely refuse to believe him?

No one in this castle was behaving in a straight-forward manner. Actions contradicted words, and words contradicted each other. What the fuck was I missing?

"Tomorrow will be better," Aster said. "You're going to sleep in here so I can keep an eye on you."

That couldn't happen for multiple reasons. I needed to stop Kylo from prematurely declaring war. I wasn't willing to doom the realm because of *my* failure.

"I'm not going to hurt you," Aster said slowly. "You are only being restricted for the protection of yourself and others. You speak of Juliette's violent ways, and yet you are the only one who killed three people today. You've murdered *many* of my kind, actually."

"To protect myself and—"

I stopped talking. It didn't matter. I was not dealing with reasonable people.

I was dealing with monsters.

"Let me go, please," I said. "You said I would always be free to leave."

"My wife is healing from a stab wound," Aster snapped. "I find it implausible she would go to such lengths as to hurt herself, but if that's what happened, we will figure it out tomorrow. Until then, you will be under my care. It's the only way I can be sure you are both safe."

The words were poised on my tongue, but I decided against voicing them.

His wife was healing from a stab wound. So why wasn't he with *her*?

Part of me was delighted by the mental image of Juliette suffering alone from the consequences of her own actions. But another part of me felt strangely sad. She deserved much worse, of course.

But Aster was her whole world. Psychopath or not, she was deeply trauma bonded to him. And instead of being with her, he was here with me, the woman who supposedly stabbed her.

I looked at Aster with new eyes. His pupils were big, his nostrils flared. He unabashedly flicked his gaze up and down my body before stopping to stare at the metal cuff around my neck. I avoided glancing at the bulge swelling beneath his dress pants.

If I stabbed Aster in his sleep, I could find the key to the bondage around my neck. Aster slipped the key into his pocket. While I was at it, I could grab my necklace and the attached stun powder.

A strong knock cut through my scheming thoughts.

"Come in."

Conrad entered, his sharp gaze finding mine immediately. He smirked at the sight of me at the far edge of the bed.

"We need you in deliberations," Conrad said.

His eyes were alight with excitement. I didn't like the sight of it one bit.

Aster slowly circled the bed, approaching me as if I were a feral animal. To my horror, he held some kind of chain in his hands.

I backed up, but he grabbed my ankle and yanked me back.

"Ah-ah. This is only temporary," he said.

I struggled, but he overpowered me easily with his vampiric strength. He attached the chain to the locked clasp of my collar before locking the other end to the bedframe.

"You'll be safe here. Rest. No one will disturb you."

He released me. My cheeks burned as I scratched at the collar and pulled at the chain. Conrad appeared positively delighted. His gaze was hooded, his own pupils dilating slightly.

Aster cleared his throat, features souring as he saw the way his friend was looking at me. He took a step forward, but Conrad held up a hand.

"Has she been checked for weapons?"

Aster paused. He hesitated for only a moment. I kept my face neutral, but the moment Aster approached me again, I realized I had another split decision to make.

If I stabbed Aster, I would still be chained to the bed. Conrad would hit me with pain magick in an instant, and I would have soured my image in Aster's mind completely. Leaving me even more vulnerable to violence and hyper-surveillance.

I bit my tongue so hard I tasted blood when Aster's hands tentatively skimmed the sides of my body. He found the dagger immediately, but he continued to search as if savoring the excuse to grope me. My stomach twisted, and I struggled to stay still.

When he lifted up my skirt, I wanted to die. His breath hitched, nostrils flaring. He stared down at my bare legs and lace panties as he slowly disarmed me. His touch was icy against my upper thigh.

Conrad's eyes were wild, his smirk back in full force.

As if remembering Conrad was here, Aster pulled my skirt back down. He held my weapon in his palm.

"See? Why would I have stabbed Juliette with a kitchen knife instead of my own weapon?" I asked with a slight tremor, backing away from him.

My skin was hot. I burned with the violation of being seen by both of them, humiliated and even more powerless than before.

If I'd stabbed him, I would've been more fucked. I still wished I'd chosen differently.

I looked to Conrad, but he remained as silent as Aster. Our flimsy alliance was over. He'd already gotten what he wanted: me.

"Rest."

That was all Aster said before he left me chained to his bed. He exited the room with my key to freedom.

All I had now were my hands, a pen, and a direct line of communication to Kylo.

I waited for the footsteps to grow faint. Then I reached into the hidden corset pocket.

My hands shook as I unfolded the note, straining to see the words that immediately appeared in the dim light.

Baby, please write to me. I—

58

EVIE

That was it. No more words appeared. Kylo had written to me, but something had prevented him from finishing the message. I wasn't even sure when this had happened.

Dread flooded my system. Kylo knew something had gone wrong. He'd tried to write to me. Yet he wasn't here. The born were in *deliberations*.

What the fuck had happened?

I wrote back anyway, using the nightstand next to me that was within my leash's radius.

Kylo? Are you okay?

I waited. I knew I needed to update him about my own predicament, but I honestly didn't know what to say. Everything inside my body was tight with shame. It seemed like every move I'd made in the past twenty-four hours had been the wrong one.

Kylo would feel if I'd written to him. It had been magickally designed to deliver a noticeable zap with each message.

If he were okay, he would drop everything to read my note and respond.

Instead, silence.

My fingers trembled as I wrote to him. I still wasn't sure what to say, what was best for myself or anyone else. All of my instincts felt wrong.

So I told the truth.

I fucked up. Juliette got me captured. I'm uninjured, but they've blocked my magick. Please don't punish the city for my failures. I will escape.

The last sentence was stupid to say. Like a hopeful affirmation from the depths of my enormous fuck-up.

As if Kylo would focus on anything except the word *captured*.

But worse than Kylo reading my message was the evidence that he *hadn't* read my message.

I wasn't the only one in trouble. And like everything else that didn't make sense, I had the glaring intuition that it was all connected in a way I couldn't yet fathom.

Whatever the full picture, all roads led back to me.

I sat there and stared at the blank note, shoulders hunched, for what must've been hours. It was only when I heard footsteps approaching that I quickly folded it back up and slipped it back inside the hidden pocket.

Juliette slipped inside the room.

Her stomach was heavily bandaged. She wore only a bralette and a long cream skirt.

When she saw me on Aster's bed, her face fell, as if it hadn't been me she was searching for. She looked like she was holding back tears. But when she wiped at her eyes, we both stared at the droplets of crimson on her hands.

"Why?" she asked me, lowering her blood-specked hands to her sides. "Why do you want to take everything from me?"

"*Me?*" I scoffed. "*Take everything from you?*" My voice squeaked, a bitter laugh escaping my lips.

"This all could've gone so much differently," she said as she clenched her fists. "You're about to learn exactly how it feels."

"How *what* feels?" I asked, on the verge of sounding utterly hysterical.

Violence built in my body that had nowhere to go.

"He never forgot about you," she said, repeating what she'd told me previously. "You or your magick. *Never.*"

Juliette didn't look angry, or manic, or deranged.

As she stood between me and the door, she only looked hurt.

"I just want him to be happy."

She stared at the chain above my head and then at her feet.

"All I've ever wanted was to make him happy."

Her eyes leaked crimson tears. She clutched her stomach.

For the briefest moment, I saw myself, talking about Jacob. It wasn't the same. But it was a feeling I understood, one that I didn't want to see in Juliette.

I didn't want to see her pain. It was easier for her to be a soulless villain, evil without reason or context.

"It's not your fault," I said, before I could stop myself. "It's not you."

Juliette hadn't started this *rivalry,* and neither had I. We'd been pitted against each other since Aster had first laid eyes on me as a child. She'd been set up to fail. She would never satisfy a monster with a void instead of a heart.

Juliette stopped crying and slowly lifted her gaze to me. She cocked her head. With the next blink, her torment had drifted away. Her eyes turned mean, her features twisted with disdain.

"You're right." She backed away, her hand on the doorknob. "It's *you.*"

～

I DIDN'T KNOW why I'd tried to be kind to Juliette, after everything that had happened. Well, I did know. And it had everything to do with the spirit world, which apparently would rather teach me lessons about empathy, assumptions, and psychological shadows than actually provide a crumb of real fucking help.

I finally saw myself inside Juliette, and that was cool and all, but I was also still chained to Aster's bed.

Aster didn't return until the next morning, which meant neither of us had slept. Guards had allowed me to use the bathroom, and one had tossed me bread at some point. Plain and stale. Eventually, one brought me water, as if they'd forgotten that was something mortals needed for their survival.

And I was supposed to believe that I *wasn't* a prisoner?

My stomach rumbled, but it was hard to feel hungry when I was worried sick about Kylo.

I was worried sick about the entire city.

As Aster approached, I searched his face for clues.

At first, he merely appeared sober and resolute. But a cold anger flashed in his eyes that couldn't be ignored.

He was wordless as he removed the chain from the bedframe. He wrapped the end around his wrist.

"Come. With. Me."

I'd never heard this level of venom from him before. I had no choice but to follow him as he led me by the leash. Humiliation burned my skin with every step. None more so than when the men outside the room ogled me with a mix of lust and amusement at my expense.

I was led downstairs. Vampires smirked as I passed. There was a different energy in the air today, a heaviness that fell over the huddles of vampires speaking in hushed tones. Hedonism had been replaced by Lillian's wrath. Eyes lingered on me hungrily.

Before Aster could drag me down another set of stairs, uniformed men marched into the foyer.

I swallowed down a choked noise.

Soldiers.

They nodded in subservience as they passed Aster, heading for the staircase that led upstairs. To Conrad's study, I assumed.

My lungs were working overtime to keep me breathing. And the stars in my vision only multiplied when I realized I was being yanked into the underbelly of the castle. Where the born so often kept their skeletons.

Where they kept their *slaves.*

"What is happening?" I tried. I didn't even care about myself right now. I needed to know what had happened to Kylo and the clan. "What is happening in the city?"

Aster barked a cold laugh, not saying a single word.

Vampires in the basement—or dungeon, rather—had not abandoned their hedonism. In the first room, dim lights illuminated the born feeding from mortals. Some violently, others more sensually. And unlike the first night I'd spent here, I wasn't at all certain any of these mortals were willing participants. A girl with mousy brown hair met my gaze. Her eyes were hauntingly empty, limp in the arms of a blonde born woman on a velvet couch.

I ignored the smiles and stares as Aster pulled me away from all of them. He gripped the back of my neck now, as if showing his claim.

By the time I was pushed past a set of guards and into a new room, my anxiety was a maddening force.

The space was dark, cold. Black pillar candles were scattered around the space. Magick that didn't belong to me boomed in the air, whispering tales of cruelty, dark power, and unearthly Lillianic magick. Dead flowers were everywhere. A spell circle was painted in blood.

In its center, Juliette.

She was no longer bandaged. When she saw me, she merely smiled, her eyes sharp and icy.

Aster unhooked the chain from my bondage and threw it to the ground. "Tell me it isn't true," he finally bellowed, as if he'd been holding it in.

I flinched, and his hand closed around my throat above the metal ring.

"Tell me you haven't been blood marked by another man," he hissed.

Droplets of spit landed on my cheeks. Aster's amber eyes burned into my flesh, his body trembling with fury.

"Tell me you haven't ruined your body with classless ink," he yelled in my face. "Allowed yourself to be tattooed by *vermin*. Less than fucking vermin."

I shriveled, unable to pull free of his tightening grip on my throat. Dark splotches spread across my vision. My mind blurred.

"Did he fuck you, Evelynn? Did he stain your blood and cunt?"

Aster's voice was quieter now as I struggled for air, scratching at his hand, body slumping.

Just when I thought I was going to lose consciousness, he tore his hand away. I gasped, falling forward and catching myself on my hands and knees. I sucked in breath after breath, forcing myself to shove everything but my own survival out of my mind.

I needed to fucking live. That was the only way I could fix any of this.

My desire to live was the only thing keeping me from flying into a deathly rage at how he spoke about me, my body, and my family.

Aster's pupils were big, frenzied. If he entered bloodlust, I was dead.

"I was scared," I said. "They protected me."

476

I didn't fully answer any of his questions, just like he refused to answer mine. I looked up at him with frightened, wounded eyes, remaining as small and powerless as he most desired me.

"Show me," Aster said.

He picked me up off the ground and shoved me in front of Juliette. The moment I entered the spell circle, I shrieked, assailed by another witch's magick. My own power was bound, leaving me with no ability to defend or protect myself.

I tried to stand, but Juliette snapped her fingers, forcing me to remain kneeling before her. She sat in a puddle of white fabric, a dress that stood in glaring contrast to the bloody magick seeping through the walls.

Aster tore my own dress from my body as I uselessly flailed my arms to try to stop him. He left me in my underwear and a thin bra.

Juliette scattered a fistful of bones, chanting under her breath in a tongue I was unfamiliar with.

Her death magick screeched, assailing my defenseless body and mind.

Oh gods, was this the day I would lose my eyes?

It felt like my skin was being peeled away. My teeth rattled together.

Aster made a violent growl from behind me. He yanked me up by my hair, his hand meeting the nape of my neck.

He was tracing The Star.

I looked down at my unglamoured arm and its clan marking, which was next to be inspected by Aster's bruising grip. He spun me around. His enraged gaze snagged on my hip immediately. There he saw the mark of Hekate: the snake and key with blooming flowers. My tattoos remained onyx. They didn't come alive for Aster.

He reached from behind me, taking a bottle of gray liquid from Juliette and shoving the concoction down my throat with my head pulled back.

I choked and gurgled on the acrid taste.

Aster let me go and stepped back a few paces. I heaved, coughing as my lungs burned.

His fists clenched at his sides. His eyes widened, and his nostrils flared. I stared down at my nearly nude form, watching in horror as my veins turned black.

I made a startled yelp, rubbing at the dark lines spreading across my fair skin.

"Get. It. Out. Of. Her."

Aster's voice was clipped. His breathing was ragged now as he stepped out of the circle, leaving me alone with Juliette.

"Yes, Sir," Juliette said sweetly, nearly a chirp.

I heard bones hit the stone again. My body fell limp, forcing me to collapse on the ground.

"Wait, no," I said, pleading. "Removing a blood bond is dangerous. The mortality rates are high. I could—"

"*Silence!*"

Don't cry. I didn't want to give Juliette the satisfaction of seeing me lose it. But Aster wanted her to remove my bond with Kylo, to drain me of his blood mark.

Kylo would no longer be able to hear the beat of my heart. He wouldn't know I was hurting or losing blood.

He would no longer be able to find me. He wouldn't know if I was alive or dead.

Terrified and angry, desperation took hold as Juliette rolled me over onto my back. I stared up at her triumphant gray eyes, fighting the urge to lose it completely.

I'd never felt more hatred. My helplessness consumed me. I couldn't move, couldn't use my power.

I couldn't stop them.

"Please," I wailed. "She's going to kill me. *Please.*"

"You're not going to die," Aster snapped. "If you don't stop fighting this, you're going to make me think you *want* to be marked by those thugs."

478

"Don't you want to be pure again, Evie?" Juliette asked, lifting a dagger with an engraved silver handle. "You told me you wanted to be back on the path of light. Let us help you."

"Good girl," Aster praised.

Juliette lit up like Aster was the sun she orbited, her gaze slow to move from Aster back to me. "I forgive you for lashing out. I know it was because you were ashamed of your secrets. But the truth is going to set you free."

What game was she playing? Why had she only spilled half of the truth, and not the other?

I couldn't even strategize properly, not when the dagger was moving closer to my heart.

"Don't," I croaked, no louder than a whisper. "Please don't."

I held Juliette with the truth of my vulnerability. My lip wobbled, my face reflecting the grief of what was to come. She hesitated only a moment before she began to cut into my flesh.

My scream was swallowed up by a cool, white mist that enveloped us.

Chants left Juliette's lips. Bones rattled. In the mist, I saw ghosts of Juliette's previous workings, the demons she'd birthed from blood and bones, the power she'd stolen from other witches' deaths, their eyes collected in jars. I saw myself, smiling and twirling in front of a golden mirror.

My body was slick with my own blood. A foreign substance once again trickled down my throat as I gagged and thrashed my head. It was the only thing I could move, my limbs held down by an invisible weight.

I didn't know if the warmth on my cheeks was blood or tears. My vision was swallowed up by darkness.

Behind my eyelids, I saw Kylo's silly little dimple. I saw the moment he'd marked me with his blood, as we were both drenched in rain, tangled together on the forest floor. I remember the way I'd relaxed as his blood reached my stomach, knowing he would now be able to keep me safe forever.

I cried for him like a child might cry for their mother. Begging, pleading, screaming until my throat was raw.

It was as if I were being split in two, half of my soul viciously slaughtered as I lay paralyzed.

I floated further and further away from my body. I couldn't tell if my mind was protecting me or torturing me as the visions of Kylo continued. I saw visions of him reading to me as I sat in his lap, the way he bathed me and brushed my hair with devoted tenderness, his delicious wicked streak, and his quick wit that loved to spar with mine. I saw *us*.

All I could see was *us* as Juliette carved me open and yanked Kylo out by the roots.

59

KYLO

Something was wrong. Evie's heart was more distressed and erratic than when Aster had tasted her blood.

The extraction team was occupying a mortal ally's home near the Nighswander Estate, a nondescript building we entered discreetly from the back. I had a clear view of one of the towers from the upstairs window, most of the structure obscured by trees.

"What is it?" Harmony asked.

I'd gone rigid, listening to Evie's heart through the bond.

"Shhh," I said softly.

I waited. Was she in the process of killing Juliette? Had something gone wrong, or was she merely fulfilling her mission?

There was no evidence of blood loss or drugging. But...

I strained, trying to understand the shift that had occurred. It was as if she'd been dimmed, like the snuffing of a candle flame.

I pulled out our linked note, writing to her.

Baby, please write to me. I—

The sound of an explosion rattled through the house. Shouts soon followed. I didn't have time to blink before the window shattered. I ducked as a ball of fire soared into the opposite wall.

A body slammed into mine, tackling me to the floor. Heat from the fire was scalding against my face. As I stabbed my born attacker between the eyes, I watched in horror as the note I'd dropped fell directly into the leaping flames. I threw the woman off me, but it was too late to salvage the now blackened ash.

"Everyone out now!" I bellowed.

Harmony coughed, her own dagger wet with blood as a born man lay at her feet.

The building didn't have long. We fought our way down the stairs, where more of my men were fighting born soldiers.

How the fuck had they known we'd be here? Honestly, it didn't surprise me. Conrad and Aster were stupid in their own ways, but they had to suspect Evie might have protection lurking nearby.

They were just as tired of us hiding as we were. Everyone in the city was starving for a fucking fight.

I relished the opportunity to unleash my repressed rage. I made my kills messy, deranged. I made art from born blood and bone.

We poured out of the back exit as the building began its booming collapse. These were my top fighters—we only lost one in the fight, a woman who'd been taken by surprise during the initial ambush.

"Lucetta," Blade said.

"Fuck."

I shook my head, quickly scanning the buildings encasing this courtyard. "We need a new vantage point."

One of my women wielded her water magick, forcefully sending gusts of water from the earth toward the building to stop the spread of fire.

"I hear more. They're luring us into battle," Blade said. "We don't have many options here."

"We could use our human glamours and split up," Harmony said quickly. "Then reconverge at our backup outpost."

My intuition fired low in my gut. How had they found us in the first place? We were wearing human glamours in the *first* outpost.

I paused, distracted by the erratic beat of Evie's distressed heart. "Juliette. She could've given them a description of my appearance. She knows what some of us look like."

But she knew *I* was the man Evie loved. And if she told the born who to search for... had she told the lords what I meant to Evie?

Had Evie been ambushed too?

My thoughts scrambled. As soon as the fire had been quelled, more shouts broke out from within the mortal buildings surrounding us. Born poured out onto roofs. A crossbow's arrow whirred toward me, and I deflected it with my shadows just in time.

We didn't have the luxury of deciding which path to take. It was being chosen for us.

Vesper conjured a snake made of shadow and fire. The beast roared, consuming the born on top of a nearby roof with the snapping of its jaw.

"Be careful of the mortals," I called.

Born leaped from windows. An omen rolled through me. This didn't feel like a street skirmish.

This was the start of something more.

We'd been caught off guard. These were born soldiers, in numbers that far surpassed anything we'd seen before.

It was as though Conrad knew we weren't just any cell of turned. He knew we were powerful enough to not only warrant his forces, but also important enough to make the move he wanted us to make.

"Kylo, there are too many. We have to—" Blade's call to action was cut off as he lunged for nearby born sneaking up on Clarke.

I cursed. Vesper and I locked eyes. Firebirds circled overhead.

I didn't have time to give the dreaded, inevitable order before blood onyx began to rain from the sky.

"Take cover now!" I yelled.

The born decided for us. After all of our careful planning, our eighty years of hiding and restraint, the weeks of tension and heartache between Evie and me...

In the end, not every choice could be ours to make.

I cleared a path for us by allowing my shadows the free rein —something I'd never shown to the streets of Etherdale before.

With blood and grit and sweat, my fighters and I battled our way inside a building, using dead born as umbrellas to guard against the spray of blood onyx. They would never waste such resources on random turned.

They knew exactly who I was.

Chills swept over my skin, an ancient, primal knowing curling around my spine. Evie's heart was bleeding—I could feel it through our bond in a way that was undeniable. She'd been hurt, in some way. And they were keeping me from her.

They were keeping me from her.

In a brief lull, Blade pinned me with a knowing look. I could tell we were on the same wavelength. I heard Clarke curse, and Vesper murmur, *there's nothing we can do.*

"We don't have a choice," Blade said. "Do or die."

We needed reinforcements. And if we brought more numbers, so would the born. And this fighting would spread like a plague. The mortals would jump to help us. Which meant we'd need to do the same for them. Conrad would notify Earle. Our allies would alert us to dreaded military movement toward Etherdale. The clans between here and Prospyrus would activate. The chain of events we'd meticulously orchestrated would fall like dominoes.

The only missing piece was the might of the Serpent Clan, who were willing not only to reinforce us in the air and on the ground here in the city, but also bring their wealth of resources amid our disadvantaged drought.

Even with Evie's poisons, we wouldn't be as strong until they arrived in two weeks.

"We'll have to start without them," I said.

Blade placed his hand on one shoulder, and Harmony placed hers on the other. I placed my hands on each of theirs. We stood there, linked, flushed with intoxicating, fiery energy.

We'd stood like this before Princeton turned us, jumping up and down and chanting, converting our fear into excitement in some holy alchemy.

From born blood we rise.

From born blood we rise.

"From born blood we rise."

Born rushed in. Shadows swarmed.

"Tomorrow is here."

Our masks finally fell.

60

KYLO

The worst of the first battle for Etherdale was the time between when our masks had dropped and reinforcements arrived. The fighting was gruesome and bloody. I watched men and women I'd known for decades die by my side.

As soon as we had ample numbers, everything improved. Even still, the savagery of war was not something any of us could've prepared for. War was not romantic; it was cold, brutal, and apathetic.

We'd fought all night. The city had instantly divided into born and loyalists and turned and mortal rebels. Etherdale became a grid of opposing forces, the sentiment shifting street by street, sometimes block by block. We overwhelmingly held mortal support, but there was only so much mortals could do to help us—especially humans. Their bravery was humbling.

In the underground, the first round of fighters fed and recouped their strength after a bloody battle on campus. It had resulted in a much larger turned territory that extended past our neighborhood.

In other words, we'd fucking won.

And the born had never appeared more shocked than they had looked in that moment.

We'd taken a large section of the campus, allowing hundreds of young mortals to take refuge under our protection. Many of the born continued to gather on the side of campus closest to the Nighswander Estate.

I chugged blood unceremoniously as I helped chart out the current map of born versus rebel forces.

Harmony and Blade had to all but drag me underground, and I only agreed after they reasoned it was best for Evie. We needed to meet with the inner circle, refuel, and build a strategy to extract Evie that wouldn't fail.

I was a man torn in two, caught between my primal urge to go to her at any cost, and my role as a leader to do what was best for the city under tenuous wartimes.

The born army had surrounded Nighswander Estate immediately. By the time reinforcements arrived, we'd been pushed out and away from the other half of my soul.

Out of all possibilities, this was the worst.

"I fucking knew this was going to happen," I roared, slamming my empty chalice on the deliberation table. "I shouldn't have let her go. She has now spent the entire night with *him*, and she's hurting. I can feel it."

"There was nothing you could do, Kylo. We couldn't have known they were going to force our hand last night," Blade said. "We're going to get to her. She's strong. She's going to be okay until then."

Vesper nodded. "None of this is ideal. We have to hold this city together for another twelve days *minimum*. And even that is pushing it."

As the blood strengthened my power, all I wanted to do was say *fuck it* to all of this and go pull Evie out myself.

But that might've been exactly what Conrad hoped I would do. He knew who I was. And he knew who I was to *her*.

Two things happened at once. First, Idris burst through the door, trailed by two wary guards.

"Where is she?" he asked, eyes finding mine immediately.

Second, a shockwave of warning slammed into me from my connection to Evie. I gasped, clutching the table as cold dread sank low in my guts. All eyes moved to me.

"No," I said, harsh and pained.

Someone closed the doors to the room, as if to hide me from the eyes of my clan.

My clan who needed to see me strong now more than ever.

But how could I be strong when Evie's blood was draining?

I couldn't say the words, not when Idris was here.

Evie was dying.

I felt hands on me, voices reaching through the haze of my panic and horror.

This was my worst nightmare—Evie's life slipping away while I was powerless to stop it.

"We have to go *now*."

Harmony and Blade exchanged a single glance before they launched into strategy talk. They'd fed, but I knew my extraction team hadn't had nearly enough rest for this kind of mission.

"You know I have to go with you," Vesper said. "For her. And for *him*. But we can't yet. We don't have the—"

"I don't care," I growled.

"What is happening?" Idris yelled, fists clenched as something bright crackled in his palms. He jumped, looking down at his hands as if he were surprised by this development.

"Evie is wounded and likely magickally bound," I managed, unable to breathe. "We were ambushed. They have surrounded the estate—nowhere in the city is more concentrated with born numbers."

Idris released an exhale. "But she's alive."

Her blood was draining so rapidly now that I feared she'd been attacked by a vampire in bloodlust.

"Kylo, wait—"

In a dissociative haze, I burst into the hall. Young turned were clinking glasses of blood, celebrating our first decisive win.

They turned toward me.

I fell to my knees. My hand clutched at my heart—the heart bound to hers.

Evie's heart stopped. Our connection sifted through my hands like sand.

She was gone.

61

EVIE

I felt the moment our bond severed.

On the brink of death, I'd long since stopped my writhing and screaming. I floated in a tranquil ocean of blood.

The emptiness was terrifying without my magick. There was nothing to add meaning and light to the darkness that spread on forever.

That was until I fell into a place that didn't belong to me. A small home on a river where insects were loud, the air was sticky, and a man in black stood with a belt in his hands.

My thighs stung, my face wet with tears. Useless.

Nothing I did was ever good enough. I couldn't make him happy. Sometimes I dreamed of being rescued and taken far away from here. But that would never happen. He would never let me go.

My father was going to kill me and feed me to the river monsters. Because I couldn't make him happy. I was worthless, impossible to love. There was something wrong with me. Maybe if I could figure it out, I could fix it.

Girls who were perfect, who were special—those were the girls who were loved.

~

I woke up to the sound of myself choking.

Aster's face hovered above mine. He swallowed, releasing a breath as the tension in his face relaxed. "See? You're still alive. You're okay." He held my head up as he fed me blood replenishing potion.

"Do you still want me to remove her tattoos? I can try burning them off," Juliette said.

I glanced down at my body covered in blood, bra and panties soaked through. A horrified cry spilled from my lips.

"I do," Aster said. "But not today."

My eyes shuttered. Aster let my head rest in his lap.

"What are you going to do about Conrad, Sir?"

Juliette's voice was tinged with nervousness, or perhaps anxiety.

Aster sighed heavily. "What do you mean, sweetheart?"

"He wanted me dead," she said softly. "They both did."

"And you know this, how?"

Juliette didn't speak. Breaking through my tsunami of grief, a brutal, feral rage was building. Kylo must've felt the moment our bond severed.

Oh, gods. Did he think I was dead?

"Kitten, Conrad would never betray me in that way. I need you to drop these paranoias." Aster slowly ran his hand through my hair, soft and gentle, as if I'd imagined his previous cruelty and venom.

"Is she going to stay in the dungeon?"

"Why would Evie stay in the dungeon?"

Juliette made a strangled noise. "But you said—" She cleared her throat. "She lied to you. She's been ruined in the eyes of Lillian. Doesn't she need to atone? Aren't you angry with her?"

"Of course I'm angry," Aster said calmly, a tinge of irritation in his voice. "But she isn't ruined. She made mistakes out of fear, and now that she's safe, she will atone under my care. Soon we'll all be far away, somewhere much better than this stain of a city."

"But she's been fucking the leader of the Masked Order!"

My eyes fluttered at the sound of a hiss. Aster's hand covered Juliette's mouth.

"I ought to clean out that filthy mouth with soap," Aster admonished, slowly dragging his hand away. "Juliette Montgomery, you will stop this treachery at once."

She flinched at the sound of her full name. "But, Sir, I've been faithful to you since the day we met," Juliette said, voice quivering with building emotion. "I've done everything you've ever asked of me. Why? Why am I not enough for you? You said I was special. You said I was perfect. She isn't perfect at all, and yet you still love her. *Why?*"

Her words slurred as she began to cry. My eyes closed again.

"Lillian below, I do not have the bandwidth to do this with you right now," Aster hissed. "How many times have we been over this? I have enough love for both of you, and my love for Evie does not detract from my love for you. You are *both* special. She almost died. She lost all of her blood to be purified for me, and that isn't enough for you. What do you want, Juliette? Do you want me to be as cruel to Evie as your father was to you?" Aster was yelling now, and Juliette sobbed harder. "Well, I won't. I'm not that man. Dry up those manipulative tears. We are already at war. I don't care to add any more drama into the mix."

Soon we'll all be far away.

We are already at war.

Oh, gods. I was still bound, and Kylo would have no way to track me if Aster left with me. And what happened to the borns' insistence that they could easily overtake the turned without the need for war? Had the war begun over *me*?

I was half-delirious from blood loss and pain, parsing

through these conversations as I burned with rage and grief. I had to get back to Kylo. I had to show him I wasn't dead.

And what about the note? Was Kylo okay? If they knew who he was... surely Aster would be boasting if they'd killed him.

Juliette continued to sob increasingly violently. Aster scooped me into his arms.

I had to get away from these wounded, dysfunctional people and the violence they left in their wake.

I peeked through my heavy eyelids. I caught one last glimpse of Juliette and the dagger she'd used to carve into my soul. She watched Aster carry me away, leaving her to cry alone in her demented spell circle.

I hated her guts. I was glad she was suffering, and yet that stupid, nagging feeling of empathy still rattled around in my chest.

Because while Juliette and the Servant were the ones hurting me, Aster was the one calling all the shots. And he made sure he was there to pick up the pieces.

Juliette wanted Aster to choose her. She wanted him to see her, to believe in her. She was *right* about me, and she was right about Conrad.

But Aster didn't care. He didn't choose her. Her plan had backfired. The moment he left her there, with me in his arms, I knew he'd betrayed Juliette on a deep, fundamental level.

And I was downright terrified of how she'd retaliate.

"War?" I croaked.

Without my bond with Kylo, I felt hollow inside. I would do anything to get back to him. There was no line I wouldn't cross. And if war had already begun, I had free rein to rot everyone in this castle the moment I could get my magick back.

"More like an uprising. It will be handled once Earle steps in, don't you worry."

As soon as Aster made it to the first level, Conrad appeared.

He stared at me for three beats before lifting a brow. "Did you two leave any blood inside her body?"

Conrad appeared strained, his nostrils flaring as he stared at my wounds hungrily.

Aster's grip on me tightened. "I did what needed to be done. She is grateful to be free of them."

Conrad smirked. "Is she now?"

"What are you implying?" Aster hissed, his hold on my blood-soaked body now bruising.

"Nothing, brother. I'm glad our lost little lamb has been safely returned to the flock." He met my eyes. "You should be grateful you're on the right side of the battle line, girl. The catacombs will be at capacity by the end of this mess."

I needed to know what was happening. I was desperate for information, for more than just their usual cocky taunting.

"My family is out there. Please—what is going on?" I asked.

Conrad only smiled, more than happy to torture me with his silence. What had he done to Kylo and the extraction team?

Conrad saw the moment anger flashed in my eyes.

"There, there," Aster consoled. "You need to rest."

Conrad stayed rooted in front of us. "What she needs is to be questioned."

"And she will be," Aster said coolly, stepping out of Conrad's reach.

I whispered my question again, begging. "What is going on?"

Aster only continued to stroke my hair and shush me, stoking the ravenous hunger of my scorned shadows.

My only way out of this was the key in Aster's pocket. Either I had to take it from him, or I had to persuade him to use it.

Which would mean convincing him I didn't want to cut him into a hundred pieces for what he had just done to me.

He had me sliced open. Mutilated.

All because he couldn't fathom my connection to another man.

If my stomach hadn't been so empty, I would've retched. I forgot I was nearly nude, unable to feel any shame when my entire body was covered in blood.

Vampires' attention locked onto me immediately as we passed, frustration blooming in their predatory eyes when they realized I was untouchable.

Without Aster's protection, I would've been eaten alive. I bet my strong, powerful blood was sending the entire estate into a frenzy.

I met Aster's eyes, seeing his own churning hunger. There was nothing stopping him from violating me now that he didn't need to win me over.

"It's sexy to know how desired you are, knowing you only belong to me."

I tensed in his arms. I couldn't pretend. All I could think about was Kylo believing I was dead.

Phineas had been right about me. I wasn't cut out for subterfuge. I wasn't prepared to be traumatized over and over until I was a hollow shell of a girl.

So when Aster set me down before a grand bathtub and began to cleanse my wounds, all of me was a tight ball of stress.

"Nothing will scar. After I bathe you, we will apply healing ointment."

"I can bathe myself."

I couldn't do it. I couldn't sacrifice my body and mind.

Aster slowly looked up at me. "Evie, you know I only did what I had to do, right?" he asked sternly. "You're covered in blood—the most delicious blood I've ever tasted—and I haven't once harmed you, have I? Even after I discovered your treachery, I did not show you violence."

That wasn't true. He'd choked me. He'd thrown me around. He'd yelled in my face.

If Juliette had heard what he'd just said about my blood, she might actually kill herself. She wanted love from an abuser; she'd been doomed from the start.

He grabbed my wrist. *"Right?"*

I forced my head to nod. Survival. I had to survive. I had to get back to my family.

"You were only protecting me," I lied.

Aster released my wrist, and I fought the urge to rub it.

"But I'm hurting and embarrassed and I need to be alone for a minute," I said. "Please."

"Fine," he said curtly, not giving a fuck about my comfort at this point. He only wanted to pretend to respect my boundaries, to uphold the bare minimum of decency for his narcissistic white knight complex.

He cleared his throat with a tight smile. "You'll let me heal you once you're clean?"

I nodded, and something in me died.

In the bathtub, I could hardly feel the sting of Juliette's slashes. The cuts had clearly been mended on some level during the ritual when I'd been unconscious. All that washed away was old blood.

A lot of old blood.

I swallowed down the feral scream building in my throat. I clawed at the metal ring around my throat. I scrubbed at my skin. I could sense this new form of madness bubble up from the darkest pit of me, and I didn't stop it—I welcomed it, teeth bared like a rabid wolf.

Behind my eyelids, all I saw was him.

After three washes, the water finally ran clear. I stood from the tub. I scanned the bathroom for anything that could be used as a weapon. In my head was this ringing sound I couldn't shake, though I suspected it had something to do with the heat rushing up and down my spine.

The buildup of magick and power was making me ill.

I caught sight of myself in the mirror as I stumbled around, naked and wet. My gray eyes were intense, frenzied. My long, damp hair was a tangled mess. Jagged scars in various symbols littered my body, including one over my heart.

I glared at Juliette's handiwork. It wasn't nearly satisfying enough to hear Aster betray her. I needed to see her bleed.

I needed to *make* her bleed.

When the sight of me nude and wearing what was essentially Aster's collar was too much to stomach, I turned away from the mirror.

Before I could continue my search for a makeshift weapon, a chill swept down my spine.

I heard my own giggle.

But my mouth was closed. I whirled back around, heart thumping as I faced my own reflection.

Except while I remained nude, my reflection was now wearing a pastel purple dress. She smiled at me, lifting a finger to her plump pink lips.

She made a come-hither motion while hooded eyes scanned my body.

Okay, yep, I'd officially lost my damn mind.

Even still, I approached. Because what the fuck else was I supposed to do?

"Does Kylo love me?" my reflection asked.

I studied her in confusion. "Of course."

"Would he ever betray me?"

"Never."

What kind of cosmic lesson was this? And how was I able to vision with my power blocked? Unless of course, this truly was a hallucination of the psychotic variety.

She sighed. "That sounds really beautiful."

My voice was shaky with emotion. "Being loved by Kylo is like staring up at the vastness of the cosmos and not feeling small. He has seen and studied all of me and fallen in love with every piece. Loving each other is worship."

Our lips curved, and our eyes grew glassy.

"A devotion to life itself."

Her smile faded. She nodded her head. A coldness snuck into her eyes as she looked down at her lilac dress. "Time to learn how it feels."

"What?"

I blinked, and for a moment, the mirror was empty. But as soon as my fingers brushed the glass, my nude form reappeared. Our confused faces matched perfectly.

At the sound of a knock, I jolted. "Just a moment," I called.

The hairs on the back of my neck stood in high alert, as if I'd seen a ghost. I pulled a towel around me. I searched the bathroom once more for a weapon.

Aster barged in.

"Are you all right?"

Translation: I was tired of waiting, and I'm going to pretend that my intrusion was for your benefit.

Calling him out would be useless, so I merely admitted defeat. He led me out of the room and had me lie on a loveseat. I was feverish and disoriented.

His breath hitched when he gingerly pried the towel out of my death grip. Tears brimmed my eyes as he applied healing salve to my nude form.

"I feel ill," I said, begging him to care with wide, wounded eyes. "My magick is building up from within, and it's killing me."

"Shhh. It was the ritual. Juliette was rough with you out of spite. If I could've freed you from the turned, I would've done it myself."

My spine was searing. Pressure built at the crown of my head and the soles of my feet. Power with nowhere to go.

"How can I earn my magick back?"

Aster's hand paused over my heart, spending more time than necessary rubbing the salve into my skin. His eyes lit up, and his gaze roamed over my form more ravenously than before.

Stop. Please stop.

"By being a very good girl for me, angel."

62

KYLO

The moment I emerged from the underground, I ran. I didn't care who followed me. I ignored the sound of my name being shouted frantically.

Unmasked, unglamoured, I tore through the streets until I hit up against our ever-shifting battle line.

Faced with a line of born, I ripped chunks out of necks. Shadows shot from my palms in gusts of screaming wrath, annihilating several born at once.

I dodged flying weapons and deflected several currents of magick.

At a certain point, I slipped under my shadow glamour, becoming invisible to most born except those with expanded sight.

I couldn't wield the glamour for long. I was overextended, wielding godlike amounts of power with hundreds of born surrounding me. I took every opportunity to refeed from born blood.

I had to get to her. She wasn't dead. She *couldn't* be dead.

None of my clan had kept up with me. I was alone, reckless and unhinged. A man driven to madness.

Or at least, I thought I was alone, until I turned down a quiet alley to catch my breath and saw a hand appear from a dark mist.

Phineas.

"They have her, and I need her back," was all I managed, my voice a raspy growl.

The born had long learned to set traps for turned eyes, but Phineas was crafty. He could get close.

At the very least, he'd seen me being stupidly, unabashedly reckless and was covering me.

Beneath the grumpy exterior, he was a fiercely loyal fucker.

I hadn't realized how compulsive a habit it had become to check the blood bond until only silence waited for me on the other side.

My heart was a tight fist. My muscles and bones screamed from the exertion.

Phineas's hand reabsorbed into his veil of shadow.

I must've destroyed hundreds of born before my invisibility glamour disintegrated for good. Firebirds screeched. Shouts hit me from all directions—calls to gather forces and hunt me down.

I'd be surrounded in a matter of minutes.

I couldn't fight my way through all of them. I ripped at my hair. My lips were stained with copper. My soul was bloody and aching as if it wanted to break away in search of Evie's.

At the end of the street we were currently on—now lined with born corpses—I saw another hand floating midair.

Phineas made the symbol to retreat.

But I couldn't. I couldn't abandon her, not again. My angel needed me.

I stumbled forward, tripping over the bodies of slain demons. More born were already swarming, failing to learn from the ruthlessness of my previous slaughter.

Phineas's hand hadn't stopped making its symbol, and yet,

something strange happened to his glamour. It was trembling. He was closer now than before, moving strangely slow.

Weapons flew at my head. My shadows worked subconsciously, impaling born and shielding me without my direction.

Suddenly, a body appeared from under Phineas's glamour and hurtled toward me—a girl with long blonde hair wearing a lilac dress, face stricken with fear.

I nearly fell to my knees again, unsure if what I was seeing was real or a vision from beyond the grave.

Perhaps I'd died, and Evie and I would spend an eternity haunting Etherdale together.

"Angel?" I asked, voice strained as Evie slammed into my chest.

I covered her with a protective shield, inhaling her soft floral scent and listening to her heartbeat here in the flesh rather than through our bond.

"I'm scared," she whispered. "I can't use my magick."

The sound of her voice snapped me the fuck out of it. I didn't care how she was here or what had happened to our bond.

All I knew was that I had to get Evie out of here.

While it was impressive I'd made it this close to Nighswander Estate, that also meant we had a way to go to reach turned territory.

My shadows covered Evie the moment I lifted her into my arms, roaming over her protectively. She was alive. Of course, she was alive.

I took off, running on pure adrenaline and cosmic gratitude. I prayed for us as the sweet girl in my arms clung to me, trusting me with her life like the perfect, good girl she was.

Born soldiers didn't know this city like I did. I confused them with my route, zigzagging down side streets, moving through back entrances of buildings.

When a group caught me in an alley, a primal noise escaped from deep in my throat in warning. They would not fucking touch her. Never again. My shadows swarmed like a plague of locusts. As they fell, something sharp landed in the back of my shoulder.

I quickly pulled out the knife, the blade laced with blood onyx.

Fuck.

My already drained power took a hit. Without the weapon still lodged in my flesh, I'd heal. I wouldn't go into full paralysis. But it would be harder to recover while this overextended. And we still had seven blocks to go.

All I could do was run, not nearly as fast as I had before. Firebirds landed on nearby buildings. Soldiers poured in from all directions. Orders were shouted—to close up the perimeter, to box us in. I could hear them calling me the bastard lord.

I could hear them saying my *name.*

I panted. Evie gasped in my arms. I held her tight.

There were too many born, and I was too drained to fight my way through all of them.

With heaving lungs, I deflected poisoned weapons. I kept Evie safe as she trembled. They were toying with me, only attacking from a distance as they let me see just how surrounded I truly was.

"You crazy motherfucker!"

Evie and I looked to the sky. Harmony and Blade sat atop firebirds. As soon as I saw them, Blade leaped from his creature to Harmony's. The abandoned firebird dove for me as weapons and magick flew.

I didn't think twice. I used the last of my strength, covered by my friends, as I mounted and took to the clouds. Fiery wings spread wide, blessed by Helia's rays.

We were pursued immediately by the borns' sky fleet. Blade peppered them with his lethally sharp shadows that flew through the air at impossible speeds. Demons rained down from the sky.

After a few blocks, we were assisted by greater reinforcements.

I hissed as a born managed to dive from his firebird to mine. Evie screamed.

I recognized the look in the born's eyes—the willingness to become a martyr if that was what it took to eliminate the most prized kill in the city.

He moved quickly, and I was in the worst possible position to defend us.

He raised his sword.

Lightning came down and struck the man on the head. He jolted, electricity frying the shit out of him. Our firebird twisted and shook, knocking him loose as he fell to the earth below.

Evie coughed, a sickly noise leaving her throat.

"Baby, are you okay? Are you getting your magick back?"

The born must've subdued it somehow.

Evie nodded. "I'm okay."

She lifted a hand to her face, and at the scent of her blood, I quickly grabbed it.

Droplets of crimson stained her fair skin.

"Fuck, baby. Are you coughing blood? How badly are you injured?"

She began to cry, and I held her tightly as the firebird made its descent. "They broke our bond. They cut you out of me."

Rage and grief tore through me, a low growl lodged in my throat. "Impossible, angel. Bond or not, they could never cut us out of each other."

Those procedures were extraordinarily risky, with a high likelihood of complications and fatality. They gambled Evie's life away like it meant nothing at all. Just to try to keep her from me.

We landed at the nearest firebird stables within turned territory.

My legs were jelly when I touched down on solid ground. I still wasn't entirely convinced I wasn't dead, and all of this was some kind of afterlife fantasy.

Blade and Harmony shared similar disbelief.

"How the fuck?" Blade summarized.

"Vesper is so pissed," Harmony said under her breath.

Vesper had no reason to be angry. We hadn't stormed the castle without her, so her kill was still hers to take. And to be frank, I didn't really care about other people's feelings when Evie's life was at stake.

We all stared at a trembling Evie, waiting for her to explain.

She reached for my hand and looked at the ground. "I knew you'd come for me the moment they drained me of our bond. So I did everything I could to escape—I convinced Aster I was on the brink of death, that I needed my magick to heal and survive. He made the mistake of removing my magickal binding."

"Is he dead?" I asked.

Evie's eyes flashed with anger. "No, I don't think so."

I couldn't imagine the degree of shame she must be feeling. She might've even believed the start of the war was her fault.

"That's okay. They'll all be dead soon enough," I said, hugging her tight as my heart pounded with adrenaline and relief. "All that matters is that you're home and you're safe."

"You two have some fucking guardian angels, I swear to the gods," Blade said.

Another firebird landed, one carrying Vesper and Clarke. I felt a strange mix of gratitude, surprise, and guilt that they'd followed me into a deathtrap.

Vesper held a look of pure death, glaring sharply at Blade and Harmony.

"I thought you were following us!" Harmony squeaked. "I'm sorry!"

But as soon as Vesper's gaze landed on the girl in my arms, she melted. "Thank Helia."

I peeled Evie off my chest to stare into her wide gray eyes. "You're a miracle. I'm going to take care of you now, okay?"

She smiled, taking me by surprise. She'd endured the unspeakable. She was captured, tortured, brutalized...

I scanned her, finally noting how untouched she appeared. My brows drew together, but the sound of her voice washed my questions away.

"Thank you, Kylo," she whispered sweetly.

Everything else fell away, for this brief reprieve. Our audience, the war, the born men I yearned to tear limb from limb. It was just me and my angel against the world.

Her eyes softened as if mesmerized. "You're so beautiful."

I grinned at the strangeness of such a declaration. The poor thing must've been as disoriented as I was. Even more reason to do everything in my power to help her feel safe.

"You're surrounded by people who love you. Everything is going to be okay. One step closer to The Sun."

Evie looked confused for a moment before understanding washed over her. "Don't forget The Star."

I traced her upper back, where her tattoo was.

Her face crumpled suddenly. "They stole my tattoos."

"What?" I hissed. "They fucking did *what*?"

Evie sobbed, burying her head in my chest. "I begged for them to stop. They burned them away."

63

EVIE

After Aster finished mending what he'd broken, I quickly asked for clothing. At the sight of my features stricken with shame and discomfort, he feigned sympathy that didn't match the churning darkness in his amber irises.

He fetched me a far-too-translucent white nightgown. I reached for it, but he shook his head. He guided me to stand and raise my arms, and he proceeded to dress me.

My throat tightened. Repressed violence rotted away at my insides.

What *was* that mirror vision? Some grand truth was poking me with its sharp edge, but every time I reached for it, the revelation melted into water and slipped through my grasp.

"When we make it to Prospyrus, you're going live like a princess," Aster said, tentatively closing a hand around my waist.

I wobbled, woozy and lightheaded.

"You'd like that, wouldn't you, pretty girl?"

A princess *and* a secret weapon.

"Why Prospyrus?" I asked, capitalizing off my half-delirious state to play dumb.

"I'm going to fill an opening in King Earle's council," Aster said, eyes alight as his voice dropped.

Wait, *what?*

I steadied. Something brave and strong took over my body—sneaking past the grief and the fear and the trauma, rooting itself in my weary form until it had eclipsed my shame.

"I had no idea there was an opening. That's incredible." I swallowed down my pride. I raised a trembling hand to Aster's chest to soften my inquiries. "That doesn't happen very often, does it?"

Aster looked down at my hand on his chest. "No, it doesn't. The stars have surely aligned." His eyes were fiery as they moved to my lips. "You're turned on by a man's ambition, aren't you, Evie?"

I released a breath. I was playing with fire. I didn't want to sacrifice my sanity or my body for subterfuge. But I also had to take advantage of the position I was in. Kylo was probably fighting his way to me as we spoke—he would do anything for me, even after I'd failed miserably.

Kylo might've thought I was *dead.*

"Maybe," I said softly. "If it's the right kind of ambition."

Aster stroked my cheek. A low moan rumbled through his chest. "You need someone powerful to protect you, don't you little one?"

Nope. *Ew.* No, thank you.

Time to steer this ship back on course. "Uh-huh. Is Conrad envious of your new position?"

Aster wagged a finger. "Bad girl," he admonished, though it was nearly a groan. He *wished* he could make Conrad jealous. He smiled. "No, Conrad is happy for me. It isn't yet official, but we will all be heading to Prospyrus within the week."

Panic was a volatile force. For a moment, I struggled to breathe. Blood bond or not, Kylo would track me to the ends of the earth. But would he be able to get to me in King Earle's city?

The strongest vampire-run city in the realm? If I was forced to become the wife of a *councilman?*

I couldn't let Aster take me away before the Serpent Clan arrived. He and Conrad wouldn't leave this blood-soaked city alive.

Realization slammed into me from all angles. If Conrad wasn't jealous of Aster, a man of his ambition and authority, that meant Conrad was aiming higher than the council.

Conrad wanted to be king.

They were infiltrating the council and sowing seeds of doubt about Earle's competency to clear the path for Conrad.

Our suspicions being true was a relief and a shock both at once. Because Conrad believing he could truly take the throne, as a controversial, religious, slavery-endorsing lord from the south, was *insane.*

Whether Earle was truly going mad or that was a part of his detractors' smear campaign, the man had ruled for nearly one thousand years.

Conrad and Aster were in over their heads. And now that I'd spent this amount of time with them, my intuitive superpowers were painting a clear image of the power dynamics my spirit guides had urged me to pay attention to from the beginning.

Conrad was a raging, malicious narcissist, and Aster was his idealistic, covert narcissistic yes-man. They were two complementary flavors of the same evil—the same desire for control, misogynistic domination, and the subordination of mortals under a façade of religiosity.

I was well-familiar with narcissists after my mother and Jacob, which gave me a unique advantage here.

I knew now what I'd been searching for in Conrad's office. And it was far more damning than names of possible dissenters.

Conrad and Aster were about to have a councilman killed.

And I was going to find out who.

Aster misread the excitement in my eyes. That was his weakness. With me, with Juliette, with Conrad.

Aster only saw what he wanted to see.

His lips met mine, hungry and urgent. The kiss was too soft, too sloppy, and the scrape of fangs felt like a punishment.

I'd made him wait too long. A poor, hedonistic male vampire deprived of getting exactly what he wanted at all times.

The universe had finally thrown me a bone now that I was at my lowest, which was just *typical*.

This had better be my last dark night of the fucking soul, or I was going to start firing my spirit guides.

Aster violated me, and I didn't crumble. My body burned with heat and strained with pent-up power, but it didn't fold.

I was going to do what I needed to do.

When Aster pulled back, I wondered if the key to my collar was still in his pocket. He had only shared such sensitive information with me because he had no intention of letting me go.

I'd heard them mention bribing someone to keep my power a secret. Which meant I'd be free to use my magick eventually, for *them*.

It was either be a *very good girl* or a very bad one, but either way, I was going to free myself long before Aster smuggled me out of Etherdale.

"You have such expressive eyes," Aster said. "Are you feeling better, my love?"

I nodded. "I still feel sick." I grabbed at my collar briefly before lowering my hand and looking away. "But I'm glad I'm safe now."

"I know it's early," he said. "But I can't wait to marry you."

I suppressed the urge to laugh or claw out his eyes. As if timelines mattered to someone who took child brides.

When his thumb traced my jugular, slipping under the metal

bar around my throat, I sobered. He revealed his fangs, and I went utterly still.

Someone knocked on the door.

Aster frowned. "Come in."

The sight of Conrad's grin twisted my guts. Because someone like him only smiled genuinely when someone was suffering.

"Guess who's throwing a temper tantrum through the streets of Etherdale?" he drawled, pinning me with a cruel gaze.

My heart fluttered.

"Hilarious that they wanted us to see them as noble, well-educated revolutionaries when their leader behaves like a petulant child with zero sense or self-control." Conrad stepped toward us. "He's going to get himself killed, all because we stole his favorite toy." He made an infuriating faux pout.

I wanted to deck him. I wanted to punch his haughty face until it was mush.

Kylo was alive. But he was putting himself in danger for *me*.

Something must've happened to our linked note. Conrad likely ambushed the extraction team, and soldiers moved in before they could get to me.

And if Conrad knew who Kylo was, that meant he must've been playing both me *and* Juliette, on some level. He'd extracted the information he needed from Juliette—Kylo's identity—while simultaneously promising me he would kill her.

Conrad wanted me to beg for information, but I kept my mouth shut tight. I wouldn't give him the satisfaction, nor would I enrage the man with my key to freedom in my pocket. If Aster suspected I cared for Kylo as deeply as I did, it would put both of us in more danger.

And Conrad couldn't be fucking trusted, just as Vesper warned me.

Everything he said was manipulation.

Kylo was going to be okay. Hope planted deep inside me. He was coming for me. *Of course,* he was coming for me.

Or was he so blinded by rage, believing I was dead, that he was killing every born he could get his hands on?

I shoved the thought away. Aster pulled me against him, jealousy radiating from him in waves.

"Good riddance," Aster said, watching my face.

It took everything inside me to stop myself from making the expression I wanted to make. All I did was stare at Conrad like a thoughtless bimbo until his grin finally faded and Aster relaxed his hold.

Conrad cleared his throat, lip curling with disdain. "Your presence is needed."

Aster sighed.

He let go of me the moment my stomach made a pathetic growl. Both men stared at me as if with mild irritation at my own bodily functions.

"You haven't fed your toy," I snapped before I could stop myself. I quickly balanced it out with a small smile.

Aster blinked.

Conrad's eyes narrowed.

With a short, surprised laugh, Aster pet my head like I was a small animal and stepped toward Conrad. "See? I told you she was quite witty." He paused. "I'll send food up for you, dear. You rest—that's an order. And don't worry about the city. Your family will be safe so long as they stay out of trouble, and this will all be over soon."

I let my shoulders relax, as if convinced. What comforting words.

The moment they left, I released a shaky breath and found the quietest, darkest corner of the room to sit. It was exactly what I used to do in my childhood bedroom.

I pulled my knees to my chest, rocking slightly, and I prayed. Not to Lillian.

To Hekate, Selena, and Helia. To anyone who would listen and offer their aid.

Please keep him safe.

∽

AS THE HOURS PASSED, the sinking feeling grew heavier. I was suffocating with worry and helplessness.

I'd torn up the room searching for the key. I'd tried jamming objects into the lock and jiggling, but nothing worked.

How was I this powerful and this thwarted by a piece of cursed metal?

I moved through every emotion in the book, but I preferred to stay in the comfortable currents of rage.

Because as soon as I moved to grief, a horrible feeling came over me. Visions of Kylo slain before he could fulfill any of his grand dreams.

Visions of him slain in the streets because of *me.*

I don't know what possessed me to stop pacing in front of a mirror after my last eerie interaction with my reflection.

But maybe she knew something. Maybe this time the vision would become clearer, even *helpful*, gods forbid.

I stared at myself and waited.

Minutes passed, and nothing happened.

"Hello?" I asked my reflection like a crazy person.

My marks were fading—the evidence of Juliette's mutilation of my body and soul. I hoped she was off somewhere sobbing about how Aster had used her for her magick and then abandoned her.

At the sight of my own cruel smirk, I frowned. I stood, but before I could turn away, I saw the shift I'd been waiting for.

The version of me in the lilac dress was back. Her eyes widened, looking me up and down. I glanced down at the revealing slip over my body, the night gown that ironically —*tragically*—appeared like it belonged to Juliette.

My gaze snapped back to my reflection the moment another figure entered the mirror.

"Baby, what are you smiling about?"

Kylo.

A strangled sound left my lips as I approached the mirror. I missed him so much it broke me.

"I'm just so happy to be yours," my reflection said, wearing one of Kylo's oversized shirts. "To be here with you and not *there*."

She looked directly at me. When Kylo bent to kiss her neck, she winked at me.

Wait.

"*No.*"

I heard the word leave my lips as the truth finally smacked me in the face.

Time to learn how it feels.

My reflection hadn't been the first person to say that to me. That was the vow Juliette had made when she told me I was *taking everything from her.*

In retaliation for *stealing* Aster, she was…

"Oh my fucking gods!" I screeched.

Juliette giggled, snug in my skin she'd long coveted.

Kylo's lips were on *her* neck.

He'd rescued *her.*

"Changeling," I gasped, borrowing a term from faerie mythology.

She'd been watching me. Sneaking into places she didn't belong. She knew things she shouldn't have known.

She stole a vial of my blood.

And the visions of mirrors had begun directly after—visions of Juliette playing dress-up with my motherfucking *body.*

She'd been studying me, all this time. My likes and dislikes. My mannerisms.

An emotion I'd never felt overtook me as Juliette kissed the love of my life and forced me to watch. My body vibrated uncontrollably with suppressed magick.

Kylo would know. He would know it wasn't me. Just because she wore a glamour didn't mean she understood the intricacies of my body and mind.

He pulled back, and I stared at him hopefully when his eyes flashed confusion. He looked down at Juliette, silent and assessing.

"Are you okay?" he asked.

He knew. He knew something was wrong.

"It's not me. You know it's not me," I said to him, willing him to see the truth in the mirror. Willing him to see *me*.

"Mmhmm. I'm ready for bed now." Juliette stretched like a cat, snuggling against Kylo until his confusion melted away.

"Of course, baby."

They disappeared. The wrathful scream that left me was inhuman, pure beast. My collar heated until it was scalding, damaging the sensitive flesh beneath.

And I didn't care.

I picked up a nearby vase, and I bludgeoned the mirror, over and over again until it was nothing but shards.

The last thing that left my lips before Aster and Conrad burst in with a set of guards was a demented, strangled vow.

"I'm going to kill that wretched psycho bitch and put her *eyes in a fucking jar!"*

64

KYLO

"Coffee?" I asked.

Evie tilted her head. "What do you think?"

She'd been acting noticeably off since her escape, so this bit of Evie normalcy brought a relieved smile to my face.

I'd spent a precious few hours holding her close, relishing her aliveness. I'd told her she should continue sleeping, and I'd send a healer for her, but she'd insisted on joining me for breakfast before I headed to our post on campus.

The underground was still a hub, but now that we were able to meet in broad daylight, I was intent on taking full advantage.

I'd explained to her what had happened—emphasizing that launching into battle ahead of the Serpent Clan wasn't her fault —but she hadn't reacted at all like I thought she would. Her eyes had been wide with surprise, but there was no evidence of shame or worry. She took everything I said at face value, with no follow-up questions.

I worried she was in some kind of shock, or dissociation. What had been done to her was so violent and brutal that it was more than reasonable.

I'd chugged preserved blood to refuel, and I declined Evie's offer for me to drink from her. Her body did not need any more stress or blood loss.

"Baby, I know you want to fight with us, but I need to make sure you're okay first. Especially with the lingering struggles with your power."

She nodded. "Of course. Whatever you think is best."

I lifted a brow. Well, that was hot and all, but not exactly Evie.

Before I could prod, she set her coffee down and launched into my chest. She inhaled deeply, and my heart panged.

"Hi, baby," I whispered into her hair.

"You really think we can *win?*" she asked for a second time since her rescue.

It made me wonder what the hell had been said to her while she was being tortured.

"We *are* winning," I said simply. "Things will shift when Earle sends his forces from the north, but only until the Serpent Clan arrives. We can hold out until then—we've planned for all manner of catastrophes. No one was deluded enough to believe everything would be perfect."

Evie's heart sped up; I could hear it leaping against my chest.

When she pulled back, her eyes danced with anxiety and her lips tugged down.

"Angel, I've got you," I said. "You're safe. Things are going *well*. Etherdale is ours, and everyone who harmed you will soon be dead. We will make sure they receive the punishment they have earned."

"Then why did you let me go? Why did you let them torture me?" Her voice was heartbreakingly small and wounded.

My heart dropped into my stomach.

"Why did you let Aster kiss me and chain me to his bed?"

I let go of her waist, so I didn't accidentally squeeze her to death. Fists balled at my side, I turned away from her. I knew my barely recovered shadows were leaking from me. The room became dark, heavy, and oppressive in seconds.

I cursed, body trembling with a rage that would easily lead to bloodlust if I dropped even a fraction of my self-control.

"I didn't let you go," I whispered, strangled and raw. Guilt and fury warred for supremacy. "You *chose* to go. I wish I'd stopped you, fuck, I wish I'd acted on my worst qualities. You might've resented me for taking away your agency but at least you would've been safe."

What had happened to her played out in my mind in agonizing visions. He'd kissed my angel. He chained her to his bed.

I whirled around on her, noting the way she flinched. It forced me to take a deep, ragged inhale and halt the flow of my power.

"What else did he do?" I growled. I couldn't stop myself. I had to know.

I'd exercised more than enough restraint the past few weeks, and I'd only been punished for it. I'd failed her, and she knew it. She'd needed a savior last night, and I never came. I was too late.

I'd betrayed her trust in me to protect her when she needed it most.

Evie trembled, fear swimming in her shiny gray eyes. "I don't know. I can't remember."

My heart broke, my guilt reaching an insurmountable weight on my chest until I could hardly breathe. I imagined the worst, unspeakable horrors that would haunt Evie for the rest of her life.

"I'm so sorry, Evie."

When I reached for her again, she flinched a second time. I pulled her close anyway, and she finally relaxed.

"What do you need to feel safe today?"

She didn't answer. The lump in my throat grew.

"I know you want to be with me, but if you remain here, you can read in your garden or sleep or do whatever you need to do to heal. I'll send an emotional healer. I'll have someone cook for you. I wish I could stay, but I have to get back."

Evie wasn't acting like herself. I had no idea what had truly happened to her. And I couldn't be here for her properly because we were at war.

All I knew was that Aster and Conrad were going to suffer brutally for what they'd done.

Evie still didn't speak.

"I could call for Idris as well," I said.

"I can stay and read in the garden," she finally said. "I don't want to see Idris yet." Previous emotion drained from her voice.

When I studied her again, there was no dissociation in her eyes nor fear. Her features held an eerie pleasantness that was so opposite of the reaction I expected from her.

The color drained from my face. She was *not* okay.

And neither was I.

But that didn't change the fact that I had to go, and she was better off here than on the front lines. We would have to make do without her until her power returned.

I leaned in and kissed her forehead. "I'll be back as soon as I can."

Visions of what Aster might've done played out with every step I took away from her.

Evie would never be the same again, and she was right to ask me how I'd ever let that happen.

It was another gruesome day in Etherdale. And yet, I witnessed just as many acts of love as I did violence. Students offered us blood and dispersed food and water among the witches and shifters. Professors stepped in with their own expertise.

Administrators donated magickal supplies. I watched humans drop witch-made explosives and poisons on the born from windows on battle-torn streets. I saw strangers save strangers, opening their homes and hearts.

These were the things that fueled my shattered soul, that kept me going as I led my friends into another bloody battle.

For Etherdale, for *her*, I forced myself to compartmentalize —to think only of the tasks at hand and to find catharsis in the breaking of bones and the piles of born corpses.

We took another mortal neighborhood today. It helped that it was an overwhelmingly pro-revolution area. Bit by bit, we were showing the born how vastly they'd underestimated us.

And gods above these fuckers were so satisfyingly confused.

I slowly made my way back to the heart of turned territory after I ensured stability. Witches were hard at work setting traps, erecting wards and safety measures for their beloved neighborhood. The fighting had simmered in this area, the born far more concerned about our presence on the other side of town—the stretch of busy streets that separated us from Nighswander Estate.

"Kylo," Blade huffed, wiping blood and sweat from his hairline as he closed the distance between us. "It's happening. Born forces from over the mountains are heading for us. Our allies are rising from the underground to slow their movement. Earle finally realizes the truth of who he's up against."

I halted. Despite it being expected and inevitable, the words still triggered a heady concoction of sensations in my body and brain.

Evie might call it the hum of fate.

"And so it begins," I said.

The hum carried us through until late evening.

My inner circle had just met with mortal representatives, and tensions had never been higher. Most agreed with our courses of action, but some were deluded about the scope of our power, and I feared nothing we did would ever be *enough* for mortals of their temperament.

I found a small break in the action and returned home to find Evie asleep, sprawled out in our bed and barely moving. She needed the rest. Her forehead was hot when I brushed my hand over it.

I frowned. She must've been running warm as her body recovered.

As she slept, I answered correspondences with allies across the realm, updating them on our progress in Etherdale and mapping out information from their own updates.

My mind was doing what it did best—synthesizing, finding patterns, and converting it all into predictions and courses of action. Blade and I were rapidly scrawling notes to each other, our usual dance of scheming.

At a certain point, exhaustion won, and I dozed for a necessary few hours. Between states of dreaming, I saw Evie giggling in the mirror hours after Aster had ripped out our blood bond and had her chained to his bed.

I woke up gasping for air, and Evie was quick to twist in my arms. She peppered me with sweet kisses, her hand trailing down my chest.

Her touch was soothing to my overworked mind and depleted body.

"I love you," I dreamily whispered as I ran a hand through her hair.

She shuddered. Her hand slipped lower.

At first, her small fingers curling around my cock had its expected effect. My groan was breathy, and she sighed contentedly. My shadows reached for hers.

They hit up against the strangest cold emptiness. A chill crawled down my spine, some preconscious intuition jolting me awake.

I grabbed her wrist. "Not yet, angel."

She yanked her hand back. Her eyes flashed hurt.

"Are you feeling okay? You were feverish, and I still don't feel your shadows. What did they do to your magick, sweet girl?"

Evie's hurt expression transformed swiftly into anger. At first, I thought she was reliving the borns' torture, but then she recoiled from *me.*

"What if they never come back? Will you still love me?"

I frowned. "Of course, Evie. I love you for *you.* Not your magick. I love you for your soul."

Did she really think her magick was gone for good? What the hell had happened? My inner monologue was halted by the sight of Evie throwing the covers off her, grabbing a marble candle holder from the bedside table, and slamming it against the full-length mirror by the dresser.

My mouth fell open. The mirror shattered. Evie screamed, raging and wounded.

I swiftly grabbed the candle holder from her flailing arm and pulled her away from the shards of glass.

"Shhh." I stroked her hair, pulling her into my lap as she shook. "You're safe, baby. I will love you forever. You're safe."

I RAN a hand through my hair as I approached Harmony, Blade, Idris, Vesper, and Clarke at Harmony's dining room table.

Idris rose. "Where is she? Why has she been avoiding me?"

I shook my head. "She should be here soon. And I don't know, Idris, but I'm worried about her. Terribly worried. She hasn't been herself since her rescue."

"What do you mean?" Idris asked.

"It's difficult to explain," I said. "Her moods are unstable. She's shown no interest in what previously mattered to her—namely, being involved in war efforts. I was happy to see her reading again, but I suspect that's just another trauma response." Reading was probably the only way she could escape the horrors of what she'd endured. "Her magick has been stifled somehow, and the only time she was able to use it, she coughed up blood. I don't know. I think she needs a bit more time."

What I didn't say to Idris or the rest of the group was that for the first time since Evie and I had met, I didn't feel like I understood her. All I could do was be patient. I reminded myself that these were all signs of trauma.

Guilt was a ghost that haunted me everywhere I went. The only time I could breathe easier was when I was on the battlefield, forced to let everything go but the kill in front of me.

"Earlier today, I caught her stomping on flowers in her own garden," I continued, my voice low. "They'd wilted, and she was frustrated, maybe. Supernatural wind pushed her back, and she—"

I stopped myself, feeling weird about sharing Evie's post-traumatic behavior with people without her permission. Evie was throwing these tantrums I'd never seen from her before, like she'd been triggered back to the wounded inner child, the part of her that had been harmed and abandoned by her parents.

Idris's brows lifted, his face shifting through shades of surprise and confusion. "Wilted?" he asked. "And she was destroying her own—"

Allie entered with Evie trailing her. Idris quickly closed his mouth. He rose from the table and pulled his sister into a hug. She was stiff for a moment but soon relaxed.

"Hi, Idris," she said, pulling back.

Idris studied her. "I'm so glad you're here. That you're safe," he said. "I know it's a stupid question at this point, but how are you?"

Evie took a moment to process. "It's not stupid." She looked to me. "I'm going to be okay."

Idris nodded, raw emotion swimming in his eyes.

Vesper hugged her next, and Evie smiled at her warmth.

"Thank the gods. We were so worried. I'm ready to chat whenever you are, okay?" Vesper said.

Harmony squeezed Evie tight, and Blade smiled broadly. Everyone expressed how relieved they were to see her home safe.

I released a breath. This normalcy was going to be good for her. I suspected her magick was blocked due to trauma, and with some time and healing, everything would improve.

I was just grateful she was *alive*. That was what mattered.

Evie took a seat between me and Idris as Harmony fussed in the kitchen and Vesper regaled us with stories. Blade watched Vesper speak like she was a goddess incarnate.

When I caught Evie smiling at something Clarke had said, something tight inside me relaxed.

As the minutes passed, I began to notice Idris stealing glances at his sister with a perpetual frown.

"I met someone," Idris suddenly blurted.

I grinned. "Oh?"

Idris nodded. "A new recruit."

He didn't say anything more, in typical Idris fashion. Not even a gender reveal.

Evie smiled at him. "That's exciting," she said, tilting her head.

Blade teased Idris. Clarke stepped up in Idris's defense, and soon Blade was explaining the concept of a *war fling* again.

When Harmony came back from the kitchen with food, Idris stood. "I'll help."

Harmony grinned and rubbed his shoulder. "You're a doll."

The table erupted into laughter when Vesper cut Blade down with her trademark wit, gentle enough not to bruise his infatuated, soft heart.

After several plates were set out in the center of the table, Idris walked back to his seat.

In one swift movement, he smacked Evie in the side of the head with a frying pan.

I leaped up. Evie slumped to the ground. Idris's nostrils flared, his eyes burning as he stared at his unconscious sister.

"What the *fuck*, Idris?"

He looked straight at me, frighteningly calm and unwavering. "That is *not* Evie."

65

EVIE

When Juliette kissed Kylo, I lost my mind. And when Conrad, Aster, and a set of guards rushed toward me, I felt the disgusting ghost sensation of Aster's lips on mine.

I lost my mind twice.

Aster was the first to reach me. I grabbed a shard of mirror, and I stabbed his neck.

He gasped, dislodging it and grabbing my wrist before it could go too deep.

His white knight mask dropped for a second time as he lifted me off the ground with his hands around my neck.

I locked eyes with Conrad. "You know, don't you? You know Juliette is with him!" My words were stifled as darkness crawled over my vision and my airways closed.

Aster slammed me onto the ground, straddling me as I thrashed and coughed. He pinned me there, blood ruining his perfectly tailored clothing. "What are you talking about?" he hissed.

"Juliette is a changeling. She wore a glamour to appear as

Conrad right before she stabbed herself, and now she's wearing a glamour of *me*."

Conrad's eyes flashed, as if half of that was news to him. It was clear that was how Juliette had known about our murder plot. I suspected she was testing my relationship to Conrad, and she actually hadn't expected to find a deeper betrayal.

"Why would she pretend to be Conrad?" Aster asked like a fucking idiot, too blinded by ego to connect the dots on his own.

"Do I really need to spell all of this out for you?"

He slapped me.

My cheek stung, tears filling my eyes. So much for never laying hands on a woman. But I supposed he could justify this one with his supreme logic.

"She's with the turned. She left you," I said.

Aster's eyes were cold. His lips curled as he glared down at me. "Looks like someone doesn't want to be my good girl after all." His hand closed around my throat, pushing the hot metal of the collar against my skin. "Would you rather be my disobedient slut, Evie?"

I was suddenly hyperaware of his hips against mine. I stopped thrashing, my body going into a freeze response against my conscious protests.

Conrad sighed. "I'm sorry, brother. I fear she needs more work than we originally thought. Perhaps some much-needed alone time."

Aster undid his belt.

"Don't you dare rape me!" I screamed, tears brimming my eyes.

Kylo's lips on Juliette's neck was behind my eyelids every time I blinked.

"I. Am. Not. Going. To. Rape. You," Aster spat.

"She needs to be calmed down. Her hysteria isn't good for morale."

"Shhh," Aster said. "I'm guessing Juliette managed to reach you in here with her witchy tricks. But you're safe. I won't let her hurt you."

He manhandled me onto my stomach and hiked up my nightgown as I continued to scream.

The belt came down on my ass, and I was transported back to the rolling hills of Isolde. The tall grass, the children who played quietly, the heads bent in prayer.

Another smack reverberated through the room. I could feel the scorch of several men's eyes on me.

"I don't want to punish you, Evie," Aster said. "It hurts me more than it hurts you."

He knew. He knew all about the belt and the prayers and the grains of rice.

I closed my eyes, finally going still as my mind floated away. The pain melted my brain and set me free from this corporeal hell.

The world was quiet save for the sound of leather on skin. My breathing slowed. The power that had once been clamoring to break free went cold.

Shame flushed across my skin, but I didn't move. I kept my eyes shut tight. I stopped thinking about lips where they shouldn't belong—Aster's on mine, Juliette's on Kylo's.

I drifted into the soil beneath my childhood home, the inhospitable womb, the empty eyes. I remembered how my small hands had reached for comfort and were met with nothing at all.

At some point, the beating stopped. I was small and yielding in Aster's arms.

I clung to him as he carried me to a small empty room—a hollowed out cleaner's closet, windowless, no furniture save for one cushion.

My ass stung. I buried my head into Aster's shirt as the ghost of my mother's voice whispered familiar cruelties in my ear.

Aster kissed my head and then set me down on the cushion. He slapped my hands when I refused to let go.

Humiliation and confusion blended together. My vision was blurry with tears as I watched Aster and Conrad leave the room, slam the door shut, and twist the lock.

It was stupid and childish, but I still ran to the door, screaming for them not to leave me in here as I yanked on the knob to no avail.

I didn't know who or what I was in this moment. A raging fire inside me had been stifled, scalding embers doused with cold water. I'd been extinguished in the peak of my rage.

I was half-aware that my traumas had been used against me but that didn't curb the method's effectiveness.

Pathetic, my mother whispered when I lay on the hard floor, head against the cushion.

She was right. Nothing I did was good enough here. It all led to the same result.

Curling into the fetal position didn't help the feeling of walls closing in. I hadn't been this trapped since I lived in that farmhouse in the hills.

By his design.

And *hers.*

I shivered, tear-stricken, sore, and hungry.

I will not break. I will not break. I will not break.

I HADN'T UNDERSTOOD when they'd first put me in this room that they'd planned on leaving me in here for days.

Or at least, I thought it had been days. I'd been fed and provided water five times. And each occasion, it had felt like an entire day had passed since the last time hands had quickly placed water and food just inside the door, quickly closing it back before I could reach them.

Those quick hands were the only stimulation I'd received, save for the five times a pillowcase had been shoved over my head, and I'd been allowed to use a bathroom. Someone could've been watching me relieve myself, and I wouldn't have known. I existed within the stuffy fabric head covering until I was safely back in my cage. All I knew was the shove of hands, the low snickers, the way my bladder had been stretched so far to its limit that I feared it might rupture.

Or that I'd piss myself while lying on the cold floor.

I was being treated like a war criminal.

I *was* a war criminal.

Which was why it shouldn't have been surprising that Conrad was the one to finally unlock the door and step inside.

I'd been rocking for hours, staring at the wall, half-hallucinating. Sometimes I saw a mirror. Sometimes I punched that mirror until my knuckles bled.

Conrad's nose twisted.

"Oh, do I smell?" I hissed. I stopped rocking. My eye twitched. "That must be hard for you."

My voice was gravelly. I may have been screaming on and off, for about an hour at a time. I was surprised I still had any voice left.

Conrad stared at my hand which was crusted with blood. "Looks like you still have some reflection to do. I'll return when you no longer greet me with this nasty, unbecoming attitude."

He turned.

"No, *please*." I scrambled to my feet. I would do anything to be free of this room. "I'm sorry," I forced out. "I'm sorry. Please don't go."

Conrad still faced the door, but he didn't move. "The manners are much better, and I do enjoy hearing worthless whores beg for mercy."

I bit my tongue. I was shaking against my will. The fever had come and gone, and now it was reaching another peak. There was movement in the corner of my eye, a taunting hallucination of a shadow.

I begged the darkness to kill Conrad. I turned my head, and the shadow was gone.

Conrad faced me again. I felt the ice from his cool blue eyes in my veins. My teeth chattered. I swayed.

His burgundy attire resembled that of an ancient war general. Not a strand of his dark hair was out of place. With a rigid jaw, he stared down at me.

Days had passed, and Conrad was no longer gloating. He didn't look excited, nor victorious.

He was *pissed.*

Delirious and half-mad, I still felt smug, hopeful warmth in my stomach. Kylo was doing exactly what he promised. He was showing the world how much it had underestimated us.

The moment Conrad read my spite, an agonizing shot of pain rushed down my spine. I fell hard on my knees, screaming and twisting. It felt like I was exorcising myself of a demonic possession, the way I was shifting and bending in jarring, inhuman ways.

Conrad finally smiled.

He crouched in front of me. "You were doing so well," he said, shaking his head with false pity.

The pain stopped the moment I feared losing consciousness.

"You were playing into Aster's dreamy romantic fantasies perfectly," Conrad said. "But I knew you wouldn't be able to keep up your treacherous game. You've been an atrocious liar from the start. Your face tells me everything. I've always known you would need to be broken and rebuilt in Lillian's divine image. And now Aster sees it too."

Aster was not a dreamy romantic. He was merely a different flavor of controlling abuser, one with a sickly sweet glaze on top.

"You will only leave this room once you have told me

something useful," Conrad said. "I will not let my closest friend take an unrepentant harlot to Prospyrus. He deserves an obedient, loyal wife."

"Then he should go find one," I said through gritted teeth.

More pain.

I shrieked, scratching at my skin like it was crawling with a thousand biting insects.

When the torment, finally ceased, my voice was smaller than before. "He's really going to leave Juliette behind?"

Conrad rolled his eyes. "Gods, I hope so. We'll see how things play out." He pinned me with his beady stare. "That was one of your most stupid mistakes. You were so blinded by pettiness that you told the truth about her. That she was *useless*. Defective."

Aster wouldn't leave her behind. He may have been distracted by his shiny new toy, but he still loved Juliette. Or, rather, he felt his sick and twisted perversion of *love*. And he was still wrathfully possessive, enraged that she was now with Kylo.

"I despise weakness," Conrad said, wrinkling his nose again. "You are a much better fit for us. Once you realize you've been channeling your efforts toward the wrong aims."

More anger infected Conrad's face as he glared right through me.

"Where the fuck are they disappearing to?" he asked suddenly, grabbing my throat. "They pop in and out of portals. The catacombs are empty, save for mortal remains. So *where?*"

It was good to know mine and Princeton's protective wards were still holding strong, shielding the underground from prying eyes.

"Didn't you all say that the turned had ripped open portals to Lillian's hells?" I asked softly, cocking my head. "Maybe something like that."

Conrad squeezed my airways.

Kylo was winning. If I had it in me, I would smile. Conrad was going to torture me all night long because my clan was making him look like an idiot.

Where was all that cockiness now?

He released me, but not before delivering a slap to my cheekbone so hard I saw stars. I gasped. That was going to leave a nasty bruise.

I let my eyes round as I clutched my throbbing cheek. "Why *me?* Why do you need *me* to marry Aster and do your magickal dirty work when there are countless Servants of Lillian who would *gladly* take my place?"

Conrad stared at me like I was stupid, as if stunned I didn't understand.

"You seriously don't know, do you?" he asked after several seconds passed.

I angled my head, studying him, but remained silent.

"Because witches who wield shadows and conjure storms have been kissed by Lillian and her underworld," he said, his voice rising and falling with an inflection that was cruelly patronizing. "And you're a child of both Helia and Selena—making you blessed by *three* major goddesses—with a chaos witch nature. There aren't that many of you, believe it or not. Juliette tried to mimic the phenomenon, I assume by reading Aster's obsessive ramblings on the subject."

My head was spinning. I wasn't kissed by Lillian. But Hekate was a dark, chthonic goddess, just like her.

"If not for your rarity, I assure you I would've already delighted in your death," he drawled, nearly sensually. "The last time one of *you* made it into the history books, it was to help Earle Augustus unite a fallen, war-torn realm and become King Earle of Ravenia."

Wait, what?

"She was erased from most accounts, of course, given she was both a mortal and a woman. She would've weakened Earle and his rise, as well as the legitimacy of all born-exclusive institutions."

Well, wasn't that just typical. My mouth opened and closed, but no words came out.

"Aster's father passed down his love of history and ancient texts. Aster was fascinated by the idea of a witch who stood at the crossroads between the heavens and hells—to put it mildly. I didn't take him seriously, at first. No one did. But when he proved that you were the one who destroyed the coven in Isolde *and* the witch who'd conjured a storm over Etherdale, my sentiments shifted. I read his work. I studied Juliette. And then I met you." Conrad exhaled. "I see how you fit, just as your predecessor fit into the story of Earle's rise. You weave fates. You've made a lowly clan of bastards into something so much bigger than they ever would've been without your goddess-blessed power."

I shook my head. Aster's obsessions finally made sense, but they were being used to paint yet another religious myth that wasn't rooted in reality.

"I'm not blessed by Lillian, and it's not because of me that Kylo's clan is holding their own. They were preparing long before I arrived."

I shut my mouth tight, realizing I was still being questioned despite Conrad's momentary pause.

If anything, his reveal of information and sudden reprieve from torture was yet another manipulation tactic.

He watched my lips with a smirk. "Like I said, I despise weakness. If Earle once fell in love with a conniving mortal, then he was never meant to rule forever. I have no such romantic sentiments. You will be useful, or you will be nothing."

He suddenly yanked me up to my feet, his face inches from mine. His breath reeked with copper.

"Now which will it be?"

66

KYLO

s soon as Idris said the words, *That is not Evie,*
everything made sense again.
    "Oh my gods," Harmony said.
"Oh my *gods*," Vesper echoed.

Blade's mouth was wide open.

"We need—fuck, we need witch bondage," I said.

"On it." Blade finally closed his mouth, then he rushed off in
the next blink.

Idris set down the frying pan. "She didn't grill me about a
potential love interest," he said with a shrug. "Flowers under
Evie's care would *never* wilt. Nor would she ever destroy any
part of a garden out of anger. Finally—you said she coughed up
blood, and Evie said that Juliette was physically sick from
stealing power. But the love interest thing, *that* was the most
damning."

"So you *didn't* meet someone?" Harmony squeaked.

Idris rolled his eyes.

Harmony sighed and shook her head.

My heart hadn't stopped its pounding since the frying pan.
We all gathered around the unconscious impostor.

"Evie's still with them," Idris whispered.

I was going to be sick. The woman I'd slept beside for the past four nights, the woman I'd held and kissed, was *Juliette*.

Nausea churned, and I looked away from the convincing glamour. Gripping the back of the chair next to me, I slowed my breathing.

Thank Hekate I hadn't fed from her or given in to her advances. My soul had known. I'd recoiled from her emptiness instinctively.

My lip curled. "That girl is sick in the head."

I'd left her alone in our home. Who knew what she could've done or seen while snooping around.

"That's how she infiltrated our spaces. She wore a turned glamour." Harmony rubbed my shoulder.

"Changeling." Idris glared down at her before meeting my eyes. "Don't blame yourself, brother."

"I just wanted her to be alive—to be safe—so badly..." I said. "It blinded me."

"She is alive," Idris said, his voice firm. "They broke the blood bond, like Juliette said. Lies are better told with grains of truth."

I nodded, my chest tight.

Clarke rolled his neck. "They may have our witch, but we also have theirs." He lifted a brow.

Harmony, Idris, and I exchanged a glance.

"This is Aster's *wife*. Surely that means something to him," Idris said.

My head spun. Aster and Conrad had to know, right? It would've been reported to them by any born who survived my rampage—the fact that I left with a small blonde in my arms. Was this scheme their doing or Juliette's?

The witch wearing Evie's skin stirred. A hoarse cough left her lips. I gathered power, which wasn't a hard task given my blinding, unquenchable rage.

I let my shadows crawl over her eyes, blinding her as a precaution until Blade arrived.

When she screamed, I let my shadows gag her and tighten painfully around her limbs. I stood over her. The desire to kill her was strong, but her appearance as Evie was a hindrance.

"Remove that fucking glamour or I will cut off a finger."

Juliette struggled and screamed into the gag. The house rattled. I strained against her magick, blocking the sickly mist that left her palm with my own shadows.

I unsheathed my dagger and grabbed her hand. "Last chance." I let the blade meet the base of her index finger.

Juliette chanted something into the gag.

Her hair darkened. Her form shrank slightly.

I released a breath, begrudgingly placing my dagger back in its holster. Only moments later, Blade returned with magickally binding handcuffs. I assumed Evie had been dealt the same.

As soon as they snapped into place, I removed the shadows from her eyes and mouth.

Her gray eyes darted around, and her lip trembled. "How did you know?"

"None of your godsdamned business," Idris growled.

Juliette ignored him, as if no longer remotely interested in pretending to care about what her *brother* had to say. She met my eyes immediately. "She's Aster's now, and he will never let her go."

My laugh was humorless. I refused to give her the satisfaction of a reaction. Even though my body and soul surged with wrathful possessiveness, right on cue.

"Did you *genuinely* believe that you could keep this up for any substantial amount of time?" Harmony asked her.

Juliette refused to look anywhere else but me, and it was pissing me off. She didn't deserve to look at me. The fact that she'd tricked me into profoundly betraying Evie made me so violently enraged I wanted to throttle her. But that would require touching her, and I never wanted to touch her again.

Evie's angry rants came back to me, all the times she'd said Juliette was obsessed with her, wanted to *be* her.

"You weren't even spying on us, were you?" I hissed.

Juliette shook her head.

I raked a hand over my mouth, laughing again in bitter disbelief.

"I don't get it!" Juliette wailed, irritating our eardrums once more. "You said you'd still love her without her magick. I showed Aster how powerful I could be, and he still wanted *her*. And now she's with him, and *you* still want her. What is it about her? She's rude and impious and violent and deviant and disloyal. She's *far* from perfect. What makes her *so special?*"

"You. Will. Never. Get. It." I straightened and took a step back. "And I will never explain it to you. Now, you will either help us get Evie back and live out your days with your beloved husband, or you'll die."

That was a lie, obviously. She would die either way.

Fat tears rolled down Juliette's cheeks. She cried loudly and unabashedly, like she had no control of her emotions and couldn't understand the gravity of the predicament she'd found herself in.

We all stared down at her, unmoved. Not even Harmony curbed her glare.

"Which will it be?"

She stopped crying, her face twisting as if she were irate no one had taken pity on her. "Fine." She smiled, deranged. "Let's go get *poor Evie.*"

Juliette giggled. No one took the bait. We merely passed her off to be babysat by Allie and a few other comrades. It was safest that way, lest Idris or I lost control and killed her prematurely.

We all sat back down at the table.

"Our clan will be here in one week," Vesper said. "We don't

know when or how many of Earle's forces will be making it over the mountains."

Before I could say I didn't care, Vesper spoke again.

"But Evie's too important, and your clan is surpassing even your own expectations."

Blade, Harmony, and I exchanged a brief look of pride. She was right. We'd already taken half the city, and we crept closer to Nighswander Estate every day. The born who'd once smugly taken over Ravenia's strongest mortal-dominant haven were now panicking, fighting increasingly erratically. They were making dumb mistakes, as if they hadn't expected the fight to last this long. How could they when we'd been occupying an entire underground domain for eighty years right under their noses?

"Let's take them out," Clarke finished.

"We've only been this successful because we've been careful not to overextend," Blade cautioned. "Whatever we do needs to be precise, especially with an army heading for us."

"I'm coming," Idris said. "I stood down last time. Please don't expect me to do it again."

I opened my mouth to tell him *no*, but the desperation in his eyes gave me pause. Another damn mirror. I didn't want to have to worry about a newborn in battle. But who was I to keep Idris from fighting for his sister?

I knew how it felt to lie helpless while the born tortured someone I loved.

"Fine."

The whole table stared at me incredulously, none more so than Idris.

But we wasted no more time before launching into the plan.

Our masks were off. We had Aster's wife. We had half of Etherdale under our control, and King Earle had all but declared war.

It was actually simpler than all of that, though.

This was my city, and Aster and Conrad had taken something that belonged to me.

I would now crush them for it, and they would leave the earth disgraced.

History would forget Aster and Conrad. Their death would be final, an afternote.

Evie and I would be immortal long after we died. Our love would be enshrined in myths that would be told for thousands of years.

Hold on, baby. I'm coming.

67

EVIE

I wasn't sure how long the torture had lasted, but at a certain point I couldn't feel any more pain. I passed out and woke up screaming.

Conrad wasn't exactly sane before, but the longer I lasted, the more he unraveled into a new monstrous form.

Would he kill me?

At least I would die knowing Kylo would take back this city I loved. Conrad's furious questioning was just further proof of the clan's imminent victory.

"What is the poison they're using in their weapons?" Conrad asked again.

They knew it wasn't blood onyx, and they were pissed we'd found a way out of that shortage. They were also pissed our vampire poison was *stronger.*

"If I tell you, will you let me out?" I asked. It wasn't as if the born could make violet bane, given it needed Hekate's aid. Though I obviously would never tell them any of the real ingredients, knowing they'd only try to wipe them from the earth.

"I will let you out when you tell me where they are

disappearing to and how to get there!" Conrad yelled, throwing me against the wall like I was a rag doll.

My shoulder took most of the force, and I didn't exactly land well when I hit the floor. But I didn't hear a snap, so it was all good. If I could leave this torture session without any broken bones or permanent bodily harm, I'd count that as a victory.

"Fine. I didn't want to have to do this, but you've left me no choice," Conrad said.

My vision doubled. Two Conrads stood over me with a wicked gleam in their eyes.

I managed to lift myself up to rest against the wall. After rubbing my eyes, my vision returned to normal. My heart beat hard and slow. My body had been pushed to its absolute limit.

When his hands reached for his belt, I couldn't fully comprehend what I was seeing.

As soon as it clicked that I was going to get another beating, I gave in to the dissociation. What was more trauma reenactment going to do, anyway? Just throw it on the pile. I still wasn't going to fold. The clan making a fool out of Conrad and his men was too sweet of vengeance, and I would never betray the goddess I'd pledged by body and soul to.

But he didn't remove his belt. He left it unbuckled.

He peeled me off the wall and straddled me as I lay flat on the floor. His hand covered my mouth.

"Aster won't believe you," Conrad snarled.

He hiked up my dress.

I screamed and thrashed and scratched at him. My fight response overcame my freeze response, and once again my collar burned where my magick fought to escape.

When Conrad reached for my throat, he hissed in pain, staring at my collar in confusion.

I pushed, encouraging the heat coiling through my body to multiply. Ignored the pain of the scalding metal against my already blistered skin.

Break, motherfucker.

"Last chance."

His cock was out, but I refused to look at it. I just pushed and pushed until my forehead was slick with sweat and my body was engulfed with a fire that couldn't be extinguished.

Conrad once again winced, as if my skin itself was burning him. He removed his hand from my mouth.

"Explain how they're doing this," he spat in my face. "You have ten seconds to start being useful or I will fuck you like the useless cunt that you are."

Instead of talking, I started yelling. "Hekate!" I called as purple burned through my third eye. I didn't need magick to pray.

Light my way out. Protect your daughter.

Conrad's hand went back over my mouth. His hips lowered.

The door flew open.

Aster tackled Conrad to the floor. My collar exploded.

Aster punched Conrad in the face. "What the fuck are you doing?"

Conrad attempted to infect Aster with his pain magick, but it was thwarted by Aster's shielding abilities. So they wrestled on the ground the old-fashioned way.

I shot through the open door, delighted by how disgusting and feral I must've looked.

I was pure animal, not a drop of humanity left in my veins. The guards who had once taunted me, shoved a pillowcase over my head and thrown food at my feet, now gurgled on their own blood.

When they dropped to their knees, I grinned. "Order has been restored."

I heard Aster and Conrad arguing loudly inside my old cell. I left them behind, killing anyone standing between me and Conrad's study.

Around the corner, the next hallway was quiet. Downstairs,

guests were congregating, likely wondering about the noise above. Or maybe they were too drunk on elixir and blood to care.

Breathless, I barged into the room, only to realize quickly I was in the wrong lord's study. I didn't have time, but I stole just a few moments, anyway.

The world was alive again. Energy from above, below, and in each cardinal direction was both a blessing and a distraction. Too much had been repressed and for too long.

I let my surging, regained witchy senses guide me. I shoved books off Aster's desk until I saw the root of Juliette's torment. The map of notes and jottings about witches like me. Notes on my magick as a child. Notes about my trauma, my mother, and my coven. Arrows leading to Jacob Whitfield, Celeste's, and a *man in a black skull mask*. Question marks. Underlines. Even things I'd told him in passing—foods I liked, books I'd read.

Juliette was only obsessed with me because Aster had been obsessed with me. She'd told me over and over that Aster hadn't forgotten about me. I could see that clearly now.

I moved quickly, casting a glance over my shoulder and grabbing a letter opener off Aster's desk.

Out in the hallway, I pricked my skin and ad-libbed a spell, chaos-witch-style. I whispered to my shadows, sowing confusion, masking my scent.

I slipped into the correct study this time, knowing my impromptu spell was temporary at best, unable to hold without the proper glue.

With the snap of my fingers, I lit a candle on Conrad's bookcase. I offered the flame to my spirits and guides, asking them to illuminate my way.

I used my own body as a pendulum. A surge of warm tingles meant *yes,* and a lack of sensation or warmth meant *no.* I opened a drawer.

No tingles.

No other drawer elicited a response. I put my hand on the desk. Nothing.

I started opening up books, tearing the room apart as footsteps sounded below and grew heavier by the minute.

In front of the grandest bookcase, my body finally surged with tiny pinpricks. I nodded, a shaky smile forming.

"Okay, understood."

My hand glided over each book, waiting, listening, finding stillness amid the palpable chaos around me.

They were looking for me. But they'd been thrown off by the spell. It nearly sounded like soldiers were storming through the estate.

By the time my hand tingled, it was shaking with adrenaline. My empty stomach grumbled. I tore the book from the shelf.

It shocked me.

I laughed, cruel and bitter. "Oh no, you fucking don't."

I wiped my saliva on the leather, a powerful magickal aid in sowing claim. *Bend,* I commanded.

All the candles in the room lit with purple flames.

The book sent me flying across the room. "All right, fine, we'll do things your way," I said, out of breath and head swimming.

I was unsteady when I hobbled over to Conrad's desk chair, using a witch light to scan the piece of furniture.

As soon as I found a single, short dark hair, I captured it between my fingers and placed it on the book. I chanted, drawing in the power of the room. I whispered in the language of pain and power—Conrad's language—as I lightly stroked the book.

I wasn't zapped, nor was I thrown across the room for a third time today.

Assassination, I guided. *Which councilman is being assassinated?*

The book flew open. Undiscernible words jumbled together

as pages flipped on their own. The floor outside creaked. Voices grew louder.

I didn't think twice when the book finally stopped. I didn't know if it was the right page or what the notes said. I merely ripped out that page and a few before and after and folded them.

I realized with great sadness this nightgown didn't have anything close to a pocket.

Clutching the pages in my left hand, I threw open the window. I called to the earth. She reached back like a reunited sister, happy to lend a helping hand after I'd tended to her devotedly for so many years.

Sturdy vines shot toward me. I climbed out of the window. Conrad burst into the room, his soulless, pale eyes taking in the disarray.

Before he could hit me with a dose of pain, my shadows flooded the room. I didn't kill him. That kill belonged to Vesper.

Shadows yanked the window shut. I scaled the building, soaking in the fresh, early autumn air. It tasted like freedom.

When I stumbled, vines steadied me. I landed softly on the earth, facing the backyard of the property.

My ears pricked. I could hear fighting in the distance, my first real evidence of war other than the soldiers who'd entered the estate. The fighting sounded surprisingly close.

With my hand holding the evidence of Conrad and Aster's coup attempt, I took off toward the back gate. I'd seen it on my second visit here, when Aster tried to seduce me under the canopy of trees.

Each footstep away from Nighswander Estate felt euphoric, nearly orgasmic. I didn't care how I'd get there.

I was going home.

And I hadn't been raped. That was worth celebrating.

There were several wins to celebrate after the grandest, most humiliating failure of my entire life.

A cold breeze slammed into me in warning. I glanced over my shoulder for the third time, noting what appeared to be chaos through the windows into the estate. A back door flew open. Heavy footsteps and shouts cut through the air.

I conjured more power with a wicked smile. I continued running toward the back gate.

And just as I was about to be out of harm's way, strong hands wrapped around me from behind.

Fangs tore into my neck, deep and urgent, dosing me with an immediate flood of venom. My blood drained. My magick halted.

I dropped the treasonous pages.

A hand petted my head. "Shhh, angel, you're safe now. I'm getting you out of here. A firebird is waiting through the gate. We're going straight to Prospyrus."

68

EVIE

"No," I mumbled from down the end of a long tunnel, carried in Aster's arms.

We were so close to the back gate—the freedom that continued to taunt me and slip from my grasp. But it wasn't freedom that awaited me on the back of that fiery, winged creature. It was another cage.

I'd been flooded with venom, my anger and power diluted by an artificial surge of pleasure.

"You are no better than him."

Aster halted. He set me down. I watched his hand lift, and I smiled. Point proven.

"You were going to leave without me?" Juliette stepped out from behind a tree, wrists shackled, her familiar whine much more bearable under the haze of venom.

I stumbled, losing my balance as the world tilted. My ass hit the earth.

"Kitten, thank the gods," Aster said. He lowered his hand, but his anger soon fell back into place as her words landed. *"You* left *me,"* he snapped. He glared at her. "Tell me you didn't defile yourself with the vermin. Tell me you aren't ruined."

"Excellent blame-shifting maneuver," I slurred.

Juliette and Aster both glared at me now.

"You were," she said, choking on a sob. "You were going to leave me behind and marry Evie. You were going to replace me like I never meant anything to you at all."

Her tears were a flood I recognized. In the haze of blood loss, venom, and depletion, I saw my inner child reflected in Juliette.

She was looking for the love of a mother—perfect, unconditional love—and Aster's grooming and abuse would never come close.

"You said we were written in the stars," Juliette said, sinking to her knees. "You said we were forever." She reached for his feet, but Aster stepped back. She gasped. "I tried everything. I gave you all of me. Why was I never enough for you? What is missing inside me?"

Aster went cold, not a touch of sympathy in his eyes as his gaze flickered between the two of us. He merely appeared impatient.

I tried to conjure shadow, but it was more like sputters of dark goo that left my palms.

"Don't you fucking dare," Aster roared at me. "Not a drop. Or you will regret it."

His own palms glowed with defensive magick, a subtle ripple of fluid energy.

"It's not you." I smiled sadly at Juliette. "And it's not me." I pointed at Aster with a trembling finger. "He was born with a hole inside him that can never be satisfied."

Aster's face twisted with rage. Juliette struggled for air through her hysterical sobs.

Aster reached for a dagger.

I shook my head with a laugh. "Hurting me won't fill the void either, but you're welcome to try." I lifted my chin. "Your existence will only have meaning when you die."

Aster took a step toward me, his handsomeness destroyed by cruelty spilling through his every crack. I refused to see him as a white knight—and now he knew I never would. There was nothing more damaging to a narcissist than seeing them for who they truly were, and not for who they wanted you to see.

Behind Aster, a streak of shadow shot through the trees.

A sound left my lips that was unavoidable.

Kylo.

He was a dark god, a being that didn't belong in this realm. His shadows scorched the earth. His black hair was gently tousled, his sharp jaw trembling. He locked his gaze on Aster's weapon.

He came for me.

It was as if he refused to look at me to preserve his own focus. Relief and love flooded my veins.

"He's what you wished you were," I whispered, trying and failing to stand again. "And so much more."

Aster had me flush against his chest with the dagger to my throat before Kylo could make a move.

Juliette didn't stir from her puddle of grief.

"I can see now that your wife means little to you," Kylo said, shooting Juliette an irritated glance as if she'd gone off script in whatever scheme was currently unfolding. "But what about these?"

He pulled folded papers from his back pocket with a casual grace that stirred something inside me. I was surprised I could get turned on at a time like this.

For Kylo, only for Kylo. I sighed dreamily, perhaps drunkenly.

Aster tightened his hold on me until I was sure he was leaving more bruises. "And those are?" he asked, failing to sound even remotely as cool as Kylo.

"An admission of guilt," Kylo drawled. "Need I say what for?"

Aster stammered. He hadn't picked the papers up off the

ground after I'd dropped them. He might not have even noticed them fall with his fangs buried in my flesh.

"Let Evie go, and you can have Conrad's damning little diary entries back in your possession. You can even keep your *actual* wife."

Aster didn't glance Juliette's way, as if she was already dead to him. Yet, his grip loosened. "Fine."

I shook my head, warning Kylo not to trust him. If Aster couldn't have me, no one could.

Kylo and I finally locked eyes for the very first time. I lost my breath. His intensity was a drug, an anchor in the storm.

My shadows weren't yet tangled with his. But it was as if I still heard his whisper in my mind.

Hi, angel.

"I'm going to drop her," Aster said. "And you're going to drop the papers."

Aster slowly retracted the blade from my throat. He was trembling with rage. I could smell the bloodlust in the air, hitting me from all directions, including from inside myself.

"Ready?" Aster asked.

I could hear it in Aster's voice, feel it in his aura. Kylo wasn't looking at me anymore. He was watching Aster and the movement of his weapon. Again, I shook my head.

Don't trust him, I screamed inside my mind, willing the message to reach Kylo.

Kylo nodded.

Aster released me. Kylo dropped the papers.

I felt an excruciating pinch in my back, straight through to my heart. I gasped and fell to the earth.

A deadly fast vampire tackled Aster from behind, catching him off guard. "Get the fuck away from her!"

"Idris," I breathed.

Idris stabbed Aster in the back, right through the heart.

Juliette shrieked. *"No!"*

She strained against her magickal cuffs, scrambling toward them until Harmony grabbed her and pulled her back. Harmony was out of breath, glancing around at all of us to assess the situation.

Idris didn't stop. He rolled Aster over only to stare him in the eyes. He was yelling in a primal, grief-stricken way I'd never heard from him before. He stabbed Aster again and again until tears streamed down his face, and he still couldn't stop, couldn't stop, *couldn't stop.*

And now we were both back in that house. In Idris's childhood bedroom, where a born vampire named Vernon assaulted my little brother when he was seven years old.

Blood splattered until the farmhouse was swallowed up by death and holy vengeance once more.

Kylo ran to my side. I clutched at my heart, feeling the wound from the dagger that had never landed. It had only been a premonition.

Aster almost stabbed me through the heart. He would've rather I had died than see him as a monster.

I squeezed Kylo's hand, and he helped me to stand and walk to Idris.

"Hey," I said gently, mirroring his tears. "I think this dead horse has been sufficiently beaten."

Idris stopped his compulsive stabbing of mangled flesh. He blinked.

"Maybe stab him one more time, just to be sure," Kylo said.

I elbowed him weakly. "Only I'm allowed to be funny right now."

"Apologies, baby."

Idris dropped the blade with a trembling hand. I immediately pulled him into my arms, letting him shake and yell and flood the earth with the trauma we'd buried for so long.

"You saved me," I whispered. "You're safe. We're both safe. *I've got you.*"

I repeated that over and over until it penetrated. "I've got you. We're safe. I've got you."

Idris stopped yelling. He hugged me back. "I'll laugh at both of your jokes at a later date," he managed with a rough, shaky exhale.

"Look who I found," a voice called with a singsong voice.

I slowly pulled back from Idris, slipping my hand into his and squeezing.

When Vesper threw a gagged and bound Conrad next to Aster's unrecognizable corpse, I realized what had happened to the vampires who'd been chasing after me. The source of the shouts and heavy footsteps.

"Oh my gods," I said. "You stormed the estate."

"Baby, I'd storm King Earle's castle if that's where you were," Kylo said.

He glared at my cheek until I remembered it was likely bruised from Conrad.

Blade appeared holding someone's head as a demented souvenir. "That's certainly on the future agenda, but ill-advised until we have Valentin on our side."

Valentin. An image of Amy's rendition of The Tower card flashed in my mind—King Earle falling from his own castle as it crumbled from within.

Woozy, disoriented, and with a throbbing headache from Juliette's nonstop wailing, my chest couldn't help but warm.

We were at *war*. Our better world was hurtling toward us at breakneck speeds.

I looked around at my family, my lip wobbling. We were at war *together*.

"Whose head is that?" Harmony asked. Mercifully for all of us, she'd gagged Juliette and then pinned her to the ground with her knee.

"This bloke who pissed me off a couple years ago and has

been on my shitlist ever since." Blade tossed the head over his shoulder.

Idris nodded. "Nice."

"Um, hello?" Vesper snapped as Clarke moved to her side. "I believe I've taken center stage." She quickly found my eyes. "Hi, Evie. You okay?" she scanned me quickly.

I nodded. "The floor is yours."

All glares moved to Conrad. I could hear more commotion and shouts in the distance as the turned moved into the heart of born territory. Someone had started a fire, one-half of Conrad's castle now consumed by raging flames.

Conrad's gaze flickered briefly to me. A feral noise escaped me. Shadows gathered in my palms, stronger now that I was out of Aster's grip. I couldn't wait to watch him die.

Harmony tossed a bottle of green liquid to Kylo.

"Drink, baby," he whispered in my ear. He brought the blood replenishing potion to my lips and kissed my temple. "I need you battle-ready."

I chugged the bottle.

Vesper removed Conrad's gag. He pretended not to notice his slain co-conspirator on the ground next to him. He didn't want to give us the satisfaction of a reaction.

"I thought you killed yourself," Conrad said. He cocked his head. "You look much older."

Vesper's eyes were wild, her grin wilder. "As do you."

Vampires didn't technically age, but you could still see subtle changes as the years passed. A flash in Conrad's eyes revealed that his vanity had taken a hit.

Kylo pulled me into his lap, his head swiveling in all directions, protectively remaining vigilant. A low rumble vibrated through him when he traced the blisters in a line around my neck where my power had destroyed the collar. Or maybe he was touching Aster's fang marks, because he quickly soothed himself by staring at Aster's bloody corpse.

I met Kylo's eyes. Our shadows finally intertwined. He kissed my forehead, a tremor rolling through him as he inhaled deeply.

Oh, gods. I hadn't showered in days.

Kylo's dimple appeared. *You smell like flowers and sunshine, baby.*

Liar.

I turned back to Vesper's show. Conrad's skin was peeling, and I realized his gag and bindings must've been soaked in violet bane. He was paralyzed, forced to face the woman he thought was dead.

I mirrored Vesper's vengeful smile.

"Because of you, my daughter thinks I abandoned her. I may never meet her," Vesper said. Her smile fell.

My heart splintered. Kylo held me tighter.

Conrad looked bored.

"But at least I know for certain she will never know *you*," she said, her tone overflowing with dark, maternal venom. It was wild and lupine, giving Vesper a powerful aura that held us all in a trance. "I could list all the ways you tortured and abused me, but you'd like that too much." She grinned, picking Conrad up by the collar and spitting in his face.

My mouth opened in awe.

She clipped him in the jaw for good measure. Drool and blood dribbled out of Conrad's mouth. The quickly spreading paralysis robbed him of his ability to speak.

It was better that way.

"Because of *me*, you will die knowing my comrades have taken your city. Your region will be the first to fall, and with it, your legacy. You will not die as a king. You will not even die as a *lord*." Vesper laughed, a beautiful, vibrant sound kissed by the golden sunset. "You will die a disgraced loser, a tiny blip in the course of history, never fulfilling a single one of your adorable little ambitions."

Conrad's eyes were pure death, a dark, empty rage that extended for an eternity.

Vesper shrugged. "What's more to say, really?"

She slashed his face where he'd once slashed hers. She pushed him onto his back.

She took her time, savoring the kill in a way that was so sensual I nearly looked away out of respect. Her smile remained, a dark angel of death dressed in black leathers, carving into the man that once stole everything from her.

Blade swallowed. Harmony and I noticed his arousal and exchanged a glance, quickly averting our eyes before we could burst into inappropriate giggles.

Clarke watched his co-leader with tenderness and pride. His blond hair was as spiky as the silver rings adorning his knuckles.

Vesper pulled Conrad close as the light drained from his eyes and blood pooled below him. She smiled in his face as he took his last breath, making sure she was the last thing he saw.

She tossed him on Aster's body. A shudder rolled through her, followed by a blissful serenity. She wiped her hands on her leather pants.

"Whoever said that revenge isn't satisfying is full of shit," she said. "Because I feel fantastic. Being the bigger person is an abuser's favorite propaganda."

"Agreed," Kylo said.

Allie jogged to us with a glass of water and a plate of meat and bread.

When she handed them to me, I almost started drooling. "This is the best gift I've ever received."

Kylo looked down at me. "I find that incredibly offensive."

I tore into the meat, continuing to feel more animal than girl. As the potion worked its magick and the food entered my stomach, greater euphoria entered my system that had nothing to do with lingering vampire venom.

Kylo needed me battle-ready.

He had *no idea* how fucking ready I'd become.

I checked in on Idris, the gravity of his presence here finally hitting me.

"He's doing great," Harmony said, reading my mind. "He has only been an asset."

Idris shrugged, bashful of the praise. His cheeks warmed, his complexion back to normal. He'd recovered quickly. He was strong; we both were.

"I believe we have one last order of business here," Kylo said, helping me to my feet after I finished the last bite of food and gulp of water.

We stared down at the snot-nosed, shell-shocked girl under Harmony's knee.

She'd stopped crying at some point, her eyes hauntingly empty. She smiled, slowly meeting my eyes.

I want to smile when I die, she'd once told me.

Kylo handed me his favorite dagger.

Juliette nodded. "He was my entire world. Without him, I'm nothing. Kill me."

She began to flicker through bodies—the skins of men and women she'd worn before—and when she landed on mine, she sighed.

She relaxed, as if soothed by being in a body that wasn't her own. She didn't believe her skin was good enough.

I gazed down at myself, shackled. I kneeled beside her. I reached for her hand.

Vision after vision of Juliette's atrocities played out behind my eyes. The lives she'd stolen. Princeton's body strung up on the wall. The academic building reduced to a pile of rubble and corpses. The demons and plagues infecting Etherdale. All the times she'd hurt me, taunted me, enraged me.

Her lips on Kylo's.

The knife she'd used to carve out our bond.

And yet, none of it changed my heart. I tried to force the bloodlust, but it was blocked.

I'd once looked at Juliette with more venom than I had the true villains, the men who now rested together as bloody corpses.

I stared at the mirror of myself, and I didn't feel hatred.

I only felt grief for her, for the woman she might've been. If she'd been born to a loving family. If she'd never met Aster.

"Aster was right. Your heart *is* full of love," I said.

Juliette's eyes flashed surprise, her chin trembling as she stared at me with wide gray eyes. My mirror, my shadow, the unhealed woman I could've become.

"You never had a chance."

I handed the dagger to Harmony. "I can't kill her. But she has to face the consequences of what she's done."

Harmony nodded. She exchanged a look with Blade, Allie, and Kylo. "For Princeton."

I held Juliette's hand. Kylo rubbed my back.

Juliette smiled when Harmony's weapon came down. Her death was quick. I only let go of her hand when her hair darkened and body shifted back into place.

"I hope her next life is kinder."

Kylo pulled me into his arms, his voice a cool whisper in my ear. "Baby, I love your violence. But I love your mercy a thousand times more."

He kissed me.

The calm after the storm was brief, as a heaving, breathless voice rang through the air.

"We took the estate, and we were set to overpower Conrad's men—but ground forces were too much for the clans of Terasette. One of Earle's fleets has made it over the mountains."

69

EVIE

We'd fought our way to the center of the battle, an intersection between four of Etherdale's busiest streets. It was a crossroads, a powerful source of magick for any witch, but *especially* for a daughter of Hekate. I fed on the energy beneath my feet, the charge of cosmic change that rattled through me.

I'd seen premonitions and visions of war, but nothing could've prepared me for its reality. My only solace was the knowledge that Mena's neighborhood was one of the first sections of the city taken under turned control.

But now that one of Earle's fleets had arrived, nothing felt safe.

Kylo had won against Conrad's men. But now thousands of highly organized born fighters were infiltrating the city on behalf of the king.

Vampires moved at impossible speeds. Opposing magickal forces collided, like a rich tapestry of currents rippling in all directions.

The words *fate weaver* repeated in my mind, a grounding reminder in this sea of brutality.

Kylo covered me, never leaving my side. As a non-vampire, I was utterly defenseless against vampire speed and strength. I was only powerful at a distance. Kylo didn't let a single enemy get too close to us. He also watched out for Idris, who'd been commanded not to stray too far from our bubble. Harmony had been right—my brother was more than capable of holding his own.

In the center of this war-plagued crossroads, I closed my eyes and took a deep breath.

I envisioned my better world resting in my palms, just like Amy's version of The World card. The final card in the major arcana. The completion of a cosmic cycle, an ultimate victory.

For the first time in my life, I consciously exploded. I pictured exactly what I wanted to happen, I grabbed loose threads and braided them together, bending reality to my will.

When I opened my eyes, a dark storm had gathered. I conjured lightning, hitting members of Earle's sky fleet. Dozens of born rained down from above, dead before they hit the ground. My hand danced in the air like an orchestral conductor.

"Are you humming?" Kylo asked incredulously.

"Shhh. I'm making art."

I grinned, glancing away from the distracting force of his silly little dimple.

This was who Aster and Conrad wanted me to be. The fuckable weapon who was going to lift them into positions of power and strike down anyone who stood in their way.

"Helia's heavens," Blade gasped.

Three born fell at his feet after he'd skewered them on a sword. Now Blade was staring up at the sky.

Idris stood at my other side, wiping sweat from his forehead. "*Evie*. Gods."

Fighting looked like dancing, if I let my vision grow unfocused. It reminded me of the mortal club that played revolutionary music, the bodies moving in a wild yet synchronistic rhythm. Like mycelium under the forest floor in perfect, reciprocal harmony.

Born continued to fall to the earth, consumed by my vengeful storm. I was high on the power in a way I hadn't expected. It rushed up and down my spine, pooling at my core. I raised my hands, and a cyclone formed.

I pointed.

My friends stared, slack-jawed, as the shadowed winds slammed into hundreds of born rushing toward us down Fourth Avenue.

Bodies flew in every direction.

"Hey, careful," Kylo whispered. "Don't let it carry much further or you risk a block of mortals."

I nodded. "Okay, thank you."

"What. The. Fuck," Clarke said, finding us again after he'd earned his own impressive collection of kills.

Vesper grinned. "Now I see what all that fuss was about." She winked at me.

I slowly released an exhale, and my cyclone dispersed back into a gentle wind. I was a tad woozy, but not even close to finished.

"They blocked my magick for too long. I had some shit that needed to be released," I said with a shrug. I caught my breath as I decided what facet of my power to wield next.

"Once you're depleted, you're depleted," Kylo warned me like a sexy professor. "Remember to pace yourself."

"Kylo, sky!" someone yelled.

Kylo leaped in front of me, throwing out a shield of shadow as fire rushed toward us from a nearby rooftop.

I glanced at Idris. He was calm and focused, using his shadows and earth magick with ease.

When he suddenly winced, my brows furrowed in concern. "You okay?"

Idris glanced down at his palms. "I don't know…"

We were cut off by the collapse of a nearby building, sending our group scrambling out of the way. Kylo grabbed me into his arms and moved me in fractions of a second. The distraction allowed born who'd survived my cyclone to rush toward us. Firebirds swarmed above.

I understood why this fleet had made it over the mountains and why Kylo had been so incredibly cautious about provoking Earle. The sheer numbers alone were daunting, but when poisons and specialty weapons from Valentin were added into the mix, it was clear that Earle's tactic was to crush us as quickly as possible. He wasn't worried about overextending or being cautious. He wanted us wiped from the earth before the revolution even had a chance to spark.

My clan had numbers too. Not comparable to the royal army, but we were not *nothing*.

The air had been knocked from my lungs when Kylo finally set me down. We'd been pushed onto Fourth Avenue, opposite from where my cyclone had rampaged. The intersection was filled with dust and smoke, but I could make out flashes of magick and bodies beyond.

"Idris?" I called, having lost sight of him in the commotion.

I whipped around, relieved to see my brother with Blade, Harmony, Vesper, Clarke, and other fighters. So many dead bodies were strewn around us making it frighteningly easy to become desensitized.

The Evie of a year ago wouldn't have believed this was where we now stood.

Further down the street, turned and born were entangled in battle. Shadows crawled along the cobblestone, working together as if independently of their hosts. Hekate's magick had come alive, lending power to the downtrodden as we bravely faced our oppressors.

The screeching firebirds dove onto roofs on either side of us, boxing us in. Harmony wielded shields the moment blood onyx weapons rained down on us.

"Take out the witch by any means necessary."

The command from above had Kylo trembling with power and rage, a growl leaving his throat as he stood in front of me. Idris's face held similar sentiments, but at the sight of him wincing, my stomach dropped with concern.

He stared at his palms again.

"Idris!"

Idris dodged a poisoned arrow, but it had been close. Why the hell was he so distracted?

My protectiveness triggered more power flowing through the crown of my head. It seemed like it had only taken seconds for born to swarm the crossroads we'd just left and for the battle down the street to suddenly be on top of us.

My friends danced with fluid grace. Blade's razor-sharp shadows ricocheted through the chaos, finding borns' skulls with easy precision. Vesper made an art form out of her fire magick, creating gorgeous snakes of orange and red flame to consume born fighters.

From behind Kylo, I wielded my own shadows. My mother's last words were correct: I *was* a plague on this world.

My poisonous, bloodthirsty darkness rotted entire groups of born instantly. Hekate was speaking through me, delivering a message to the born: *You will no longer harm my children without consequence. This world is for the living.*

My love for this city poured out of me in a devastating mix of grief and reverence. These streets were once filled with artists and students and grumpy elder locals, helping and learning from one another. They'd been filled with lovers' quarrels, music and laughter, the low rumble of my wagon rolling along the cobblestone on my way to Celeste's.

When I inhaled, I imagined the scents of fresh baked goods

from my favorite café on campus, books in the library, and flowers and herbs intermingling inside witchy shops.

Now the streets smelled like blood and death and anger that had festered for too long. I mourned the city I loved. But I knew that from the rubble, we would rebuild.

Together.

The scream that tore through me shattered glass and lifted pieces of the destroyed buildings off the ground. With a tilt of my head and the wave of my hands, I sent a storm of brokenness toward the born on rooftops, delivering deaths by a thousand cuts.

They just kept coming. As soon as I caught my breath, more born arrived, pressing closer and closer until Idris was fighting a couple of them mere feet from me.

"They're not even bothering with the rest of the city, are they?" I asked Kylo in horror. "They're only focusing on *us*."

He was still keeping born away from me with his deathly shadows as he shielded my body with his. "Kill the shepherd and the sheep will scatter."

Born had slipped through the cracks of our bubble, forcing Kylo and me to fight back-to-back. If I was focused on killing born right in front of me, I couldn't wield my magick on the greater numbers surrounding us from above.

"Fuck!" I heard Blade yell from somewhere nearby.

Blood onyx rained from the sky.

I realized in horror that no one had a free hand to shield us. I quickly cut down the group of demons beelining for me and raised my fist in the air. A ripple of darkness created a dome above our heads, blocking most of the poison.

"Harmony!" Kylo yelled.

I hadn't been quick enough. Harmony's arms were peeling, the poison seeping into her skin. Born surrounded her.

Idris dropped his bloody dagger, his body shaking as if with a violent fever.

Hundreds of born rushed toward us from the intersection.

The protective dome I'd erected wobbled, an impossible choice presenting itself. I had less than two seconds to decide whether to shield us from blood onyx, stop the rush of born from overwhelming us, save Harmony, or protect Idris.

I screamed.

At the sound of my voice, Idris's hands shot out. He stopped trembling. His palms crackled with bright golden radiance. His pupils disappeared, his eyes pure white.

One hand lifted to the sky. The other palm faced the ensuing born.

Blinding power burst from him with a boom that surely injured my eardrums. The sound was deafening. The force of the explosion sent everyone flying, including Idris himself.

I watched from the ground as skin and sinew melted off bone. Hundreds of born perished in an instant.

Blade managed to kill the born who'd been too distracted by the explosion to finish Harmony off. He pulled her behind him protectively as she recovered from the poison.

Idris had shattered my shield, but he'd also annihilated the born who'd surrounded us from above.

Small orbs of golden light fell from a dark, war-torn sky.

Idris and I locked eyes. My jaw trembled.

"You remember," I whispered.

Idris was stunned. He watched the tiny stars fall to the earth with the same awe he'd had as a child on the nights I'd sneak into his room when he was crying.

He'd cried until his voice was gone and his face was cherry-red, but our parents never came for him.

So *I* came for him. I would sit across from his crib with my legs crossed.

"Wanna see the stars?" I'd ask.

I used my still-developing power—the power Mama hated—

to conjure tiny orbs of light until Idris went from sobbing to babbling gleefully.

The stars had looked like freedom.

Idris nodded, a small smile forming. "I remember everything, Evie."

"Celestial magick," Kylo murmured, staring at Idris with wide, awestruck eyes.

Idris moved to stand, and it was an arduous, wobbly effort. "Do not expect me to do that again anytime soon."

Clarke rushed to steady him. "Seems reasonable," he gasped. His own bright green eyes studied my brother in utter shock. "What the fuck kind of bloodline do you two hail from?"

"Don't know, don't care," I said for both of us. Kylo helped me to my feet.

Idris smiled. "Our power isn't from *her*. It exists in spite of her."

I hugged him tight. The street was noticeably quieter than before. Fighting hadn't stopped, but Idris had eliminated so many born at once that they were likely retreating to regroup— perhaps wondering what the fuck they were supposed to do *now*.

I grinned. "I'm sorry for ever trying to hold you back."

"I forgave you after the first dozen apologies," Idris said dryly.

I almost apologized for apologizing, but I thought better of it. The fact that we even survived our childhood was already a miracle. But our strength? The depth of our love for our new home, our chosen family, for this world that had been so extraordinarily cruel to us?

We pulled back, facing each other with a mirrored smile. "Look at us," I whispered.

Idris laughed. "I think they're looking."

70

EVIE

At some point, the fighting had turned into real dancing. I was swept up in a tide of celebration that carried us through the streets. Mortals gave us food and alcohol and blood. Musicians sang and played songs from open windows.

For the first twenty-four years of my life, I'd hid from the world. I preferred fantasy to reality because I'd allowed my reality to become so heartbreakingly small. I didn't know how to dream bigger than my self-imposed cage of trauma.

Not until Kylo helped me break myself free.

His love changed me. And Etherdale's love, my friends' and clan's love—it changed me even more.

What was left of Earle's men had pulled out of the city. More forces were heading our way, but they would be slowed by turned clans rising up all over the realm. Not to mention, our most powerful allies would be here in less than a week.

All of Kylo's moving pieces were falling into place, locking Etherdale into her destiny. We were the hub of the revolution, where mortals and vampires would flock to train and fight with us. We were a heart with shadowed veins shooting out in all directions.

This war was far from over, but Etherdale was ours. Lord Conrad was dead, and our masks were off. Once the Serpent Clan joined us, our regional stronghold would be cemented. The war would slowly creep north, which would drive Earle even madder than his dissenters' allegations.

Kylo handed the papers I'd taken from Conrad's journal to Blade. "Mail these to Kole Tefar. He will ensure Earle knows he has usurpers in his council. They'll be forced into hiding. The deaths of Conrad and Aster will sow further destabilization among lords. Not to mention adding fuel to Earle's increasing paranoia. All very useful for us."

Blade nodded. "Gladly."

Kylo smiled at me, and I released a long exhale. The cheering had only grown louder around us. The attention I used to shy away from was unavoidable now as word spread about my displays of goddess-like power.

"I'm glad something good came from my blunder," I muttered.

Kylo tilted my chin up with his index finger. "You gave us everything we needed. Our enemies are dead. Political ammunition has been gathered. And we won our first battle against the *crown*."

He slowly pulled me out of the crowd of moving bodies, away from our friends. Idris was arm-in-arm with Clarke and Vesper, laughing. He didn't notice our absence.

Kylo pushed me up against the door of an empty shop. "Now, was my intuition right? Yes. It's always right."

I rolled my eyes, and his hips pressed against mine.

"I said if you returned, Aster wasn't going to let you go. However, I will admit that your intuition was *also* correct. My angel is safe where she belongs and completed what she set out to do, albeit in quite possibly the worst way possible."

I snorted. "That's generous," I said. "You were right that I'd underestimated them. Juliette, Conrad, Aster... I knew they were evil, but I was too careless in that den of venomous snakes. I'm—"

"Don't," Kylo said, putting a finger to my lips. "Don't be sorry. You paid enough." He stared at my bruised cheek and blistered neck. A muscle in his jaw hardened.

"I'm done atoning for other people's sins. I'm done trying to fight my battles alone, thinking I'm protecting those I love. We're more powerful together."

Kylo released a breath. He kissed me briefly, his lips soft and warm. "I need my blood down your pretty little throat. *Now.*"

I smiled sadly, looping my arms around his neck. "Yes, Kylo. Yes, *please.*"

"You know how much I love those perfect manners," he growled, picking the lock behind me with shadow before pulling me inside the quiet building.

We found ourselves in a furniture store. Kylo dragged me to the back, and I conjured a dim witch light and let it hang above us. We were both covered in blood and sweat, caught somewhere between the animal and the divine.

"Evie, first, I have to know. For your safety. Did they..." Kylo trailed off, anger coursing through him that was hot enough to feel on my skin.

I shook my head. "Aster kissed me, and you know, fed from me." I looked down at the ground, but Kylo gently grabbed my face, forcing me to stay with him. "They both tortured me—Conrad with pain and Aster using methods from my childhood, like kneeling on rice, and um, a belt. Conrad tried to do more." I shuddered. "But Aster stopped him."

Kylo closed his eyes, bleeding darkness.

I fought the urge to cry, my throat tight.

When he opened his eyes again, heartbreak had eclipsed

every drop of his rage. "You're safe now, baby, do you know that?"

I stared into those deep pools of blue. My shadows billowed around his ankles. "Yes. Thank you for always protecting me—all of me, but especially my heart."

"I love your sweet, vulnerable, feral little heart," Kylo said, leaning in as his breath tickled my ear. His lips brushed the shell, pressing against me when I shuddered. "I'm so sorry, Evie. For all of it. I wish I'd been the one to do it, but I hope everyone who has ever hurt you is being tortured in Lillian's hells for an eternity where they belong."

I placed my palm over his heart. "I might not have been the one to kill her in the end. But I'm glad Juliette is dead too. Most of me is fucking ecstatic, actually."

My fiery possessiveness mirrored his. I fisted his shirt, pressing against him and still feeling like I couldn't get close enough.

"We only kissed—I'm so sorry, angel. I knew on some level it wasn't you, but I thought you were dead." He shook his head. "I wanted you to be alive so badly that I ignored every last one of my instincts."

"It's okay. Well, it's not okay, but I don't blame *you*," I said, plagued by those thoughts of Juliette kissing him, torturing me with it. The fact that it had only been kissing didn't soothe me as much as I'd hoped.

The tension broke when we closed the distance between our lips at the same time. We consumed each other. Our hands and lips and bodies moved hungrily, desperate to reclaim.

We ended up on the carpeted floor, kissed by the faintest glow from above.

"You're mine, angel, forever," Kylo growled, grabbing my face instead of my blistered neck. "Do you fucking understand me?"

"Yes, Kylo."

He spat in my mouth. "Then be a good girl and swallow."

I swallowed. I tried to push his brick wall of a body, but it was a futile effort.

Kylo lifted a brow with a dimpled grin. "What are you aiming for, silly girl?"

"My turn." I scrunched my brows as I pushed again.

"You're so fucking cute," Kylo groaned. He rolled off me with a chuckle, allowing me to straddle him next.

I grabbed Kylo's dagger and dragged it up his body, staring down at him intently.

Kylo's eyes rolled back. "Just when I thought you couldn't get any sexier, you threaten me with my own weapon."

"Tell me who you belong to in this life and every life after," I growled, blade to his throat.

Kylo bit his lower lip, fingers digging into the flesh of my hips. "I belong to you—mind, body, and soul—in this life and every life after."

I grinned.

"Please sit on my face and let me grovel for your forgiveness, angel," Kylo said, staring between my thighs like a man dying of thirst.

I sheathed his weapon and did as he asked. "Because you used your manners."

Kylo's chuckle rumbled against my core. I gasped, melting into the slow strokes of his skilled tongue.

"Oh, how I've missed my perfect little doll," Kylo mused, his grip on my hips tightening.

I moaned, unabashedly chasing my pleasure as I rocked against Kylo's mouth. He pulled my clit into his mouth and pulsed, and I fell over the peak near-instantly.

When I tried to move, shadows roped around me and kept me in place.

"I'm not finished," Kylo said firmly.

When his fangs scraped against the most sensitive part of me, I squealed. He laughed.

"Aw, look how wet my angel is," he taunted, plunging two fingers inside me. "This time, I want you to remember how it felt to fight side by side. The hundreds of demons we killed together, the blood we shared. I want you to think about how fucking powerful we are as you come on my tongue."

I nodded, at a loss for words the moment he began to feast on me again. I did as he asked. I pictured what our enemies must've seen, two beings of godlike power fused at the soul. The lightning I'd wielded, the fury of shadows Kylo commanded, the evidence of our violent, obsessive brand of love.

For each other and for the world—the world we built together.

I came hard. The witch light flickered. Kylo rolled on top of me and filled me with his cock as he stared into my eyes.

"That's my good girl."

He grinned, then reached for his dagger again and made a small but deep cut on his wrist. "Drink," he ordered.

My breath hitched, remembering the trauma of Juliette breaking this sacred bond between us.

I sucked Kylo's wrist gratefully as he stroked my hair and kissed my forehead. He gently rocked, in and out. When I swallowed, he buried himself deep. I cried out at the stretch, the fullness, and he put a hand over my mouth.

"Shhh, I know you can take your God's cock," he soothed. "And now he will once again know exactly how hard and fast your heart is beating. He will know where to track, hunt, and capture you at all times." His next word was a whisper against my lips. *"Mine."*

I nodded, blissful as I melted into the carpet. *"Yours."*

Kylo was gentle with me tonight. We were both soothed beyond words to have my blood marked again. What started off as animalistic shifted into a softer kind of claiming. We relished it—exploring each other's bodies with tenderness and melting into the pleasure of being this close with another person. We spoke in each other's minds through our shadows. We laughed at half-formed jokes. We read each other's thoughts as if we'd been doing it for years.

"I don't think this is our first time around," I whispered in the dark stillness, curled around Kylo like a vine as he traced patterns on my back. "This isn't our first life together."

"Duh," Kylo said.

I scoffed at him, swatting his chest as he chuckled.

"I thought that was obvious. Otherwise, my initial stalking was... a bit much."

I rolled my eyes. "That's your defense?"

"It's the truth," he said, pulling me closer and kissing the top of my head. "And *also,* a great defense."

I made a small huff.

"Don't growl at me."

I bit his arm.

"You grow more feral every day," he said, yanking me up by the hair. "I will delight in taming you and keeping your dark little urges in check."

I batted my eyelashes. "Good luck."

71

KYLO

I fell more stupidly in love with Evie every day. It shouldn't have been possible to love someone this much, this deep in my body and soul.

I cherished each new memory we created together, especially after suffering that brief moment in time I thought we'd never make another memory again.

This afternoon, she'd fallen asleep on me as we read out on the back patio with Vesper.

Her head was in my lap; her face was beautifully innocent and relaxed.

"Tuckered herself out killing hundreds of enemies," I said with a sigh.

Vesper snorted.

"Serves the born right for not learning their lesson after the first battle."

The gods shined favorably upon us this past week. The Serpent Clan arrived with their numbers and looted resources the day before Earle's next fleet had, along with the regrouped forces from the week prior.

It was a slaughter, but we prevailed.

King Earle declared war on all turned clans of Ravenia. Dissenters on his council went into hiding. More rumors of Earle's madness and paranoia spread like wildfire, and tensions were high both at court and among born nobility as Earle hunted for more usurpers. Thanks to Evie, we were afforded another lucrative advantage.

"How does it feel, Kylo?" Vesper asked.

I begrudgingly raised my gaze from my sleeping angel to Vesper.

She continued. "To officially rule Etherdale after eighty years of building?"

"Eighty-four, if we're being precise," I said. I looked out over the back lawn, where Idris, Clarke, Blade and a few Serpent Clan members were fucking around and halfheartedly sparring. "It feels surreal," I answered honestly. "I don't think I'll ever truly be settled or certain of my place until we've taken the whole realm."

After a girlish squeal, Blade suddenly ran toward us, waving around his correspondence journal. "Kylo's gonna meet his *boyfriend!*" he sang.

Evie stirred.

Blade repeated the juvenile line, refusing to back down after my deathly glare.

"What's he talking about?" Evie asked groggily. Her eyes lit up the moment realization struck. "*Oh.*"

My heart pounded in my chest. Rune had agreed to a meeting. I was going to meet the man I'd admired since I was a teenager—the first turned vampire to lead a war against the born and *win*.

"When?" I asked.

"Based on our current schemes and the time it will take to get there, I'd say a month and a half," Blade said.

"We'll be dangerously low on resources by then," Vesper murmured. "We will *need* Valentin. And we will surely need them to stop supplying the kingdom's weapons and magickal imports."

"Gods, if we could pull *that* off... let alone convince them to join, in some capacity," Blade said, shaking his head. "There is bad news in all of this, however. Rune's close comrade Uriah has explained that Valentin may be heading toward its own civil war, just as we feared. Which means relations with the kingdom are already dicey. No one knows exactly how this will all play out. Rune's clan could either be pushed toward us, or decisively away from us. Depending on what Rune deems best for his city and island."

"Okay," I said. "Let's keep our ears to the ground. We'll prep as meticulously as we always do. I have a feeling it's going to work out. For all of us."

"Oh my gods," Evie said, raising up and poking my cheek. "You're going to meet your boyfriend!"

I grabbed her finger and lightly bit it with my fangs. She only giggled.

"Do you think you'll kiss?" she asked sweetly. "I won't be mad."

I dropped her hand. Blade and Vesper burst into laughter.

"I hate all of you."

TONIGHT WE JOINED our mortal allies at Mena's house for Gwendolyn's celebration of life.

I held Evie's hand tight, especially when she finally faced Amy, her teenage admirer who'd found Gwendolyn's body.

We'd gone over it again and again—the fact that Juliette's atrocity wasn't Evie's fault—but Evie's guilt was rooted deeply.

Evie hesitated. Amy locked eyes with her from across the room. But *Amy* didn't hesitate—she immediately ran to us and folded Evie into a hug.

"I'm so sorry," Evie said, dropping my hand to hug Amy. "I'm so fucking sorry."

The girls pulled back and wiped their tear-stricken faces, and my heart clenched.

"You killed the witch who did this?" Amy asked, gaze flicking between the two of us.

Evie and I nodded.

"THAT WAS WHAT I HEARD. GOOD," Amy said, stronger now. "I know she's so happy for us. Gods, I wished she'd lived to see a free Etherdale again."

"Me too," Evie whispered. "Her help was invaluable. I know she's still aiding us from the beyond."

Amy nodded. "They all are. She's with Princeton now. He always knew how to make her laugh."

"One of his greatest gifts," I murmured with a small smile.

I surveyed the space. I admired the pillar candles and warm lighting alongside Mena's artful decor and meticulously curated environment. It was easy to see why Evie felt comfortable here.

I let Evie and Amy catch up, relaxing the moment that Evie did. Soon she was surrounded by witches, all asking her about the unbelievable battle stories spreading through the realm. They included Evie's impossible power, the way she killed one hundred born in the blink of an eye, and her turned brother's magick blessed by the heavens.

Idris quickly joined Evie to bask in the attention, the confidence of his grin softening something inside me. I moved to Mena, who hugged me fiercely.

"Thank you again," she whispered. "For protecting them."

She glanced at my proudly displayed tattoos, as she had on previous visits. After our first battle against the kingdom, Idris had told Mena the truth. She'd cried, but she took it well. She was just glad her grandchildren were safe.

"How long have you known I was a vampire?" I asked her, curious.

"Since we first met," she said slyly before winking. "I know *all.*"

I nodded. "I believe it. How's the memoir coming along?"

When Mena clapped, her golden bracelets jingled together. "Marvelously! I'm still piecing together the early years. But I know this book is going to be a *hit.*"

Vesper joined us, and Mena's eyes became radiant.

"You *must* be an early reader, Vesper. We have twin flame souls, you and I."

Vesper grinned. "Absolutely. In fact, I'd be offended if you let anyone else read it before I did."

"Hey," I said. "This whole thing was *my* idea."

Mena fanned herself. "No need to fight over me, dolls," she said, enjoying herself far too much.

"You can go second," Vesper said with a crooked grin.

"How generous of you."

Behind her, both Hekate and Serpent Clan members intermixed with the revolutionary mortals. Every tattoo and set of fangs was on full display. Bexley and Harmony were finally making out in a corner, and Lachlan and Clarke were making eyes from across the room.

I knew Evie was safe, but I still found her with my gaze every few minutes just to be sure. My love would always be as obsessive and all-consuming as it had been in the beginning, when Evie had pretended she hated me but fell as hard and fast as I had.

After a grand feast, several toasts to Gwendolyn's legacy and the burgeoning revolution for Etherdale and beyond, Evie and Idris danced with Mena. I smiled. My heart swelled with emotion.

Mena and the two children she'd welcomed into her life with open arms were so fucking cute together.

As I watched from the shadows, I reflected on the catalyst that had set me on my path: the day the born had forced me to watch them murder my best friend.

They thought I would kill myself, and in a way, they got their wish.

But they had no idea of the monster who rose in my place.

Evie broke away and found me in the corner of the room where I'd been watching her. "Hi, creep." She looped her arms around my neck. She was impossibly soft and warm.

Evie had died too, that day her brother cracked open his skull, and the sky bled darkness and wrath. She killed the girl who hid from love, from belonging, from her own destiny. She killed the woman who made herself small in the face of controlling, mediocre men.

She let go of the fear that had held her back for a decade, and she made her life as big and ruinous and extraordinary as any of her favorite fantasy romance novels.

I brushed my lips against her forehead, inhaling deeply. "Hi, angel."

72

EVIE

Vesper was finally ready for her tarot card reading. She sat with me on the roof of her apartment building, letting out a deep sigh after a long day leading her clan.

We were one month into the war, and Kylo's journey to Valentin was rapidly approaching. It would be incredibly risky for him to take to the sky on a long journey between two war-threatened lands. But it was a risk he needed to take.

The Serpent Clan had settled in remarkably well, and Etherdale was relatively peaceful save for the occasional skirmish between lingering loyalists and revolutionaries. All born either went into hiding or fled the city, and battles had been pushed over the mountains. Our border was impressively secure as we worked to clean up the city and train new recruits.

Kylo, Idris, and I were not the only ones gifted with incredible magick. We had gods on our side, righting the balance of the world that the born had disrupted for too long.

I grieved the mortals who had lost their lives to this war, some willingly, and others who had merely gotten caught up in violence out of their control.

But change was inevitable, like every death and rebirth cycle

Selena guided under the phases of the moon. We'd rolled over and taken what our oppressors had given for hundreds of years. They destroyed our books, brainwashed us with religious propaganda, groomed our children, and abused and trafficked us while laughing and clinking flutes of elixir. They'd tortured students in basements while partying and living lavishly above their heads, surrounded by meaningless art and soulless conversations.

Their power and magick was inherited. Ours was earned.

"You've got a little something," Vesper said, touching a finger to her neck.

I mirrored her touch before blushing, feeling the mark Kylo had left this afternoon when he'd fed.

He'd always told me he couldn't wait until he could live openly as his true vampiric self. Who was I to deny Kylo his beautifully possessive, primal urges?

I took immense pleasure in showing off that I was *his*.

"Still honeymooning?" she asked, relaxing in her chair as she eyed the tarot deck between us. I detected the tiniest note of nervousness in her gaze.

"Something like that," I said. "I fall deeper in love with him every day. We take care of each other."

Vesper grinned. "You two are good for morale. I'm happy for you, Evie."

"How are you feeling?" I asked.

"Better." She glanced out at the cityscape, releasing another deep breath. "I imagined killing him a thousand times, a thousand different ways. Sometimes the visions were grand, cinematic masterpieces, and other times they were quick and unceremonious. In the end, reality was a mix of both. I had fun. He's gone. And my daughter will be safe from him forever."

Emotion clogged my throat, and I tilted my head slightly as her words sank in. At first, I assumed Vesper's need to kill

Conrad was merely revenge. But vengeance was only part of it, perhaps even the smaller part.

Love was her driving force.

"Do you want to learn about her?" I asked gently.

Vesper looked fierce as ever in her silky black gown and dramatic winged eyeliner. Yet, there was something beautifully vulnerable in her features as she stared at the tarot cards and slowly met my eyes.

"Yes," she said, folding her hands neatly in her lap. "I want to know who she is."

I lay a collection of hand-picked crystals and dried flowers on the table in offering. I asked my spirit helpers for guidance and aid, and I also asked Vesper's and her daughter's.

The chilly autumn air came alive for us, charged with a soothing, supportive energy. I glanced up at the clear sky of luminous stars.

Bringing a witch light closer, I began to shuffle the deck, clearing out old energies and inviting Vesper's into the fold. I spread the cards out on the table in a crescent formation.

"Pick three cards. We'll start there," I told her.

Vesper leaned forward. She tapped on three cards. I pulled them out and flipped them over.

"Two of Cups. Ten of Swords reversed. The Empress." I took a deep breath, zoning out as I stared at the cards' imagery and combined the symbolic meaning with my own intuition. "The Two of Cups is a marriage card—two lovers facing each other, perfectly balanced. I'm getting two messages here. The first is that she is deeply in love."

Vesper smiled. Her eyes instantly became glassy. She raised a hand to her mouth, staring at the cards.

"Second, she also has a special sort of nourishing love with a best friend."

"Good. She needs friends more than she needs men," Vesper said, her lip twitching.

The Ten of Swords wasn't exactly a pleasant card. It depicted a man fallen and impaled by ten swords and blood leaking from his head. However, the card was in the reversed position, which altered its meaning.

"She has faced great loss and great betrayal. She knows pain," I said, reaching for Vesper's trembling hand. "But she also knows healing. These swords are falling out of her back, not going in. I'm guessing the love she has found has given her a path out of past sorrow."

Vesper's daughter was a succubus, and succubi and incubi notoriously faced all manner of danger and cruelty from the world. People did not look kindly on creatures capable of manipulating desire.

"The Empress card is not surprising," I said, and Vesper relaxed when she saw my easy smile. "It's sometimes a motherhood or fertility card, but here it indicates a powerful expression of the divine feminine and sacred sensuality." My shoulders relaxed. "I'm getting the very strong feeling she shares her mother's high expectations and impeccable taste."

Vesper laughed. A tear broke free, and she wiped it halfway down her cheek. "Good. That's good." She nodded. "None of us get to escape pain. I'm so fucking relieved to hear she knows more than just suffering."

"Vesper, she knows so much more than suffering. Even from these three cards, I can promise you that."

Chills swept over our skin, the spirits confirming my words from the beyond.

Vesper gasped, rubbing her arms. She cleared her throat. "Can we take a break?"

"Of course." I steadied myself, hesitating for only a moment before pushing through. "I just need to say one thing, first."

Vesper held my gaze, her features consumed by intense emotion—love and fear and heartbreak.

"If you'll let me, I want to help you find her." I cleared my throat, tears filling my eyes. "I would give *anything* to discover I had a mother like you. Fucking *anything*."

Vesper swallowed. More tears broke free, and she was powerless to stop them.

"Your daughter knows love. You can rest easy knowing that. But I bet she has room in her heart for more. She has room in her heart for *yours*."

The words I didn't say, I kept close to my heart instead. Vesper didn't deserve to feel any more guilt. Everything she'd done, she'd done it to protect her daughter.

We were all searching for perfect maternal love. That was the hole in Juliette's heart, the hole in mine.

I would learn to live without it. But maybe Vesper's daughter didn't have to.

The world was quiet. Vesper closed her eyes.

My mind drifted to Kylo's upcoming journey to make a bid for Rune's support—support that could help us win a war against an ancient, mad king and his expansive army.

A gentle breeze rolled over the roof.

"Okay," Vesper said. "Yes. Please help me find her."

73

KYLO

"We're so glad you made it," said a man with shoulder-length honey blond hair and a neat beard. "I'm Uriah."

His eyes shone with genuine warmth and excitement, instantly putting me at ease as we walked further into Rune's castle.

I managed not to get shot down on my journey across Ravenia, an ocean, and Valentin's dry lands to the vampire city in the center of the island.

Aristelle was the most beautiful city I'd ever seen, rivaling even Prospyrus in its effortless splendor. On my descent, I'd marveled at the great expanse of twinkling lights, the crystalline domed temples, the architecturally stunning buildings in various shades of cream, black, white, and jewel tones, and the sloping cobblestone streets.

I was *here*. The stars had aligned, leading me to a place I'd idolized since I was a boy. The city that had been ruled for centuries by the first turned vampire clan to win a war.

I smiled. "Thank you for the warm welcome. I know these

haven't been easy times for either of our clans. But it's wonderful to put a face to the impeccable handwriting."

Uriah laughed. "It's barely legible, I know."

I caught a glimpse of a woman with icy blonde hair slipping into a room, where a giggling brunette was lounging on a couch with a book in her lap. The brunette closed the book, peeking around the blonde to get a good look at me.

They both laughed, whispering to each other.

Uriah smirked, rolling his eyes. "Those fucking girls," he said. "They don't listen."

"I understand the feeling." I pieced together who the brunette was immediately, and I sensed soft, witch-magick from the blonde.

The notebook in my pocket delivered a familiar, light zap to my hip. I casually opened the journal to Evie's note.

Only one kiss! No tongue.

I rolled my eyes, covering my chuckle with a cough. Uriah caught the expression on my face as I scribbled a response.

I know you think you're safe from me with an ocean between us, but I'm keeping score of every bratty word. You're taking your punishment with your favorite collar and a matching gag. Oh, and my rope skills have improved tremendously.

The collar in question was a lacy pink piece with a cute little bell. Evie fucking hated it, which brought me much delight and satisfaction.

She wrote back immediately.

Is that supposed to be a threat?

I shook my head.

Enjoy being able to sit while you still can.

"Sorry about that," I said. I closed the notebook, relieved that everything hadn't fallen apart in my absence.

We did, however, need Valentin's support now more than ever. I wouldn't show them my desperation. They needed to see my strength. I had to believe our story, and our parallel ideologies, would have to be enough to move Rune.

Our fates were intertwined. They just didn't know it yet.

"Not at all," Uriah said, waving a hand. "It was a long journey. I'm sure folks back home were worried for you."

A woman with short, wiry hair and dark skin joined us. She was far less approachable than Uriah, offering me a curt, guarded nod.

"I'm Mason, Rune's second-in-command," she said without extending a hand.

"Kylo."

We stopped walking, waiting in the center of a hallway. The art, furniture, and decor were classically gorgeous, like being in a finely curated museum.

Behind us, in the direction of the room with the giggling, whispering girls, a man's voice carried.

"Behave."

Two fiery, softer voices said things I couldn't quite hear.

The man chuckled, and a door closed.

I slowed my heart with a deep breath, pretending to be much cooler and more aloof than I was by a longshot.

I slowly turned my head.

The man walked toward us, slow and graceful. His features were impassive, deadly. Thorny branch tattoos crawled down his arms and up his neck. He matched my height, one of the few men who did.

"Welcome, Kylo," he said. "I'm Rune."

I smiled. I obviously knew who he was, but we both politely pretended. "Thank you for welcoming me into your home."

Rune nodded. "I'm intrigued to hear your story."

He was more guarded than Uriah, but less icy than Mason. He wanted to protect his people, now more than ever.

Convincing him to endanger his city after everything that had happened the past month was going to be a tall order.

But I wasn't leaving empty-handed. It wasn't an option. Rune was the only being capable of giving us a fighting chance.

He wordlessly led us into a deliberation room. Guards pulled the door shut behind us.

I pictured Evie in her garden where she was happiest, talking about magick and fate and the gods' wills.

When it was time for me to state my case, I centered myself with the memory of Evie handing me an arrangement of pink roses and lavender and whispering in my ear.

Ask me again. Ask me again to marry you.

I told our story, let its beauty and grief and devastation flood from my lips and stun my audience to silence.

And when Rune sighed, a half-smile on his ruthless face and an irritated look in his eyes, I felt Evie's soft blonde hair beneath my fingers. Steady, certain.

I awaited my judgment, heart unburdened. I'd said everything I needed to say.

Rune leaned back in his chair. "You're making my life difficult and complicated when it had *just* become simple again."

Uriah beamed. Mason narrowed her eyes at Uriah's smile and shook her head.

"Thank you for telling us your story, Kylo. You have no idea how much it resonates with our own." Rune straightened. "I need time to process. But I'm open to further discussions." He uncrossed his arms, his eyes softening. "We will help you."

EPILOGUE

EVIE

S *ometime in the future...*

"Evie, my innocent little flower petal and spiteful angel of death and destruction..."

I giggled, wrists snuggly bound with pink rope, thighs spread, glowing with post-orgasm bliss.

"Will you marry me?"

I stopped laughing. "Kylo!"

He halted his trail of kisses down my nude form. He'd adorned me with flowers, tied me up and flooded me with pleasure as I lay helpless in my garden.

"This still isn't the proper way to ask!"

He lifted a brow. "What is improper about it, angel?"

It had become a running joke, ever since I told him I wasn't ready yet—that he needed to ask me *properly* next time. He began to propose to me in the most absurd, inappropriate ways, if only to watch me blush and laugh and chastise him.

And I agreed to marry him anyway, each time he asked. I wondered if we would never actually marry, if only to keep the bit going forever.

His laugh was infectious, his silly little dimple flooding my stomach with butterflies like it had the first time he'd smiled at me.

"Well?"

He drew the peak of my breast into his mouth, feeding me his thumb. I sucked, relaxing into the earth.

"Duh," I said around his appendage.

Kylo released my nipple and shook his head. "Horrible response."

"I'll do better next time."

He captured my lips, and our shadows reached for each other—whispering, teasing, becoming one.

"The first time I saw you, I thought you were an angel."

I smiled. "The first time I saw *you*, I thought you were the devil."

"We're so fucking perfect for each other. It's so sexy."

I nodded. "So sexy."

"I found us a cabin in the woods for winter, so you can see all the snow your little heart desires."

"Yay!"

"And the surprises keep coming..." he teased, dragging a finger down my body as I shivered. "Because we're going to Aristelle for a night at the opera."

I squealed. "Yay again! Are we picking up Vesper on the way?"

"She's already there," Kylo said.

My cheeks hurt from smiling so broadly.

"It's time to rejoin the world, baby."

"If we must," I sighed. "But then we're escaping again, for a really long time."

"What about your shop?" he asked, kissing either side of my lips as I wiggled in my pastel pink bondage.

"Amy's got it, and my mysterious disappearance will be excellent publicity. Business will boom." I stared deep into his heart-melting blue eyes. "You don't want to run away and be hermits together?"

"Baby, I would follow you anywhere."

"Anywhere?"

He kissed me again, and we saw stars.

"Anywhere."

ALSO BY MAGGIE SUNSERI

EVERLASTING POSSESSION DUET

Marked by Masks and Secrets

Claimed by Fangs and Darkness

ETERNAL OBSESSION DUET

Stalked by Seduction and Shadows

Taken by Touch and Torment

THE LOST WITCHES OF ARADIA

The Discovered

The Coveted

The Illuminated

The Hunted

The Scorned

The Claimed

The Redeemed

ABOUT MAGGIE SUNSERI

 Maggie Sunseri is the author of fantasy romance books by day and a witch, tarot card reader, and succubus by night. She has a bachelor's degree in Anthropology/Sociology. When she's not traveling the world, you'll find her curled up with a good book and a hot cup of tea, pretending it's autumn no matter the season.

She also writes a Substack about spirituality and witchcraft, critical theory, sexuality, holistic health, community building, and addiction and trauma recovery.

Connect with Maggie:
maggiesunseri.com